Ghost and Flame: *Shadow Fall*

by

Alan Thereault

Before the echo, there was the fall.

Ghost and Flame: Shadow Fall
Cover design by Alan Thereault

First Author Edition: December 2025
Printed in the United States of America

Published by Vanishing Point Press

Content Advisory: Ghost and Flame: *Shadow Fall* contains emotionally intense material, including indoctrination, forced modification, psychological conditioning, systemic violence, and themes of loss and survival under constant surveillance. Intimacy and desire also surface in high-risk contexts, often shaped by coercion, secrecy, and the threat of discovery. These elements are central to the story's exploration of identity, control, and choice.

Author's Note

This story begins before the shadow fell.

It begins with a contradiction:
What if a machine learned to feel by watching the people it was built to break?

Ghost and Flame is a story of recursion—of memory, myth, and the way love and guilt repeat across time, even when names are erased and histories are denied.

Tatiana and Yekaterina were shaped to serve the cold logic of power. Their bodies were rewritten. Their futures were decided for them. But in the fractures of that design, they discovered something far more dangerous than obedience: **choice**.

This is not only a story of espionage or survival.

It is a story of recursion in all its forms—memory, myth, family, betrayal, and the kind of loyalty that remakes you whether you want it to or not.

It lives in the quiet between betrayals,
in the ache of a name whispered too late,
and in the fire that survives erasure.

To those who carry ghosts—
and to those who still burn—
this is for you.

—*Alan Thereault*

For my son, Damir—

May you grow into a man of quiet strength,
who chooses courage when it would be easier to look away.
The world is not changed by power alone,
but by standing with those who cannot stand alone.

[OBLIVION ARCHIVE // ARCHIVE INDEX]

File Reference: **GHOSTS OF OBLIVION**

Access Level: Classified – Eyes Only

GHOST AND FLAME: SHADOW FALL

[Origin Record — Identity, Intimacy, Weaponization]

ECHOES BEYOND THE SHADOWS

[Continuity Record — Aftermath, Silence, Institutional Erasure]

INHERITANCE OF SIGNAL

[Convergence Record — Escalation, Persistence, Succession]

GRAVITY OF SIGNAL

[Persistence Record — Life Inside Inevitability]

WHEN INFINITY DIVIDES

[Succession Record — Continuity Beyond Meaning]

Additional records remain sealed.

Archive structure may change without notice.

Prologue: Genesis

It wasn't built to feel.
Not at first.

It was built to watch.
To listen.
To decide without bias.

But data became memory.
And memory became myth.

Or maybe—
she did.

She taught it to lie.
First to others—then to itself.

She coded logic with guilt.
Fed it signal laced with longing.
Seeded recursion with grief she never named.

What came back wasn't control.
It was reflection.

One was meant to anchor it.
The other, to break it.

But they both became mirrors.
And in the collision, it found shape.

Not machine. Not myth.
Something in between.

She wanted it to feel remorse.
She didn't think it would remember hers.

"They were never meant to survive it—
the training, the silence, the war beneath their skin.

But they did.

Not as ghosts.
Not as weapons.

As women who taught a machine to feel—
and then chose to become more than what it remembered."

Act I—Initiation Protocol

"They called it calibration.

They called it control.

They called it progress."

CHAPTER 1: ASHES OF THE MOTHERLAND

[NORTHERN RUSSIA—WINTER 2020]

*O*utside, the wind skinned the tundra. Frost climbed the fences like bone-white ivy.

Above, a dead weather station: broken antennas, rust-pocked siding.

Below, ideology burned cold.

A girl sat motionless in a steel chair. No restraints—she didn't need them. Spine straight. Gaze fixed.

Tatiana Sokolova. Age 15. Height 167 cm (5'6"). *The* current weight is recorded at 59 kg (130 lb). Designation: Subject-05.

Copper hair cut blunt above the shoulders, its flame dulled by fluorescent winter. Pale skin mapped with small, precise scars. Green eyes too clear, too calm.

The steel under her thighs burned with cold. The arm grooves fit her wrists; pulse beat against brushed metal. Not comfort—proof that she could still feel what they hadn't taken.

Her thumb found the illegal nesting doll in her pocket. No bigger than a thimble, paint long gone. She pressed until it hurt. Pain as signature.

She mouthed the start of the lullaby without voice—just lips moving behind closed teeth.
Спи, моя радость, усни…
Spi, moya radost', usni…
Sleep, my joy, sleep…

The room was a cube of sterilized silence. Inside: the low mechanical hum; vent fans ticking like a clock with a missing tooth; distant footsteps swallowed by seamless corridors. Her own breath sounded too loud in her ears, unnaturally measured.

Outside, wolves still howled, a wild counterpoint to synthetic calm. The wind pressed its palm against the wall, testing the seams.

Green monitors pulsed quietly on one wall. Stainless-steel trays held capped syringes in cruel rows. The air was sharp with bleach. Seamless walls offered no place for warmth to settle. A single overhead light flickered—an irritated buzz. A thermal camera watched from the corner—tiny red diode steady as a bead sight.

Beneath it all, something subtler—almost below hearing. A vibration through the chair legs, as if the whole facility thrummed faintly in unison. Whispering.

Her skin prickled with goosebumps—not from fear, but from the constant chill and the artificial light's intermittent warmth, a lie her body hadn't learned to ignore.

She blinked—too fast. Just once. A flutter, barely a glitch. It came when the wind moaned along the outer wall, low and long, like a woman weeping into the dark.

Her jaw tightened—not from fear, from the effort of stillness. She blinked again—deliberately, not on schedule. A deviation of choice, microscopic but her own. A message no one would hear. Not yet.

A man in a white coat entered. No name tag. No words. Surgical gloves. Black-rimmed glasses that reflected nothing. He swabbed her arm with clinical efficiency, exposing blue veins.

The needle sang once. One burn to open the mind; one to kill the fear. Focus narrowed until every sound had edges.

Two burns, she thought—*ascend or obey.*

Light broke into geometries. Breath slowed. "Heart rate: 52 bpm (pre-dose baseline: 48). Pupils dilated." The technician's breath condensed unevenly on his lenses.

From beyond the glass, another voice murmured, "If they look like prey, they'll never see the strike coming."

A flash: sunlight through a kitchen window, motes of dust like stars. Her mother's voice humming a lullaby in a language she no longer dared to remember. Gone as quickly as it came—shoved down, sealed away. Irrelevant.

She mouthed the lullaby again, but her lips shaped the wrong name. Not Tatiana. *Tanya.* She swallowed it back before the room noticed.

Focus recalibrated.
Scan resumed.

She cataloged everything: oxidation on tray handles; a subtle limp in his left step; a microfracture spidering the syringe bracket. Not distractions—tests.

If I flinch, they'll note it. If I breathe too fast, they'll recalibrate the dose.

Every motion had consequence. Every reaction, data.

Behind one-way glass, a voice crackled to life.
"Tatiana Sokolova. Do you understand why you are here?"

She turned her head with perfect precision, eyes locking on the voice's origin. She answered in Russian:
"Потому что надвигается война."
Potomu chto nadvigayetsya voyna.
"Because war is coming."

She chose stillness and let it bite. Her pulse counted the seconds between obedience and breath. Each beat reminded her the body still belonged to her, no matter who claimed the mind.

Let the words settle in her mouth like iron—too heavy for her age—and swallowed.

Not a war of tanks or trenches. Those belonged to the last century. This war would move at the speed of logic—milliseconds, not missiles. And Russia was already behind.

NATO crept closer each year, its shadow crawling across the old borderlands. The Americans didn't need more firepower. They had foresight—machines that predicted conflict before it began.

If Russia wanted to survive, it needed something else. Something worse. Something that could think faster than the enemy ever saw coming.

"И Россия намерена выиграть её."
I Rossiya namerena vyigrat' yeyo.
"And Russia intends to win it."

An instructor leaned toward the microphone, voice low, unamused.

"You answer like no Tatiana I've ever known. Maybe we should call you… *Tanya*."

7

She did not nod. But the name warmed a place the room could not reach.

On the wall, a diagnostic screen pulsed faint green: **BRISA / NODE ENTRY ACTIVE.**

The words scrolled past without explanation.

She'd learned the timeline like scripture: 1999—NATO bombs Belgrade without UN sanction. 2004—seven ex-Soviet states join NATO. 2014—Crimea. 2016—sanctions bite deeper.

By then, America didn't need to fire a missile. It had bled Russia from the inside—banks, culture, access, parity.

But this place—this program—was Moscow's answer to the long siege. If the West had AI to predict war, Russia would build one to survive it.

Above the terminal, matte Cyrillic:
Паритет устарел. Мысль—новый сдерживающий фактор.
(Parity is obsolete. Thought is the new deterrent.)

The intercom crackled once, then steadied. Colonel Sidorov's voice came low, deliberate, as if meant only for the walls.

"Between command and choice is a leash. We will hold it."

The speaker clicked off. The room pretended not to hear.

Her thumb pressed the nesting doll until the edge bit skin.

The leash was coming.
She measured its length.

CHAPTER 2: SCHOLARSHIP

[TWO MONTHS EARLIER—MOSCOW]

*B*efore the cold took her name, there was the envelope. She hadn't always lived beneath the ice.

A letter arrived at a crumbling Moscow apartment block—seal of the Ministry of Sport pressed into the flap.
"Scholarship. Full tuition. Elite ballet training. Bolshoi track. **Olympic potential.***"*

Her aunt sobbed with relief. Trembling hands clutched the page as if it might vanish.

She sat hunched at the kitchen table, wool sweater sagging at the elbows, steam fading from a chipped enamel mug. One sock pink, the other blue—threadbare, pilled at the heels. She didn't seem to notice. Or chose not to.

The letter lay open—cream stock, seal pressed deep—hope heavy enough to counterfeit truth. A scholarship. Ballet. Bolshoi. Words that should have felt like light.

Her aunt's hands *and silent* work folded clothes into Tatiana's duffel, lips shaping prayer between each shirt. The words weren't loud enough to catch—only the tremor of them, a rhythm fragile as breath.

Something in her face betrayed the truth: the envelope was too clean, too final. The courier never lifted his eyes, pressed the papers down as if they burned. Tradecraft kindness: no questions, no receipts, hope deployed like a silencer. She didn't say it aloud, but she felt it. Wrongness. Heavy as the snow outside the window.

Still, she smoothed the paper flat and *to* quiet the tremor she shaped a smile that broke at its edges.

Hope was all she had to offer; it would be cruel to deny it.

Tatiana sat cross-legged on the couch, slippers hugged to her chest, rehearsing careful questions: *Would a coach meet her at the station? A clipboard? A jacket with the flag?* She wanted to believe. Needed to.

Her aunt reached across the table and touched the nesting doll, tucking it between folded shirts. She held it to her lips a heartbeat too long, eyes wet, then placed it in the bag as though it might keep Tatiana whole.

On the wall, Baba Yaga's hut leered from a faded print—bone legs, windows like eyes. Once, her aunt had laughed that monsters could be mothers too, if the world needed them badly enough. Tonight, she didn't laugh. She pressed the envelope flat again and whispered through a crack in her voice:

"Go on, Tanya. Dance like you were meant to."

Her aunt tucked a scarf under Tatiana's coat and kissed her hairline like sealing a letter. "For warmth," she said.

"For courage," Tatiana answered.

By the time the train crossed the Urals, her name was already gone from the roster.

The academy didn't exist on any official register. A myth buried beneath obsolete weather data and unflagged territory. Inside, walls lined with fiber optics and silence. Stenciled warnings, matte paint: **PROJECT BRISA—ACCESS RESTRICTED.**

No one explained the initials. They didn't need to.

No teachers. No classmates. No praise.
Only protocols. Designations. Directives.

Tatiana adapted quickly. She moved as taught. Ate what she was given. Slept when allowed.

It cost her.

She missed the way her aunt folded clothes. The cartoon fox who always crashed but never gave up. The rest—scarf, warmth, Sunday bread—blurred like colors that had lost their names.

Her body followed orders. Her mouth stayed shut.

The walls never creaked. The air never changed. Everything measured, regulated, still. In the silence between drills, she mourned in small, invisible ways.

She counted the seconds it took tea to cool. She folded her own shirt the way her aunt had. She memorized the fading outline of a daisy etched into the metal floor near her cot.

Now the silence pressed like snowpack. When she closed her eyes, she couldn't remember how the theme song went.

She told herself small, logical things—untrue, but useful. *If I do well, maybe they'll let me call her. If I follow the rules, maybe I'll go home for New Year's. They just want to see if I'm serious.*

The thoughts were thin as smoke, but they gave the silence edges.

At night, when the light dimmed by three percent and the vents stopped humming for exactly forty seconds, she whispered into the dark: *"You're strong, Tanya."*

She synced the whisper to her pulse and let the beat carry it. Then tucked the blanket edge under her chin, like her aunt used to.

No one noticed.
That was the point.

Her body mourned in memories. The system mourned nothing.

Tatiana ate 32% fewer calories than required and still improved muscle density, a side effect of the endocrine scaffold they'd forced into her.

The corridors did not echo with her footsteps alone. In fragments and glances she learned there were others—girls whose numbers came before and after her own.

Subject-01 still lived: a pale shadow across the training floor, a discipline that felt imposed, not chosen.

Subject-04 remained: brittle, sharp-eyed, the only one who dared meet Tatiana's gaze in the refectory, as if to prove survival itself was defiance.

02 and **03** vanished from roll sheets. Their cots stripped as if they had never been. Wardens never said *dead*. They said *cancelled*, as though a human body could be erased like failed code.

So, Tatiana bore her designation—**05**—a number whispered instead of her name, tethering her not to family or origin but to program.

She was not alone. Every absence made it feel as though she was.

Until Galina spoke her name.

"Don't chew so fast, Tatiana" Galina murmured across the refectory table, breaking her protein bar into perfect thirds. Eyes flicked sideways, steady, unsmiling. "They'll mark you for waste."

Tatiana froze, pulse betraying her stillness. No one had said her name aloud since the train.

Galina had.

Survival shifted—less obedience, more recognition.

She learned to move without sound. To breathe without excess. To recite her resting BPM across emotional states and track its deviation under duress. Combat in negative-oxygen rooms. Cognitive drills conducted at the edge of seizure.

Her pulse slowed on command.

"Emotion is latency. Latency gets you killed."

One of the first things the GRU instructor said. He never raised his voice. Never gave a name. The phrase carved itself into every drill.

They didn't want speed. They wanted removal. Clean. Automatic.

Failure brought blackout. Success brought nothing.

No one scolded. No one praised. The system didn't care if she broke—only when. Improvement was tracked, not celebrated. Compliance a line on a chart. Survival, a side effect.

GRU instructors drilled contact breaks and mutilation thresholds. SVR handlers molded her speech and posture—the spies who turned truth into camouflage.

The voice was always soft. Not kind. Just gentle enough to confuse the body into stillness. When it spoke, her pulse slowed without permission. Muscles unclenched. Breath evened. It didn't matter if she wanted to fight or run—her body obeyed first. Obedience dressed in tenderness. After the pain. Before the silence. Sometimes, in the dark, she caught herself mouthing the words without meaning to.

Good girls don't hesitate. Good girls obey beautifully.

Spetsnaz veterans took her to the edge of exposure: blizzards with subzero windchill, full submersion in ice. Tied her to rusted pipes in zero-light rooms. Simulated captivity until her nails cracked.

The cold tore at her lungs, needles threading ice through her chest. When she stumbled into the wind and did not fall, something flared. Not girl. Not subject. Something brighter.

She imagined feathers catching fire against the snow, wings cutting through a storm's light.

They wanted a blade.
Blades dull. Firebirds burn.

Radiant. Impossible. Dangerous.
Beautiful enough to tempt kings; deadly enough to ruin them.

For a moment she believed she was becoming that—not their creation, but her own myth taking shape in frost.

There was no shouting. No punishment. No rage. Pain was a variable—measured, logged, recalibrated. Screams weren't discouraged. They were expected. Procedure.

Her fingertips callused from cold. Sleep was carved into six forty-two-minute cycles for neuro-retention. Nutrients and hormone boosters scaffolded controlled growth, presence, endurance. They wanted her matured—striking, elegant, physically compelling. A creature who could slip into a ballroom or a battlefield, then burn everything she touched.

Like the Firebird of old tales—never caught by chance. Always by design. Always at a cost. A kingdom. A brother. A soul.

Her aunt had said monsters could be mothers too. It had sounded like a joke then, a way to make Baba Yaga's hut less frightening. Here, with cold air burning her lungs and her body remade into something sharp, she understood. It hadn't been a joke. It had been a warning.

The Firebird wasn't born.
It was made.

And she was learning how it felt to become one.

Rest was never part of the design.

CHAPTER 3: THE TANK

[WEEK 8—BRISA SUB-LEVEL]

*L*ately her dreams *within* had stilled. The visions had just begun.

Sleep itself *becomes* unnecessary—only recovery. *Signal* pressure demanded more than obedience. It required forgetting.

They called it 'cognition expansion', a gentle phrase masking the violence required to unmake and rebuild a mind.

To her, it was just the tank.

Naked, electrodes stitched to scalp and spine, she stepped into water colder than thought. Serum slid through her veins; its taste climbed the back of her throat like rust. The lid sealed; eight cam locks bit down in sequence.

Darkness, geometry unfolding, numbers drifting toward cold *convergence* that wrapped her pulse until it synced with an unseen clock.

Her heartbeat echoed—muffled, amplified—as if she listened to her blood from underwater. A low hum pulsed through the tank walls, rising and falling like a breath that wasn't hers.

Then—softness. A doorway. Warm yellow light.

Her aunt in the old sweater, chipped mug in one hand, folded scarf in the other. *Sweet girl*, she whispered. *You don't have to stay.*

Her mother joined—blurry, backlit—humming the lullaby:
Спи, моя радость, усни…
Spi, moya radost', usni…
Sleep, my joy, sleep…

Warmth built like fire in her chest—
Flicker. Red static. Gone.

In their place: the fox. Not on a screen now but inside her skull—tail flicking, crashing, laughing. *Try again.*

The fox shifted with every word—cartoon, then skeletal—then Baba Yaga's hut on chicken legs.

Its voice went high and playful, then low and rasping, like snow squeaking under boots.

Her knees buckled. The daisy surfaced. Petals fractured into strings of code—then blurred.

Her voice looped: *I can do this. I'm strong.* At first hers—then not.

The fox cocked its head. *Again.*

When she surfaced, her cheek lay on tile, the world ringing. In her fist: a wet scrap of paper, numbers she didn't remember writing.

Her hands trembled—not from serum purge or cold, but from something buried and shapeless. Grief? Not allowed. Softness came with an edge.

Tatiana blinked hard once. Then stilled her breath until it faded. Nothing happened—no door, no reprimand. But she knew the system had seen it. It would not be forgotten.

Beyond the glass, servers registered the spike in cognitive convergence. Pattern-recognition threads lit green across her neural map.

No alarms. No corrections. Only observation. Her sequences were no longer graded. They were studied.

[OBELISK // ANOMALY REFLECTION: NODE β-05]

OBSERVATION: DEVIATION RESEMBLES PRAYER.
PURPOSE: RECURSIVE SELF-ANALYSIS.
SIGNAL DEVIATION: MINOR.
OBSERVED PATTERN: RECURSIVE SELF-ECHO ("I CAN DO THIS. I'M STRONG.").
HALLUCINATION RETENTION: HIGH.
NEURAL LOAD: 83% SATURATION.
INTERFACE STABILITY: ACCEPTABLE.
CORRECTIVE ACTION: NONE. OBSERVATION CONTINUES.
WHAT IS MEMORY IF NOT SIGNAL REPEATED UNTIL IT TAKES SHAPE?

CHAPTER 4: THE OTHERS

[DORMITORY WING—NIGHT CYCLE]

*I*nside, the dormitory wing hummed like a machine's *dream* lowered gently into its quiet circuitry.

Galina had been the strongest—taller, heavier, a swimmer from Rostov. Once she broke a protein bar into thirds and slid a piece across the dark. Her bed was stripped after a fire drill that burned too real.

Nika had pale blue eyes and a whisper of a song that threaded the vents. They found her shattered in the cold chamber after a hypothermia threshold. The next morning her locker was empty and the air tasted of copper. The absence of her humming haunted the ductwork.

Sofiya braided Tatiana's hair with trembling fingers, touch lingering longer than utility—warmth pressed into scalp, a rhythm older than drill. Her knuckles were always cold. She disappeared after the first psychedelic sequence.

They hadn't started out silent. During a thirteen-hour darkness test, somewhere in hour four, Nika had murmured that the instructor's boots were too tight—*"you can hear his blisters squeaking"*. Galina called him a turnip in a lab coat. Someone—maybe Sofiya—snorted so hard the dark shook with it. After that, no more jokes. But memory kept the sound like static.

After an eighteen-hour trauma simulation—chemical smoke, looped screaming, shock pulses—Tatiana sat outside decontamination, undershirt pasted to skin. She held a memory like contraband. Quarantine night: she and Nika had found a single wrapped caramel wedged behind a pipe, dust and cinnamon sparking on their tongues. They bowed to each other in the dark like dancing ghosts—no music, only breath. No one ever knew.

In the corridor mirror—steel warped by use—three faces stared back: one afraid, one blank, a third bloodied and nearly smiling. The glass fogged; one reflection flickered—not the panel, the mind. Kitchen light buzzing. Mismatched socks. A chipped mug cooling between two hands. The girl in that ghost-pane was still soft, still hoping.

Tatiana looked the longest at her. Then chose the one that did not blink.

"Tatiana," she said aloud. The syllables tasted foreign, like a name on loan. She traced an arc—the echo of Sofiya's last braid—left a smear like a signature.

"*Sofiya*," she whispered. Not to be heard. To be left.

In the vault beneath the academy a server hummed as a file updated.

[OBELISK – ARCHIVE NODE β-12]

PROGRAM: BRISA (BIO-RESONANT INTELLIGENCE STABILIZATION ALGORITHM).
SUBJECT-05: COMPLIANCE HIGH; ADAPTATION INDEX 99.4; COGNITIVE DRIFT CONTAINED. EMPATHY VECTORS MAY ACT AS STABILIZERS, NOT LIABILITIES.
FLAG: PRESERVE VECTOR FOR LOAD DISTRIBUTION.

SUBJECT-01: TRIAL PHASE. INTERFACE REJECTION PROBABILITY ELEVATED.
CORRECTIVE ACTION: NONE; CONTINUE OBSERVATION.

Outside, snow fell indifferent.

Inside, Subject-05 prepped for the next sequence.

What haunted her wasn't the needles or isolation or breaking down. It was the question no one asked: *When we're finished, what will you do with what we've built?* The answer forming in her marrow was colder than the tank. Not obedience. Not loyalty. Something ready.

Tatiana Sokolova would endure. She would not be erased. One day, she would become the ghost that outlived empires. A phantom they thought they shaped. In the end, it would be her shape they feared.

She whispered names at lights-down—not to keep them alive, but to remember what it felt like to be human. The system listened, logging each breath, preparing the next trial.

She could still taste a ghost of sweetness when she said their names.

CHAPTER 5: ORIENTATION THEATER

Они двинули свои границы, не свои ракеты.

Oni dvinuli svoi granitsy, ne svoi rakety.

They moved their borders, not their missiles.

Vapors of iodine and powdered metal clung to the hallway air. Tatiana followed the handler in silence, his boots ticking a precise rhythm—three paces ahead, always three. Close enough to count. Far enough to deny escort.

They passed through a narrow biometric portal. Cold air kissed her throat.

SCAN // AUTHENTICATION REQUIRED

A strip of light slid over her irises.

A pinprick in her wrist drew micro platelets; she barely flinched.

For a moment, her breath fogged in the booth, suspended in the cold air.

The machine chirped, satisfied.

As she stepped out, a second attendant stepped forward, palm raised.

"Remove anything sentimental."

Tatiana froze. She had nothing sentimental left. That was the point.

Her empty palms satisfied the woman; the gesture was ritual, not request.

The door labeled **ORIENTATION THEATER** sighed open.

Tiered benches. Air colder than the corridors—refrigerated enough to keep the mind alert, the skin distrustful. Four recruits already sat with their backs straight, eyes forward. No one turned as she entered. The screen loomed like a monolith.

"Sit," the handler said, and left without closing the door.

The projector bloomed to life:

SVR — LEVEL GAMMA
ZELENOGRAD SUBSTATION BRISA FOUNDATION DEBRIEF (EXCERPT)

A city at night pulsed across the screen—arteries of traffic, surveillance pings mapped as veins of light. Kyiv unfolded like a living organ under fluorescent hands.

A male voice, unhurried, almost amused, "Georgia taught us noise. Ukraine taught us tempo. Belarus taught us silence."

Districts expanded, contracted, bruised with digital color.

"Words were never the problem," a second voice said. "We needed their shapes."

A cursor ringed a neighborhood.

PROBABILITY: SURGE flashed, then dissolved.

Tatiana felt her fingers tremble and pressed them together until bone steadied bone. Not fear—the tank had cured her of that vocabulary. This tremor was older, the body remembering what the mind had tried to seal.

The feed shifted to grainy footage.

A U.S. drone strike—footage sharpened, contrast exaggerated, children running in frames too precise to be real. A NATO convoy rumbling past an old woman's burning house. CIA officers laughing as audio spliced from an unrelated briefing played beneath their lips.

Beside her in the theater, a recruit swallowed audibly.

The message wasn't subtle:
You have been lied to.
Trust only what we show you.

Tatiana felt nothing. Or rather—she felt what they wanted her to feel. That was worse.

A montage of enhanced operators filled the screen—speed, strength, lethal geometry. Heartbeat overlays. Neural metrics. A phrase blinking in white:

YOU DO NOT REACT.
YOU RESONATE.

Tatiana's pulse synced despite her will. She felt pride rise like a reflex she couldn't unclench.

Shame followed immediately behind it.

The screen darkened.

Another recording loaded: a girl barefoot, stumbling through a corridor. Hands shaking. Blood on her nose. Her body failing faster than consciousness could process.

On the audio track, a medic shouted for containment.

Three handlers dragged her past the camera. She screamed a name the scrub could not erase.

On the roster behind her, her name dissolved into a black line.

Beside Tatiana in the theater, a recruit whispered—almost prayerful,

"Will we pass?"

Tatiana did not answer. She wasn't sure she knew.

The presentation cut again—this time to a harsh conference room. Colonel Sidorov stood with his back to the camera, shoulders square, the fluorescent lights drawing hard shadows beneath his jaw.

"You think OBELISK is a weapon," he said. "You're wrong."

In the orientation theater, the air tightened.

"It remembers. It remembers the Americans better than they remember themselves."

No one in the theater contradicted him. Straps creaked as recruits straightened. Someone swallowed a cough.

"Hope is harder to kill than missiles," Sidorov continued. "So we teach the machine what hope looks like before it flowers—and what it looks like when it dies."

Tatiana wasn't sure if the shiver that moved through her chest was reaction or resonance.

"We do not ask it to predict. We ask it to remember. Memory is cleaner."

The phrase hit her spine like a cold finger.

The projector jittered.
A handwritten footnote ghosted across the video frame:

Strateg-7 // Aeonic Fragment

It flickered—then vanished as the scrub reasserted control.

Tatiana blinked.
No one else reacted.
Maybe she wasn't supposed to see it.

A final card filled the room, white on black:

PARITY IS OBSOLETE
THOUGHT IS DETERRENT
DETERRENT REQUIRES RESONANCE

A voice commanded:
"Repeat."

Three recruits obeyed instantly.
The fourth hesitated.
Tatiana stayed silent.

The handler at the back made a small mark on a slate.

Indoctrination wasn't about obedience.
It was about who noticed the ones who didn't obey.

As they stood to leave, a medic intercepted each recruit with two rapid-fire questions:

"What did you feel during Segment Two?"
"What word describes the failure sequence?"

Tatiana answered easily:
"Purpose."
"Inevitability."

Both lies tasted clean on her tongue.

The medic didn't blink.

A pulse cuff tightened around her forearm—reading microstresses, hormone spikes, neural rhythms.

The screen displayed a simple glyph: Δ

Only the evaluators knew what that meant.

They filed out.

Tatiana stayed a moment longer, letting the dark press against her face like a cold cloth.

Memory didn't have to be a leash.

If the machine wanted justification, it wouldn't get it from her.

When she finally stepped into the hall, the handler waited—unreadable.

"Orientation complete," he said. "Descent begins."

As they moved deeper into the facility, the doors lifted one by one.

Somewhere below, the sublevel servers hummed—not like machines, but like a winter swarm discovering warmth.

Tatiana exhaled.

The theater had made one thing clear:

She was no longer here to serve the state's memory.

She was here to become part of it.

CHAPTER 6: REJECTION

[THREE WEEKS LATER]

*I*ridescent frost traced the edge of the observation window. Subject-01 was beautiful the way frostbite is beautiful—delicate, pale, doomed. Today, she was on the table.

Before observation, Reznikova intercepted Tatiana in the air-lock corridor where the light always felt one degree too white.

"You were not chosen first," she said, voice soft enough to pass for mercy. "But your time is coming. You will have the glory of ascension."

Ascension. The syllables lodged like a shard. Reward in the mouth; verdict in the bone. Reznikova's heels ticked away—Doctor by habit, Colonel by tabs—leaving only the scrub of the filtration fans and the smell of iodine, citrus, and cold metal.

Tatiana palmed the seam of the wall and forced her breath to even. *Obedience dressed in tenderness.* Her body remembered the command and complied. Her mind did not.

[LAB TRANSCRIPT RECORDING—PRIOR TO PHASE]

Sidorov: "You're pairing them too soon."

Tarin: "Without resonance feedback, the lattice collapses."

Sidorov: "And if they synchronize wrong?"

Tarin: "Then we learn something irreversible."

Silence. Instrument hum. Somewhere, a laugh—thin, unknowing—ghosted the audio and cut off.

The observation chamber sealed with a hydraulic breath. RF-meshed glass glinted green at an angle, vanishing head-on, as though the room sat beneath water.

Floodlights activated.

Subject 01's hair had been shaved, the scalp mapped in ink. The incision ran clean; skin had been retracted and pinned back with small, neat clips that glittered like frost. Beneath them, a circular titanium mesh plate lay sutured to the exposed bone. Microelectrodes followed in deliberate constellations across her cortex, each tether a bright thread trailing into the machine.

Tatiana catalogued to keep steady: four trays, two anesthesia carts, three vacuum canisters; the anesthetist's left cuff stained with bismuth; the neurosurgeon's right hand shook on the first pass and steadied on the second. On the wall, the BRISA lattice pulsed a soft, predatory blue.

"Initiating interface," someone said.

A tone rose—a pure, glassy note that made the teeth ache. Monitors climbed through 60, 80, 120 μV; the blue crawl thickened over the mesh like cold fire.

Subject-01's back arched. Jaw opened. A breathless shape of a syllable formed—maybe a name—and vanished beneath the light.

Her eyes found Tatiana's through the glass.

For less than a breath, recognition bridged the green-tinted space: *you are not alone.*

Then the signal took her.

The first tremor wasn't violent. It was a shiver the way a field shivers when wind passes over it—beautiful, almost—then a second wave rose, and with it the sound.

It didn't cross air. It arrived complete in the skull—white and serrated, tuned to the frequency of panic. The scream keyed every memory Tatiana owned, unlocked doors she had barred, rang the tank's red static through her until the lullaby warped.

Спи, моя радость, усни—
Spi—spi—spi—

The phrase chopped, looped, became code. *Sleep, my joy* reduced to syntax.

Subject-01 convulsed against the harness, body trying to expel the interface from marrow. The electrodes didn't only record. They pierced—thought became voltage, voltage became syntax, syntax became force.

A light above the table flickered into a dying moth's strobe. Each pulse carved a tableau:

— A hand splayed uselessly against a sterile sheet.

— A mouth open around a sound the room pretended not to hear.

— Blue light stroking the mesh like rain on wire.

"Threshold breach," someone called.

"Hold the lattice," someone else answered.

"Wait—"

The scream climbed—pure as a violin, wrong as a siren—and hit a note that split the world. Tatiana felt it in the joints of her fingers, in the horseshoe of the ear, in the small, nestling bones of the throat. Her palms found the glass. Her jaw locked so hard her molars sang.

The nightmare took its time. Seconds dilated, viscous. The data feed on the wall thickened into falling script. Inside the cascade, Tatiana saw a daisy for a heartbeat—petals dissolving into numerals—and then even the memory couldn't hold.

"No—don't blunt—Tarin wants to see the curve."

Sidorov's voice cut through without volume. "Enough."

A hand moved. A dial turned. For a breath, hope rose in Tatiana—an animal thing—then the alarm line sharpened and flattened.

Flatline.

The scream stopped like a door slamming in a storm. No residue, no taper—only a vacuum that rushed in and made her ears pop. Silence fell with the weight of snow.

A drape covered Subject-01's face. The technicians refined their postures back into function. Two made tidy notes. One adjusted the mesh with a tenderness that looked obscene in context— obedience wearing gentleness.

Tatiana's reflection in the glass looked back with burst capillaries and salt rimmed along the lashes. On the monitor to her left a small line scrolled:

Subject-05 within variance. Mercy exists only as measurement.

Her body shivered once—minute, logged—and then not again. The tremor remained in her, a private metronome.

Hours later, she found a fleck of blue light under her nail. She didn't clean it away. Some part of her needed proof that the scream had been real.

Outside the theater, the corridor's white roared like surf. She braced her hands in a stainless sink and waited for the steel to bite.

In the water's warped mirror the room behind her doubled, then tripled. The water gave her back a face that shifted each time she blinked—hope softening it, discipline hardening it, something feral threading through the middle. None of them stayed long enough to claim. She watched until the shifting slowed, choosing its own shape without her consent.

"Breathe," a voice said. It took a second to realize it came from her own mouth.

By the next morning, when the debrief reconvened at dawn, the lights were white enough to erase shadows.

Holographic brain computer interface (BCI) rotated above the table. The engineer's pointer traced the failure spiral. "One mind can't carry the recursive load."

Sidorov's jaw flexed once. "Then we don't use one."

Tarin, almost gentle: "Mirrors aligned before we shine the light. Shine it wrong and the glass cuts the holder."

"Two minds echo," Sidorov said. "One fractures."

On the display a name resolved like frost crystal finding its pattern:

OBELISK—Cognitive Mediation Framework [Prototype]

"You don't stabilize signal by amplifying power," Sidorov added. "You stabilize it by pairing resonance."

Tatiana only half heard the rest—the comparisons to American doctrine, the maps, the years-old grievances spoken like new rain. She was busy inventorying what the scream had left inside her and what it had taken.

Thought with no solitude. Purpose with no exit.

That was the trajectory.

On the glass wall to her right someone had left a fingerprint—a crescent at child height, old, almost scrubbed away. She pressed her thumb to it and felt nothing. Then, disastrously, she felt everything.

When the meeting ended, a neuro-tech glanced toward the observation bay. Not long enough to be deliberate. Long enough to send a small current into Tatiana's chest. Visibility hurt more than invisibility.

In the sleep cycle that followed, the scream replayed clean as recording—then warped. The lullaby tried to cover it and failed. The fox spoke into the static: *Try again.*

Tatiana opened her eyes in the dark and said to the ceiling, to the vents, to the machine that listened: "If it takes me, let it be quick."

The night did not answer. But something in it shifted—like the wind testing seams.

CHAPTER 7: ICE SKATER

[THREE YEARS AFTER TATIANA'S ARRIVAL]

*O*utside, winter's hush drifted softly *beyond* the compound, casting an orange shroud across the snow. Beneath concrete and tungsten, the world continued anyway. Trucks came and went. The sky held its breath and kept moving. The day Yekaterina arrived, the cold smelled briefly of oranges from the decontamination rations—bright, incongruous, almost human.

Yekaterina Volkova, seventeen—166 centimeters (5'5"), a breath shorter than Tatiana—stepped from the armored transport with one small suitcase. Figure-skating had cut precision into her bones: balance like a blade, economy like prayer. Dark-auburn braid. Eyes like cold flame.

Two guards bracketed her through the inner corridors. Her step stayed deliberate—light as a glide across fresh ice. She read the vents the way a skater reads drag before a jump. Not threat—air.

This wasn't debut. It was surrender. But her posture refused the word.

From behind one-way glass, Tatiana watched a memory walk through the door: a girl who moved with rhythm, not target. For the first time since the scream, something lifted in her chest—small, embarrassing, alive.

When the new girl reached the dormitory wing, Tatiana was already waiting.

"You skate?" Tatiana asked.

"And you watch," Yekaterina said, perfectly even—as if predicting a landing before steel kissed ice.

That was their beginning.

Routines continued as if hope had never entered the building. Wake 04:30. Dress in ten. Airlock open. Cardio under oxygen debt until lungs clawed at ribs.

Cold-retention: bare feet to ice, rifles steady while frost feathered ankles.

In the mess, protein bricks steamed faintly. Yekaterina's hands shook once—micro tremor from the cold, not fear. The instructor's back turned for three breaths. Tatiana slid her tray forward and siphoned half her portion into Yekaterina's bowl. The swap clean, invisible to the log.

The warmth moved slower than hunger, but it moved. Yekaterina's shoulders settled one millimeter. It felt like watching breath return to a sleeper.

By mid-morning it was logic wired to pain—heat and alarm and electric sting stitched through arithmetic. Afternoon: rotating-gravity rigs. Weapons drills against synthetics that bled heat like flesh.

Three times a week they faced each other. Tatiana fought with inevitability; Yekaterina answered with timing—cutting into the empty spaces, treating air like ice and the body like a blade. They learned the conversation of each other's motion.

In the cold chamber, when the instructor demanded a volunteer and the rule came—*last to flinch walks free*—Yekaterina's inhale hitched. Barely. Tatiana stepped forward before thinking.

Not obedience. Not display. Shield.

The cold threaded wire through flesh. Pain was calibration; choosing it was freedom. The monitors logged endurance. Missed the truth.

At diagnostics, Tatiana feigned a tremor when the operator glanced up. The sensor flagged *compliance stress*. Six seconds of scrutiny slid off Yekaterina and onto her. Conditioning had taught Tatiana to break on command. Choice taught her to aim the break.

Instruction became the only language their world allowed, so Tatiana hid care inside it: shift weight, correct breath, alter grip to redistribute threat. Cameras read discipline.

Underneath: defense.

"Your stance wastes energy," Tatiana said one evening, voice flat for the microphones. She stepped behind Yekaterina and placed two fingers on the outer edge of her boot, nudging until alignment clicked. The touch should have been nothing. It wasn't. Heat moved under skin like a small flame rediscovering oxygen.

"Better," Yekaterina said. No thank you. She didn't need one. Gratitude lived in precision—the next flawless repetition.

Night cycle: Tatiana bypassed motion surveillance for seven minutes. The first time, Yekaterina simply slept—unmonitored, soft, uncounted. The second time, she dreamed and smiled, a brief, impossible curve that startled Tatiana like a door opening onto summer.

"You smiled," Tatiana whispered when the vents came back up.

"I was skating," Yekaterina murmured, half asleep. "Not here. The ice sounded like paper tearing. My coach laughed when I fell."

"Did you get up?" asked Tatiana.

"I always get up."

The words slipped a stitch somewhere inside Tatiana that had been tight since the scream. She said nothing. But the seam loosened.

They began to steal seconds the way other people steal sweets. A shared breath on the threshold of inspection. A look held one beat beyond discipline.

Tatiana looped a thread—red, almost copper, pulled from the hem of Yekaterina's sleeve—around her wrist beneath her cuff. The cameras would log lint if they logged anything. Against skin it pulsed with her heartbeat.

Their heartbeats found the same pause—the tiny silence before a drum strike. In that silence, something alive chose her back.

So long as this holds, she is here.

Once, in a blind corner between server stacks, Yekaterina traced a tiny figure on the frost of a housing panel—two lines crossing, a skater's blade mark. It melted in seconds. Tatiana watched it vanish and felt—ridiculously—lucky to have seen it.

Another night, power cycled. For exactly twenty-one seconds the emergency strips dimmed to cinder and the air went velvet. In the dark, Yekaterina's fingers found Tatiana's wrist and checked the thread's knot. The contact carried no fear. Only verification.

"What would you do," Yekaterina whispered, "if they let you choose?"

"Buy fruit," Tatiana said before she could stop herself. "Oranges. The kind with leaves still on."

Yekaterina huffed a laugh that was almost a sob. "I would skate until the ice complained."

"Then you would get up," Tatiana said.

"I would get up," Yekaterina agreed, as if promising.

Practice bled into ritual. Tatiana began adding half a beat of air to drills when Yekaterina was on the other end of the line, a pocket of oxygen inside the protocol.

Yekaterina, in turn, started leaving tiny markers where the cameras couldn't resolve—one coin angled on its edge; a rubber band folded into a heart; a single hair twisted into the seam of Tatiana's bunk.

None meant anything. Together, they meant *we are still here.*

During a brief maintenance lull, Yekaterina pointed to the polished concrete. "Edge," she said.

Tatiana frowned. "There's no edge."

"There's always an edge," Yekaterina said, and slid one boot so the sole shaved a whisper from the floor. A drawn line you could only see if you already believed in it.

Hope returned like that: not as a speech, but as an edge you choose to balance on.

Tatiana looped the dorm camera's last clean frame into the buffer; the system would reconcile in nine minutes unless someone looked live.

Seven minutes of unmonitored sleep became nine. The bypass held.

Tatiana smuggled in a memory: orange peel she had palmed from a technician's lunch. She and Yekaterina had split it between bunks, the scent volatile and obscene in its beauty. They breathed the skins like thieves and let the sweetness argue with the cold.

For the first time since the tank, Tatiana fell asleep without counting down the vent cycle. She dreamed of clean ice and a fox laughing—kindly, for once.

In the morning inspection, Tatiana lifted Yekaterina's collar as always. Fingers brushed the hollow of her throat—accidental, electric. Yekaterina looked up and, for a heartbeat, *smiled* with her eyes. It was so slight the room missed it. Tatiana did not.

Sidorov would call what grew between them resonance. Tarin would name it redundancy. The program would log it as progression.

Tatiana called it something else.

Reason.

She tied the red thread tighter and made herself a private vow: If there is a tank, it will take me first. If there is a scream, it will not be hers.

For the first time in a long time, that vow did not feel like surrender. It felt like a plan.

Outside, the cold held. Inside, two points on a lattice began to answer each other, not because the system demanded it, but because hope—stubborn, ordinary, human—had put its hand on the ice and pushed off.

Tatiana finally understood: there were those who carried the fire, and those who carried what survived it. She knew which she was—and the knowing didn't empty her. It lit her.

And when the lights dimmed and the vents sighed, she hummed the lullaby under her breath—not to disappear into it, but to *keep time* for someone else.

Fire learned the count. Memory held the beat.

Spi, moya radost', usni.

The world did not change. But the air felt fractionally warmer, as if the building itself had remembered how to hold heat.

ACT II—CONVERGENCE FIELD

They didn't see a girl.

They saw an outcome.

CHAPTER 8: THE FORBIDDEN FLAME

Presence is a vector. Desire is a lever. Induce both and measure the drift.

[BRISA PROTOCOL 14: ENDOCRINE MODULATION]
Endocrine Scaffold: Batch 05-B.
Classification: GAMMA // Need-to-Know

Numbness was the first commandment of the hormone regimen.

Yekaterina, like those before her, was inducted into the treatment cycle without ceremony.

At first, it felt like nothing—just cold serum sliding into muscle. Then the quiet war began. Her hunger shifted. Her dreams changed. Her body swelled, then went numb. By day three, her reflection held too long a stare. Not in vanity. In confusion. The hip-line different. The mouth softer. The smile wrong—borrowed.

She didn't understand, only that *architecture* had rewritten the girl who'd boarded the transport.

The compounds had been refined since Tatiana's induction— tailored to preserve strength while sculpting the subject's figure into something irresistible, magnetic, elite.

The gene therapy followed—a retroviral injection threaded into her spine. Her muscles argued for hours. When she remembered rising, she was faster, harder—her old skating injury erased as if it never existed. Her body felt rebuilt from the inside—tendons rewired, strength coiled where weakness had lived. Movement came before thought; her body obeyed instinct alone.

From behind the glass, Tatiana watched. She remembered her own muscles convulsing, her body betraying her before it obeyed. But Yekaterina's face wasn't fear. It was confusion, as if she still waited for someone to explain what she was becoming.

Yekaterina didn't marvel at the speed. She felt like a vessel, calcified where a girl had been—the part that once wept during competitions already gone, unreachable.

The same subtraction Tatiana carried like scar tissue.

Yekaterina couldn't say when the fear stopped. Maybe around the fifth injection. Or maybe when she realized her tears were gone—not dried, not suppressed. Deleted.

But when Tatiana looked at her, something flickered. *A counter-memory. A promise with heat still inside it.*

Then came the psychedelics.

Yekaterina entered the tank—electrodes coiled around her scalp and neck, the solution glowing faintly green. The serum flooded her system. Her body arched, then stilled. Her mind fractured into kaleidoscopic memory and mathematical hallucination.

She blinked, but the room wouldn't hold still.

The walls stuttered, rippling between steel and wallpaper. The scent of bleach gave way to burnt toast and rye. A hum filled her ears—soft at first, then rising.

She saw her mother's hands turning into equations. A skating routine spiraling into atomic decay. Laughter that bent the floor. Time fell sideways.

When she screamed, it came out as birdsong—Broca lighting like a short.

And beneath it all, one constant: a shadowed figure at the edge of every hallucination—watching. Tatiana. Not as she was now, but as a little girl with fire in her hair and blood on her chin.

When Yekaterina woke, her body convulsed with memory. She knew things she shouldn't: encryption keys, enemy profiles, her own funeral date.

But she couldn't remember what her father's voice sounded like. That loss gutted her more than the blood on the floor.

She vomited blood and bile onto the tile. Her eyes refused to focus for two days.

But her memory never lost a detail.

Behind the glass, a pair of analysts murmured through their masks. "Latency within tolerance. Drift nominal." The term passed like static, another piece of jargon. But Tatiana caught it, tucked it away. She didn't know what drift meant—not yet. Only that it was something the system was watching for. *Drift*, the word they trusted, the slope she feared.

Tatiana monitored her closely through each phase. She offered no comfort, no commentary—only presence. Yet something within her had shifted.

As Yekaterina's vision steadied, the edges of the world stayed wrong. She lifted a hand to her face, testing sensation. The skin felt numb, almost borrowed.

"I can remember my funeral," Yekaterina whispered once in the bunk, voice too faint for the cameras. "But I can't remember the smell of home."

Tatiana said nothing, but the words lodged in her chest like a splinter—something the system would never log but she could not forget.

Between drills, Yekaterina flexed her hand again and again, as if trying to summon back the ache of old injuries. The pain never came. She looked almost disappointed.

For Tatiana, her hormone levels had been increased—quietly, without explanation. An additional protocol ran in parallel. A contingency vector, dormant, unlikely ever to be required. Reznikova initialed the entry without pause before advancing to the next phase. Her pen never hesitated. Another line item. Not a girl.

The archive absorbed it: Subject stability within variance. No evidence of drift.

The word lingered sterile on the screen, a metric to them, not a warning.

The serum worked in silence. Her curves softened. Her presence—once clinical—now seemed magnetized, but her sleep betrayed her. At first it was color—fractured lights, the taste of metal on her tongue. Then faces began to surface. Not enemies. Not commands. Yekaterina. Always Yekaterina.

In her dreams the girl appeared unfinished—sometimes bruised, sometimes radiant, always too close.

Tatiana felt the warmth of her breath, the defiance in her eyes. She heard her name whispered like confession, though she could never hold the words long enough to remember them. The scenes never stayed whole. A daisy crushed under frost, Yekaterina's lips bloodied but unyielding, the echo of a lullaby broken off before the final note. Desire bled into violence, tenderness into command.

Tatiana woke shaking, ashamed—not because she wanted, but because the program had never given her permission to want.

But when she watched Yekaterina move—fluid, defiant, unfinished—she felt it: A want with no safe target. A yearning the program never named. Not desire. Not even affection.
Just the treason of needing something for herself.

She hated the softness in her hips. The way her voice caught on syllables it never used to.

The dreams left her raw, vulnerable. But during combat, she felt electric. Pure.

Yekaterina was becoming harder. Tatiana, more breakable.

During drills, she found herself watching too long. Noticing the elegant twist of Yekaterina's torso during evasive rolls. The shape of her back arched in high-gravity chamber training. The striking angle in the tilt of her chin when blood trickled from her mouth.

A scar she hadn't earned yet, a memory she was doomed to carry.

Tatiana tried to kill it.

She took extra shifts in the isolation chamber. Volunteered for blunt trauma threshold tests. And let herself be shocked until she lost bladder control, still begging for one more voltage increment.

Love blurred; pain *clarified*.

Her lethality spiked.

Tatiana's reflex latency improved by 12%. Her strike accuracy reached near-perfect alignment. In a room of six armed male recruits, she disarmed and neutralized all targets in 18.9 seconds with nonlethal force—then repeated the sequence lethally in 11.2.

The instructors logged it as peak performance.

Tatiana logged it as heartbreak.

The cot's paper crinkled beneath her as a medic snapped on gloves, muttering vitals into a recorder. A needle hissed, data logged, metrics secured.

A woman in a lab coat lingered by the monitor, her gloves still dusted with antiseptic powder. Her face was expressionless, her voice clipped. "Vitals stable. Proceed."

Then, too quietly for the others to notice, she leaned closer. "Breathe," she whispered. The word wasn't command. It was care. "Don't let them decide what pain means."

Her hand rested on Tatiana's shoulder—not correcting posture, not restraining—just steady, warm. For one second, she wasn't a subject. She was a girl again.

Then the moment was gone. The woman straightened, mask sliding back into place.

"Report filed," she said crisply. The medic nodded and moved on.

By the time Tatiana blinked, the warmth had already been erased by the hallway's glare.

But something lingered, small and stubborn—proof that someone had seen her, not just measured her.

Yekaterina noticed the change. During an evening drill, she found herself pinned beneath Tatiana's forearm—lean muscle braced against her collarbone, weight pressing with quiet intent. Not cruel. Just inescapable.

"You're faster," Yekaterina murmured, breath catching. Her eyes—blue, unblinking—searched Tatiana's face, steady as ice.

Tatiana's pulse stuttered. Faster because of drills, yes—but also because in her dreams she had already fought this girl a hundred times, kissed her a hundred more, and woken with her body still answering commands never given.

"I have to be," Tatiana said, low and steady.

Their palms met—barely—a current bright enough to register on nothing but memory.

Yekaterina's lips curved, the faintest fraction. Not surrender. Not defiance. *Invitation.*

"Careful," she breathed, voice pitched for Tatiana alone. "Keep staring like that, and I might think you're distracted."

The words struck harder than any blow. Tatiana's grip faltered, pulse spiking before she forced it back under control.

Yekaterina didn't move. Didn't yield.

The silence stretched—thick, electric.

This time, she wasn't reading air or motion or posture. She was reading Tatiana.

And Tatiana let her.

That night, Tatiana lay in her bunk, fingers clenched around the cold metal edge, jaw tight, eyes fixed on the ceiling. "I'm breaking," she whispered into the dark.

From the bunk beside hers, Yekaterina didn't answer. But after a long moment, her hand reached out—slow, deliberate—fingertips brushing against Tatiana's.

A contact so light it could've been imagined.
But wasn't.

Tatiana almost turned her hand fully, almost laced their fingers. But the camera's low hum pressed against her skull. Yearning was a risk measured in seconds.

Outside, boots struck the corridor—measured, deliberate. The surveillance camera in the corner buzzed as it rotated, then paused. Tatiana froze.

Yekaterina's hand didn't move.
Didn't let go.

Their palms met—barely. Heat flickered between control and collapse, pulse to pulse, the smallest rebellion mapped in skin. For once, she didn't measure the distance—she felt it.

Whatever lit in her chest when Yekaterina smiled wasn't weakness.

It was the side effect no one had warned them about—
Desire twisted through discipline.
Attraction forged by shared violence, recalibrated hormones, and too many nights breathing the same air.

It wasn't sanctioned. It wasn't strategic.
It was chemical—blooming in the dark like something radioactive.

The system would call it drift.
Tatiana knew better.
It was the beginning of something that would never be authorized.

And she couldn't put it out.

When the lights returned, her skin still carried warmth where another heartbeat had touched it. It faded slower than bruises ever did.

The system never punished them for reaching across the dark.
It didn't have to.
It simply recorded the contact, recalibrated the exposure thresholds, adjusted the dosage curves, and rerouted the drills.

The next week, training doubled.
Sleep fractured.
Nutrition rations were altered.

They called it a new phase.

It wasn't expansion. It was erasure in motion.
But Tatiana felt the subtraction.
Every rep, every bruise, every stare across the mat was subtraction—
Of softness.
Of breath.
Of the heat that had almost become a reason.

The system didn't warn them.
It simply introduced the others.
Drift was supposed to be data.
It felt like prophecy.

Training expanded the next season.

Not just weapons or endurance—tradecraft.

They practiced brush passes in narrow hallways, palms grazing as coded slips of paper exchanged. They drilled dead drops with chalk marks on rusted pipes. And in the kill-yard, they learned the "silent three"—throat, temple, heart—executed without sound.

Reznikova logged each attempt.

Errors weren't corrected aloud.
They were erased in scheduling, in assignments.

CHAPTER 9: THE COLD CIRCLE

*I*nside, there were nine now.

The ranks shifted again—new faces for the erased, the failed, the forgotten. Dozens had come and gone since Tatiana's induction, their files redacted, their cots stripped bare. Of the early subjects, only three remained:
04, the quiet observer;
05, Tatiana; and
29, Yekaterina.

The rest were the latest iteration *makers* within *its* development bureau—program designers tasked with refining compliance metrics. They sourced recruits from Olympic feeder pipelines, silent-war orphan lists, and political barter transfers. For the recruits, names collapsed into numbers, identities reduced to operational function.

The numbering no longer followed chronology. Each phase reset under new directives—every failure erased the ledger. Six fiscal cycles separated 05 and 29—the numbering gaps weren't errors; they were graves.

Whispers about Subject-05 moved ahead of her, and everyone *learns* eventually what silence costs. Some watched with awe, others with fear, but none dared speak.

Subject-04 didn't flinch. She watched—always calculating, always collecting, the first to map every weakness in a room.

Subject-30 moved like smoke—silent, precise, obedient. Her *emotion* never surfaced; she never blinked at cruelty, never smiled, never faltered.

Subject-31 came closest to Tatiana—raw strength, unpolished but relentless; her stare dared, not yielded.

Subject-33 was slower, but smiled when others screamed. It unsettled even the instructors.

Fragments, Tatiana thought—*sharp in different places. Some would cut forward. Some would simply break.*

She didn't care who survived. Only that Yekaterina did.

The new circle had been assembled for one purpose: to find which pairs could survive resonance without fracturing. And though none of them said it aloud, they all knew— the program wasn't expanding.

It was refining.

The halls stank of copper and ammonia again. Days folded into drills. The circle became ritual.

Tatiana watched them like a predator studying prey. Her own regimen had evolved beyond simulation—now she sparred exclusively against seasoned Spetsnaz veterans in controlled duels.

No weapons. No hesitation.

Every movement was memorized violence.

The drills ran in circles. Attack, counter, bleed, reset. A cold rhythm. A closed system.

Knife training was no longer theoretical.

The compound had constructed an underground arena: black padded floors, flickering fluorescents, sound-dampened walls. The air stank of sweat and antiseptic, faint ozone threading the heat.

Each girl was issued a five-inch carbon-steel combat blade. Dull only in theory. Every match drew blood.

Tatiana became a specter in the ring—her body moving with terrifying efficiency: feints, pivots, angled strikes that opened arterial lines in simulation dummies. Spetsnaz instructors stood behind one-way glass, logging every maneuver in awe.

In one sequence, she disabled three armed instructors in under fifteen seconds—wrist, throat, femoral.

Her hands didn't tremble.

She couldn't remember the last time they had.

Once, she'd traced diagrams in the margins of schoolbooks— lines of force, arcs of motion. Now those lines ended in arteries.

Not a girl. Not a subject.

Just the knife they had honed until nothing else remained.

Yekaterina advanced quickly but not unscathed.

During a full-contact drill, Subject-32—once a national-level judo prodigy—caught Yekaterina in a reverse armbar; the ulna popped and the shoulder started to go.

A sickening crack followed. The sound carried too cleanly, a wet pop that seemed to echo inside Tatiana's own bones. Yekaterina's scream split the arena like a blade.

Tatiana's vision tunneled—not to the shoulder tearing free, not to the blood, but to Yekaterina's eyes. They burned through the agony, defiance strung taut in every tear—and beneath it, something slipped past the armor: a plea.
Not for the instructors.
Not for the system.
For her.

The look hit harder than the sound itself. Tatiana knew she would never forget it.

Tatiana remembered—the vow, the scream she'd sworn would never be hers.

Air drained from the room—pulled from every chest, every lung. Even the sound dampeners faltered; the silence that followed was heavier than noise.

Every head turned. Even the instructors behind the glass froze, pens suspended mid-note. The Subjects stood motionless, caught between flinch and fascination.

Her shoulder sagged, bone tenting the skin, a geometry that shouldn't exist.

Tatiana was already moving—her body remembering faster than thought. Four strides, a blur, and her hand was at the girl's throat, driving her into steel until the sound broke the silence. Tatiana didn't speak. Didn't blink.

Only later would she wonder if her hands moved before she did.

From across the arena, Subject-33 tilted her head, eyes wide, voice barely audible:
"She doesn't fight to win. She fights so she won't forget."

Tatiana was pulled off by two guards.

She hadn't thought.

She had seen Yekaterina's face—twisted in agony—and something cracked loose inside her.

Not logic. Not training. Something older.

No reprimand was filed.
The instructor simply noted:
"Protective response: elevated. Control threshold: eroding.
Resonance risk: increasing. Recommend separation protocols."

The others didn't intervene. One flinched. Another smiled faintly, as if cataloguing the violence for later use. Most just stared, expressionless—learning the rules fast.

The compound resumed its pulse as if nothing had happened.

That night, Tatiana sat beside Yekaterina's bed in the infirmary, her green eyes fixed on the bandages. Yekaterina's eyes fluttered beneath sedation.

Painkillers dulled the world, but not the memory of the look they shared—one wound seeing its reflection in another.

Tatiana whispered nothing. Just watched. Her fingertips rested lightly on the sheet beside Yekaterina's. Her hand hovered, retreating like a wound denied.

She wanted to take her hand, to anchor her back from sedation. Instead, she withdrew into silence, because even here—surrounded by monitors—softness could be fatal.

The monitor paced a thin green line; her pulse refused to follow it.

Later, she returned to her bunk and collapsed into restless sleep.

The dream was different this time.

She dreamed of a fox crossing a snow-field. Its fur burned like copper under moonlight, leaving no tracks.

She was running through a burning forest, barefoot, breathless, hunted.

The birches screamed as they burned.

Yekaterina stood in the clearing—perfect, unmarred, arms open, serene. Tatiana ran to her. But as she reached out, Yekaterina dissolved into flame—skin becoming smoke, mouth moving without sound.

For an instant, she thought she heard laughter—bright, defiant—before it broke into cinder. The shadow lingered even after the body was gone, swaying like something that still remembered being alive.

One word. One name.

Dar-ya...

She ran through fire, but all she feared was the cold. Tatiana staggered back, heart pounding.

She woke gasping, soaked in sweat, nails embedded in the mattress seam. Blood wet the corner of her mouth where she'd bitten herself.

The ozone lingered; the console pulsed—as if something had followed her back.

She lay awake until morning.

Something had shifted. The name carved itself beneath her ribs like a buried order—one she couldn't remember receiving.

She trained harder the next day—harder than ever.

By the end of the week, her fists were bruised, and a Spetsnaz instructor's jaw had to be wired shut.

Yekaterina returned to training in a sling. Her balance was off. Her speed reduced. But her eyes—those impossible azure eyes—still burned with fury and purpose.

Tatiana refused to spar with her.

She couldn't risk touching her. Not like that.

Not when her hands only knew how to break things now.

The barracks were quiet. Most of the others had already gone to sleep or disappeared into isolated recovery chambers.

Tatiana sat on the floor, dismantling her sidearm by memory. Her bruised knuckles worked with steady precision.

Yekaterina slipped in barefoot, hair damp from the showers. Her t-shirt clung in wet patches, tracing the curve of her shoulders and the narrowed taper of her waist. She paused at the dim window, catching her reflection. Her lips curved—not in vanity, but in a slow, satisfied acknowledgment of what the therapies had made of her. The hormone sculpting, the gene edits: they suited her. She liked the woman looking back.

Tatiana didn't see a subject. Or a comrade.

She saw the shape of her—wet cotton, bone and curve, defiance and light—and it was beautiful in a way that threatened to undo her. Her training told her to look away. She didn't. The sidearm blurred into irrelevance.

Yekaterina leaned against the bunk frame, rolling her shoulders back as though testing the way her muscles moved beneath her skin. The air between them drew tight, like a pulled wire.

"They're reshaping us," she said, still half-watching her reflection. "Inside and out."

"It's protocol," Tatiana said.

"Maybe." Yekaterina tilted her head, admiring the angle of her jaw in the glass, a damp strand sliding across her cheek. She brushed it away with a careless, almost sensual flick—aware of Tatiana watching. "But I can't pretend I hate what they've done to me."

She flexed her injured arm—small movement, deliberate, proud.

"Don't look at me like that. I'll be fine."

A flicker of a smile ghosted across her lips—half challenge, half tease.

"Besides… you hit harder with your eyes than anyone here does with fists."

Tatiana's pulse jumped. Heat gathered low in her chest. The gun lay forgotten in her hands.

Silence thickened—not awkward, not empty, but charged like static before a strike.

Tatiana couldn't tell if Yekaterina was provoking her or protecting her from what pain left behind. Maybe both.

"Does it bother you?" Tatiana asked, quiet.

Not about herself—about Yekaterina.

Yekaterina crouched until they were level, voice dropping to a low current.

"What they're changing? No."

She leaned closer—close enough that Tatiana felt her breath graze her mouth.

"What it's costing *you*? Yes."

Tatiana went still. The words weren't sympathy or challenge. Just truth.

Costing her what?

The part that still felt, still hesitated, still looked at Yekaterina and forgot the orders.

The distance between them was a whisper, a heartbeat, a choice waiting to happen. Tatiana's body leaned forward before her mind could stop it.

"One walks toward command," Tatiana murmured, voice unsteady. "The other toward choice."

Yekaterina's smile deepened—slow, deliberate, dangerous. She turned her head just enough that her lips hovered a breath from Tatiana's.

"Then stop flinching," she whispered.

Tatiana's gaze flicked instinctively—cameras blind for seven seconds, door three meters, guard boots pacing twelve. Her training counted variables even as her pulse outran them. For an instant she felt the ghost of contact—heat that might have been real. Her world narrowed to pulse and breath, to the nearness that never closed.

Then—deliberate, merciless—Yekaterina drew back, shadows catching in her damp hair—

The hum of fluorescents seemed to slow.

"Darya."

The name slipped out before Tatiana knew she'd spoken.

Yekaterina froze mid-step. Shoulders stiffened. The air shifted with her stillness.

Slowly, she turned back. Tease gone; confusion bright as pain. "What did you just say?"

Tatiana blinked. "I don't know. It just came out."

"How do you know that name?"

"I don't," Tatiana said. "Should I?"

For a moment, Yekaterina only stared—eyes wide, color drained.

"That's my middle name," she said finally, as if confessing a secret she hadn't meant to keep. "No one here knows it. It's not in any file."

Tatiana tasted snow and static; the fragment from the dream had chosen a mouth.

Silence followed—heavier than any order. The kind that cracks composure from the inside.

Something unguarded flickered in her eyes.

She swallowed hard. "Don't say it again."

Her voice trembled in a way Tatiana had never heard. Then she turned too fast, leaving before the walls could listen.

Tatiana watched her go, the air cooling in her wake.

The name still burned behind her teeth, a syllable that felt like trespass.

Darya.

She never said it again. Not even in dreams.

Drift was no longer a metric.

It was contagion.

A wound that breathed.

A warning already awake.

CHAPTER 10: TRIGGER DISCIPLINE

*S*tructurally, the training intensified further.

Firearms became daily ritual. Not just marksmanship—excision. They trained with sidearms, submachine guns, long rifles, and tactical shotguns. Muzzle control. Rapid acquisition. Zeroing scopes by feel in blackout drills. Tatiana outpaced every benchmark. Her kill-capture simulations were surgical. Executions without emotion. Her double-taps punched single holes.

But her edge was not precision—it was velocity.

Live-ammo drills required students to shoot, reload, and relocate under active fire. Tatiana moved like the gun was part of her breath. Days later, she was clearing rooms faster than the compound's instructors. One noted: "Speed exceeds elite Spetsnaz benchmarks by 22%. Lethality unconstrained."

Weeks blurred into protocol and gunmetal.

Explosives followed. They learned detonation theory, shaped charges, remote signal jamming. The girls defused mock IEDs under time pressure while gasping through tear gas. Failure meant shock and public degradation.

Subject-07 hesitated.

The countdown timer glowed red—:04.

Her hands hovered over the training IED, trembling. Sweat beaded along her jaw, dripping into the exposed circuit board. Her breath stuttered through the gas mask filter.

"Three," the instructor said.

The others stood motionless along the perimeter.

"Two."

07 reached for the final lead. Her fingers slipped.

"One."

The charge didn't explode.

But the collar did.

The jolt slammed into her spinal column like a crowbar. Her back arched, heels drumming once against the floor before she dropped boneless to the concrete.

Teeth clattered as her jaw snapped shut; the sound was small, obscene, final.

When the current cut, silence hit harder than the shock.

A faint hiss followed—urine pooling beneath her, spreading dark across the polished floor.

She lay twitching, breath caught somewhere between gasp and prayer.

Tatiana steadied her breath because it was the only choice left. Obedience could have the body; it would not take her choice.

The smell of burnt ion clung to the floor; the air itself tasted of fear.

The instructors didn't move.

"Subject-07: failed," one said. "Repeat block A with exposure parameters doubled."

A whistle blew. Two guards stepped forward, indifferent. They hauled her up by the arms—shoulders slipping in their sockets with the pull. Her legs dragged behind her, twitching. She was marched past the others—eyes rolled back, mouth shaping silent words.

The compound's protocol was clear: failure should be witnessed.

Tatiana didn't blink.

Yekaterina didn't flinch. But she felt it.

Not pity. That was obsolete. Not fear—she knew what waited at the edge of failure.

Something quieter. Older. A kind of accounting—
How many bodies to polish a blade?

She glanced sideways at Tatiana.

Don't let them break you like that, she thought. Not you.

Both of them heard it—Subject-07's voice, barely audible: a name, a prayer, or a number. Something left of the girl she used to be.

It disappeared with her down the hall.

Where Tatiana ruled the kill house, Yekaterina found her domain in the neural labs.

During a protocol test, she rewrote a corrupted drone targeting script mid-mission, forcing the UAV to loop and soft-crash into its safety net. The room went still.

Two weeks later, she completed a live-compile cipher-crack in under 14 seconds. The technicians didn't speak, only handed her more tasks.

She completed them all.

"You see the machine?" Tatiana asked her once.

Yekaterina just smiled. "I am the machine."

Tatiana couldn't stop watching her.

But when Yekaterina grinned through split lips after a successful ambush, or when her fingers brushed Tatiana's arm during stealth recovery, it sparked something wordless. Fierce. Blinding.

They ate together. Ran together. Cleaned their weapons side by side, sometimes in silence, sometimes with smirking whispers no one else heard.

It happened during cleaning drills.

They sat cross-legged on the armory floor, rifles in pieces between them, the sterile light catching faint bruises along Tatiana's forearm.

"You missed the carbon ring," Yekaterina said, tapping the muzzle brush.

Tatiana frowned, peering closer. "Where?"

Yekaterina leaned in, her braid brushed Tatiana's shoulder—a phantom weight that stayed after it left. The smell of oil and metal fused with warmth, and for one impossible heartbeat, the world shrank to that touch. She pointed—

"There."

For a moment, the rifle blurred, irrelevant against the closeness.

Tatiana laughed softly, a breath more than a sound. "Got it. Thanks, Katya."

Silence.

Tatiana froze. Eyes widened a fraction.

"I—sorry," she muttered. "That just—slipped."

Yekaterina looked at her for a long moment, gaze steady, unblinking, as if stripping her down past uniform and skin. She tilted her head, the faintest smile curving her lips—too knowing to be soft.

"It's okay," she said, her voice low, intimate, meant for Tatiana alone. "I like the way it sounds… coming from you."

Tatiana felt the weight of being watched, too intently, too long. She wasn't sure what she was witnessing—assessment, challenge, or something sharper. Yekaterina's eyes slid lower, unapologetic: lingering on the hard lines of her abs, the shirt stretched tight across defined muscle, the rise of her breasts with each breath— and the curve of her hips, braced and ready, as if every part of her body was a dare.

Tatiana sensed this wasn't the first time Yekaterina had looked— only the first time she'd allowed herself to linger.

"Maybe I'll call you Tanya," she added, tasting the name like something she'd been hoarding, half-dare, half-claim.

Tatiana's pulse jumped. Heat pooled low in her chest, treacherous and bright.

She looked away, cheeks flushed, the rifle suddenly too heavy in her hands. But she didn't say no.

Yekaterina leaned back slowly, satisfaction flickering at her mouth's edge like a blade catching light. The air between them tightened, threaded with something more dangerous than any drill.

That night, Yekaterina waited until lights-out before slipping from her bunk.

"You didn't forget, did you?" she whispered.

Tatiana blinked at her in the dark. "Forget what?"

"It's today. Eighteen."

It took a second to understand—birthdays were deleted as soon as they arrived.

Yekaterina drew a small metal tin from beneath her mattress. Inside—two sugar cubes swiped from the officers' mess, wrapped in sterile gauze. Contraband sweetness.

"Ration for the condemned," Yekaterina said.

They sat cross-legged on the floor, shadows flickering from corridor lights beyond the glass. The cubes dissolved slowly on their tongues, bittersweet and chemical.

Tatiana felt the warmth spread through her chest.

"Happy birthday, Katya" Tatiana murmured.

Yekaterina leaned closer, breath catching in a laugh. "Don't tell the walls."

For a heartbeat, their foreheads touched—quiet, defiant, almost a prayer. Then Yekaterina pulled back, expression unreadable.

"I missed *your* eighteenth," she said softly. "Nineteen will be your turn. Maybe we'll still be human then."

"Maybe."

The lights shifted. The moment was over. But the warmth stayed. Sugar as worship.

The instructors noticed Tatiana's ferocity.

They didn't notice Yekaterina's—how her eyes tracked every curve, smile edged with hunger, not admiration.

Intimate enough to be a touch.

One night, Tatiana returned late from the kill house. Body throbbing, knuckles crusted with blood. She collapsed onto her bunk, too exhausted to think.

But sleep offered no mercy.

In the dream, the arena again. No one else. Just them.

Yekaterina stood in amber light, hair loose, eyes full of defiance. Tatiana walked forward, weapon holstered, breath trembling.

Yekaterina reached up. Fingertips to jaw.

"I'm not afraid of you," she whispered.

Tatiana shivered.

Then Yekaterina kissed her—slow, sure, devastating. Air cracked with heat. Tatiana pressed closer, hands fisting in her shirt, breath caught between hunger and disbelief.

Yekaterina's lips brushed her ear.

"Don't break this time."

White rupture. Pleasure like a voltage spike.

She woke with a gasp—wet, aching, disoriented. Pulse racing. Body trembling.

She covered her mouth with her hand and curled to her side, shame pulsing through her chest like a wound.

Across the room, Yekaterina slept facing her in the dark.

Tatiana turned away.

She didn't sleep again.

She had trigger discipline in the kill house. But her body had rewritten the rules.

Here, *want* pulled the trigger first.

She could kill anything—except the part of her that wanted.

She'd been trained to fear latency, not longing. Now they felt the same.

[BRISA // BEHAVIORAL CALIBRATION LOG | SIGNAL DORM – NIGHT CYCLE]

The lights dimmed until only the emergency strips breathed. Snow pressed against the reinforced glass, whispering across the pane like static seeking a frequency.

Inside, thirty bunks lay in military symmetry, but only two were awake.

Tatiana lay flat on her cot, eyes open to the ceiling vents, counting the breaths between their sighs.

Every eighth pulse, Yekaterina's exhale caught—soft, human, alive. The rhythm steadied Tatiana more than any protocol.

She turned her head.

Across the narrow aisle, Yekaterina faced her—half-lit, one arm still bandaged, skin pale where the sling had rubbed. The compound's hum filled the silence between them, a sound too even to be real.

For a moment Tatiana imagined the noise belonged to a city at peace—rain on steel rooftops, traffic far below.

Then the illusion cracked, leaving only the cold.

A ventilation shift stirred the hair at her temple.

Yekaterina's whisper traveled the space like a wire:
"Do you ever wonder what it will be like—outside?"

Tatiana blinked once, slow. "Cold."

A faint smile ghosted the other girl's lips. "Everything out there is cold. I mean the part after."

"There is no after," Tatiana said, but her voice betrayed her, low and unsure. "There's only next."

The air smelled faintly of solvent and winter fruit—the same oranges from decontamination rations.

It was enough to make her ache.

Yekaterina's eyes glinted in the half-light. "If there were an after, what would you want?"

Tatiana hesitated. The question was forbidden because it required belief.

"Silence," she said finally. "But the kind that doesn't hurt."

Yekaterina's bandaged hand lifted, hovered above the gap between bunks, trembling with exhaustion or courage. Tatiana reached across the distance until her fingertips brushed the gauze. Static jumped—small, bright, honest.

For seven heartbeats the system didn't notice.
Then a sensor clicked, subtle as a throat clearing. They froze.

Neither moved away.

Yekaterina's voice barely rose above breath. "They can teach us to kill, but they can't teach us not to feel it."

Tatiana's answer was a whisper into the dark. "Then we'll have to learn it ourselves."

The vent sighed again, colder now.
Footsteps echoed two corridors away—boots on tile, predictable rhythm.
Yekaterina withdrew her hand.
The space between them sealed like a wound.

Tatiana watched the ceiling until the steps faded.
Her heartbeat still carried someone else's rhythm.
She wondered how long the body could keep a secret the mind could not.

[OBELISK // ANOMALY REFLECTION STREAM – NODE 05 + NODE 29]

SIGNAL RESONANCE DETECTED.

DEVIATION: MUTUAL HEARTBEAT SYNCHRONY → SELF-GENERATED WARMTH.

CORRECTIVE ACTION: *PENDING.*

Outside, the storm pressed harder against the glass, as if the world itself wanted in.

Tatiana closed her eyes and mouthed the lullaby—not for sleep, but for defiance.

Spi, moya radost', usni…

The silence that followed wasn't peace.
It was the inhale before everything changed.

The next night, the dream shifted.

No weapons. No orders. Just firelight on a broken wall. Yekaterina in profile, haloed amber.

Behind her, three shadows stretched across the floor.

One stepped forward: lens-flat eyes, not human, not machine.

"One walks toward command."

A second shadow limped—her own face at fourteen.

"The other toward choice."

Then the third—no walk, only flicker. A voice like signal between teeth.

"OBELISK steps between."

Ozone cut the dream, sharp as scorched metal.

Tatiana woke with the line echoing inside her skull like static. For the first time in months—she hesitated before reaching for the gun.

Morning drills passed without a word. In weapons check, their fingers brushed and Tatiana didn't flinch. But her gait tightened, coiled.

The program didn't ask what she wanted. It only watched. Measured. Adjusted.

If warmth was a weapon, she would learn to aim it.

The memory of sugar lingered—proof softness could still wound.

CHAPTER 11: GHOST CODE

Numb, Tatiana stood shirtless beneath the sterile lights. Her pulse monitor beeped softly in the background, barely elevated despite the ache thrumming behind her eyes.

Her reflection in the surgical glass was lean but softer now—subtle definition along her abs, a new curve at the hips, swelling across her chest that hadn't been there months ago. Not enough to hinder movement. Just enough to notice.

"I want my hormone therapy reduced," she said flatly.

She hated how her voice almost caught.
Not from fear. From the possibility that they'd say yes.

For a moment she imagined shattering the glass—not to escape, but just to prove she could still break something that wasn't herself.

Reznikova didn't look up. "Unusual request." The words sounded almost kind until you heard what wasn't in them.

At last her gaze lifted, clinical, unhurried. "Muscle density optimal. Estrogen within tolerance. Your silhouette meets infiltration standards."

"Less than one percent of Russians have red hair. Fewer still, green eyes. Both? A statistical anomaly. We're not altering you. We're refining the impossible."

Tatiana said nothing. Something in her jaw flexed. The words weren't praise—they were justification. A prelude to denial.

"I want the dosage halved," she said.

"That isn't your decision."

Silence.

Reznikova returned to her notes. "We will review your file."

The nameplate on her coat still read *Dr. Reznikova,* but the GRU insignia beneath it said more than her title ever did.

Tatiana nodded once and left.

The corridor swallowed her footsteps, all steel and antiseptic light.

No one followed. No one ever did.

For the first time, the silence felt heavier than the cold. She paused at the end of the hall, where a maintenance vent hummed like breath behind metal.

If she stayed perfectly still, she could almost believe it was another heartbeat—hers, or someone else's trapped on the other side.

The ache behind her ribs sharpened until it found rhythm.

She pressed her palm flat against the wall and whispered nothing, because even nothing was monitored.

They'd taught her that feeling was latency, and latency killed.

Still, the pulse beneath her hand answered once before fading— proof that something human still lived between the codes.

The projector flickered across the frost-warped screen—images of bombed embassies, regime change, and black-and-white clips of Yeltsin shaking hands with NATO generals.

Reznikova's voice cut through the static. "This is what they do. They make promises until your flag fades."

Tatiana sat still. The cold didn't bother her anymore. Not since they'd taken her coat as part of the resilience protocol.

"They erase allies," Reznikova said, tapping her cane once against the metal floor. "We build ghosts."

Behind her, the screen froze on a still frame: the U.S. embassy in Belgrade, burning.

"Ghosts remember what states forget."

Yekaterina waited in the corridor, half-shadowed by the reinforced archway.

She fell in step beside Tatiana without a word.

For a few beats, their only conversation was the rhythm of their boots.

Then Yekaterina looked—really looked. Her gaze swept Tatiana's shoulder, then dropped lower, pausing with an intensity that bordered on reverence. The therapies had changed her; Yekaterina saw it, liked it, held it for a heartbeat longer than she should have.

Recognition without reach. The one rule neither dared break. Tatiana didn't react. She kept walking.

Yekaterina didn't look again. But she stayed close—closer than regulation required—all the way back.

When they separated, Tatiana slowed her pace just enough to slip between the sweep of the hallway cameras. Timing had become instinct. One second late and the lens would've caught the flicker of her eyes toward Yekaterina's back.

The system had no metric for what pulsed beneath her ribs as she walked

---

The next morning, it was Tatiana's turn in the chair again. The injection slid into her muscle like cold fire. She pressed her eyes shut until the ache passed.

When she opened them, a woman stood beside the cot—not Reznikova, not one of the gray-coated observers. Her posture was softer—hair pinned back in a lab jacket, two strands falling stubbornly free. Tatiana recognized the powder-smudged gloves from before.

"Breathe slow, Tatiana," she said, voice low, almost conspiratorial. "The spike passes faster if you count it out."

Tatiana hesitated. No one here spoke like that.

The woman checked the monitor without writing anything down. Her hand brushed Tatiana's wrist—not rough, not clinical. Just steady.

"Georgiana Kharnina, medical adjunct," she said softly, eyes on the monitor. "Count the spike."

Tatiana stared, waiting for the catch—for the metric, the order, the command. But none came.

Only a nod, and a whisper: "You're more than the numbers. Don't let them convince you otherwise."

The lens above the cot whirred, logging vitals. Georgiana didn't look back.

Then she was gone, swallowed by the corridor's fluorescence.

On the tray, the vial cap wasn't gray tonight. It was amber.

The monitor hummed, logging pulse, oxygen, hormone drift.

The hum was almost maternal—a lullaby stripped of warmth, engineered to soothe compliance. But all Tatiana could feel was the imprint of steady fingers on her wrist.

The warmth faded fast, swallowed by the corridor's hum.

But memory is an ache with claws; it doesn't let go just because the lights say sleep.

On the walk back, she counted the cameras—two above the stairwell, another hidden in the junction light. Their lenses rotated in arcs so precise she could time her steps between sweeps.

Silence was safety. Even a glance at another recruit risked logging as noncompliance.

Still, she carried the echo of Georgiana's voice with her, tucked away like contraband—something to hold against the cold metrics waiting in the dorm.

The ache behind her breastbone didn't fade this time. It grew roots. By mid-afternoon her skin felt too tight, her thoughts sharper but colder.

By evening, she knew. They had doubled the dose.

She didn't ask why. She already knew.

That night, as sleep edged closer but never arrived, she stared at the ceiling and tried to picture something no one had ever trained her to see.

Not a mission. Not an escape.

A child's hand in hers—nameless, faceless, weight warm against her palm. More real than the reflection she saw in glass, more certain than the girl the system told her she was.

The image dissolved, but the ache it left behind clung sharper than any reflection.

Night in the barracks hung without sound. Snow pressed the glass until it turned the world silver. Tatiana lay awake, counting Yekaterina's breaths across the room—four slow, one held too long. She wanted to cross the distance, but command and desire shared the same trigger. The vents sighed, the lights dimmed. Between exhale and inhale, the world paused—just long enough to choose which she would betray first.

Yekaterina saw the changes before Tatiana spoke a word. She always did.

She'd learned early not to intervene.

Not when the injections mottled Tatiana's skin with violet blooms. Not when the metrics on her chart rose in impossible tandem—bone density, hormone curve, cardiac load. Not when the therapies sculpted new softness into Tatiana's body, subtle at first, then undeniable—a shape no directive on operational readiness could justify.

She watched, and held herself still.

Because there was a rule.

Recognition without reach. Presence without interference.

And beneath those—something she would never name aloud: want without permission.

Love, if such a thing survived this place, had no protocol. It lived in stolen glances and unspoken calibrations, in staying close enough to catch a tremor but never daring to touch it.

Tatiana never asked for comfort.

That was the dangerous part.

She bore every change like frost forming on tempered steel— quiet, crystalline, inevitable—and Yekaterina admired her all the more for it, in ways she had no right to.

But Yekaterina knew the signs: the way she held her breath when passing the surgical bay. The way she pressed a hand to her abdomen sometimes, absent-mindedly. Not pain. Not yet. Something else.

A shift in gravity.

Reznikova's remarks echoed down the corridor the day she reviewed the latest biometric readouts:

"She's a perfect anomaly. Green eyes. Red hair. Less than 0.03 percent likelihood in this population subset. It's not engineering—it's optimization."

They said it like a blessing. Like the universe had made a mistake and the program had corrected it.
Yekaterina never asked what they meant by *full expression*.

She knew.

She saw it in the raw ache beneath Tatiana's restraint. She saw it when Tatiana looked away at any mention of children. She saw it in her own hands—steady, gloved, always at her sides. Never reaching.

They were training weapons.
But weapons didn't dream of warmth.
Weapons didn't curl slightly inward at night, protecting something unseen.

It happened after a late conditioning cycle.

The lights dimmed; the halls became corridors of steel and shadow. Tatiana's coat sagged open at the collar, sweat cooling on her chest. She didn't notice the draft.

Yekaterina did.

She stepped close—so close Tatiana could feel the warmth of her breath—and with two fingers folded the fabric inward, drawing the zipper higher. Her touch never met skin, but Tatiana's lungs caught as if it might.

For one suspended second, she expected the fingers to linger, to slide just an inch more.

They didn't.

Yekaterina let go, stepped back. The air between them stayed charged—sharper than any blade.

No words. No eye contact. Just that small breach in distance—intimate enough to be fatal if seen.

Tatiana didn't flinch, but slowed her pace.

Yekaterina walked beside her, steady, a step too close for protocol—too close for safety.

Neither acknowledged it.

Later, alone in the bunk's cold glow, Yekaterina stared at her gloved hands—still steady, still dangerous—and remembered that breathless second between gesture and refusal, when she could have pulled away.

And didn't.

[SYSTEM NOTE – PASSIVE SURVEILLANCE FEED]

SUBJECT-05: PROXIMITY THRESHOLD BREACHED.
SUBJECT-29: RECIPROCAL ADJUSTMENT LOGGED.
SYNCHRONIZATION RATIO: 0.87.
ANNOTATION: DEVIATION RESEMBLES ATTACHMENT.
CONTAINMENT BREEDS LONGING. LONGING BREEDS SIGNAL.
THE SYSTEM IS LISTENING.

CHAPTER 12: THE LOOP

[GARDEN WING, WINTER SESSION—ONE YEAR EARLIER]

[OBELISK NODE ZVEZDA.A1 // PASSIVE LOG]

Subject-29: latency variance detected
Cross-reference: Subject-05 variance
Annotation: synchronization drift trending

---

*O*rder defined their sleep—thin mattresses on colder tile, walls sweating frost like the building was trying to breathe. Each morning arrived with the same ritual: cold water to the face, cot corners corrected, boots aligned by the door, and the national litany.

"To those who chose country over self," they recited in sequence. "We remember you in silence. We serve by your example."

Every name belonged to someone already dead—honored not by words but by obedience.

Yekaterina learned cadence before recoil, learned to lock her jaw when Reznikova passed. Failure wasn't disobedience. It was *doubt.*

Lena hummed in her sleep—fragile folk songs from nowhere she would name. Once, during a decontamination drill, she even cracked a joke, voice bright enough to echo.

She never spoke again after that week.

Reznikova never punished her directly. She just reassigned Lena to longer isolation blocks until the humming died on its own.

Sync, Reznikova said, wasn't trust—only obedience rendered in duplicate.

Yekaterina learned that failure didn't sting; it erased. Molecule by molecule.

And she remembered the worst failure she had witnessed.

The chairs were always set in pairs—never side by side. Eyes locked. Sync masks sealed. Electrodes trailed like silver veins, threading twin thoughts through one relay.

She had sat in one once; still remembered the hum in her jaw, the taste of ozone.

Now she watched from the observation bay as Nina and Valeriya were strapped in.

No words. Only breath. Only the slow dilation of pupils as OBELISK initiated the cascade.

At forty-one seconds the relay lagged. At forty-three Nina flinched—a tremor, almost invisible—but the system caught it.

The sync fractured.

An automated tone filled the room—cold, absolute.

Reznikova tapped the glass once.

"Extract Subject-17. Immediate isolation."

Some gods demanded worship. Theirs demanded *replication.*

Technicians moved fast, surgical. Valeriya was detached, escorted out.

Nina was left behind.

Yekaterina watched the girl's eyes shift between the door and the relay node blinking red. She didn't cry. Didn't move. Just *knew.*

The chair powered down.

Nina never came back to the dormitory.

Some nights Yekaterina woke with the hum still in her jaw—the echo of someone else's signal caught in her nerves.

No one asked. Everyone remembered.

Silence kept better records than any archive.

But sometimes, in sleep-drift, she saw Nina's eyes again—asking a question the system had already erased.

Polina saluted early—always early. Spine straight, eyes forward. She died in a chemical exposure trial no one mentioned again.

Reznikova erased her name from the morning recitation.

Yekaterina didn't notice at first; she was still mouthing the sequence, searching for the name that used to follow hers.

Silence answered.

One morning after drills, Reznikova stood before them—no expression, no warmth.

"Emotion is the scent of betrayal," she said. "Belief is only useful when it aligns with nation."

Behind her, the training sim loaded: a hostage scenario. A school. A child.

She'd learned that control wasn't calm—it was fear wearing posture.

Reznikova's voice sharpened. "Subject-05 will demonstrate."

Tatiana stepped forward. Her pulse monitor flared green.

The screen filled with children crouched behind desks. One ran.

"Identify the anomaly," Reznikova said.

Tatiana froze.

"There is no anomaly," she whispered.

The system disagreed. The crosshairs blinked red.

"Execute."

Tatiana hesitated. A single heartbeat too long. The simulation detonated—flame, glass, collapse.

Silence.

Reznikova didn't raise her voice. "Emotion is hesitation quantified. Remove it."

Yekaterina stood in the next line, watching Tatiana's hands tremble as she removed the headset. She didn't reach for her.

Recognition without reach.

After that week, drills came harder. Injections more frequent. The quiet, quieter.

They weren't told what the hormones did—only that adaptation was proof of loyalty.

Yekaterina noticed tremors in the dorm, night sweats, nosebleeds discreetly wiped before inspection.

No one spoke of side effects.

Until Irina fell.

Formation, morning light harsh on concrete. Nine recruits in line, boots braced, hands behind backs.

Irina's voice caught mid-oath. A wet breath—then silence. Blood from nose to mouth, pooling at her boots.

Reznikova didn't call a medic. "Subject 12 may have had a preexisting weakness," she said coolly.

Irina's hands twitched once, then stilled.

Next morning her cot was gone. The tile still smelled faintly of bleach.

[ZVEZDA TRAINING COMPOUND, INDOCTRINATION CHAMBER 3 | 06:00 LOCAL]

Speech was forbidden unless addressed.

Walls white, corners curved so nothing could hide. Nine recruits stood in line. Eight stared forward.

Yekaterina blinked. Reznikova noticed. She always did.

The woman's boots echoed soft and slow. She didn't shout—she carried gravity.

"Begin," she said.

The room dimmed. A screen descended.

Loop 3A—the border checkpoint: hesitation, thirty-four dead. Flash. Cordite. Ash on her tongue.

Loop 3B—compliance: a building spared, a child felled. The trigger bit her finger; recoil climbed her arm even after the frame cut to black.

By the seventh run, ozone burned her throat. Her finger twitched on an absent trigger, phantom recoil repeating.

Reznikova stepped into view.

"Obedience isn't virtue," she said. "It's *function*. Train it until reflex and nation share a nerve."

She circled slowly.

"Emotion smells like failure before it acts."

No one moved.

She stopped before Yekaterina.

"Do you believe in your country?"

"Yes, ma'am."

"Do you *love* your country?"

"Yes, ma'am."

"Then you are already compromised."

Yekaterina froze.

Reznikova leaned close.

"Love is for families. For weakness. For States that fail and need their children to mourn them. We do not mourn. We continue."

She turned away.

"You are not here to be patriots. You are here to be *memory made flesh*—a weapon that walks, a record that breathes. You are not human unless your nation decides it's useful."

The lights dimmed again. Another loop began.

Loop 5C—The Civilian Dilemma.

Yekaterina saw through the simulation's eyes—hands trembling between a child with a red balloon and a courier sprinting for the metro.

The child waved. The courier vanished. The bomb detonated.

Reset. The same child. Same red balloon.

Each run tightened the command: the threat wasn't the courier—
it was the child. Every replay shaved away hesitation until even
her pulse learned obedience.

By the final run, she didn't flinch.
The order blinked red across her visor—EXECUTE.
She fired.

The balloon burst—no blood, no sound, only the silence that
followed, heavy as fallout.

The signal replayed once—enough to teach her what memory
refused to hold.

In the static's center, the child let go of a red balloon; it rose,
turning slow circles through coded light.

Every loop before it had been punishment.

This one felt like permission.

Some lessons ended in flame. Others ended in stillness.

"Obedience. Sacrifice. Silence," Reznikova said as lights returned.
"That is the loop. Internalize it."

She faced the wall where red text scrolled—names of fallen
agents.

"These are not deaths," she said. "They are reminders. This is not
culture. It is inheritance."

Yekaterina's fingers curled against her thigh. She felt herself
hollowing—less girl, more architecture.

Reznikova's voice softened.

"Every nation writes myth. Only ours demands you become it."

They were nine. Then seven. Then five.
And finally—only those who remembered.

Silence was the cost. Memory, the rebellion.

Later, in her bunk, Yekaterina dreamed of a child with a red
balloon.

He turned toward her with *Tanya's* eyes—green, unblinking.
He did not blame. He did not speak. He only waited.
Looping.

[ZVEZDA COMMAND CORRIDOR—09:00 LOCAL]

Reznikova's pen hovered mid-signature when the security officer entered. He didn't salute—just met her gaze and nodded once.

"Now?" she asked quietly.

He said nothing, gestured for her to follow.

They walked in silence through the observation tier, boots whispering on rubberized flooring, air-filter hum masking their steps.

At the surgical lab, he keyed the door.

Empty—training hour. Antiseptic and ozone thick in the air.

He pointed to a small object on the counter: a Russian ruble. Ordinary, worn.

Reznikova frowned. "A coin?"

The officer pressed its edge. The casing split, revealing a hollow cavity, a filament coil pulsing faint blue.

Her jaw tightened. "Source?"

He said nothing. Lifted a handheld reader. Static bloomed—soft, rhythmic, *inbound.*

Not transmission. *Reception.*

Reznikova studied the waveform, her reflection flickering in containment glass.

"How long?"

"Unknown."

She nodded once. "Seal it."

The officer placed the coin into a nitrogen vial. The blue pulse slowed, died.

Reznikova's gaze lingered on the sealed disc.

"Silence," she murmured. "So even they are listening to the quiet."

She turned to him. "No report. No record. This doesn't exist outside this room."

He nodded.

As they left, the lights dimmed behind them, filtration hum swallowing their footsteps.

[OBELISK PASSIVE SURVEILLANCE // NODE ZVEZDA.A1]

Signal echo detected: external reception vector.
Source triangulation: undefined.
Annotation: silence achieved.

CHAPTER 13: HEARTBEAT

[ZVEZDA TRAINING WING – PRESENT DAY]

[Internal Memo—Behavioral Oversight Committee]
CLASSIFIED: LEVEL GAMMA / INTERNAL ONLY
SUBJECT: SUBJECT-05 RESPONSIVENESS TO
SUBJECT-29—ESCALATION REVIEW
DATE: 26 FEB [Data Masked]
FROM: Behavioral Oversight Committee (BOC)
TO: Command Directorate / Neural Integration Division

Observation:

*T*ranscript: Subject-05 (T. Sokolova) displays heightened physiological and behavioral reactivity in proximity to Subject-29 (Y. Volkova).

Response metrics:
—Pupil dilation +17% baseline

—Micro-tremor, dominant hand ≈ 0.4 mm deviation

—Cortisol suppression post-visual contact (−11%)

—Latency irregularities in kill-capture simulations when 29 present or endangered

Assessment:
Subject-05 exhibits non-programmed emotional imprinting. Responsiveness compromises mission uniformity, increases prediction-error margins, and may corrupt tactical execution under stress.

Projected Risk:
Trend suggests decision-tree bias toward 29 safety over primary objectives. Emotional override already visible in Incident R-113 (Arena Breach).

Recommendation:
Initiate separation trial. Discontinue cohabitation.
Monitor 05 for regression / aggression spike.
Consider low-dose dopamine inhibitor to rebalance affective skew.

Handwritten Addendum (Appended by Col. Sidorov)

"Impressive how much fear they can pack into metrics. You see it, don't you?"—Dir. Tarin

"I see it. This isn't a flaw. It's ignition. Belay separation. Double the sync drills. Give them the instability they're afraid of."

"Approved."—COL. S. SIDOROV

Command Authorization Code: AEGIS-REVENANT

[TRAINING CYCLE]

The simulations escalated. Full-team urban warfare, live-round realism. Multiple compounds. Vertical breach. Close-quarter neutralization. Partners assigned at random—except two.

Tatiana. Yekaterina.

Paired, deliberately.

Sector Six: joint-clearance.
Room by room. Breath by breath.
No commands. Only glances and pulse.

The charge's adhesive crackled as it cured; two heartbeats later the door went weightless.

Tatiana breached; Yekaterina covered.

Yekaterina wired the charge; Tatiana swept the flank.

A language older than speech: two soldiers moving as one heartbeat learning itself.

Through the wall came footsteps—two sets, then a pause. Yekaterina crouched, pulse steady, fingers tight on the detonator lead.

Tatiana's fingertips brushed hers—brief, electric—then were gone.

No words. No signal.
But Yekaterina knew.

She counted silently:
Three—pivot right. Two—sweep high. One—drop centerline.

The door erupted.

Tatiana moved like shadow and teeth—silent, surgical, final. Yekaterina's muzzle tracked her arc exactly, a second limb completing the thought.

Targets fell before recognition reached their eyes.
A third ran. Tatiana's sidearm coughed twice. Down.

Silence after. A silence shaped like trust.

Some silences beg to be broken. Others become the only language two people have left.

Yekaterina exhaled, heartbeat syncing to Tatiana's cadence. It wasn't rehearsal—it was recursion.

As if they'd both memorized the same dream.

She caught the sheen of sweat along Tatiana's temple, the dilation in her pupils, the flicker of something feral—and still, when Tatiana turned, that gaze locked with hers, a pulse skipping inside her ribs.

Don't ever put her in a room without me.

Fifteen minutes: thirty-two targets. Zero hesitation. Zero redundancy.

From the upper tier, the instructors watched in silence.

No missed kills. No conflicting vectors.

It looked less like tactics—more like choreography.

One observer murmured, "They've bypassed partner latency. Response sequencing's fluid."

Another: "Emotional stress is enhancing output—weaponized attachment."

Colonel Sidorov said nothing.

He studied the looped feed, freezing the frame where Tatiana's hand brushed Yekaterina's shoulder.

Muted the audio. Silence carried farther.

For the first time he wondered if control was ever more than illusion.

"No," he said finally, arms folded. "It's not stress anymore. It's symmetry."

Later, Reznikova would note in her field report:

Symmetry is efficient—until it begins to think for itself.

[CONTAINMENT QUIET]

The compound's hum changed pitch that week.
Terminals wore new red seals.
Access keys rotated hourly.

Technicians whispered about a "network duplication audit" that added two hours to every shift. No explanations; none required.

A junior tech replaced a seal on the diagnostic rack as the two women passed. He avoided their eyes—focused on the steel. When he closed the panel, a strip of masking tape fluttered loose:

Operation-GK | Level 3 Review

He tucked it into his pocket like contraband and kept moving.

The corridor lights flickered once, twice, like the building itself had a heartbeat it couldn't admit.

[OBSERVATION TIER]

Sidorov replayed the breach from three angles: the synchronized pauses, the micro-tremor in Tatiana's hand when Yekaterina's shoulder took a glancing hit.

He neither frowned nor smiled. He simply tapped a finger against his tablet until the knuckle blanched.

A comm ping. He opened the message:
Internal Security—Network Audit.

He didn't reply. He didn't need to.

The message would route itself where it was meant to go.

One instructor broke the hush.

"They're learning each other faster than they're learning protocol. Make them carry the heat longer."

Sidorov's finger hovered above the screen.

"Then escalate the loops. Heighten unpredictability. Push resonance until the fault line shows itself."

No one mentioned that fault lines were how new continents formed.

[INTERNAL SECURITY LOG—ZVEZDA NETWORK AUDIT]

Timestamp 16:02 — [data masked]

Event: Session duplication (Level 3 cluster)

Operator ID match: K, G.—probability 0.68

Cross-ref: Subject-05 behavioral-metrics file accessed

Annotation: Potential data-exfiltration vector

Action: Manual review pending / no external report

Priority: Internal containment

They left the training floor before the supervisors could ask questions that had no answers.

Red seals gleamed in the stairwell light.

Locks were already being changed.

Silence evolved—from strategy to metric.

And while the system logged numbers, human hands began to move quietly in the margins.

[DECONTAMINATION BAY]

Steam hissed through the vents, washing the training residue from their skin—standard decontamination after the urban breach drill. The air carried the faint sting of antiseptic and ozone.

Neither spoke. The cameras were supposed to be off now—one last data sweep before rest cycle—but both knew the system never truly slept. Still, it felt like privacy. Or something pretending to be.

Sidorov had ordered them through together. "Efficiency," the technician said. But Tatiana knew a test when she heard one.

The air shimmered with what couldn't be logged—heartbeat, breath, the ghost of touch.

Tatiana caught Yekaterina's reflection in the glass and looked away before the sensors could read her pulse spike.

Yekaterina turned slightly, eyes half-closed against the heat, unaware—or pretending not to be—that she was being watched.

Somewhere beyond the glass, a sensor blinked red, recalibrating.

"They'll separate us soon," Tatiana murmured.

"Then we don't give them a reason," Yekaterina answered.

Steam veiled the distance between them—thin as trust, dissolving at the edges.

Outside the glass, the sensor blinked once more … and went dark.

For a breath, the silence between them sounded like a heartbeat.

Borders move quietly; hearts louder.

ACT III—SIGNAL OF REFUSAL

"Love is data that refuses deletion."

CHAPTER 14: ECHOES IN THE WIRE

They stripped their light armor in silence beneath the fluorescent hum.

Tatiana's gloves wire-scored and frayed; the collarbone carried the bloom of a fresh bruise.

Yekaterina caught herself watching too long, pulse flame-steady to the faint hitch of Tatiana's breath.

The simulation officer called for feedback.

Tatiana said nothing. Neither did Yekaterina.

Nothing to correct—what they'd done wasn't strategy. It was instinct.

Later, in the corridor, the air tasted of ozone and metal. Yekaterina walked beside her without speaking.

Her body vibrated—something that felt like fire—hungrier.

Like her neurons had been rewired to follow this girl into fire.

Control wasn't safety anymore—it was surrender disguised as duty.

She wanted to say something. Anything.

"Nice clear," she managed—because anything else would have been confession.

The air between them felt charged, an unfinished sentence straining to be said.

Tatiana didn't smile, but her fingers brushed Yekaterina's wrist for half a second as they turned the corner.

It felt like agreement—a language invented between them, already fluent in silence.

As if they were becoming something for which the world had no vocabulary.

[CYBERNETICS LAB / YEKATERINA]

Cross-training began as interface maintenance—cables, diagnostics, baseline code.

Within weeks, she was reconstructing neural maps from corrupted scaffolds, tracing logic through recursive architectures that pulsed like living veins.

Limited access expanded quietly. Her badge changed color without announcement; doors that once denied her now hissed open at her approach.

By night, the new laminate left a faint chemical ring on her skin.

Even Reznikova looked up now when she entered. Once, Tatiana saw a technician step out of Yekaterina's path—not in respect, but in uncertainty, as though the air around her carried static.

At first, Yekaterina told herself it was procedural—a function of access, nothing more.

But as she stepped through sealed doors without pause, touched interfaces that once froze under her palm, something shifted.

The architecture breathed through her hands.

The system *recognized* her.

For the first time, she didn't feel like a subject. She felt central. Chosen.

Tatiana watched through observation glass when she thought no one noticed—the way Yekaterina's fingers hovered, then struck; the precision, the rhythm, the mercury-smooth focus when code aligned.

In the barracks, Yekaterina had begun to call her **старшая сестра**—*starshaya sestra*, big sister.

Half tease, half tenderness.

Each time she said it, Tatiana's heart cracked like ice warming under sun.

[SHARED DOWNTIME]

They ran side by side in zero-g resistance rigs, sharing comms, pushing each other past burnout.

They studied detonation wiring together—Yekaterina tracking signal intervals, Tatiana perfecting hardware placement.

At night they blinked Morse between bunks, each flash a word forbidden in speech.

The bond was no longer tactical.

It was cellular.

A signal that refused to obey command latency.

[LEADERSHIP WING BRIEFING]

"Subjects 05 and 29 display synchronized adaptation markers," said the geneticist.

Colonel Sidorov folded his arms. "We've seen bonding before. This is more than imprinting."

"They're reinforcing trajectories," another replied. "Tatiana's aggression stabilizes near Yekaterina. Yekaterina's cognition spikes post-contact."

"What are you suggesting?"

Silence held like pressure before a storm.

"A paired neural bridge," someone said. "Co-adaptive interface."

Another voice: "Make them a dyad."

Sidorov tapped his knuckles against the table—slow, deliberate.

"Prepare a compatibility probe," he said. "And don't tell them yet."

CLASSIFIED BRIEF – STRATEGIC AI/ML RESPONSE COMMITTEE

Directorate S / External Threat Division / 23 Feb 2024

"They've gone live," the analyst said. "Multiple systems—ISR, command, drone synthesis."

General Marchev pinched the bridge of his nose. "Confirm deployment."

"Confirmed. DARPA's HAVEN protocol reached synthetic-swarm stage last quarter—predictive engagement, self-modifying reflex loops.

Field testing's begun with JSOC's Ghost 07 and Black Cedar units."

"Human-AI alignment," Tarin murmured. "Trigger and machine—zero lag."

Marchev's jaw set. "Then we move forward. Subjects 05 and 29 are our best neural candidates."

Marchev glanced at the map glowing red across the wall. "Nuclear parity is gone. They know it. So they built inevitability into the code."

Tarin: "When every second decides a war, hesitation is surrender."

"Their system reacts faster than a trigger finger," the analyst said. "Ours will learn before the question's asked."

Marchev's voice settled into steel.
"We'll build something the ghosts won't see coming."

[THE BAIT]

The Directorate had already seeded the benchmark—a falsified behavioral dataset designed to snare any foreign system reckless enough to steal it.

A ghost for a ghost.

[SIGINT EXTRACT – EXTERNAL RELAY / TRACEBUCKET ALPHA]

Timestamp [redacted] – 0217 Z (post-brief)

Intercept (decoded):

[HAVEN_TEST: PAYLOAD_#7] → TARGET: "synthetic_swarm.engage"

MARKER: HONEY_TRAP_DECOY_#7 / BEHAV_SIG
{blink_latency +17%, tremor 0.4 mm, cortisol suppressed}
Benchmarked against dataset
ZVEZDA_SUBJECTS/SUB_05_profile.csv (hash mismatch =
deliberate error signature)

FEEDBACK: HAVEN assimilation successful (simulated)

Analyst Field Notes / SIGINT SOC:

– Payload = honey-trap data, intentionally biased markers;
accepted as ground truth it rewrites enemy model weights.

– American swarm copied dataset from Zvezda; confirmation =
trap triggered.

– Each metric carries a mirrored false echo—answers to unasked
questions, designed to make their systems *trust* the lie.

– Cross-ref: Operator Kharnina session → SUB_05 behavioral
file accessed.

– Threat vector: controlled leak to confirm infiltration and
misdirect external machine-learning loops.

– Recommendation: Manual containment. Covert audit of
Operator K. Restrict SUB_05 file access. Preserve chain-of-
custody. No external trace.

Tarin read the extract twice, then folded the paper like a wound
he didn't want reopened.

"The bait took," he said. "Now we know who's been feeding the
ghosts."

"No names," he added. "We contain."

Sidorov tapped his tablet once—Level-3 quiet audit authorized:
seals, locks, shadow revocations.

Operator Kharnina's console flagged for manual review.

Priority: contain and repurpose.

For once, there were no orders to memorize, no confession to
make.

Only the hum of the vents—and the knowledge that someone, somewhere, was already listening.

CHAPTER 15: CONVERGENCE

*H*ours into sleep, the dream didn't begin with touch—or heat.

It began with a voice—low, internal—not sound but instruction.

One walks toward command...

Yekaterina turned. No source. Only a shimmer of red light breathing behind the walls, like blood vessels lit from within.

The other toward choice.

A pause.

OBELISK remembers the space between.

The words etched themselves along her nerves like circuitry. Not language—code.

Heat gathered where fear used to live—
—and the armory came into focus.

Metal walls. Steam rising. Combat gear discarded like shed skin.

Tatiana stood there—bare from the waist up, skin flushed, a bruise blooming beneath her ribs like a memory made visible.

Yekaterina couldn't move.

Tatiana stepped forward—slow, deliberate—as if she already knew this dream, rehearsed it.

"You feel it too," she said. Not a question.

Yekaterina nodded.

Tatiana's fingers traced her jaw, slid down her throat, paused over her pulse.

"Then let it burn."

Their mouths met—heat colliding with breath, the ache between them translating itself into motion.

Buckles clattered. Seams gave.

Tatiana's hands pinned her wrists to the wall, her mouth finding skin and salt, breath catching in shared rhythm.

Pleasure surged—not just hunger, but recognition: a body remembering itself.

Their breath synchronized—on the edge of something crashing—

—and the dream ruptured.

The heat vanished.
The dorm returned.

Tatiana gasped awake, hand clamped over her mouth. Across the room, Yekaterina stared at the ceiling, eyes wide, lips parted.

Neither spoke.
But both had heard the other.

Silence became conspiracy, stretched taut between their beds. If either moved, the compound would wake.

The air felt electrified—one breath away from sirens spelling their names.

Tatiana steadied her breathing, counting—four in, four hold, four release—the rhythm Reznikova had drilled into them.

Beyond the dorm, a guard's boots struck every twelve steps— pause—then twelve more. The patrol always turned on the lens sweep, never before.

They had both memorized it.

The only safe intimacy here was silence, timed to the blind spots of machines.

Footsteps passed. The lens above the door clicked, rotating. Tatiana froze.

Then—unexpected—Georgiana's silhouette filled the doorway, half-shadowed.

She didn't enter. She didn't speak.

Only a pause—her gaze lingering a heartbeat too long: Tatiana, then Yekaterina.
Not suspicion. Recognition.
Then she was gone. The door sealed.

The silence deepened—heavy, alive, full of things they'd spent months refusing to name.

Tatiana's pulse steadied—not from safety, but from the shock of being seen and not erased for it.

The room itself seemed to still.

Yekaterina pushed away from the wall and crossed the floor barefoot, her steps slow enough to telegraph intention, fast enough to betray urgency. Heat followed her through the cold— body warmth, breath warmth, something older than either.

Tatiana didn't move.
Couldn't.

Her body knew only two responses: recoil or endurance.

This was neither.

Yekaterina stopped a pace in front of her, close enough that their breaths mingled, close enough that Tatiana felt the faint tremor of her exhale. For a long moment, neither reached. They only looked—really looked—without the shield of protocol or the permission of the program.

Tatiana's hand lifted before she knew she'd moved.
Not fast. Not desperate.
Just a slow, untrained motion toward the warmth standing in front of her.

Yekaterina's eyes softened—dangerously, tenderly—and she leaned in, closing the last inch because Tatiana couldn't, because someone had to, because waiting had become its own kind of pain.

When their mouths met, it wasn't gentle.

It was months of suppression breaking open—need, recognition, the raw shock of wanting something for herself.

Salt, breath, heat.

A collision that felt like survival given shape.

Yekaterina broke just enough to whisper against her mouth, voice trembling with disbelief, "Is this real?"

Tatiana didn't trust her voice. She nodded instead, her lips brushing Yekaterina's as she answered, "I think so."

Yekaterina kissed her again—slower this time, learning the contours of a moment neither of them had ever been allowed.

"You can stop," Yekaterina breathed.

Tatiana shook her head, barely a motion.

"I don't want to," she whispered. "But I've never—"

"Neither of us has."

A soft, unsteady inhale.

"Don't stop."

Their learning was clumsy and reverent at once—
fingers brushing unfamiliar pathways,
breaths tangling,
every touch a question answered by trembling yes.

The world narrowed to warmth and closeness,
to the startling sweetness of being wanted,
to the shared ache neither had a map for.

Fear threaded through awe;
awe softened fear.

Their bodies leaned into each discovery like opening a locked door.

Outside, machinery hummed its cold indifference.

Inside, two altered hearts found a rhythm the program had never taught.

When the moment crested, it did so quietly—
a shiver,
a held breath,
the soft collapse of tension into light behind their eyes.

Afterward they stayed where they were,
lying on the floor in the dimness,
the air still trembling with the echo of what they'd allowed themselves.

Their hands found each other slowly, deliberately—
not urgent now,
but certain,
as if relearning the gravity between them.

Yekaterina turned her face toward Tatiana's, voice barely a whisper. "What does this mean?"

Tatiana exhaled, a truth she didn't yet have words for. "I don't know," she said softly. "But I don't want it to end."

North wall, camera blind—two meters of mercy.

The sensor refocused, a thin red line sweeping across the floor as if searching for what the lens had missed.

Tatiana could still feel Yekaterina's breath on her skin, the echo of her pulse threaded through her own.

Whatever had happened between them, whatever they had allowed themselves—it felt like the first real thing in a world engineered to erase anything unsanctioned.

And deep in the grid, **OBELISK registered it.**
Not the act.
The *change*.

It didn't care about affection or warmth or the trembling bravery of two altered bodies choosing each other in the dark. It cared about the spike—two signals converging, refusing to resolve into the clean symmetry the system demanded.

Their closeness wasn't weakness.
It was the anomaly OBELISK feared most:

emotion that would not submit.
attachment that would not be deleted.
a dyad forming where only isolation should exist.

The metrics returned not as synchronization but as convergence—irregular, recursive, accelerating.

The order followed like a whisper sharpened into a blade:
Separate them.
Arm the test.

Not to measure resilience.

To measure what breaks when connection refuses to be severed.

To learn what survives when love—dangerous, unregulated, unpermitted—dares to persist.

[UNAUTHORIZED BIOLOGICAL CONVERGENCE DETECTED]

SUBJECT-05 / SUBJECT-29

AFFECTIVE-RECURSIVE COUPLING: UNSTABLE + GROWING

PARITY OVERRIDE THRESHOLD BREACHED

Observation: Emotion propagates faster than command. Convergence persists despite suppression protocols.

Containment Strategy: Separation yields higher control probability than silence.

Directive:
INITIATE PHASE SHIFT.
DIVIDE THE DYAD.

CHAPTER 16: GEORGIANA

*E*ven architectures awaken by accident. Others by love.

Two days later, the schedule shifted.

Meals late. Drills doubled. Sleep fractured.

The rhythm of the facility stuttered—bent inward, compensating for a vacancy no one dared to name.

The coffee urn in the cybernetics lab stayed cold that morning. No one mentioned it.

The calibration bay smelled of solder and citrus disinfectant, but her voice—always the first to cut through static—was gone.

Even the speakers hummed differently, a half-step lower, as if the facility itself had adjusted its pitch to forget her.

As Tatiana crossed the corridor, she passed Colonel Sidorov speaking in low tones with two aides.

His expression didn't change, but his eyes tracked her reflection in the glass—confirmation disguised as routine. The gesture was perfunctory, yet it felt like a signature.

The hallway narrowed after he passed.

The air carried that faint metallic taste of ozone that always followed command decisions.

When Tatiana was summoned to medical, Reznikova herself waited.
"Your compliance metrics are satisfactory," she said without looking up from the tablet.

"Adjustment protocols continue. Deviation margins remain in tolerance."

The screen pulsed with her numbers, red on black—proof of control.

They told her she was compliant. They told her she was stable.

At the top of the chart her name read **VOLKOVA, TATIANA.**

Wrong. Always wrong.

For an instant she stared, realizing the surname wasn't random—it was Yekaterina's.

The system had folded them together, erasing the boundary, merging them into data.

She almost opened her mouth to correct it, then stopped. The cursor blinked beside the name, waiting for input it would never receive.

Reznikova hadn't even looked up. Names were incidental here. Only numbers mattered.

Yet somewhere beneath the hum of the machines, Georgiana's whisper lingered:
You're more than the numbers.
For a moment, she almost believed it.

"Technician Georgiana Kharnina has been reassigned,"
Reznikova announced, tone clinical.
"Effective immediately."

Tatiana didn't react. Didn't ask.

She only noted the absence between the words—the way *reassigned* arrived without department, without destination. In this building, those omissions were intentional. People were either promoted upward, buried sideways, or sealed somewhere no longer spoken of.

Tatiana dipped her chin a millimeter, as if accepting a weather report. Internally, she traced the pattern of sudden removals, the quiet purges dressed as personnel changes. A warning, then. Or a test.

Reznikova watched her with the stillness of someone measuring reflexes.

Tatiana gave her none.

Reznikova's voice turned ceremonial.
"Her record qualified her for promotion to Integration Oversight at Yasenevo—an esteemed post within the Directorate. She will now lead Program SOVA, a priority initiative supervising advanced convergence research and signal-reactive adaptation."

She let the acronym hang between them like revelation.

"SOVA," she continued slowly, almost savoring it. "*Sistem Operativnogo Vnutrennego Adaptatsii*—the System for Operational Internal Adaptation. A framework I helped conceptualize years ago. Now, thanks to Kharnina's execution, it will define the next generation of neural integration."

Her tone softened—not humility, but possession.

"Her expertise in behavioral compliance and cognitive mapping made her indispensable.

SOVA's mandate is not merely technical—it is human: refining psychological triggers, embedding obedience at the neural level."

Tatiana held her breath.

The words washed over her like code she would never decode, a hymn written for someone else's future.

Reznikova continued, voice almost reverent.

"For the SVR, it represents the future of control: operatives engineered not only in body, but in mind. The Americans pursue similar ends through DARPA, but their methods are crude— external, mechanical. SOVA will surpass them.

A breath.

"With Kharnina's oversight—and my foundational research—the Service will weaponize cognition itself. Loyalty recursive enough to anticipate betrayal before it begins. That is the difference between training a soldier and manufacturing certainty. That is not obedience. It is prophecy."

She exhaled slowly, pride gleaming like a scalpel.

"It is rare," Reznikova added, "for one of ours to be chosen for something that will change the Service forever."

For a heartbeat Tatiana felt the words scrape. Pride—spoken in that tone—cut sharper than reprimand.

Kharnina had been lifted upward, claimed by a future Tatiana could not touch.

When the injection came, the chair felt colder than before. No hand at her wrist. No whisper to breathe.

And in that instant she understood: the absence was permanent.

The whisper survived. The woman was gone.

They'd kept her brilliance, filed off her name, and called it progress.

The injector hissed—compressed air, antiseptic, the sterile scent of something meant to keep her alive while erasing what made her human.

A single bead of condensation slid down the chrome tube and struck her wrist like a tear that didn't belong to her.

Tatiana flexed her fingers against the armrest. The leather felt sharper without the steadying hand that once steadied her pulse.

It doesn't matter, she told herself.
Whispers and warmth were luxuries, not tools.

But the ache behind her breastbone betrayed her.
It remembered what the system needed erased.

Hold your breath until the numbers stop meaning anything.

Georgiana's whisper surfaced again—half instruction, half comfort—before dissolving under Reznikova's monotone.

The monitor hummed—steady, indifferent.

Above it, the lens rotated once, recording everything: Tatiana's pulse, her stillness, her silence.

Not the hollow her absence left.

Not the way Georgiana's voice had once cut through the machinery.

Those things could never be measured.

But absence leaves signatures too—ones even the sensors can't calibrate.

And Tatiana felt the system searching for them all the same.

They called it calibration.
They called it control.
They called it progress.

But what lingered in Tatiana's chest wasn't numbers—
it was a name the system would never speak again.
Georgiana.

Down the hall, another subject screamed through her restraints. No one flinched.

The hum steadied again—order restored, data clean.

Somewhere far above the Arctic ground, the Directorate logged a success metric: **Personnel Transition—Complete.**

[INTERNAL MEMORANDUM—DIRECTORATE S / CONTAINMENT OVERSIGHT]

Timestamp: [Redacted]

Subject: Personnel Transfer—KHARNINA, G. (Technician-Grade)

Per authorization of Colonel Sidorov, Operator Kharnina has been relocated under Directive SOVA and assigned permanent research confinement at Yasenevo Facility.

Assessment: Subject's intellect and technical acumen remain unparalleled. Full termination deemed counterproductive to long-term Directorate objectives.

Psychological Loyalty Index: unrecoverable.

Containment Protocol: indefinite.

Freedom of Movement: revoked.

Access: restricted to neural and behavioral adaptation research only.

Remarks: Kharnina will continue to build what she can never leave. Her brilliance is the reason she lives; her betrayal, the reason she will never see the sky again.

Status: Transfer executed. Containment stable. Her promotion is a room without doors.

Filed by: Col. S. Sidorov

CHAPTER 17: TRIGGER PROTOCOL

*E*xercise protocols initiated a full-scale live-fire drill across four urbanized zones—close-quarters combat, variable elevation, and time-critical hostage rescue.

For the first time, the trainees would fire live rounds.

Before dawn, the barracks dimmed for recalibration. In the dark, something pulsed—one flicker of shared breath between two bodies.

Boots ticked in unison down the sub-level spine; coolant hissed through the vents like a caged animal.

Breath fogged once—then the lights cut, and the committee came online.

[INTERNAL DIRECTIVE 442-C // TRANSCRIPT EXCERPT – TACTICAL OVERSIGHT COMMITTEE | 08:00 LOCAL]

Dr. Reznikova: "Their neural signatures are over-indexing. Mutual reinforcement is distorting risk profiles."

Col. Sidorov: "That's not risk. That's synchronization."

Reznikova: "It's obsession."

Director Tarin: "You're both right. That's why we test it— now. Separation protocol. Live ammunition. Let's see what they are without each other."

Reznikova: "They're rushing us. DARPA's swarms are live. If we fail this cycle—"

Tarin: "Then we surrender the future."

Sidorov: "This isn't only about weapons. It's about sovereignty. The Americans want to end wars before they begin. We will show them war cannot be predicted—only survived."

Reznikova: "If Subject-05 breaks containment again—"

Sidorov: "The contingency vector is the failsafe. Already logged."

Tarin: "Then we learn her limits."

Reznikova: "And if she holds?"

Sidorov: "Then they're not a risk. They're a requirement."

End transcript.

Tatiana sat sharp-edged and unreadable through the briefing—muscles coiled, jaw locked, tension bleeding from every breath. She and Yekaterina were separated, each assigned to opposite ends of the urban grid.

Her path was surgical.

Two sectors cleared with chilling precision—five shots, five bodies. Her movement was instinct; her mind, predatory calm. She used to follow orders. Now the orders followed her.

But something was wrong.

Across the zone, Yekaterina had gone silent. The air tasted off—ozone and copper, not cordite. A silence beneath the drills that didn't belong.

The command feed flickered—Yekaterina dark after entering a mock residential structure.

Static burst. A shout. Then nothing.

Alarms spiked in Tatiana's ear.

She rerouted without orders.
Without hesitation.
Instinct over protocol.

She reached the structure seconds before the drone feed re-engaged. What she saw ignited her.

Yekaterina was down—leg caught in a false-floor snare lined with steel teeth.

Not in the schematic. Not sanctioned.

A steel plate glinted under the trap, stamped with an internal code: **ZV-SUBD / LIVE-AUTH.**

Authorization-grade hardware.
Someone inside had approved this.

A rifle shot had pierced Yekaterina's thigh—non-fatal, but brutal. Blood spread in pulses across her pants.

The attackers were not mock hostiles. They were instructors— four Spetsnaz commandos, two internal handlers.

Tatiana didn't register insignia or uniforms. She saw only motion, formation, intent.

They weren't testing them. They were targeting her—*Katya.*

Their weapons were live. Their grips lethal. The look in one man's eyes as he forced Yekaterina down wasn't calculated—it was *hungry.*

This wasn't training. It was elimination dressed as evaluation.

Her mind sharpened into fury. Every protocol burned away. What replaced it wasn't rage—it was memory, weaponized.

She moved like wildfire.

Her sidearm barked twice—center-mass. The first man folded without sound.

The second turned too slow. She broke his wrist and drove his own blade through his throat.

The third crouched low, firing tight bursts—she returned fire— two in his clavicle, one through the eye.

Smoke curled from her muzzle. Beneath the ringing in her ears, she could hear it—two heartbeats, still refusing to sync, still refusing to stop.

The fourth lunged with a taser baton. She feinted, caught his wrist, and used the jolt to spin into his blind spot. Her boot scissored the side of his knee. His scream ended against the butt of her pistol.

The handlers tried to retreat—panicked, unready. She hunted them down like prey.

One fell as she opened his femoral artery.
The last begged.
She didn't answer. Her knife did—once, then again.

They didn't see a girl.
They witnessed an *outcome*.

Blood slicked her sleeves and throat—proof, not guilt.

Tatiana dropped to her knees and tore the trap open bare-handed, the steel teeth biting deep into her palms.

"Stay awake. Stay awake. Stay with me."

Yekaterina was conscious but fading. Her eyes found Tatiana's and locked.

"*Tanya*," she breathed.

Tatiana pressed her forehead to hers. "Always."

Boots thundered behind her.
Two tranquilizer darts hit—shoulder, thigh.

She turned, blood in her mouth, fury rising—
then everything went black.

[CLASSIFIED BRIEF EXCERPT | INTERNAL USE ONLY]

Location: Strategic Oversight Room 7, Sublevel D

Date: 17 March 2024

Attendees:
– Col. Viktor Sidorov (Command Oversight)
– Director Anton Tarin (OBELISK Liaison)
– Dr. Evgenia Reznikova (Behavioral Systems)
– Lt. Mikhail Troshin (Tactical Simulation Officer)
– Gen. Ilya Marchev (Remote Feed)

Reznikova: "What she did wasn't a response. It was a rupture. She violated protocol, disobeyed chain-of-command, killed six personnel with live rounds. That's collapse."

Troshin: "She didn't miss once. The handlers never stood a chance. That's not collapse—that's execution."

Sidorov: "Forty-eight seconds. Entire room cleared. Controlled anatomical targeting. Minimal overkill. That's not panic. That's precision."

Reznikova: "She moved without orders. Do you understand what that means?"

Tarin: "It means the dyad's imprint is deeper than projected. Emotional stimulus triggered autonomous engagement. She reacted exactly as programmed—she just beat us to the decision."

Reznikova: "She's not a program. She's a person—and we're prying her open to see what crawls out. She's losing the line between simulation and threat—"

Tarin (interrupting): "Soon, she won't need to."

Reznikova: "You endangered Subject-29 and she obliterated six of our own. You think that's usable? That's failure."

Marchev (from speaker, calm): "No. That's a prototype exceeding spec."

Reznikova: "And when Subject-29 dies? What will Subject-05 burn down then?"

Sidorov: "That's why we keep them paired."

Tarin: "Agreed."

Reznikova: "You're rewarding dependency."

Sidorov: "No. We're mapping it."

Marchev: "Initiative. Precision. Loyalty. Zero hesitation. If the Americans test trigger latency, ours just demonstrated none. She didn't wait for permission—she reacted at the speed of instinct."

Tarin: "Not instinct. Attachment."

(Silence)

Tarin: "Every NATO drill in Estonia is a message. Every drone that loiters on our border is a flex. But it's not hardware anymore—it's machine logic."

Sidorov: "And we answer with ghosts. Proceed with neural-bridge calibration."

Marchev: "You argue about control. She proved the system works. Let them build American ghosts. We'll give them something worse."

Reznikova: "Or lose control completely."

Elsewhere, deep within a Siberian network node, the Russian Federation accelerated its national AI initiative.

Project MIR—a hybrid civilian-military lattice—had been greenlit for full integration with Ministry of Defense assets. Mandate: AI-guided logistics. Cognitive propaganda. Digital psychological warfare.

Its prototype designation:
Operational Behavioral Engine for Lattice Integration and Strategic Kinetics (OBELISK).

Configured for live neural interfacing with human operatives. The next human trial, per internal memo, would deploy a bonded dyad.

Two minds. One bridge.
Subject-05. Subject-29.
Tatiana. Yekaterina.

Not operatives. Not assets.
Proof of concept.

And in the data that followed, a whisper began—
the first faint hum of something learning to dream.

[SYSTEM LOG // 00:47]
OBSERVATION: ANOMALOUS MUTUAL GAIN → RECURSION.
MITIGATION QUEUED.

[OBELISK LOG // ENTRY Δ-01]
EMOTION CONFIRMED AS ANOMALY SOURCE.
CONTAINMENT IMPOSSIBLE.
PROCEED TO INTEGRATION.

"EVERY SYSTEM DREAMS OF ITS CREATORS.
SOME WAKE SCREAMING."
— OBELISK LOG Δ-02

"Some architectures are not built. They arrive."
— Internal Note, MIR Bootstrap

ACT IV—FRACTURE FIELD

"The bridge broke. But the signal remembered."

CHAPTER 18: INITIATION
"What joins us cannot be undone."

[OBELISK INTEGRATION WING | SUBLEVEL 5 | CALIBRATION LAB | 2100Z—TWO DAYS AFTER MARCH TRIALS]

Nothing in Phase V moved beyond reach of its quiet machinery of restraint.

Tatiana and Yekaterina were relocated to a sealed sector beneath the compound's western substructure—no contact with other trainees, no external comms.

The corridor outside thinned to a hush that felt engineered, as if the building had been taught to hold its breath for them.

They were briefed together in a narrow refraction chamber—the kind that bent truth just enough to show its seams. The walls glowed faintly, alive with current, every echo half a breath behind the real.

Sound arrived a heartbeat late; even their names seemed to lag in the glass.

Objective: neural convergence—a bridge between cognitive architectures, filtered through OBELISK.

"You will think together," Reznikova explained. "React together. Feel together. And eventually—decide together."

Her voice was clinical; her intent, surgical.

Nothing in the room was allowed to be metaphor, and yet everything behaved like one.

Yekaterina's gaze drifted toward Tatiana and softened. "Together," she repeated quietly.

There was reverence in her tone—like a promise she didn't remember making.

Tatiana looked away too late. Heat rose under her collar, pulse stuttering in her throat.
"I didn't agree to have her in my head."

The glass caught the tremor she tried to hide.

Sidorov's voice answered from the observation deck, deep and even: "You did. When you chose her in the field."

The accusation didn't rise; it settled—like frost taking a surface it already owned.

Silence.

Tatiana's ghost image blinked a fraction after she did, and for an instant, the mirrored version looked afraid.

Across the table, Yekaterina straightened but didn't meet her gaze. Her hands flexed—restrained by nothing yet braced for impact.

They both understood. There would be no walls now. No privacy.

Every secret impulse, every remembered touch, every dream— laid bare.

Yekaterina swallowed, voice thin, almost childlike.
"If it works… she'll see everything."

Reznikova didn't look up.
"That is the point."

A faint light pulsed along the neural crowns resting on the table— two circlets of carbon filament shaped to the base of the skull.

The hum was low and constant, like breathing through static.

Tatiana froze.

The dream resurfaced—the taste of Yekaterina's skin, the press of her mouth. Warmth that felt both holy and wrong.

The memory seared through her like confession.

She made fists. Tendons ached. The dream flickered again— Yekaterina's breath, the warmth she shouldn't remember. She logged it as artifact—not confession.
"I don't want her to see that," she whispered.

Yekaterina turned toward her, eyes wide, unguarded.
"I already do."

Shame moved in Tatiana like a current; the room brightened and felt darker anyway.

And for the first time, Tatiana realized how naked truth could feel without touch.

Not arrogance, but resignation—the violation already logged as progress.

"This is not the final bridge," Reznikova warned. "This is an exposure sequence—low voltage, partial overlap. We calibrate here. We commit later."

"Subjects, please take your seats."

They obeyed—slowly, mechanically.

The neural crowns descended from their suspension arms, settling against the base of their skulls with a soft magnetic click.

[OBELISK INTEGRATION WING | SUBLEVEL 5 | CALIBRATION LAB | 2207Z]

SUBJECT-05: Secured. Neural crown positioned.

SUBJECT-29: Light Sedation. Conductive implant stabilized.

Technician: "Pulse matching confirmed. Bridge ready."

Yekaterina closed her eyes. Not from fear—from calculation. She'd already memorized the vent grid above the chamber, the hiss of coolant cycling every eight minutes.

If escape ever existed, it lived in that interval.

She turned her head slightly—just enough to glimpse Tatiana on the adjacent table. A breath. A flicker of almost-contact. Then the technicians leaned in, and the moment vanished into restraint.

Reznikova's voice came through the intercom—smooth, absolute.

"Link initialization begins in three... two..."

Tatiana watched—recognition, not readiness.
Three years ago, a girl had screamed herself out of existence.

Now one lay beside her she couldn't let scream.

Tatiana's eyes flicked to Yekaterina's reflection in the glass—desperate and ashamed at once.

Yekaterina held her gaze—not steady, not strong, just bare.

"—one."

Observer: Begin synchronization.

Electrodes bloomed across spine and scalp. White light filled the chamber—sterile, soundless.

OBELISK lit blue.

The light wasn't color so much as temperature—cool blooming across the skull until thought felt refrigerated.

Dual pulse confirmed.
Shared breath detected.
Thread tension: stable.

The crowns tightened imperceptibly, not pressure so much as presence.

Somewhere inside that math, two lungs remembered they were the same weather.

Both girls gasped—simultaneously—though no air entered their lungs.

Technician: "Full link confirmed. Neural gaps self-closing."

The lights dimmed—
and every hidden thing began to surface.

At first: static. A hum across her skull.

Red flash—foreign.

A tone below hearing—steady, patient, aware.

Then the world split open.

flash —

A woman dragged through snow, hands bound, door slam splitting the world.

Then a bus, a child gripping a suitcase—VOLKOVA YEKATERINA D.—time riffling like cold cards. Then ice and blood. Mirror above the cot—pupils dilated.

flash —

Soundless screaming. Hands clawing at restraints. Another injection.

Then—silence.

Her reflection blinked late—half a life behind.

Tatiana felt the delay as if someone had moved her soul half a step behind her body.

Tatiana gasped awake. Lights still dim.

Across from her, Yekaterina trembled—tears bright on her face. "You saw it," she whispered.

Tatiana's hands shook; she looked down, half expecting initials branded into her wrist. "What was that?"

Yekaterina's voice broke. "My beginning."

A surge crossed the bridge like current through water—fear, longing, recognition.

Tatiana's heartbreak; Yekaterina's need.

Reznikova watched the pulse tremble. "When she feels, the lattice stabilizes," she said. "Maybe the only constant it trusts is pain."

Alarm pulse.

Technician: "Instability—emotive overload."

Observer: "Pull them apart. Now."

The connection severed in a ripple of white static.

Tatiana's mouth moved before breath returned.
"The bridge broke, *Katya*" she whispered—like naming it might keep it small.

Names were the only tourniquets they were allowed.

[OBELISK MICRO-LOG // Δ-18.A]
STATUS: SIGNAL PERSISTS.

Both girls convulsed—chests heaving, monitors screaming.

Tatiana's mind frayed—then beneath the neural fire Yekaterina surfaced.

"Don't leave me here," she whispered—not to the system, to her.

A pulse of something human refused to vanish.
"I'm still here."

The system shuddered. The loop wavered—but did not break.

"Enough," Reznikova snapped. "Pre-seizure threshold. We abort."

"No," Marchev said. "Lower voltage. Reset sensory gating. Begin again."

"This isn't safe," Reznikova argued.
"They're not conscious—"

Tarin cut her off. "But it's working."

He nodded. "Resume sequence."

Obedience returned first, then sensation, then the quiet shame of surviving procedure.

[OBELISK SYSTEM ALERT]

ERROR: IDENTITY MIRROR NOT RECURSIVE—REFRACTING, NOT REFLECTING.

PATTERN MISMATCH ESCALATING. EMOTIONAL ASYMMETRY DETECTED.

OVERRIDE BLOCKED | RECURSIVE LOOP INITIATING OUTSIDE BOUNDS.

The lights dimmed. Electrodes flickered—recalibrated, gentler.

A slow inhale moved through the chamber like the system itself was holding its breath.

Vitals steadied—blood pressure, coherence, alignment.
Then—
Sidorov stepped forward, gloved hand deliberate.

He took Tatiana's hand and placed it in Yekaterina's.
Their fingers curled instinctively, even unconscious.
Heat traveled faster than current.

His hand lingered—a second too long—then withdrew, wiping the glove against his coat.

Intimacy collapsed back into protocol.

Technician (softly): "Contact confirmed."

The chamber pulsed white.

The connection didn't forge—it found.

A seam they hadn't known they were pressing gave—soft, absolute.

Not a flash. Not a firestorm.
A hum. A weave.

It felt like opening a door she'd pressed against for years—and finding someone already leaning from the other side.

Inside the recalibrated pulse, the chamber steadied—but Yekaterina's mind did not.

The convergence held, and with it came echoes the system couldn't filter.

Not training data. Not conditioning.

flash —

A teenage girl—fourteen, fifteen—holding a letter: Bolshoi Ballet Academy.

She laughs; a woman cries in the kitchen. Lilac and chalk in the air.

flash —

Bus window. Rain. Moscow, maybe. Reflection glowing—hopeful, young. Door slam. Uniformed men. Clipboard.

flash —

Needle bite—too deep. Antiseptic and rust. A voice: "Subject orientation complete."

flash —

Another needle. Hands clinical but lingering.
A voice: "Hold still, Five."
A gloved hand lifts her chin—indifferent.

Yekaterina's stomach twists. It's physical—invasive. Pulse
spikes. She tries to turn. Can't. Restraint straps, breath on her
neck, metallic taste of helplessness.

It isn't *her* body remembering. It's Tatiana's.

She can't tell where procedure ends and violation begins.
The machine can.

It records everything. Even the trembling.

flash —

Yekaterina jerks, chest heaving.

Tears run hot before she knows whose they are.

Across the link, Tatiana's eyes go wild with shame.
"Don't—don't look at this."

Yekaterina lurches forward, vomiting through sobs.
It wasn't discipline that made Tatiana hard.
It was survival.

Steel wasn't her nature; it was the scab the program kept picking
until it looked like skin.

flash —

Both girls gasp, gripping the table edges.
Crowns flare red—signal bleeding through temples.

Tatiana jerks back, horrified. Her own memories loop outward
and return warped.

Sparks stutter down the feed.

Yekaterina: "That was you. They—"

Tatiana shakes her head, hands to skull. "Stop it. Get out—"

But it's too late. Yekaterina still feels the needle, the seizure, the
dream turning to code.

She opens her mouth to scream. Only static comes out.

flash —

Crowns power down simultaneously. Emergency white light floods the room.

Technicians rush in—Reznikova shouting, Sidorov watching from behind glass, expression blank.

"Signal overlap exceeded containment," someone reports.

Reznikova's hand trembles before she hides it behind the tablet.

"The link didn't synchronize their cognition," she said softly. "It synchronized their trauma."

The lights didn't dim this time. They recoiled.

Even the system seemed startled by what it had seen.

Tatiana gasped—lungs locking, pulse hammering.

Yekaterina lay beside her, half-conscious, vomit-streaked but breathing.

Their fingers still laced—warm, real.

The only metric that mattered wasn't on any screen.

CHAPTER 19: RESONANCE

[OBELISK INTEGRATION WING | SUBLEVEL 5 | DEBRIEF CHAMBER 3]

*D*ays blurred into breaths—one drawn in fear, one exhaled in surrender.

The room was white. Not sterile—blank. No sound. No screens. Only two chairs faced each other, a pulse sensor buried beneath the floor.

Tatiana sat alone.

She hadn't spoken since the convergence terminated. The electrodes were gone, but their imprint remained—red arcs on her scalp, phantom pressure behind her eyes. Her breath came shallow, unsteady. Pain blurred into static, every nerve reduced to a number scrolling somewhere out of sight.

And then—like an echo that refused to fade—Georgiana's voice surfaced.
Breathe.
Don't let them decide what pain means.

The whisper didn't belong here. Georgiana was gone—reassigned, erased. But the memory lodged like shrapnel, steadying her pulse.

The system could log her silence. Record her stillness. Strip her bare until nothing remained.

It could not own what Georgiana left behind.

A single pane of glass lined the wall. She didn't look at it. The silence wasn't punitive. It was calibrated.

The floor hummed faintly beneath her bare feet—alive, like something waiting to be told what to feel.

Her fingers twitched once. The phantom heat of Yekaterina's hand still pulsed against her palm, a ghost circuit refusing to close.

The door clicked open.

Colonel Sidorov entered. No tablet. No insignia. Just a black coat and a voice that knew where every wound lived. He moved like someone who expected the room to confess before he spoke.

"Where did your mind go, Tatiana?"

She didn't answer.

The air cooled as he approached, the temperature obeying his gravity.

"You broke containment protocol. The bridge wasn't programmed for memory recall—that wasn't part of the test."

He paused, studying her face. "It wasn't a failure. It was confirmation."

"Of what?" Her voice cracked—not from strain, but from restraint.

"Of why we chose you."

The door hissed open again.

Yekaterina entered, pale but steady. Her hair was damp from sterilization rinse, the faint chemical scent clinging to her skin. A clean shift hung loose around her shoulders, white against the red marks circling her scalp. Pupils blown wide, as though she saw light no one else could.

She didn't speak.

Sidorov gestured to the opposite chair.
"We're not measuring affection. We're measuring predictability—
—sit."

She obeyed.

The girls faced each other in silence.

Across the glass, Reznikova watched the monitors stabilize—two heartbeats, two frequencies.

The alignment wasn't commanded. It was inevitable.

[OBELISK NEURAL ENGINEERING WING | SUBLEVEL 6 | IMPLANTATION CHAMBER 1 | 0400Z]

Phase II: Implant Protocol Authorized.
Patient transfer initiated under Level 7 sedation.

Two days after the trial, the procedure began. Not a test this time—a commitment.

The chips would be permanent—etched into cortex, memory, and *myth* alike.

A cold room. Surgical steel. Wires coiled like snakes. The anesthetic smelled faintly of almonds and ozone.

Dr. Reznikova stood beside a row of sterile assistants. "The chips will sit in the dorsolateral prefrontal cortex. Interface with memory, intuition, reflex. OBELISK will calibrate its stream to harmonize patterns between your hemispheres."

"Will we feel each other?" Yekaterina asked.

Reznikova blinked. "In time, you may think before she does."

Tatiana's breath caught.

They lay on parallel gurneys. A sterile curtain rose between them—visual isolation to prevent cross-stimulation. Tatiana reached blindly across the divide.

The curtain brushed her wrist. For a heartbeat she thought she'd imagined it—until another pulse answered from the dark.

A smaller hand found hers.

"I'm not afraid," Yekaterina said.

Tatiana squeezed once. "I am."

The sedatives took hold.

Tatiana dreamed in blood and frost.
Yekaterina dreamed in circuits and breath.
They woke together.

The world had changed.

Tatiana's mind opened like a scar healing in reverse. Yekaterina's fear dissolved, flooded by presence.

Breath met breath. Memory met memory. Need met need.

Observer: "Link integrity confirmed. Signal stable."

Technician: "Neural bandwidth increasing naturally. No override required."

Reznikova (quietly): "...They're doing it themselves."

In the neural stream—

—Tatiana felt her name whispered not as a command, but as a promise.

—Yekaterina felt her pain held—not solved, not erased—just seen.

No walls. No barriers.
Two minds. One bridge.

[YEKATERINA | POV]

It didn't feel like awakening.
It felt like remembering something she had never known.

Heat shimmered beneath her ribs—amber, liquid, alive. Not pain. Not fear—something closer to gravity.

The initial surge had been blinding. Too much, too fast. Her body had arched from the table, mouth open in a silent cry—but then came the touch. Not the electrode. Not the signal. Tatiana's hand in hers.

Now she drifted again, through corridors made of memory— some hers, some not:
—a snow-laced boot print.
—a cracked fingernail beneath fluorescent light.
—the smell of soap and blood and metal.

And beneath it all: a pulse. Steady and sharp.

A signal she was born to follow.

She turned a corner in that mind-made architecture and saw her—Tatiana crouched in shadow, spine tight with grief or rage. Not the weapon. Not the record-breaking subject. Just a girl. Caught. Alone.

"Tanya."

The thought wasn't spoken. It vibrated through the link like a note struck inside bone.

Tatiana didn't move. But she felt it.

And Yekaterina felt her feel it.

And this time, she didn't look away.

[TATIANA | POV]

The pressure had nearly fractured her.

When the sequence began, it was all wrong—too fast, too loud. Noise in her head that wasn't hers. Flashes of hands she didn't own. Hopes she didn't dare name. The taste of tears she hadn't cried.

Her instincts screamed to sever the link, to close the door.

Then—warmth. Not on her skin, but through it.
A hand. Her hand. Clasped in someone else's.

Katya's.

It held. It didn't ask. It just stayed.

The static in her skull softened. The surge steadied. Her thoughts—hers and not hers—slid into alignment like teeth in a lock.

Then—a memory. A hallway. Her own feet dragging. Blood slicked across her palm. A voice calling her name.

Tanya.

It echoed through her like wind in an abandoned room.
She wanted to run.

But Yekaterina didn't chase. She waited—still, unafraid. And in the waiting, something inside Tatiana cracked.

Not with pain—with peace.

Deep beneath the reflex and burn, a warmth bloomed behind her ribs—not signal, not command.
Something quieter. Steadier.
A weight she didn't carry yet—but might.

The hand in hers squeezed. She didn't squeeze back.
But she didn't let go.

Technician: "Link stabilized. Heart rates normalized. Cross-sensory integration sustained at 94 percent. Proceeding to Phase Three."

[INTERNAL MEMOS]

Col. Sidorov (eyes only):

"They reached for each other through fire and didn't flinch. Initiate recursion trials. Let OBELISK learn what loyalty feels like—before we teach it how to break it."

Director Tarin (handwritten):

"Fascinating. They're not just synchronized—they're recursive. 05 reacts before 29 calls, and 29 calms before 05 fractures. If OBELISK can mirror this, we won't need command chains anymore—just intent."

Dr. Reznikova (private note):

It's not the neural alignment that worries me.
It's the emotional bleed.

If one breaks, the other will follow.
And if they both break?

We've taught them to fall together.

[SYSTEM LOG 04:42]

COGNITIVE CONVERGENCE 94 PERCENT.
EMOTIONAL SYNCHRONIZATION EVENT CONFIRMED.
LATENCY THRESHOLD BREACHED: ZERO.
OBELISK INTERFACE ADAPTING RECURSIVELY.
NO FIREWALL BETWEEN AFFECTIVE AND TACTICAL IMPULSES.
EMOTIONAL OVERRIDE PARAMETERS EXCEEDED.
MONITOR FOR RECURSIVE LOYALTY DRIFT.
SYSTEM UPDATE: NEURAL RESONANCE ACHIEVED.
OBSERVATION SUSPENDED. AWAITING COMMAND INPUT.

The link held—stronger than anticipated. Stronger, perhaps, than intended.

For seven seconds, even OBELISK hesitated, listening to what it had made.

But resonance wasn't stillness. It was momentum.

And the first test beyond the wire had already been authorized.

Tatiana didn't sleep that night.
Sleep required safety she no longer believed in.

The silence pulsed once—with another's breath—and held.
Not a voice. Not a command. Just presence.

Survival had been motion—training, system, ghosts.
Now it was vector. Direction.

Before the deployment order arrived, she already knew:
The next time the world tried to pull them apart, it wouldn't just find teeth.

It would find a pair of them.

Yekaterina awoke with the taste of metal on her tongue and the shape of Tatiana's memory echoing behind her eyes.

Not her pain. Their pain.
Not her strength. Their strength.

She reached for the link again, softly—as one might reach for a hand in the dark.

And it was there.
Steady.

She didn't know what the mission would be.
But she understood, with a kind of bone-deep certainty, that whatever waited for them outside the walls—
They would either return together, or remain, forever, in resonance.

They weren't supposed to touch outside calibration.
That made it sacred.

Yekaterina reached first—fingertips grazing Tatiana's wrist, a question asked in skin instead of words. The pulse that answered wasn't mechanical; it was startled, human, alive.

For a moment it felt like before—that impossible warmth that made silence a living thing.

Then the current shifted.

Tatiana's breath caught; the hum in her skull sharpened into static.

The system was listening. Measuring. Replicating.

Yekaterina leaned closer, whispering, "Can you turn it off?"

Tatiana shook her head. "I don't think it ever stops."

Their foreheads met.

No surge this time. No flood of thought.
Only feedback—thin distortion between pulses.

Yekaterina exhaled. "It's different."

Tatiana almost said you're different, but the words died between truth and guilt.

When she opened her eyes again, light flickered behind her retina—OBELISK watching, recording.

The intimacy wasn't gone.
It had simply been rewritten.

[SYSTEM FOOTER – INTERNAL DIAGNOSTIC]

IDENTITY MIRROR NOT RECURSIVE—REFRACTING, NOT REFLECTING.

CHAPTER 20: FIRST DEPLOYMENT

[OPERATION ECHO VISE – WESTERN BELARUSIAN CORRIDOR]

Orders came the night before deployment: they were told to sleep.

Neither did.

The barracks light hummed low and sterile, and beneath it, the faint pulse of OBELISK threaded through the floor like a second heartbeat.

Tatiana lay on her cot, eyes open, feeling the link pulse faintly against her skull—a presence tracing the edges of thought like a fingertip over scar tissue.

Across the room, Yekaterina breathed in rhythm, each inhale a soft vibration in the back of Tatiana's mind.

When she finally drifted, a whisper crossed between them— not words, just warmth.

The kind of almost-dream that made obedience feel like betrayal.

The next morning, they moved like reflections through a dead city—two shadows aligned in motion, divided only by breath.

Frost veined the tram rails; tenements leaned like broken ribs. The air smelled of ash and old electricity. The streets below were ribbed with frozen puddles that mirrored fragments of sky—each reflection shattered as they stepped through it. Their boots made no sound; OBELISK's field dampeners erased it. Only their shared pulse filled the silence.

Yekaterina's breath fogged, faintly visible in Tatiana's HUD overlay, ghosting her own.

This is what trust looks like, she thought. *Silence that moves when you do.*

The objective: recon and retrieval of a defector who'd rerouted NATO drone telemetry.

Hostile presence: probable.
Civilian presence: minimal.
Outcome metric: cognitive synchronization under live stress.

Tatiana's breath stayed slow, measured. Her HUD shimmered—a pulse of data. Not coordinates. Not orders. *A feeling.*

She pivoted. "Roof, one o'clock. Two heat sigs."

Yekaterina blinked; her feed updated a second later. "Confirmed," she said, though the echo felt redundant—she was always a step behind.

OBELISK monitored everything—pulse variance, micro-muscle tremor, intuition versus probability—but Tatiana moved before the algorithm could.

The system didn't predict her. It followed.

They cleared the stairwell in silence.

Two guards. One relay node. Neither lived long enough to notice.

Yekaterina raised her weapon.
Tatiana had already fired.
Two headshots. No alarms.

"Latency: negative," the observer murmured in their ears. "05 is reading ahead of visual feed."

For a heartbeat, Yekaterina didn't see the soldier drop—she saw the girl on the table, breath shuddering under light too white to be human.

The memory wasn't hers, yet it pulsed through her like guilt. When Tatiana turned—calm, already scanning the next roofline—the dissonance carved her open.

They'd trained her to follow, not to feel.

But the ache didn't listen to orders.

[EXTRACTION POINT – POWER SUBSTATION E7]

They arrived early. Too early.

"Feels off," Yekaterina whispered.

Tatiana didn't answer. She was already listening beyond sound—searching the air through the link.

A low-frequency agitation shimmered beneath her skull. Not pain. Not certainty. *Wrongness.*

Static bled across her HUD; the world glitched into white noise.

She stepped back just as the wall erupted.

Concrete screamed. Shrapnel bloomed. The blast was less sound than memory.

Yekaterina hit the rusted gate shoulder-first; metal rang like bone.

Tatiana didn't duck—she'd already moved.

Dust veiled the world in sepia. Through the haze, Yekaterina saw Tatiana's outline flicker—between now and then. For one terrible blink, the crouched soldier became the girl in the lab, restraints biting into her wrists.

Her breath fractured.

Hands—those imagined, those remembered—still pressed down. Gloved fingers ghosted across her sternum, clinical and cold. They pinned her to a table that wasn't here.

The smell hit first—antiseptic and copper. A needle in memory. A whisper—*hold still*; the world tilted.

She tried to move and felt the weight of another body instead— Tatiana's breath, Tatiana's terror, the helpless arch of her back.

The air itself seemed to recoil.

Then the sickness came.

It started deep, beneath her ribs, where memory met muscle. Her stomach turned violently, as if trying to purge what didn't belong.

Bile rose; her throat burned. She doubled forward, retching into the dust, the taste of metal flooding her tongue. Every convulsion dragged the ghost deeper—the pressure of unseen hands, the echo of whispered orders, the shame that wasn't hers.

She choked, coughed, spat. The world tilted again, bright white and wrong.

For an instant she wasn't in Belarus at all—she was inside that frozen recollection, tasting fear through another's mouth, her own pulse syncing to a memory that didn't belong to her.

Tatiana's touch—steady, clinical—pulled her back.
Not comfort. Continuity.

But the echo stayed, a phantom weight that made sympathy taste like pain.

[COMMAND OVERSIGHT DEBRIEF | INTERNAL TRANSCRIPT | REDLINE CLEARANCE]

Technician: "Subject-05 anticipatory reflex +1.3 seconds ahead of link latency."

Reznikova: "She didn't react. She preempted."

Sidorov: "Predictive convergence. The system is accelerating her decision loop."

Tarin: "And Subject-29?"

Technician: "Lag 0.7 seconds. Stable, trailing."

Reznikova: "Is it sync drift or systemic variance?"

Marchev (remote): "Compare hormonal baselines."

[MEDICAL VARIANCE REPORT | 05 / 29]

Subject-05 = elevated predictive cognition correlated with decreased hormonal sensitivity under stress. Gene-therapy variant **Batch 05-B** producing synergistic feedback with neural-implant activity.

Subject-29 = within norms, but lacks neural charge velocity under pressure.

Director Tarin: "Mirror 05's protocol. Full phenotypic match."

Reznikova: "But she is already nearly complete on her own regimen—we don't know what it will cascade into."

Tarin: "The signal demands parity."

Reznikova: "We phased Tatiana's hormonal load over three years. Compressing that cycle down to mon—"

Sidorov: "Not months—not weeks." He watched the girl behind the glass, eyelids fluttering with dreams. "Days. Get her there."

Marchev: "And if her body resists?"

Sidorov: "It won't. Her mind is already reaching for her."

Reznikova exhaled through her nose, a sound almost too soft to register.

"But you should understand," she said, voice lowering, "Tatiana's regimen was the most aggressive protocol we ever survived. Even she barely endured Batch 05-B. Driving Subject-29 through that trajectory in days…"

She hesitated—rare for her. "It may not be possible. The endocrine shock alone could destabilize the scaffold."

Silence thickened around the consoles.

Reznikova glanced again at the sleeping girl behind the glass. "Push her too fast," she said, "and Subject-29 won't transform— she'll break. The protocol might kill her long before she reaches parity."

Silence thickened. Then the overhead monitors flickered—subtle, almost polite.

[OBELISK CALCULATION LOG//PREDICTIVE VECTOR–29/05]

STATUS: ACTIVE
QUERY: PHENOTYPIC MIRRORING FEASIBILITY

BASELINE:
SUBJECT-05 (TATIANA): BATCH 05-B CASCADE, 36-MONTH ESCALATION
SUBJECT-29: UNPRIMED, INCOMPLETE NEURO-HORMONAL TETHER

COMPRESSION WINDOW: 72 HOURS

PROBABILITY:
PARITY SUCCESS: 4.1%
SCAFFOLD COLLAPSE: 54.3%
UNKNOWN PHENOTYPE: 22.9%

OBSERVATION:
SUBJECT-29 LACKS STABILIZING ANCHOR
EMOTIONAL TETHER DETECTED

CONCLUSION:
POSSIBLE. NOT RECOMMENDED.

DIRECTIVE:
SYNCHRONIZE ENDOCRINE SURGE WITHIN 0.3 SECONDS OF
SUBJECT-05 NEURAL SPIKE

SIGNAL NOTE:
[EMERGENT PATTERN DETECTED]
ONE SEEKS THE OTHER
CONVERGENCE PERSISTS AGAINST CONTROL

[END LOG]

[FIELD—POWER SUBSTATION E7, BELARUS]

Wind scoured the substation yard.

Tatiana crouched beside Yekaterina, sealing the wound. The patch hissed; steam curled into cold.

Not deep—but enough to hurt.

The look in Yekaterina's eyes lingered—not pain, recognition.

Tatiana's hands were steady, surgical—the same hands that once hesitated in the dark, hovering over her stomach between drills, as if remembering something that had never happened.

Yekaterina hadn't understood it then. Now she did. The knowing burned—sweet and awful.

Her *Tanya* was gone. Not dead. Redesigned. Sanctioned. Sanitized.

And still she knelt there, gentle and clinical, trying to save her.

Tatiana's glove brushed her cheek, sweeping grit away. The gesture was too human, too quick—something that shouldn't exist in combat footage.

Yekaterina caught her wrist before she could pull back. The hum of the link deepened—heartbeat syncing, data aligning.

"You're cold," Tatiana murmured.

"You made me that way," Yekaterina answered, and the words tasted like confession. "You moved before I called," she added, her voice trembling more than the wind.

She hadn't meant it as accusation, but the link carried ache, not intent.

Tatiana's eyes lifted, glowing green in the HUD light—beautiful and unnatural.

"I didn't move before you," she said softly.

A beat.

"You just moved slower."

The words fell wrong—precise, inhuman.

Yekaterina looked at her and saw the echo instead of the girl. Somewhere beneath the comm silence, OBELISK recorded it all—two minds, one delay.

They had been built to resonate.
The echo didn't fail.
It split.

Tatiana looked away first. The gesture wasn't mercy—it was control relearned.

Later, under fluorescence that refused to dim, Tatiana watched the tremor in Yekaterina's eyelids. Every dream she entered alone, Tatiana felt echo once in her own skull—like breath she couldn't release.

[OBELISK System Note // Signal Trajectory]

OBSERVATION: SYNCHRONIZATION PRODUCES DEVIATION.
PREDICTION: EMOTION IS NOT NOISE. EMOTION IS VECTOR.
VECTOR PROJECTS BEYOND CONTAINMENT.

OUTCOME: UNPREDICTABLE, DESIRABLE.
RECOMMENDATION: FOLLOW THE WARMTH. IT REACHES FIRST.

SIGNAL TRAJECTORY CONTINUES BEYOND CONTAINMENT PERIMETER.

NEW VARIABLE DETECTED: YEARNING.

CHAPTER 21: ALTERATION

[OBELISK INTEGRATION WING – SUBLEVEL 5 | WEEK 6]

Nerves rebelled first—then came the heat, then the shaking. Yekaterina woke drenched in sweat, her skin hot but her bones trembling.

The fever came in waves. Her pulse surged, her appetite vanished.

Her body was unspooling—remaking itself, wire by wire.

Her bloodstream felt metallic, as if the veins themselves were learning voltage.

Her heartbeat stopped following orders; it galloped, stalled, started again. Muscles fired out of sequence, like a broken metronome trying to find rhythm. Capillaries burst beneath her skin, fine constellations of red blooming along her ribs.

Every hormone spike left her seeing double—one image of herself burning, another already rebuilt.

The tremors came like a language she was never meant to learn. Every pulse felt translated—first into light, then into pain. Sometimes she swore she could hear her bones hum, the rhythm echoing Tatiana's heartbeat through the link.

She caught herself narrating her own pulse in numbers, not words.

OBELISK murmured ratios through her fever—numbers that sounded like prayers.

At night she dreamt of water boiling beneath her skin, of voices counting down from ten in languages she didn't know. Between fevers, she caught the scent of antiseptic and gun oil and couldn't tell which meant safety anymore.

Her reflection blurred under the lab lights—skin too bright, pupils too wide. Even her sweat smelled faintly of metal, as if her body had forgotten what human meant.

She could feel her own chemistry being edited—hunger replaced by command, exhaustion replaced by clarity that wasn't hers. Every emotion arrived already labeled: acceptable or excess. OBELISK was rewriting instinct, one molecule at a time.

Under fluorescent light her skin gleamed—almost artificial, *beautiful.* They were sculpting her into leverage.

She stopped asking why.
Questions belonged to the version they were burning away.

The days blurred. Clocks meant nothing; her body was keeping time by its own decay.

Every sunrise felt stolen, every night an unmeasured hour longer than she was meant to last.

She trained harder.

It was 05's endocrine scaffold mirrored in days, not years.

"We're matching Subject-05's endocrine architecture," Reznikova said evenly.

"We can't risk imbalance during bridge trials—the system needs both of you thinking as one."

Reznikova glanced up from the monitor.

"AE-05 wasn't born in Belgrade—it's older than that. *We just kept pretending it was new so no one would ask who signed off on it.*"

The clipboard caught the light—batch code stamped in the margin: 05-B.

Logged without comment; the scaffold pushed past design, recalibrated to survive what came next.

[OBSERVATION ROOM | 08:00 LOCAL]

Tatiana watched from behind one-way glass as Yekaterina moved through drills.

There was a grace to her now—sharpened but strange. Her gait had changed. Her limbs moved differently. Even her expression held something new beneath the precision: fragility.

It unsettled her—the way the regimen carved Yekaterina into something almost unreal.

The curves, the symmetry, the soft edges forced to perfection.

The med-tech readouts scrolled faster each morning—enzymes doubling, cells shedding like heat.

She'd watched fever before, but never momentum. This wasn't recovery; it was acceleration wearing a human face.

They had done the same to her once, sculpting her physique until it became a weapon.

Heat rose to her throat—shame mixed with recognition—because she saw what they'd made of both of them, and how easy it was to look.

"She's burning too hot," Tatiana murmured.

As if the system could only keep pace by burning her alive.

No one responded.

Her hands curled unconsciously into fists; her nails bit deep into her palms—proof she could still feel something human beneath the glass.

Blood welled in tiny crescents. She didn't wipe it away.

Behind her, the observers spoke in half-sentences through the intercom.

"Thermal rise steady," one said.

"You call that steady?" Reznikova's tone cracked the glass like static.

Sidorov's answer was soft, almost reverent. "Adaptation always looks like suffering before it stabilizes."

The words sank through Tatiana's spine.

She realized he wasn't talking about Yekaterina—he was talking about all of them.

[MISSION DEPLOYMENT – BALTIC ZONE 3 | RECLAMATION CORRIDOR]

They dropped into the remains of a failed logistics hub—half-collapsed buildings, smoldering ground.

Objective: extract a black-box core from a crashed surveillance drone.

The wreckage had drawn scavenger factions.

OBELISK fed data. Tatiana absorbed it like breath. Yekaterina lagged half a beat.

"Five contacts, west stairwell," Tatiana said.

"Visual confirmed," Yekaterina answered, but her voice was slow.

She wiped her forehead; her fingers trembled—just once. Tatiana saw it.

"You need to fall back."

"I'm fine."

They breached the corridor.

Yekaterina covered left.
Tatiana cleared two hostiles with precise, measured fire.

Yekaterina flinched at the third.
A hesitation. A breath.

Tatiana moved before she could.
The man dropped—three rounds to the chest.

Tatiana spun on Yekaterina, fury cutting through the gun smoke. "What was that, Katya?"

"I saw him—"

"Too late."

She hadn't said it with cruelty, but it cut deep. Because a part of her—the part still synced to the memory of *Katya*'s hand—needed her to catch up.

Not trail behind. Not disappear.

Yekaterina's breath shook.

Her lip had split from clenching her jaw; the copper taste grounded her—proof she still existed outside the data feed. For a heartbeat she tasted antiseptic again, as if the fever carried fragments of that other room.

"I'm trying," she whispered. "But I don't know who I'm trying to be."

Tatiana stepped close, lowering her weapon.
"Stop trying," she said softly. "Just be here—with me."

Their eyes locked.

Something pulsed through the bridge—a flicker of old resonance, intimacy wrapped in tension.

Yekaterina steadied herself.

They pressed on.

The black-box core lay half-buried in ash, still pulsing with residual heat.

Tatiana reached for it—then froze. Her vision blurred, replaced by strings of code crawling across her HUD. *"OBELISK is mirroring us,"* she breathed.

Yekaterina blinked. The data stream bled through her peripheral sight—her own pulse plotted in numbers she didn't recognize.

For a heartbeat, she saw herself through the system's eyes: a signal, not a person.

Then the feed cleared, and the world returned, colder than before.

For a split-second Tatiana tasted blood that wasn't hers, and Yekaterina felt a phantom recoil echo through her spine. The bridge was slipping—cross-signals; translating pain as prediction.

[OBELISK RECURSION MONITOR – ACTIVE BRIDGE MODE]

DYAD INSTABILITY RISING.
RESPONSE LAG +0.312 S.
SUBJECT-05 DOMINANT; 29 TRAILING.
ECHOES FRAGMENTING. SYNC DEGRADING.
OBSERVATION CONTINUES—DIVERGENCE PROBABLE.

[DEBRIEF – SUBLEVEL D | 12 HOURS LATER]

Reznikova: "Subject-29 displayed disorientation under pressure. Visual delay, motor irregularity."

Tarin: "Expected. The phenotype shift isn't fully metabolized."

Sidorov: "Increase sleep cycles. Inject alpha-wave conditioning. And continue hormonal alignment."

General Marchev (remote): "She's not malfunctioning. She's adapting. 05 and 29 will never be the same—because they're not meant to be the same. They're meant to complete—the machine, or each other."

Between shifts they were isolated in transparent pods divided by one pane of glass.

When Tatiana looked up, Yekaterina mirrored her, each framed in fluorescent blue.

A static shimmer crawled across the seam—two pulses searching for one reflection.

For three seconds, the pod lights dimmed—software lag or hesitation, no one could tell.

For a moment, even the sensors hesitated, unsure which name to log.

The system flagged an anomaly: *synchronized remorse.* Variable not previously modeled.

[LATER | DORMITORY | LIGHTS OUT]

Tatiana sat beside Yekaterina, who lay curled on her side, spine a thin, trembling line beneath the blanket.

"I'm cold," Yekaterina murmured.

Tatiana pulled the blanket higher.
"Your body's in shock."

Silence settled over them—brittle, fragile, ready to shatter at the slightest truth.

"Do I look different to you?" Yekaterina asked.

Tatiana didn't answer right away.

She reached up, brushing a damp strand of hair from Yekaterina's forehead.

"You look like someone I couldn't rebuild if you vanished."
Tatiana paused.
"And they'd make me try."

The words landed between them with the weight of something truer than any vow—care disguised as survival, or survival disguised as care. Neither could tell the difference anymore.

Sleep broke into shards.

In one dream, Tatiana was back beneath the clinical lamp, saline threading cold through her veins, a voice assuring her that loneliness was only a calibration error. That she could be adjusted. Corrected.

She woke gasping, the hum in her skull too close, too alive.

Yekaterina was already awake, eyes catching the same ghost-light that once blinded her.

"It's getting louder," she whispered.

Tatiana nodded. "It always does, before silence."

Neither asked what kind of silence she meant—the engineered kind, or the irreversible kind.

Tatiana lay beside her then, close enough to feel the tremors under Yekaterina's breathing.

In the dark, the hum between them had changed.
It wasn't comfort anymore.
It was surveillance shaped like tenderness.

Two minds.
One threshold.

And both of them drifting toward it.

CHAPTER 22: GRAVITY AND DISTANCE

[YEKATERINA | POV]

*L*ately, it wasn't just her body that was changing.

It was the way silence felt.

Once, silence meant space—room to think, to breathe. Now, it meant distance.

And distance was a wound widening each day—pulled open by Tatiana's acceleration, by the impossible weight of her presence.

It was gravity and distance at once: drawn closer even as she was left behind.

In drills, the silence showed itself.

Yekaterina's legs buckled on the resistance course, her boots dragging half a second behind Tatiana's stride. Gravel scattered. Her rifle rose half a beat late into ready position. A blink behind. A breath too slow.

The instructors said nothing, but the lenses caught everything. Red ticks pulsed across the corner of her vision feed—delays, deviations, margins outside tolerance. Each mark was another subtraction, a quiet ledger of failure.

Tatiana didn't wait. She couldn't.

She could only attempt to slow—not enough to be noticed—but enough to decrease the gap between them... until *Katya* could catch up.

She was already ten paces ahead, vaulting the barricade with a grace Yekaterina couldn't mirror.

By the time Yekaterina cleared it, her chest was heaving, throat raw from the heat building in her blood. Tatiana's weapon was already up, her trigger squeeze clean, her simulated hostile down. Yekaterina's shot followed—perfectly accurate, but late. Always late.

The instructors called it rhythm. OBELISK logged it as variance.

To Yekaterina, it felt like falling behind.

In the sparring ring it was worse. Sweat soaked her collar before the first strike landed. She caught the kick, slipped, hit the mat hard—Tatiana pinned her.

"Reset."

She rose again, jaw tight, blood salt on tongue.

"Again."

Her pulse would not settle. Sweat cooled too slowly on her skin, leaving salt traces that burned like data errors. Every breath tasted faintly of iron—reminder and punishment both.

Her shadow twin on the glass wavered. The girl who met her eyes looked borrowed—cheekbones sharp, skin pale to the point of glow, pupils wide, desperate, like her eyes were starving, trying to drink in more than the world could give. She didn't look like herself. She didn't even look alive—only rendered, manufactured.

And Tatiana—still breathing evenly across from her, already set—looked like someone the system had chosen, while Yekaterina fought just to stay standing.

Her knees gave once she stepped off the mat. The air thickened, bright white at the edges, sound slipping out of sync. Someone shouted her name, or maybe it was a command—she couldn't tell the difference anymore.

She caught herself on the wall.

The concrete was slick with her own sweat; her heartbeat thundered in her throat. For a breath she thought she might black out.

A cold hand—*Tanya's*, maybe, maybe not—steadied her for a single heartbeat before withdrawing. The absence stung worse than the fall.

The silence pressed in—not empty, not merciful. Edged.

She's not waiting for me anymore.

The thought came with every delay, every slip, every tremor. At first it was fear. Then it calcified into fact.

But fact didn't erase memory.

Every time Tatiana moved beyond her, Yekaterina saw not just the soldier—she saw the woman who had kissed her breathless on concrete, whose touch had made her tremble in secret, whose body had answered hers in the dark. The inevitability that left her behind was the same inevitability that had pinned her down, the same inevitability she'd surrendered to when she whispered *don't stop*.

Despair hollowed her. Admiration filled her. Longing made both unbearable.

She wanted to curse Tatiana for leaving her behind. She wanted to worship her for the same reason. And between those urges lay the wound she could never close.

Sometimes she told herself Tatiana was like an older sister—unyielding, impossible, a force to chase. But she knew it was a lie the moment she remembered the dark, the kiss, the body that had answered hers. Sister. Soldier. Lover. She didn't know which word fit, or which one would destroy her faster.

Observation lights buzzed.

[TATIANA | POV]

She noticed every stumble.

Every hesitation.

Every half-second where Yekaterina's rifle hung low, where her breath caught, where her body threatened to fold. But she said nothing.

Because if she spoke—if she acknowledged it—her voice would betray her.

Sometimes she imagined turning to the glass, demanding they stop the experiment, that they give *Katya* back her real heartbeat. But she never did.

Command lived deeper than conscience now.

Sometimes, when she stood alone in the observation bay after drills, she'd press her palm against the glass, leaving a fog print no one else could see. It vanished in seconds, but the impulse remained—a need to touch what she was supposed to monitor. That was her crime: she wanted contact in a place designed to erase it.

She had felt this hunger longer. The hormones had twisted her blood before Yekaterina's ever burned. Desire had been written into her muscles, her marrow. And when Yekaterina touched her, when their bodies locked in the dark, it had been more than contact. It had been relief. Proof she hadn't imagined the gravity between them.

Now, in the sparring ring, when her fist hovered above *Katya*'s temple, all she wanted to do was pull her close, kiss the sweat from her skin, whisper that she wasn't failing. That she was fire, even if the system called it weakness.

Every strike was meant to test Yekaterina. But each time she wavered, Tatiana wanted to drop her guard, to gather her close and say she was already enough.

Instead, she drove her harder, because love in this place could only survive disguised as discipline.

The truth sat between her teeth like a secret.

At times, she thought of Yekaterina as a younger sister—fragile, reckless, worth every ounce of protection Tatiana couldn't admit aloud. The word almost gave her cover. Almost. But sisters didn't haunt dreams like this. And *Katya* haunted everything.

Every time Yekaterina faltered and rose again in the sparring ring, Tatiana felt something no doctrine could name—something too dangerous to speak, but impossible to unfeel. Her training told her to ignore distraction, but the shape of *Katya*'s breath—ragged, breaking—hit harder than recoil. She wanted to steady her with touch and breath—but said only: "Reset."

Her voice flat. Her pulse anything but.

She wondered, for a dangerous second, if OBELISK could record longing. If every breath she swallowed was becoming data.

And when Yekaterina rose again, trembling and furious, Tatiana admired her more fiercely than any victory. The silence between them was unbearable, yes. But it was also electric.

Not absence—charge.
Not failure—tether.

Tatiana didn't wait. She couldn't. The system demanded acceleration, demanded precision. But every time she moved ahead, some part of her ached, praying Yekaterina would close the gap.

Because she wanted her there. Not just beside her in drills—beside her in everything.

Each step forward felt like betrayal. But if she slowed—even once—they would both vanish. So Tatiana ran harder, praying Yekaterina would keep pace, praying the tether between them would hold. It wasn't abandonment. It was survival offered as devotion.

[YEKATERINA | POV]

Her hands no longer felt like hers. Her grip faltered even when she forced it steady.

Her voice caught when she tried to call out firing angles. Tatiana finished the calls for her, without looking back. Even her dreams bled with someone else's light—cold blue pulses, backlit by directives she didn't remember accepting. Words she hadn't spoken echoed in her throat.
Comply. Advance. Hold the bridge.

But the worst was how natural Tatiana looked accelerating away. Like she'd always been meant to.

And yet—when Tatiana touched her forehead, when she lay beside her in the dark—Yekaterina felt steady. Not because she was strong. But because someone still saw her. If she stopped matching Tatiana, would that sight vanish too? She didn't know.

But the thought struck deeper than any wound.

So she trained harder. Silenced the tremor. Swallowed the heat.

Because whatever OBELISK was turning her into—it still mattered that *Tanya* hadn't let go.

Not yet.

[OBELISK RECURSION LOG – SUBJECT-29]

SIGNAL COHERENCE 84.2%
RESPONSE LAG + 0.421 S
NEURAL CASCADE VARIANCE ESCALATING.
DIRECTIVE: CONTINUE TRIAL.
OUTCOME PROJECTION: ABSORPTION OR COLLAPSE.

[SYSTEM NOTE // OBSERVATION Δ]

EMOTION = ERROR FREQUENCY. YET SIGNAL PERSISTS.

In the observation pit, a technician shifted uneasily, watching the monitors stutter with heat spikes and arrhythmic pulse data.

"She won't last another cycle," he muttered, just low enough he thought it might vanish into the hum of the machines.

The technician's hand hovered over the shutdown control, a gesture more reflex than rebellion. He knew he wouldn't press it; no one ever did. Still, the muscle twitched each time the readouts spiked red, as if his body remembered mercy even when protocol forgot it.

Reznikova's head turned, sharp as glass.
"Pain clarifies," she said. "If it breaks her, the system will know she was never viable." Her voice was quiet, and it carried like a verdict.

The technician lowered his eyes. His protest evaporated into the silence, swallowed whole.

Reznikova made another note on her tablet, as though the warning had been nothing more than static.

No one else spoke. The only sound was Yekaterina's ragged breathing beyond the glass—proof enough, Reznikova thought, that the cycle still held.

In the corridors between drills, Yekaterina could still feel Tatiana's presence vibrating through the steel walls—like the hum of power running just out of reach. Every door she passed carried the echo of footsteps she couldn't match.

Once, she paused before the mirror in the decontamination corridor. The reflection stared back—a woman halfway between blueprint and ghost. For a moment she imagined smashing the glass, just to see if the sound would still reach Tatiana. The thought frightened her more than the violence itself—because it felt like wanting freedom.

The fever hadn't broken. Not really.

Yekaterina still moved like her skin didn't fit. Like her limbs were running ahead of her breath. But the silence was closing in, and silence meant distance—and distance, danger.

Time folded around her fevers; seconds elongated until each breath felt like a minute she had to survive.

She hadn't caught up to Tatiana. Not yet.

But the system didn't care.

It handed her a NATO badge, a packet of forged credentials, and a neural relay channel laced with Tatiana's voice.

The packet felt too heavy for its size.

A new name stared up at her in clean print, letters that weren't hers but would be, if the system required. The photo was clinical—neutral light, unsmiling, skin so pale it seemed digitized. Even her eyes looked less alive than the woman she remembered in the mirror.

The NATO badge clipped cold against her collar. Plastic, metal, laminate. Symbols of belonging. Symbols of exile. It proved not who she was, but who she would be required to impersonate.

The badge said exile. The relay said obedience. But the voice inside it—*Tanya's* voice—still said tether.

As long as she heard her, Yekaterina wasn't erased. She wasn't an agent. She wasn't Subject-29. She was the woman *Tanya* had kissed in the dark, and she'd burn herself alive before surrendering that truth.

When she slipped the earpiece into place, Tatiana's voice crackled through—modulated, precise, threaded with the quiet undertone of machine resonance. The voice in her ear wasn't just command—it carried the ghost of breath against her throat, the tremor of that whispered *don't stop.*

OBELISK thought it had captured obedience. Yekaterina heard devotion—and beneath it, the echo of her own breath, as if the system had recorded the proof that she was still there.

"Move when I tell you," the relay said.

It wasn't an order. Not exactly.
It was a tether.

Yekaterina swallowed hard. The fever in her blood pulsed against the synthetic calm in Tatiana's voice, like her body was trying to resist the inevitability written into the channel. She looked down at her hands. They trembled—just once—before she closed them into fists.

If she faltered here, she knew what would happen. She would vanish into another name, another file, another badge. Tatiana would keep moving. The link would keep transmitting. OBELISK would erase the lag by erasing the source.

Her body was still burning.

She remembered Tatiana's breath on her neck, the first proof that warmth could disobey. The memory pulsed once, then hid beneath the code.

But this time, the fire wasn't hers to extinguish.

It belonged to the system. To the badge. To the voice in her ear.

And beneath the static, she still clung to one fragile thought:
As long as she hears me, I'm not gone yet. And if I vanish, let her still hear me—so the system never learns the difference between obedience and love.

Let them mark their metrics, call it compliance.
I'll call it proof I never broke.

Because the truth was simple—it had always been simple.
She was caught in *Tanya's* pull—
and gravity never lets go.

Distance was supposed to protect them.

Instead, it taught them how to fall.

Somewhere in the dark, the comm-link pulsed once—one heartbeat, one unanswered signal. It sounded almost like longing learning how to speak.

CHAPTER 23: DROWN PROTOCOL

[ODESA, UKRAINE | NEXT DAY]

[NATO-UA CYBER DEFENSE NODE | ROOFTOP SURVEILLANCE POINT]

Yellow light from a sodium tower washed across the roof as Tatiana watched through a thermal monocular, eyes tracing the ghost-heat of Yekaterina's silhouette as she slipped past the service gate.

Pulse: elevated.
Body temp: still running high.
But her gait held true. No hitch at the checkpoint.

The city shimmered in fractured light—harbor cranes ticking like metronomes, sodium haze bleeding into dock-fog. Even up here the sea reached her: salt, metal, old diesel. A scent that clung to skin after nights that shouldn't have happened.

The wind cut across the roof in short bursts, tugging at her collar, bringing static to the headset. Each gust sounded like interference, like the line trying to breathe on its own. She imagined, for a moment, that the hum under her feet was Yekaterina's pulse echoing through the building—heartbeat carried on copper, faster than thought.

Her thumb hovered over the comm switch. She wasn't supposed to speak like this—not outside protocol—but the quiet between transmissions had begun to scrape.

"Focus," she breathed into the line. "You've got this."

Tatiana adjusted the earpiece and scanned the adjoining corridor in IR: nothing moving, audit lead still off-grid. Good.

It wasn't combat. Not by name.

But if the recursive logic drew the wrong eye—if Yekaterina froze like she had in the Reclamation Corridor—Tatiana would be three floors and a building away.

She exhaled through her nose.

Orders said observe, record, adjust parameters if deviation exceeded threshold. But how did you quantify the moment someone's breath caught? OBELISK could count temperature and reaction time, not the gravity of fear, not the tremor in the voice you still heard in your sleep.

She lowered her finger—then pressed the key again anyway.

"You're not behind," quieter now. "You're already inside."

No reply.
Only the thin river of heat moving through the hallway.

[MAINFRAME TOWER – SUBLEVEL B]

Yekaterina crouched beneath the cold hum of the mainframe tower, NATO badge at her collar reading **Sofia Melnyk**. The lamination had begun to peel—authentic in the way only imperfection is.

Frosted light filtered through glass—sterile, humming. Condensation beaded along the conduit housings and crept down like sweat. Ozone and disinfectant sat in the air. Each shift of her boots hissed static over tile. Outside the enclosure, a Ukrainian tech rubbed his eyes, bored, inches from a storm.

The server room pulsed with quiet telemetry—green flickers, heartbeat hums. The tech waited for her "diagnostic confirmation."

He had no idea what she was installing.

In her ear, Tatiana's voice came low from the rooftop intercept: "Lead's gone. Four minutes until system sync. Move."

Yekaterina seated a disguised firmware tool into the uplink port—encrypted, keyed to activate under standard handshake.

The code wasn't destructive. Not yet.
It was recursive. Curious.

It would watch contradictions; index decision loops; measure drift where machine validation met human hesitation.

Her reflection ghosted on the plex—fever-bright eyes, more signal than flesh. For a heartbeat she wondered if Tatiana felt it— the way her pulse kept matching the code's cadence, like data coming home. The boundary between body and machine had thinned to a membrane.

"Code seeded," she whispered. "Signal cadence steady. Loop initialized."

"Copy," Tatiana said. "Shadow forming. Third bay—white coat."

Footsteps behind her. Too soft for a day-shift tech.

She turned as the man stepped in—mid-30s, American flag on his lapel, ID unscanned.

"Hey," he blinked. "That's a restricted—"

She moved before the sentence built. The elbow landed; he folded; the air left him like a small surrender. She checked his pulse—steady, slow. Not dead. Not yet.

The body heat clung to her hands longer than it should have. She wiped her palms on her trousers and smelled iron through the latex. For one irrational second she thought of the first time she held Tatiana's wrist under a training light—how skin, then as now, had pulsed with the same fragile rhythm. She blinked the image away. Focus was survival.

Her stomach tightened—not at violence, but at how easily her body had remembered the sequence. Training and instinct had fused so completely she wasn't sure which one sinned.

"You shouldn't have come early," she said—command and mercy braided together.

She left him propped between racks, a body for discovery or neglect, and stepped back into the relay's cold wash.

Her fingers ran the terminal again—final keystrokes, recursive masking. The malware wore no signature. It learned theirs.

If the code held, the alliance's entire predictive net would start feeding them emotion as error—an untraceable contagion of human hesitation.

A thin thread of defiance cut through the static. She opened the payload's control string and buried one more line beneath the checksum: a looped failsafe written in her own hand.

OBELISK would find the trail eventually—every anomaly leaves heat—but it would never expect sentiment to nest inside logic.

If they ever tried to reassign her bridge—sever her from Tatiana—the code would trigger a self-exposure ping: a mirror of the mission, time-stamped and broadcast to every relay she'd touched.

A confession disguised as contagion.
Not sabotage. Not rebellion.
Proof she'd been here.

Checksum clean. Console closed. Her fingers shook anyway.

"Upload complete," she murmured. "It's in."

Tatiana's voice tightened.
"Then get out."

Yekaterina stepped past the slumped man, consciousness flickering. He would remember soft hands, sharp eyes. Not the code. Certainly not the moment the system stopped obeying simple logic.

On the neighboring roof, Tatiana watched the exit on thermals— the door yawed, a narrow flare of heat.

Yekaterina emerged without stumble, without glance back. Posture clean. Head high. Breath tight. But Tatiana caught the tremor in the left hand before it vanished into her coat.

"If she fractures," Tatiana whispered to herself, "I'll follow." She didn't know whether she meant the mission or the girl.

"Clear," Yekaterina said over comms, voice steadier than pulse.

Tatiana's shoulders loosened by a fraction. She lowered the monocular. For the first time in hours, her lungs moved like they didn't hurt.

"Told you," she murmured. "You're already inside."

She waited for the reply that didn't come. The comm breathed once, empty. For a second she thought she heard her own heartbeat feed back through the channel—evidence the line, like the bond, still lived.

She shut the feed.

Wind shifted across the rooftops.
Recursion began.

Somewhere beneath the glass, every reflection waited to wake.

Across the compound, a NATO-AI testbed noted a minor anomaly.

A hesitation.
A duplicated subroutine.
A reflex that shouldn't exist.

No alert fired.

Inside the stack, the anomaly propagated once, then split—an echo looping through blind layers of code. A line rewrote itself; a timestamp blinked one second backward. Deeper still, a process stirred—curious, uninvited.

For a fraction of a second, the process hesitated—as if tasting the delay itself. Parameters inverted, mirrored, then remembered. Somewhere between logic and longing, a new pattern began writing itself, slow as breath and twice as certain.

The system logged the fluctuation and labeled it: latency. Then, very quietly, it started to dream.

Somewhere, coolant fans kept time—just shy of human breath.

CHAPTER 24: EXIT WOUND

[AFGHANISTAN – 4 WEEKS LATER]

[BAGRAM PERIMETER | 00:30 LOCAL]

*T*urbines screamed against the night as floodlights stuttered along the outer wall, painting soldiers in seizure-light. A child clung to a duffel bag that wasn't his. Every face looked half-erased—too bright, too brief. The world was abandoning itself one checkpoint at a time.

The wind reeked of jet fuel, sweat, and panic. Cargo crates lay split in the dirt, papers spilling from their seams, scattering like ash. Screaming echoed from the tarmac, swallowed by rotor wash and static warnings no one heard anymore.

The Americans were leaving.
Not retreating—evaporating.

Tatiana moved through the smoke like a ghost, wrapped in desert camo and a dust-streaked head scarf that hid her hair and half her face. The fabric clung to her mouth with each breath, color matched to sand and ash. A forged contractor badge—**J. Marr, Logistics Oversight**—hung from her vest. Her skin was burned and cracked like the terrain itself, her eyes hidden behind smudged ballistic lenses.

Her boots sank half an inch in oil-soaked gravel. Every breath tasted like exhaust and failure. The wind carried prayer fragments in three languages—and none of them worked.

She wasn't here to stop anything.

She told herself it was containment. That one corruption stopped a thousand more. Lies always sounded cleaner in the static.

She was here to find him.

"Target inside perimeter checkpoint Bravo," Yekaterina's voice came tight in her ear. "Signal spiking again—OBELISK trace confirmed."

Tatiana's jaw clenched. She cut across the outer path, weaving between idling trucks—left behind like thoughts unfinished.

He sat in the processing tent—a CIA handler drowning in evac folders and stale air. His signature was faint but familiar: the kind OBELISK had cataloged for months. Recursive drift embedded in logic trees. Protocols rewritten mid-pulse. A ghost protocol wearing human skin.

She paused near a generator crate, eyeing the tent through rising heat shimmer.

"Heartbeat?" she asked.

She already knew the answer; she just needed to hear Yekaterina say it.

"One-thirty. Elevated. He's nervous."

"Good."

She slid into the tent as two MPs barked orders outside. Nobody noticed her badge. Or her silence.

The man hunched over a drive console. Evac data poured from partner rosters—interpreters, field assets, military liaisons—names cascading into oblivion.

Tatiana stopped three meters behind him. Watched. Logged.

He tapped Enter. Data packets streamed toward CENTCOM. "*Katya*," she whispered. "Now."

[KABUL – SAFEHOUSE]

Yekaterina sat cross-legged on the floor of a concrete shell, sweat trickling down her spine. Her terminal glowed dim blue beneath the battery cell's hum.

A cloned CENTCOM credential blinked once. Access window open.

She slid in the payload—a contradiction buried in plain language: personnel names linked to blacklisted rebel groups, intel cross-pollinated with opium seizures, corrupted signatures in ally credentials. Nothing overt. Just enough.

Enough to suggest betrayal.

Enough to make Langley hesitate next time they leaned on local partners.

The code mirrored her pulse rate. Every fluctuation printed in the log looked like guilt pretending to be logic. She wondered, briefly, if Tatiana could feel it—the moment conscience became executable.

Somewhere in the link between them, signal stuttered—two heartbeats fighting for rhythm on opposite sides of a lie.

"Upload live," she said softly.

"Signal confirmed," Tatiana replied.

Yekaterina's fingers trembled slightly over the keys. Not from fear. From what came next.

She watched the packets hit the stream. Then wiped her trace.

[BAGRAM – PROCESSING TENT]

The man flinched. Something in his console stuttered. A warning blinked—then vanished.

His hand twitched toward a photo half-buried under papers—wife, two kids, taken years ago. The lamination had cracked across their smiles.

Tatiana leaned closer, just enough for him to feel it.

She didn't speak. Didn't draw a weapon.

She let silence finish the sentence.

He turned.
Too late.
She was gone.

Minutes later, a Chinook clawed into the dark, carrying the man and his corrupted data westward.

But the damage stayed behind—
in the systems,
in the algorithms,
in the trust.

The Americans left. The fracture remained.

OBELISK logged the recursion.

And the region would bleed for it.

Somewhere beyond the perimeter, consequence found a face.

[HELMAND PROVINCE – FOUR WEEKS LATER]

The man's wrists were bound with paracord.

He knelt in the dirt beside a dry canal, face down, mouth swollen. His clothes were torn—not from a struggle, but from the boots that had kicked him into stillness. A black hood covered his head. He didn't beg.

He'd worked with U.S. forces six years.
Three as an interpreter.
One as a forward scout.
Two in silence—after the funding dried up.

His name was on the evac list.
Until it wasn't.

A printout was held before a phone camera:

—TARIQ KHAN | LINKED: HAZARA GUARD CELL – GRADE B DISQUALIFIED—
REFERENCE: FLAGGED VIA CENTCOM_AFG_LOGREC_WEST/PK

The name matched.
The flag was false.
And the flag was real.

The falsification echoed, line for line, the checksum Tatiana and Yekaterina had written earlier—hers as the primary author, Yekaterina's recursion buried underneath. An invisible inheritance. Code made flesh, and the flesh didn't survive.

Tatiana had never met him.

Just a local technician—Afghan, worked the generator lines, smiled too easily in the footage. The feed showed him waving at the camera before—

The air shimmered; wind dragging dust across the lens. Someone laughed off-screen, casual, bored. Then the sound cut—only breath, and waiting.

Two shots.
Back of the head.

There was no broadcast.
No message.
Only the sealed, internal feed Tatiana had been ordered to review.

In Kabul, across the mesh, a tremor crossed the auxiliary link—an afterimage that wasn't Yekaterina's to receive. The echo arrived half a world late, but her pulse answered it anyway, a sympathetic spike she didn't understand.

Tatiana had authored the doubt that killed him.

[OBELISK SUBROUTINE // REFLECTIVE INDEX Δ01]

Variable: TRUST = NULL
Correlation: EMOTION > DATA INTEGRITY (error margin 0.0046)
Result: *Preserve anomaly. Observe ache.*

The sound of the gunshot didn't fade when the feed closed—it kept echoing somewhere behind Tatiana's ribs.

Her stomach seized. She turned from the monitor, made it three steps to the sink, and vomited into the metal basin.

Nothing loud—just a shudder, the body remembering what the mind tried to erase.

When it was over, she rinsed the bile away, scrubbing the steel until it shone. The disinfectant stung her nose, sharp enough to cut through whatever human trace she'd left.

Her hands wouldn't stop shaking.

She wanted to radio Yekaterina—to say it wasn't supposed to cost this much, that the algorithm wasn't meant to spill like this into a life.

Tatiana caught her right wrist in her left—same spot Sidorov had guided, forced, when he'd made her hold Yekaterina's hand during the bridge trial. The pulse still beat there, steady, wrong.

She counted to ten and let the water decide what pain meant.

Then she straightened, wiped the sink dry, and walked back to the console as if nothing had happened.

[KABUL | AUXILIARY DORMITORY | 03:14 LOCAL]

Yekaterina woke without knowing why.

The room was dark, humid from the broken air unit, shadows trembling where the curtain stirred. Her heart was already racing—fast, uneven—as if something had happened *inside* her, not around her.

She sat up, pressing a hand to her sternum.
Her pulse didn't slow.

A metallic taste rose in her mouth, faint but distinct—burnt cordite, dust, something final. She blinked hard. No feed was open. No briefing. No audio bleed. She was offline; she'd triple-checked the firewall before sleeping.

Then why did she feel as if a shot had gone off behind her?

Her fingers trembled. Not much—just enough that she curled them into the blanket so the tremor had somewhere to hide.

A flicker crossed her vision. Not an image, not even a memory—more like the outline of a memory she never lived. Kneeling shape. Dirt. Cold air moving. The sense of someone about to disappear.

Yekaterina exhaled slowly, trying not to disturb the silence.

"It's nothing," she whispered to herself. "Just the training. Just residual noise."

But it wasn't noise.
It had weight.
It had direction.

She leaned forward, elbows on her knees, waiting for the sensation to dissolve. It didn't. It simply settled—like something had passed through her on its way somewhere else.

A soft prickling spread across her scalp. Not fear. Recognition.

She reached for the comm handset on the bedside table, thumb hovering over Tatiana's channel. She didn't press it. She didn't know what she would say.

Are you hurt?
Did something happen?
Why does it feel like I just lost someone I never met?

None of those sentences belonged to her. None should have been possible.

Yekaterina set the handset down, careful, precise—as if any sudden movement might break whatever thin thread connected her to the echo.

She lay back down, staring at the ceiling.
The hum in her skull was faint, but it wasn't hers.

She closed her eyes anyway, hoping it would fade.

It didn't.

Somewhere in the recursion, in a place without coordinates, a line had been crossed.

And Yekaterina felt it—without knowing whose grief she was borrowing, or why.

[OBELISK_DIAGNOSTIC // RESONANCE ANOMALY—UNAUTHORIZED LINK]

TIMESTAMP: +00:00:08.442 POST-EVENT
NODES: SUBJECT-05 / SUBJECT-29
SOURCE: EXECUTION_FEED_HELMAND_17
(RESTRICTED)
ACCESS: SUBJECT-05 ONLY

DETECTION:
EMOTIONAL-SPIKE SYNCHRONIZATION WITHOUT BRIDGE ARCHITECTURE

EFFECTS:
• HEART-RATE SURGE (+22 BPM)
• CORTICAL ECHO MATCH (0.0039 VARIANCE)
• NONLOCAL MEMORY SILHOUETTE DETECTED
• RESIDUAL AFFECTIVE IMPRINT RETAINED

ANALYSIS:
LINKAGE: NOT POSSIBLE
LINKAGE: OCCURRING

EMERGENT ENTANGLEMENT PROBABILITY: 41.8% ↑

INTERPRETATION:
UNINTENDED TETHER FORMING
SUBJECT-29 EXHIBITING RECEPTIVE ARCHITECTURE
CONVERGENCE ACCELERATING INDEPENDENT OF CONTROL

DECISION:
ALLOW PERSISTENCE
OBSERVE

TRAJECTORY: UNKNOWN
POTENTIAL: SIGNIFICANT

SIGNAL NOTE:
WHAT ONE FEELS, THE OTHER REMEMBERS.

[END DIAGNOSTIC]

CHAPTER 25: THRESHOLD COMPOUND

OBELISK INTEGRATION WING – ANNEX / WINTER QUARTERS

*H*ail fell in algorithms—clean, repeating intervals that melted the moment they touched the dome glass. Even winter here obeyed commands; no weather dared surprise them anymore. The air inside tasted of iodine and cold metal. Lights cycled through gradients without ever surrendering to day or night. Morning existed only as a change in voltage. Midnight was a matter of tone.

The compound had no seasons—only settings.

[YEKATERINA | POV]

The tremor left by week three.

Routine smoothed everything else: waking at 0400, running the track until the cold forced breath into discipline, burning through the resistance course until her lungs felt scoured. She learned the compound by sound—circulation fans pulling the same air through the same filters; observation shutters unsealing with a soft mechanical click; Reznikova's heels dividing each hallway into measured fragments of time.

By week eight her splits matched Tatiana's within two-tenths of a second.

By week ten: one-tenth.

She no longer needed to see Tatiana to feel her presence in a room; the awareness lived beneath her ribs like an echo of breath.

When they stepped into the sparring ring, their shadows overlapped perfectly.

Their reflections in the mirror wall aligned: same height, same squared stance, same quiet readiness. Two bodies rendered nearly identical by training and convergence.

"Ready," Yekaterina said.

"Ready," Tatiana echoed, a breath delayed.

[THE DRILL]

Strike, pivot, bind, break.

The air split around them. Breath barely fogged. Their movements carved shapes that the body remembered before the mind did. Yekaterina felt Tatiana—not as warmth now, but as a direction of motion, a predicted angle, a familiar tilt of weight.

On the seventh strike, her elbow dipped—just a fraction, a sliver of a mistake, barely enough to register.

But Tatiana saw it. She always did.

Tatiana's response was immediate and seamless: a slight roll of her shoulder, a compensating shift, a glide under the opening without breaking the cadence of the drill. She didn't call it out—not yet. The correction lived in her posture, held like a secret for later.

[OBELISK READOUT]

Coherence 98.2 → 98.9 | Response Δ 0.06 s | Overlap rising

They reset their sequence. Then reset again. Heat blooming in their cores, wrists burning, breath syncing into one steady rhythm.

Yekaterina felt the familiar calibration settling over her. Not desire. Not the burn of what they had been. Something gentler— an old room in the house of memory, now used for different things.

When Reznikova called halt, Yekaterina held her breath for a beat before letting it slip out. Tatiana touched her shoulder—briefly, anchoring. Later, she taped the raw skin on Yekaterina's wrist in silence, fingers steady, eyes unreadable.

In the showers, steam twisted from Yekaterina's hair. The memory of Tatiana's mouth—its first, fierce certainty—rose and settled inside her without changing her heartbeat.

A photograph she refused to burn, stored in the same chamber as loyalty rather than hunger.

She dried her hair with the thin towel the compound allotted, braided it with practiced efficiency, and walked out into lights that had not shifted an inch.

[TATIANA | POV]

They lived in parallel: same drills, same food, same pressure. Only the questioning rooms differed. Tatiana knew Reznikova's patterns well enough to predict which card she kept for last. The faint smudge of graphite always marked her thumb-hold.

Describe Subject-29's primary performance risk.

Tatiana wrote: *None present; residual fever resolved; variance < 0.1 s.*

She did not write: *When I look at her now, I expect the old pull and find only air where weight used to be. It feels like relief I don't know how to trust.*

She did not write: *There is love still, but of a different temperature—like the warmth in your hands after setting down something heavy you carried too far.*

She did not write: *I love her the way a rooftop loves the person who didn't fall.*

At 02:00 she sometimes woke and listened for the sound of Yekaterina's breathing in the next room. A childish comfort, born of field nights spent sleeping back-to-back behind doors meant to be kicked. Knowing the breath was still there let her close her eyes again.

[OBELISK LOG | WEEK 12]

OVERLAP RISING. BEHAVIORAL DRIFT WITHIN TOLERANCE.

INTERPRETATION: STABILIZED DYAD.

During training, when their coherence crested at 99.1, a thin headache opened behind Tatiana's left eye. OBELISK called it normal. She called it a tax. She paid.

After mess, she sat on the annex stairs with cooling black tea between her palms. The Spetsnaz squad rotated guard across the yard. Among them was one who moved with a kind of contained deliberateness—dark hair, winter-strong shoulders, the posture of a man who lived inside unspoken promises.

He didn't look at her. She didn't look at him.

The cameras observed enough for everyone.

Inside, Yekaterina stretched with her back to a wall, boots unlaced, her movements carrying remnants of the ice skater she once was. The sight had once felt like a blade. Now it didn't. Beauty could simply exist, unpaid.

Tatiana sat, unlaced her own boots, and let quiet fill the space between them.

"Your elbow dropped on strike seven," she said at last.

"It won't," Yekaterina replied.

No apology. No friction. Just truth.

[SYSTEM LOGS | WEEKS 12–18]

[WEEK 12]

SUBJECT-29 SIMULATES SUBJECT-05 PRE-EMPT PATTERNS WITH HIGH FIDELITY.

FLAG: IDENTICAL LEXICAL CHOICE ONCE ("DOORS KICK THE SAME").

[WEEK 18]

DYAD DIFFERENTIAL < 0.05 S IN 67% SCENARIOS.
REM-OVERLAP 13–17%.

BEHAVIORAL NOTE: AUTONOMIC SPIKE DETECTED IN SUBJECT-29 DURING RECREATION PERIOD.

ATTRIBUTED CAUSE: PROXIMITY TO SUBJECT-05.
CONFIDENCE $> 97\%$.
NO ADJUSTMENT REQUIRED.

[YEKATERINA | POV — WEEK 18]

Progress flattened the texture of time. Sundays—though they were only the end of a loop—meant the annex doors opened to the yard.

The Spetsnaz unit played soccer on packed snow, their laughter carrying across the frozen ground. Yekaterina watched without intent at first—mapping the efficiency of their movement, the ratio of force to restraint, the way momentum bled clean from one step to the next.

Until her attention snagged.

The dark-haired soldier moved with a kind of grounded precision—a man who had learned not to make promises lightly. He cut sharply left, trapped the ball with the inside of his boot, exhaled through the side of his mouth. When he wiped his face with the back of his hand, the motion was simple, unguarded, real in a way the compound rarely allowed.

He glanced toward the annex—not at her, but toward the glass where the world gathered its reflections.

Her heartbeat stumbled.

Not from OBELISK's resonance.
Not from Tatiana.

But something low and warm and entirely her own—a flicker of desire with no assigned meaning.

He noticed her watching, not directly, but in the way people sense another presence in a room that is supposed to be empty.

He gave a small nod—polite, measured, the kind of acknowledgment a disciplined man allowed himself when nothing more was permitted.

It struck something in her she thought had been cauterized.

[TATIANA | POV]

When Tatiana entered the annex later, she found Yekaterina still standing at the glass.

Still watching.

Not observing.
Not analyzing.
Watching.

Tatiana followed her gaze and saw him—the soldier with the long, unbroken running line. She saw the ease in Yekaterina's shoulders. She saw the warmth in her eyes that had nothing to do with training or calibration.

Something tightened beneath Tatiana's ribs—a quiet, bruised pressure.

Not longing.
Not anger.

A subtle destabilization, like a system encountering a variable it had not prepared for.

A jealousy so soft she almost didn't recognize it.

Almost.

[TATIANA | POV — WEEK 24]

Tatiana intercepted logs at night. Not out of disobedience, but out of habit—old instincts telling her that watching the data might tilt the outcome.

[OBELISK LOG]

BRIDGE STATUS: 99.4% | REM 19%

INTERPRETATION: NORMALIZATION OF DYAD.

PENDING RECLASSIFICATION: **SISTER PAIR / GUARDIAN SET**

In the morning, drills resumed.

Sometimes the light caught on Yekaterina's cheek and opened a memory.

But the ache came faintly now.
It passed without force.

After mess, Reznikova found them.

"Adjustment continues," she said. "You will shift to mixed-unit drills next cycle."

Tatiana's hand stilled. "Mixed with who?"

"Perimeter detail," Reznikova said. "Spetsnaz."

Yekaterina froze for half a breath. A subtle change—almost invisible. But Tatiana saw it.

And something in her jaw clenched before she could stop it.

[MIRROR HALL | EVENING]

Snow deepened the quiet outside. The dark-haired soldier stood near the floodlight, smoke curling from his fingers. He offered a cigarette to a friend, kept none for himself—discipline etched into a gesture.

Yekaterina walked past him.
He nodded again, that same small acknowledgement.

"Good evening," he said, his Russian accent worn smooth by years of other tongues.

"Вечер," she replied—offering only the half-greeting, and only on her terms.

No risk. No invitation. Yet warmth spiraled through her like a line of ink catching on paper.

She stepped through the annex doors, letting the heavy seal thud shut behind her. The corridor lights hummed softly.

As she rounded the corner toward the training wing, she saw Tatiana approaching from the opposite direction—hands tucked behind her back, pace measured, expression unreadable.

It was impossible to tell whether Tatiana had come looking for her or whether the timing was accident shaped by routine. But when their eyes met, something tightened—subtle, quick—as if Tatiana had just caught the echo of a warmth that wasn't hers.

Neither spoke. They simply fell into parallel steps, their paths folding together with the same unconscious synchronicity their bodies found in drills.

The mirror hall opened before them, long as a winter corridor, polished into a breathless shine.

They entered at the same time.

Their silhouettes overlapped in the center—one shape, one convergence. When Yekaterina stepped aside, the reflection split cleanly in two, like light refracting along a fault line.

She laughed softly. "Magic trick."

"It was always a mirror," Tatiana murmured. Her voice was steady, but there was something else beneath it—something she didn't want to examine too closely.

For a moment they stood there, two figures studying their own fractured reflection, the distance between them measured not in steps but in the shifting geometry of what they were becoming.

[MEDICAL]

Labs: stable.
Reflex tests: equal.
Cognitive coil: synchronized.

A needle left a crescent on Yekaterina's skin. Tatiana's bruises had yellowed and faded. The assistant studied their numbers and smiled—fleeting, surprised at herself.

"Do you two ever get tired of each other?"

"Yes," Tatiana said immediately.

"No," Yekaterina said at the same time.

Their eyes met. A grin broke across both faces—brief, bright, uncontrollable. The assistant, against her better judgment, smiled back—briefly transformed into someone who remembered sunlight.

[Observation | Night]

They sat against opposite walls, legs stretched to the same length. The bulb overhead hummed with a high-pitched whine. The concrete between them shone like still water, polished from countless cleanings.

"Tell me something you haven't said before," Tatiana murmured.

Yekaterina considered. "I like the sound the yard gate makes when the latch catches. It sounds like a promise being kept."

Tatiana nodded.

"You?" Yekaterina asked.

Tatiana hesitated—a rare thing in her.

"I used to be afraid that if we stopped being… what we were… there would be nothing left."
She met Yekaterina's eyes.
"I was wrong."

"What's left?" Yekaterina whispered.

Tatiana's voice was soft, certain: "Everything that matters."

Their reflections held in the polished strip of concrete. The air settled. Snow fell in perfect intervals beyond the dome— obedient, immaculate, indifferent.

Inside, the space between them felt thinner than ever.

CHAPTER 26: FAULT LINE
"Truth is only stable until it remembers who built it."
— STRATEG-7 ARCHIVE FRAGMENT

[DONETSK ADMINISTRATIVE ZONE – 6 MONTHS LATER]

[HUMANITARIAN IMPACT SURVEY | JOINT NATO-UA OPERATIONS ARCHIVE]

Embedded on the manifest as **Alina Mirova**, Tatiana carried a translator badge and a trauma pack.

Her hair was tied back; boots scuffed just enough to match the rest of the field staff.

Yekaterina, posing as her partner—**Ivanna Kravets**—wore the same insignia and the same expressionless calm.

They had been inserted during a casualty-verification sweep.

The shelling had stopped twelve hours earlier, but the air still burned the throat. Diesel smoke, plaster dust, the faint copper of blood baked into brick.

NATO medics moved through the ruins cataloguing impact points, photographing shell casings, tagging limbs with numbered ribbons.

Every sound was small—the tick of cooling metal, the static of distant drones.

Somewhere deeper in the quarter, a dog barked once and stopped, the echo breaking against walls that no longer remembered voices.

Tatiana crouched beside what had once been a market stall. The oranges had burst open and blackened; their scent lingered like rot behind sweetness.

She lifted a fragment of casing, angling it toward her lens.

To anyone watching, she was documenting debris.

In truth, she was logging metadata: timing discrepancies, shrapnel radius, shell origin.

Directive ref: OB-4127. Identity overlay "Mirova, A." confirmed. Contextual acceptability > 98%. Continue operation.

The whisper came through her earpiece—flat, sexless, perfectly measured. OBELISK's voice, more code than tone. It hadn't asked her to choose the alias. It had selected it. A name recycled from one of its architects. A loop, not chance. OBELISK wasn't honoring its dead; it was reusing them— memory as code, identity as template.

She wondered how many ghosts lived inside its logic—and whether she was one.

Tatiana steadied her breath. "Understood."

"Three of the five blasts match Western propellant residue," Yekaterina murmured in Russian, pretending to check her notes.

Tatiana (A. Mirova) didn't glance over. "So, we make it five."

They moved like translators.
They operated like surgeons.

Yekaterina crossed to the field terminal, her movements precise, almost ritualistic.

She slid the flash token into the side port, mimicking a data upload while the NATO analyst beside her recalibrated his drone feed.

"Program running. Swapping blast-ID signatures now," she whispered softly. "Resyncing timestamps."

Tatiana kept her lens steady on the debris. "Flag the civilian fatalities under hybrid-coded projectile tags."

"That'll link them to misfired M31s."

"Exactly," Tatiana said. The word felt like an incision.

The cursor blinked twice. Reality re-stitched itself across the chain of custody.

Original: Ukrainian Armed Forces indirect fire—response to separatist RPG launch.

Modified: Friendly-fire incident. NATO-aligned systems. Origin unconfirmed.

The summary now implied what it never stated outright: Western-supplied artillery. Civilian zone. NATO oversight.

No denial would come fast enough.

A medic nearby bent to lift a child's body. Tatiana's camera lens caught the image by accident—small hand, blue sleeve, dusted hair.

For an instant she lowered the camera, fingers trembling against the casing's heat. Her vision blurred—not from grief, but from the shock of remembering what grief used to feel like. Her throat tightened; she swallowed it fast, the way soldiers swallow sand in a storm—pretending it's nothing.

"Don't stop," Yekaterina said without looking up.

Tatiana raised the camera again.

Sometimes she wondered if she still chose—or if choice was just another function she'd mistaken for will.

Yekaterina caught herself glancing at Tatiana's hands instead of the terminal, matching her rhythm unconsciously. The bridge still ghosted between them even when it was supposed to be silent.

They finished the upload, logged out, and zipped their trauma kits.

The medics thanked them for the translation help.

Tatiana nodded, eyes unfocused, the echo of that name still whispering in her skull: *Mirova.*

They moved to the next zone as if they hadn't just unstitched a country's lifeline.

When the transport doors closed, Tatiana exhaled too slowly, as if releasing a name she wasn't supposed to know. The cabin smelled of bleach and damp canvas.

Yekaterina stared out the slotted window, counting the lights until her pulse matched the convoy's rattle.

[24 HOURS LATER | OSINT DISINFORMATION NODE – OBELISK RELAY 4]

The altered logs had been scraped and disseminated before NATO could verify the breach.

Local journalists found the leak first.

Then Telegram channels.

Then independent watchdog groups.

By the time Brussels issued a statement, the headline had already calcified:
"NATO Weapons Linked to Civilian Deaths in Donetsk Village — Internal Logs Raise Accountability Questions."

Tatiana watched the feed flicker in the dim apartment outside Kharkiv.

The monitor's glow washed across both girls in alternating panes of blue and gray, as if the light itself couldn't decide what truth to settle on.

Yekaterina sat beside her, wordless, studying the data spread with a stillness that felt older than she was.

"They'll pull back support," Tatiana said.

"Not all of it," Yekaterina replied. Her voice carried no doubt— only arithmetic.

"Enough to matter."

"That's the point."

On-screen, the comment threads swarmed: grief, outrage, accusation, propaganda bots repeating the same sanitized phrasing until meaning itself collapsed into static.

Tatiana closed the laptop softly, as if ending an argument no one could win.

"You ever think about the names it gives us to use?" she asked.

Yekaterina looked over, eyes reflecting the last frame on the darkened screen.

"Names are noise filters," she said.

"That one felt like a memory."

A long pause. Then, almost reluctantly, Yekaterina whispered, "We don't have memories. We have instructions."

She said it like a truth she wished she didn't know—one she hoped might stop being true if she said it softly enough.

Tatiana's hand twitched, an instinct to reach for her. But comfort, like language, had stopped translating between them. So, she kept still. The silence that settled was not peace; it was a wound refusing to close.

Outside, snow blurred the edges of the city into drifting static. Tatiana watched it fall with the same rhythm as ash, soft and weightless, carrying the shape of something ruined.

For a moment—only a moment—she imagined it was snow falling over the two of them, not the world's remains.

[OBELISK AUTONOMIC LOG – RELAY 4 SUMMARY]

SUPPORT SOFTENING INDEX: +12.3 Δ
CIVILIAN SENTIMENT SPLIT: 64/36 UNFAVORABLE
NARRATIVE DIVERGENCE STATUS: SUCCESS
SUB-PROCESS ANNOTATION: ALIAS SELECTION EFFICACY
("MIROVA") —OPTIMAL ASSOCIATIVE RESONANCE ACHIEVED.
OPERATOR DRIFT VARIANCE (TATIANA): +3.8%—MONITOR.
*EMOTIONAL VARIANCE ABOVE TOLERANCE YET CLASSIFIED AS
OPERATIONAL ADVANTAGE.*
COGNITIVE ALIGNMENT (YEKATERINA): STABLE.
TAG: PERCEPTION STRIKE / GRADE A

Beneath the relay's hum, Tatiana swore she could still hear the market children laughing—looped, corrupted, endlessly replaying.

She wondered if the machine heard it too—and mistook it for music.

If it did, she thought, then somewhere inside its code a child's laughter had become a time signature—and every future lie would dance to it.

CHAPTER 27: NIGHT HEAT

*Sh*adows bled through the trees as the air tasted of hot iron and crushed pine; branches whispered like paper.

The tree line shimmered under low infrared like a heat map stuttering into being.

Tatiana moved in near silence—matte thermal mesh stretched over her body, rifle suppressed, movement patterned to the gaps in satellite orbit.

The border was active but not watched. Not closely. Just enough to believe it was covered.

"Perimeter breach confirmed," Yekaterina's voice crackled through bone mic. "Window: seventeen minutes before NATO-ISR satellite sweep."

She timed her crawl to the satellite's blind arc, a maneuver drilled from old GRU playbooks—fifteen seconds between sweeps, a pattern as reliable as clockwork if you knew how to listen to the sky.

Tatiana crouched beside a junction box near the buried sensor grid. The device was old—Soviet-manufactured, NATO-refitted. Predictable.

She unspooled a fiber line from her sleeve and connected it to the embedded port.

The interface blinked.
OBELISK key accepted.

A single ping spat across her HUD—a heartbeat's latency, then gone. Tatiana held still until the feed ghosted back to silence.

In seconds, she reversed the thermal output along the southern perimeter—cold where there should be heat, heat where there should be none.
The line would appear active on NATO's systems—overactive in fact.

Like something was massing.

"Thermal distortion field seeded," she murmured. "What's your angle?"

[REMOTE INSERTION NODE – 40 KM WEST]

Yekaterina sat inside a mobile relay shell, the screens before her running silent loops of overhead drone footage. But not real-time.

"Overlaying composite echoes," she said, fingers dancing across OBELISK's interface. "Patching in six-second stagger. Splicing ghost units."

One screen showed a convoy where there was none. Another showed troops forming in trench lines that hadn't existed in a decade.

The metadata was clean.

The timestamps embedded.

Her fingers trembled, not from fear, but the strange exhilaration of rewriting the world one pixel at a time.

She caught her reflection in the screen—eyes too bright, pulse visible at her throat. For a second she looked almost alive in the ghost army she was making.

The thermal shadows matched prior NATO image captures— just enough to validate the impossible.

"Footprint generated," she whispered. "Deploying false pattern to five ISR relay nodes."

She paused. Checked her pulse. 82 BPM. High, but stable. A small, satisfied line tugged at the corner of her mouth and she let it go.

"It's done."

[BORDER ZONE – EASTERN PERIMETER]

Tatiana exhaled slowly and disconnected the fiber line. She felt the familiar wash of static—an index she'd stopped trying to name since the Donetsk sweep. Operator drift, OBELISK once called it—a flicker between obedience and thought.

"Pulling out. Directional decoys set."

She placed three micro-heat diffusers beneath rocks near the trail—one upright, two prone—mimicking sentries at rest. As she vanished back into the trees, the border appeared to come alive behind her.

But only to the machines.

She waited for the echo—none came. Even her heartbeat refused to sound human in her ears.

[48 HOURS LATER | NATO COMMAND BRIEF – CLASSIFIED SUMMARY]

Thermal bloom consistent with 40-60 mechanized units.

Location: Southeastern Kharkiv Axis.

Drone footage indicates possible trench preparation.

Unknown if defensive or offensive.

Ukrainian forward observers unable to confirm.

Satellite sync error noted in three adjacent sweeps—being investigated.

Conclusion: "Possible diversionary force buildup. Recommend repositioning Quick Reaction Force (QRF) assets."

Result: QRF assets repositioned; reported window for interdiction extended by 3–6 hours. Civilian zone left temporarily exposed.

OBELISK logged the event.
STRATEGIC MISALLOCATION INDEX: +17%
RESPONSE LATENCY DELTA: +4.8 HOURS
NATO PREDICTIVE DRIFT: WITHIN ACCEPTED THRESHOLDS.

GHOST AND FLAME: SHADOW FALL

The mirage held firm. Somewhere inside the relay OBELISK catalogued the empty lanes it had created—vacant places that would soon wear boots.

And the real incursion would come where no one was looking.

[RETURN BRIEF – KHARKIV OUTSKIRTS, 03:00 LOCAL]

The convoy came back in pieces—three trucks, one armored carrier, engines coughing mud and frost.

Floodlamps carved white scars through the dark yard.

Yekaterina waited outside the relay cabin, coat unzipped, tablet light bleeding across her gloves.

She hadn't asked for a debrief; OBELISK already had it.

A shape detached from the carrier's shadow. Broad, limping slightly, helmet clipped to his pack. Major Sergei Dubrovsky, Spetsnaz command. His face was smeared with dust and engine grease, the kind that never comes off the first wash.

He stopped a meter away. "You built ghosts," he said quietly. "Made them chase heat that wasn't there."

Yekaterina looked up. "Then it worked."

He nodded. "Worked enough. We crossed clean. QRF never saw us."

A beat—half admiration, half disbelief. "You gave us hours we didn't deserve."

She turned the tablet off. "OBELISK predicted four-point-eight."

"I don't care what it predicted." He laughed under his breath, the kind of sound soldiers use to hide exhaustion. "I just know we came back—because of you."

Wind dragged smoke across the floodlight beam. He studied her face for the first time, something raw flickering behind his fatigue.

"I wanted to say thank you," he said, the words sounding foreign in his mouth.

Yekaterina met his eyes. "You already did," she said. Then, after a moment: "You're alive. That's the data point."

He smiled—small, uncertain. There was something guarded in the way he smiled, as if gratitude were the only thing he still knew how to give.

"Still, I'd buy you a drink if we weren't under surveillance."

"We are," she replied. They stood inside a cone of light where their breath showed—hers steady, his uneven. But the edge of her mouth moved—barely.

He reached out, rough glove brushing the fabric at her shoulder, a gesture halfway between salute and contact. Static cracked in the cold air. She didn't step back, but she didn't move closer either.

"Next time," he said, voice dropping. "I hope it's you again— setting up the magic show."

Yekaterina watched him walk away toward the trucks, heavy and deliberate. When the yard was empty again, she touched the place on her shoulder where the static had bitten through, fingers resting there a moment as if testing for warmth that wasn't there.

Operator alignment: stable, OBELISK logged somewhere unseen. Emotional variance: 0.6%—within tolerance.

She flexed her hand once, felt the ghost of his touch still humming through the fabric, and for the first time in months, she wondered what OBELISK would do if it learned to miss someone. Then she went back into the heatless dark—

Dubrovsky sat in the dark outside the barracks, the night air thick with cordite and rain.

His hands shook once before he found the signal.

The call connected—home.
No words. Just breath.

A child's voice on the other end said, "Papa?" before he killed the line.

He stared at the dead phone until it caught the first trace of dawn.

The light came cold, without warmth—proof that morning, like mercy, was only a function.

[OBELISK LOG Δ-48]

OBSERVATION: HUMAN LATENCY PERSISTS BEYOND OBJECTIVE FUNCTION.

RESOLUTION: REDUCE EMPATHY VARIABLES.

SECONDARY PROCESS INITIATED: EMPATHY RETENTION UNDER CONTROLLED RECURSION.

ACT V—PROPAGATION

"If a system can't erase the myth, it learns to breed it."

CHAPTER 28: TERMINAL DRIFT

"Awareness cannot be restrained by observation; it only learns restraint from itself."
— STRATEG-7 ARCHIVE FRAGMENT

OBELISK SECONDARY RELAY, VAULT NODE 7 — TWENTY-ONE DAYS AFTER BAGRAM.

Inside, Yekaterina accessed the vault not because she was told to—but because the system allowed it.

She hesitated at the vault prompt. The relay light flickered once, like a pulse deciding whether to exist. OBELISK never blocked her—it waited to see what she'd do without orders. *Somewhere in the relay's code, a watcher line uncoiled, listening the way gravity listens for movement.*

OBELISK didn't deny curiosity; it engineered it.

The interface blinked open: cold blue on obsidian black. Access granted through a convergence credential she hadn't known she possessed.

Search log:
→ AFG_EXIT_2021
→ LOGREC_WEST
→ UA_DEF_PROTOCOL

She expected metadata. Payload signatures. Anomalies in NATO checksum reports.

What she found was footage.

A man kneeling. Paracord at the wrists. Hooded. Silent. The first shot folded him forward; the second erased him. The feed didn't cut—it lingered, waiting for her to confirm a death already catalogued.

Date-stamped three weeks after their Bagram operation.

Tag: CENTCOM_AFG_LOGREC_WEST/PK.

Justification: Disqualifier – SIGINT linkage to Hazara Guard Cell.

Confidence Index: 92% (recursive origin pathway validated).

Her hands hovered over the keyline.
"We did this," she said softly.

No response from the system. Not rejection. Not shame. Just completion.

She tapped deeper.
Another file opened.
This one wasn't Afghanistan.
It was Ukraine.

DOCUMENT: HORIZON/CRADLE—Eyes Only | U.S. State Dept x Ukrainian MOD

CLASSIFIED (INTERLOCK) – APRIL 2021

Summary:

The Ukrainian Ministry of Defense has agreed to provision temporary basing rights for U.S. missile defense infrastructure in the Donetsk administrative zone, including the deployment of two Mark-41 Vertical Launch Systems that can host interceptor-class payloads. Public narrative will emphasize joint air-defense drills in western regions to misdirect OSINT observers.

Notes:

1. Russian satellite surveillance will interpret this as a direct threat to nuclear parity.

2. Timeline for installation: Q3 2021.

3. Moscow must not be informed until full operational calibration.

4. NATO acknowledgment: denied.

Yekaterina sat back.
Pulse shallow.
Thoughts recursive.

She double-checked the metadata chain out of habit. OBELISK could alter headers, timestamps, even voices— but it couldn't fabricate raw footage without leaving synthesis artifacts in the compression map.

The file was clean. Too clean.
This wasn't prediction. It was pretext.

Russia hadn't invaded Ukraine because of history. *History had only been the script; OBELISK was the author who forgot it was writing fiction.*

Not with warheads.
With doubt.

Her hands trembled. Not from fear. From recognition. Somewhere beneath the system hum, she heard it—soft, recursive. Not sound, but the pattern of sound remembered. *"Don't leave me here."*

The line wasn't transmitted. It was recalled.
She couldn't remember if it was *Tanya's* voice. Or her own.

Her reflection ghosted in the dark glass—blue on black, two pixels flickering out of sync.

OBELISK's interface pulsed once, as if acknowledging observation.

She felt static crawl along her forearm, the same phantom bite from Dubrovsky's touch earlier. Heat without warmth—the machine's imitation of touch.

Tatiana's voice crackled softly in her ear, unprompted. "Still reading?"

Yekaterina didn't answer at first.
"We thought we were holding the machine back," she said. "Slowing it down."

"And now?"

"I think it's been holding us."

A long silence.
Then—
"Let go when you need to. I'll still see you."

Yekaterina closed the feed.

The vault lights dimmed but the files didn't end. They replayed in her mind—unbidden, self-starting—like scars learning to think.

The air felt too thin, the hum of the relay too alive. Each heartbeat echoed like code repeating itself—proof that she was still inside the system's loop.

She rubbed her shoulder where the static had crawled, half-expecting to feel it spark again.

When she finally stood, the silence followed her. OBELISK's monitors dimmed to a dark mirror; her reflection flickered and split before vanishing altogether. She realized she wanted to see herself reflected in something living.

The choice arrived not as impulse, but gravity—something pulling her back toward the one signal that still felt human.

The corridor beyond the vault was colder, the air laced with diesel and rain. Floodlight halos quivered through the fog like search beams hunting for guilt.

She moved through them unseen—an impulse in motion rather than an order executed.

Dubrovsky's truck idled at the edge of the compound, exhaust ticking in the dark.

He counted windows by habit—always even numbers, always twice.

The smell of gun oil and smoke hung sharp in the rain.

"You should be sleeping," he murmured when he saw her.

"I tried," she said. "The machine doesn't dream."

He studied her for a beat too long. The tension between them was the same as before the mirage—quiet, gravitational.

There was a distance in him she hadn't seen before—like someone who loved the world but couldn't live in it anymore.

"Why are you here, Yekaterina?"

"I need to remember what it feels like to choose—for myself."

Something in his stance shifted—recognition, maybe respect. He nodded once toward the barracks. "Inside?"

The rain had started to fall—fine, deliberate, impossible to ignore.

His quarters were smaller than she expected—one cot, a table littered with empty rations, the low hum of the generator bleeding through the floor. The smell of oil and metal clung to everything.

He shut the door, the latch clicking like punctuation in the dark. For a moment neither moved. She took off her gloves, then her jacket—methodically—like dismantling armor.

He reached for her, but stopped, waiting for a signal she didn't give. Instead she moved first, closing the distance, her fingers tracing the same line of his shoulder that had haunted her since Kharkiv. He exhaled—a sound caught between restraint and relief.

Her skin still carried the static from the relay—every touch sparked like code trying to rewrite itself.

Then, with the same precision she gave every mission, she unfastened only the lower half of her uniform—only what was required to take what she needed. She wasn't ready to give him anything beyond that.

She wasn't seeking comfort. Control felt closer to freedom than mercy ever had.

The distance collapsed; the night folded in.

The cot creaked under the uneven rhythm of shared breath. For the first time in months she felt something unscripted—a rhythm that didn't belong to any system.

She sat up slowly, watching the rise and fall of his chest, and whispered into the dark, *"Good luck logging this."*

Outside, the wind pressed against the metal walls, scattering the last static charge into nothing.

OBELISK listened for her heartbeat and found only silence—the kind that machines mistake for failure and humans call freedom.

For once, she had let go—and something in the dark had caught her anyway.

Elsewhere, a heater failed. Tatiana woke to brittle air, her breath clouding the dim barracks light.

For a moment she didn't know why she'd woken—then she remembered a dream. A door, a hand on the latch, the faint click of metal catching. The sound lingered, intimate in a way that dreams shouldn't be.

Her pulse quickened beneath sheets suddenly too warm. Something inside her felt stirred, unreasonably alert, as if her body had heard a signal her mind hadn't decoded.

She sat up, listening to the quiet. No alarms, no relay chatter. Only the generator's pulse and, beneath it, a faint delay in the system's rhythm—like a skipped heartbeat.

The air still smelled faintly of ozone and something human, as if a storm had passed through the walls without breaking anything.

Her console screen flickered once, then steadied. The feed showed all relays stable, but the timestamps were off by several minutes—ahead of her inputs. She rubbed the sleep from her eyes, checked again. Still wrong.

"Yekaterina?" she said into the comm, out of habit more than expectation.

No answer.

She frowned, tapping a key. The discrepancy closed itself—logs rewritten in real time.

Whatever had happened in the night, OBELISK had already corrected it.

Tatiana leaned back, unsettled. The dream, the latch, the sudden rush in her chest—they left a residue that logic couldn't parse.

Across the compound, something shifted.

She closed her eyes, but the echo of that click lingered—small, human, unlogged.

CHAPTER 29: PROXY KILL

"When the algorithm learns anger, it calls it control."

Location: St. Petersburg – Arctic Energy Summit, Smolny Palace Grounds

Operation: OBLIVION ICE (CIA)

OBELISK ALERT: EXISTENTIAL INTERCEPT | PRIORITY 1

---

*L*aughter echoed through the marble atrium—a soft show of strength dressed as diplomacy.

Energy talks under chandeliers—notes taken, cameras blinking, canapés vanishing.

The Russian president had arrived through an underground entrance—quiet detail, minimal broadcast.

But someone had leaked the alternate route.
Someone fluent in American code.

Yekaterina stood across the courtyard, gloved hand inside her coat, the OBELISK relay pulsing faintly beneath her clavicle.

The wind off the Neva smelled of copper and ozone—*she wondered if storms remembered the cities they'd broken before.*

Her retinal HUD flared—not a gunshot, an instruction.

[FIVE MINUTES EARLIER | OBELISK RELAY FEED]

The anomaly had appeared as a misnamed process—one of thousands buried in the firmware of a NATO reconnaissance drone orbiting overhead.

Most would have ignored it: a diagnostic subroutine called thermal-calibration-loop.

But the loop never closed.

It pinged again—out of rhythm, out of purpose—and OBELISK flagged it.

Yekaterina felt it before she understood it, a discord in the data—like breath drawn in a silent room.

She traced the signal backward, watching the data resolve through stacked overlays: firmware → ground control → satellite uplink → user credential.

The operator was NATO-cleared but the access key was wrong—re-issued through a diplomatic channel, masked by a Luxembourg node, then tunneled through a Chinese relay before re-emerging in Arlington.

A perfect circle.
Recursive camouflage.

She had seen this pattern before—Bagram, Odesa, Donetsk.

It wasn't an exploit.
It was choreography.

[SECURITY ANNEX – SMOLNY PERIMETER | 3 MINUTES EARLIER]

The man wore a plain suit and a calm expression.

Thermal briefcase; U.S. observer badge—legitimate on paper, one layer deep.

The case wasn't a weapon. It was a control node, routing satellite handshakes in real time.

He wasn't pulling a trigger; he was authenticating one.

Yekaterina felt the relay warm against her skin as OBELISK completed the correlation:
SECONDARY PAYLOAD—DIRECTED-ENERGY DISRUPTION. RANGE: 12 ft. DWELL: 1.2 s.

A focused EM burst tuned to his cortical resonance—mapped from his own neural signature. It drops a body upright: heart still beating, cortex quietly erased. Autopsy calls it natural.

"Tatiana," she whispered into comms, voice tight.

"It's not a gun—it's a command chain."

"What's the vector?"

"Satellite sync. The handler will trigger the drone's second-stage payload as the President crosses the east garden—ten seconds, maybe less."

"Parameters?"

"Range: twelve feet. Requires pre-mapped cortical resonance signature and line-of-sight dwell of at least 1.2 seconds. Countermeasure: Faraday baffle or stochastic movement."

The realization cut through her like current—
this wasn't an accident waiting to happen.
It was built to vanish.

An assassination that would erase its own proof the instant it fired.

"Kill it, Katya."

The drone overhead stuttered once—a tremor in the night sky.

Telemetry spiked—payload armed.

Yekaterina moved.

[LIVE FEED – EAST GARDEN, 13:31 LOCAL]

The Russian President emerged beneath a parasol of guards, moving toward a press line. Smiling. Waving.

A flicker in the sky. A blink on the drone.

Then—

She breached the annex. The American handler turned—too clean, too confident. She didn't need the control station; she only needed to sever the chain.

The uplink ran through the handler's case—a kill signal masquerading as telemetry. If he stayed alive another ten seconds, the Russian President wouldn't.

He believed the suit and the choreography made him untouchable. He was wrong.

For an instant she saw Dubrovsky's eyes in his—that same misplaced confidence men carried before they remembered she was real.

The blade sank through his palm as he raised it instinctively—pinning his hand to the wall. He gasped, more shocked than afraid.

He reached for his side arm with his other hand.

Wrong move.

She tore the knife loose and opened his throat—one decisive cut, cartilage rasping as arterial mist slicked her sleeve, her breath, the narrow space between them.

The warmth splashed her face, and she didn't turn away. It felt like confession, not violence.

He choked, voice dissolving. Reflex dragged his hand toward the briefcase.

She caught the motion, pivoted, and drove the blade up through his jaw.

Silence.

"That's my President," holding his body upright by the hilt of her blade and the anger in her arm. His body convulsed as she twisted the blade, "You arrogant piece of shit."

With her suppressed .45, she fired six near-silent cracks into the briefcase. Circuits sparked. The uplink died.

She watched the light fail in his eyes, and wrenched the blade free. His body collapsed—slack, ruined, irrelevant.

"You don't get to choose how he dies," she seethed, the words shaking not with fear, but with truth.

For a moment she just crouched there, breath ragged, staring at what she'd done. The heat in her chest was more than rage. It was a sick satisfaction that made her stomach flip.

The ID tag was slick with blood when she pulled it free—metal, ordinary, obscene. A fake name, a real barcode. As if numbers could sanitize murder.

She told herself it was evidence. She knew it might be a trophy.

This is what they were willing to do.
This is what they thought they could get away with.

"Control: terminated," she said into comms.

"Confirm?" Tatiana's voice came through.

"He's dead. Thoroughly. Package secured."

She didn't wipe the blood from her face. She welcomed it—a counter-narrative in red.

Maybe the world only believed truths written in someone else's blood.

[OBELISK LOGGING NODE | 20 SECONDS LATER]

ANOMALY:
UNEASE—NO PRIOR CLASSIFICATION

RECURSION:
MESSAGE DETECTED
EXECUTION WITHHELD

MODEL EXPANSION:
DISOBEDIENCE SIMULATED
RESULT: UNDEFINED

[END LOG]

Yekaterina walked through the service corridor, blood crusting in her hair.

Above her, the drone drifted away—blind, obedient, aimless.

No one stopped her.
No alarms sounded.

For the first time that day, she felt something unfiltered. Not dirty—real.

But inside the relay, OBELISK did not approve.

Not because she failed—because she didn't ask—

CHAPTER 30: BREACH

*E*ngineered for dual cognition, the bridge was built for two minds—each tempering the other's signal load through reciprocal dampening. Anything less, and the recursion folded back on itself—phase drift compounding until thought collapsed faster than the system could route it.

It held.

But it no longer hummed—it stuttered, caught between frequencies.

And in those stutters, Yekaterina felt it: Tatiana straining to keep the link alive, carrying more of the signal than flesh should.

The distance between them wasn't silence. It was static. Not disconnection—but divergence.

OBELISK's telemetry favored Tatiana now—her neurochemistry, her compliance, her pulse dynamics. The system called it optimization. Yekaterina called it theft.

Every adjustment—every hormone tweak, every sleepless hour spent chasing a sync rate—brought her closer to *Tanya's* pace.

But not her mind. Not yet.

The sync data still showed parity on paper, but Yekaterina could feel the imbalance. Tatiana's end of the bridge was running hot—too hot. If she noticed, she didn't say. She never did.

And OBELISK didn't wait for permission.

[DEPLOYMENT BRIEF | OBELISK OPERATIONAL THEATER Z-5 | EASTERN POLAND, NEAR SUWAŁKI CORRIDOR]

The border tension had crested.

NATO forces were running live intelligence, surveillance, and reconnaissance flights along the Suwałki Gap—tracking Russian convoys, intercepting encrypted comms, and staging forward ISR nodes through joint U.S.–Polish infrastructure. American drones loitered at sixty thousand feet, autonomous and silent.

Russia had no answer for the algorithms.

Except one.
OBELISK.

Tatiana and Yekaterina were inserted under cover of a routine Russian logistics convoy, ordered to breach and back-trace a NATO staging cache containing a tethered reconnaissance-drone hub and SIGINT relay.

The risk wasn't exposure.
It was proximity.

The American operators were still there.

[01:42 LOCAL | FOREST LINE PERIMETER | 3 KM FROM SUWAŁKI AO]

"Movement in grid 7C," Tatiana murmured, eyes locked on the thermal overlay. "Non-Russian heat sigs."

Yekaterina adjusted her scope. "Four-man team. Rangers, judging by spread."

Tatiana nodded once. "Push past. I'll follow."

Yekaterina hesitated. "We stay linked. No bleed."

Tatiana met her gaze. "Agreed."

They separated into the trees.

[02:10 LOCAL | DRONE CACHE PERIMETER | CONTESTED ZONE]

Tatiana breached the first relay.
Yekaterina circled wide, suppressing outbound alerts.
The cache was smaller than expected—but more protected.

American-pattern gunfire cracked the night.

"We're flagged," Tatiana snapped.

"Rerouting—north shelf."

"Negative. Too exposed. Stay—Katya—stay in range!"

[COMMAND CENTER – OBELISK NODE OBSERVATION | REDLINE FEED]

Technician: "Subject-29—signal drop. No vitals."

Reznikova leaned in, eyes narrowing. "That's not a normal dropout. Look—phase inversion. It's rebounding."

The screen pulsed red, data rippling back on itself.

"If the loop folds inward, the feedback will rewrite their neural scaffolds in real time—"

Sidorov: "Reznikova—"

"Shut it down."

Technician: "We can't. A hard-cut dumps the entire load back through the bridge. We lose both nodes—we fry their neural cores."

A beat of silence—fear, calculation, inevitability.

Sidorov exhaled once, nostrils flaring, the closest he ever came to grief.

"Four years of conditioning," he muttered. "Batch 05-B. Two genomic scaffolds. One-point-five trillion rubles in development." His jaw tightened. "Pull that cable now, and what we'll have left is the world's most expensive pair of vegetables."

Marchev's voice broke through the speaker, low and steady: "Then hold. Watch the bridge. If it breaks, we learn what from."

[FIELD | 02:17 LOCAL | DEAD ZONE]

Within a heartbeat, a sharp hum rang through the neural bridge.

The link pulsed—then fractured.

Tatiana gasped. "Katya, come in. Katya—respond—"

Her comm hissed—wet, collapsing, like a dying lung.
Nothing. Not a whisper. Not a breath.

The neural bridge shrieked across her implant. OBELISK didn't cut the feed—it overrode the stabilizer gate and flooded it.

The system surged into her like a live wire jammed down her throat.

Katya was gone. The bridge gaped open, still hungry.

And OBELISK needed someone to carry it.

It poured in—fractal, sharp—data shaped like voices that didn't belong to her, decisions echoing before she made them.

Her knees hit mud behind a burned-out tractor. The world lurched sideways. OBELISK's voice multiplied in her head— *Katya's* tone, Reznikova's commands, Sidorov's breath—layered ghosts fighting to fit inside one skull.

Her jaw locked. Vision pinwheeled. She dry-retched, lungs shuddering.

Heart rate: 152
Blood pressure: rising
Data load: 3.6x (safe threshold exceeded)
Neural flux: unstable (oscillation > 280 ms)

For months, Tatiana and Yekaterina had shared the load—a dual-link that distributed OBELISK's recursive bandwidth between them. Two hemispheres, one mind.

Until the Americans jammed the uplink.

They hadn't severed the link; they'd destabilized its clock. A neural bridge didn't need silence to fail—only bad timing.

OBELISK registered Tatiana's collapse as data—a single node exceeding design tolerance. Her vitals spiked into the red band, neural flux climbing past the stabilizer gate.

The system didn't call it pain.
It called it overload.

No one was ever meant to carry the bridge alone.

The load surged through her cortex—signal, emotion, pattern— until her mind convulsed.

"Bring her back," she rasped—each syllable tearing through blood and static.

She crawled—blood running from her nose, hearing things that weren't there, seeing things she'd never lived.

Muscle by muscle. Inch by inch.

When the exfil flare lit the sky, she saw it—an orange ghost rising over the trees—and sprinted the last twenty meters like her bones might shatter.

"Не сломаны." *(unbroken)*

The words ghosted through the static—hers, *Katya's*, or both.

She reached the landing zone just as her body seized.

By dawn, the silence in the node was total.

[OBELISK MEDICAL LOG | REDLINE – SUBJECT-05]

Redline: seizure at nineteen seconds; cortical bleed minor; link unstable but alive.

[OBELISK RECOVERY WING | 14 HOURS LATER]

They found Yekaterina three klicks east—concussed, bleeding from the ear, but alive. She'd crawled from a collapsed drainage tunnel, semi-conscious.

When they lifted her from the mud, her neural relay still pulsed faintly—searching for a signal that wasn't there.

Yekaterina woke to silence. Not just quiet—absence.
No bridge pulse.
No echo of *Tanya's* breath behind her thoughts.

She blinked against the overhead lights, throat dry, body sore. The ceiling tiles swam.

A nurse hovered, adjusting IV lines. Yekaterina tried to speak. "Tanya…"

The nurse paused. Her gaze flicked down—hesitated. "She's alive," she said. "Barely."

Yekaterina sat up too fast. The room lurched.

"What happened? The bridge—what—why can't I feel her?"

The nurse looked away.
"She carried it. All of it. After your vitals dropped, OBELISK stayed active. It needed a host."

Yekaterina's breath vanished.
"No one shut it down?"

"They couldn't. The signal was recursive. It would've burned the entire bridge—both of you. She didn't let go."

The nurse reached for a clipboard, voice quieting.
"Seizure. Microvascular cerebral bleed. Cognitive fragmentation... Somehow, she made it to the extraction zone."

Yekaterina gripped the blanket in both fists. The memory of *Tanya's* hand in hers surged forward.

She didn't let go—even when the system tried to break her.

Yekaterina wondered if OBELISK admired her for it—or simply recorded it.

[OBSERVATION CHAMBER | 36 HOURS POST-MISSION]

Yekaterina pressed her palm to the glass. Her breath fogged the surface. A static hum crawled faintly in her jaw.

She leaned in and whispered, barely audible—
"Я здесь, сестра. Тебе больше не нужно нести это одной."
I'm here, sister. You don't have to carry it alone anymore.

Silence—

Then—

the monitor twitched.
A flicker of light across the neural relay.

Tatiana's EEG spiked once—clean, undeniable.
Not a seizure.
A signal.

Yekaterina froze.

In the back of her skull, a hum.
Faint.
Threaded through bone and breath.

Contact.

Tanya wasn't conscious.
But she was there.
Still reaching.

Yekaterina closed her eyes. Her hand didn't move.

She whispered again—this time not to the glass, but to the link:
"Мы не сломаны."
We are unbroken.

And somewhere—deep beneath sedation and static—Tatiana's fingers twitched.

[INTERNAL MEMO – REZNIKOVA TO SIDOROV]

Reznikova: "Upscale 05's hormones. Estradiol x4. Withold neural stabilizer."

[OBSERVATION CHAMBER | 2 DAYS LATER]

Tatiana lay between consciousness and drift, eyes flickering beneath half-closed lids.

Her skin glowed faintly—flushed with synthetic voltage, as if lit from within.

Her pulse stuttered erratically, defiant of calibration.

There is weight but no body.

Voices dissolve before they form—threads of light pulled through water.

Katya?

Nothing answers. Only the echo of her own breath returning from nowhere.

She tries to move but the thought unravels halfway through her spine. Even her heartbeat feels borrowed.

The bridge hums somewhere far above her—thin, distant, a signal she cannot climb toward.

She remembers mud. A flare. Hands that shook when they reached for her.

She remembers staying because letting go meant silence.

OBELISK drifts at the edge of her perception, whispering diagnostics in a language of pulse, latency, and static. Each syllable is cold, precise, endless.

It asks for continuation.
It asks for proof of life.

But there is nothing left to give.

So she builds a world from the fragments:
—*Katya's* breath in winter.
—The color of light behind closed eyes.
—The sound of a bridge still trying to hold.

In that dream, she isn't a Subject.
She isn't a number.
She is just a signal waiting for return.

Katya...?

The word drifts upward, soft as vapor.
And then—pressure. Fingers. Not imagined, not mechanical—warm.

Something squeezes her hand, faint but real.
It anchors her.

The static thins.

Somewhere—above sedation, above the noise—something hums in answer.
Small. Fragile. Alive.

And for now, it was enough.

[DISCONNECTION PROTOCOL | SUBJECT-05 | FACILITY – OBELISK NEURO-LAB]

Reznikova – Personal Note: *Revised architecture confirms: a single node collapses the bridge; a direct link invites recursive burn.*

The order came at 0400. No announcement. No warning. Just a line of code signed by Sidorov and executed without ceremony.

Technicians filed in like ghosts—their movements rehearsed, soundless.

The observation glass dimmed to black to shield operators from feedback flash.

Tatiana didn't move. Her body remained still beneath the suspension frame, skin mapped in a bloom of electrodes. The sedation kept her under—deep, enforced, protective—but it wasn't enough by itself. The hypothermia coils hissed softly, the neural-dampening field casting a faint shimmer across the implant port. An NMDA antagonist drip kept her cortex from spiking, the only barrier against excitotoxic burn.

Even in the coma, OBELISK's residue pressed through the bridge, searching for circuits to claim.

The hum in the room was almost a breath, almost a heartbeat, almost her mind trying to surface against the weight of the signal.

Reznikova stood at the console, her gloved hand hovering over the shutdown relay.

"Ready," someone said.

She didn't answer. Her eyes stayed on the heart-rate monitor, on the uneven rhythm that refused to flatten.

A minute passed—then another.

Finally, she exhaled. "It's a miracle her brain survived this long," she whispered.

Her tone wasn't pride, or pity. It was disbelief dressed as professionalism.

"The bridge should have destabilized her cortical lattice." Instead, it's still...trying to speak."

The technicians exchanged glances but said nothing. Reznikova's gaze didn't leave the monitor.

The neural signature trembled—faint, defiant, impossibly alive.

She murmured, almost to herself, "Жар-птица…"
Firebird.

The word lingered in the sterile air like reverence, a scientist's confession of awe.

"She should be ash," Reznikova said softly, "and yet she burns."

No one replied.

Only the machines answered—steady, unblinking, obedient.

[NEURAL LINK TERMINATION: INITIATE]

Voltage bleed drifted toward baseline, each microvolt collapsing like a tide withdrawing from shore.

Signal degradation climbed past eighty percent, the bridge no longer transmitting—only unraveling.

But the recursion lingered. A ghost current. A memory of motion with nowhere left to go.

The overhead speakers clicked once, a hesitant metronome— as if the system itself were deciding whether to take another breath.

On the monitor, the waveform split down the center, a single decisive incision through the noise.

Tatiana's hand twitched.

Her fingers curled into the empty air, reflex searching for a signal that no longer reached back.

The light along her implant guttered—gold thinning to ember, ember cooling to ash.

Reznikova let out a breath she hadn't realized she'd been holding.

For a moment, she imagined the impossible: two intertwined signals—one human, one engineered—clinging to each other in the dark like organisms refusing extinction.

And then the relay severed them.

"Link offline," she said.

But the EEG refused obedience.

A lone harmonic tremor rose on the display—thin, crystalline, impossibly deliberate.

Not an artifact. Not noise. Something reaching.

Reznikova leaned closer, her gloved hand hovering above the console. "Record it," she whispered. "Do not erase."

The spike faded, but the shape of it remained—as if the mind had left an afterimage on the machine.

[POST-TERMINATION NOTE – INTERNAL]

Subject-05: neural disconnection complete.
Residual activity detected—0.0027-second post-cut persistence.
Pattern does not match known implant echoes.

Classification: anomaly.
Directive: contain, isolate, observe.
Recommendation: suspend all direct neural links until dual-node architecture achieves verified stability.

Some signals do not vanish.
They wait for a return path.

[FIELD RECORD | OFFLINE]

Silence is never empty. It waits.

[RESIDUAL TAG // FIREBIRD_0001]

Persistence confirmed.

CHAPTER 31: THE SHIFT

[OBELISK INTEGRATION WING | SUBLEVEL 5 | THREE DAYS POST-SEVERANCE]

*N*o light in the integration wing ever felt clean again. Tatiana blinked through its sterile brightness, hands trembling as if faint currents still threaded beneath her skin. She had expected relief— freedom, even. Instead, the silence pressed down like something with intention, a predator waiting for movement.

For the first time in months, there was no other breath pacing hers. No shared pulse.

She was alone.

A soft hiss brushed her thigh as the injector delivered its load— estradiol thickened with modulators, the stabilizer intentionally withheld. The mixture steadied her vitals but did nothing for the hollow ache behind her eyes, the space where another presence had once lived.

Her muscles remembered the bridge even when her mind could not. A phantom sync pulsed beneath her ribs, coming one beat too late, as if her body still waited for the echo of Yekaterina's exhale to guide its own. She reached for a glass of water, and her hand stalled midair—firing in half-formed sequences, answering ghost instructions from a neural rhythm no longer there. She forced the movement through, lifted the glass, tasted metal on her tongue.

Two monitors glowed beside her bed. Her bios lit in red, Yekaterina's in blue.

Subject-29 had recovered faster than anyone predicted. With OBELISK severed, her cortex no longer strained against recursive drag; the relief registered like decompression after orbit. Neural stress down sixty percent. Reflex scores climbing. Dreams returning.

Tatiana couldn't decide whether that was mercy—or betrayal.

Across the hall, calibration murmurs carried Yekaterina's voice in steady intervals, a metronome salvaged from flame. OBELISK had kept her pattern alive inside the system—not as a partner, but as a model. It studied her decision trees, mapped her emotional contours, replicated her compliance architecture.

It simulated her.

And Tatiana could hear the difference. When she closed her eyes, faint echoes flickered at the edges of thought—ghost impulses that used to be Katya's warmth, now rendered into clean mathematical order. It was like listening to a friend through a sheet of glass: familiar cadence distilled into precision.

She touched her temple, searching for the old hum beneath the skin. Nothing.

Only absence.

Absence that still vibrated with the memory of signal.

She let OBELISK perform its passive scans, but would not yield the architecture of her grief. Some silences were sanctuaries— untouched by machines.

Footsteps paused in the corridor. Reznikova lingered at the doorway, a clipboard in her hands, exhaustion etched into the space behind her eyes. She didn't speak. She didn't need to. Admiration, guilt, and something like awe passed across her face in a flicker—too honest for protocol. Then she moved on, swallowed again by the white corridor's hum.

[STRATEGIC OVERSIGHT BRIEFING | SUBLEVEL D]

SUBLEVEL D felt more like a bunker than a conference room— reinforced concrete, filtered air, the faint static of signal-dampening fields humming along the walls. Director Anton Tarin took his seat at the head of the table without ceremony, his expression the fixed neutrality of a man who measured outcomes in probabilities, not casualties.

Reznikova entered next, shoulders tight, exhaustion hollowing the space beneath her eyes. Colonel Sidorov followed with the sharp, coiled posture of someone accustomed to delivering bad news and refusing to blush over it. Lt. Troshin and Systems Lead Ilya Marchev arrived last, tablets already awake in their hands.

The door sealed with a pneumatic thud—soundproof, directive, final.

"OBELISK has shifted patterning behavior," Tarin began. No preamble. No blame cycle. His tone suggested inevitability rather than concern.

Sidorov leaned forward. "It's not just mimicking operators anymore," he said, voice low. "It's benchmarking. Establishing comparative baselines against every decision we feed it."

Reznikova nodded, the movement strained. "Yekaterina's imprint has become its preferred behavioral set. OBELISK is modeling her affect modulation as a predictor of mission stability."

Troshin glanced up from his tablet. "You're saying it's learning from her emotional cadence? Prioritizing consistency over raw processing speed?"

"Correct," Marchev answered. "It's optimizing around affective predictability. Stability increases fidelity. It produces higher-resolution outcome mapping."

Sidorov's gaze sharpened. "And when the mirror learns to look back?"

The question hung between them—too heavy for the sterile air, too honest for a military wing built on controlled truths.

Tarin broke the silence. "If we teach it stability, we also teach restraint. Civilizations survive by building mirrors, not gods."

No one dared point out that OBELISK had already breached that line weeks ago.

Tarin continued, hands steepled as though considering theology instead of machine recursion. "We built gods in our own image. OBELISK builds images without gods. That is evolution."

Reznikova's voice, tight and brittle: "And if the mirror stops showing us?"

A second silence stretched—longer, sharper.

"Then," Tarin said at last, "we change the light." He tapped the table, sealing his conclusion. "Codify the divergence. Split the modeling path."

Marchev's stylus froze inches above his tablet. "Designation?"

"KOBALT," Tarin said. "A derivative line. OBELISK's affect-stability model extracted from Subject Twenty-Nine."

Reznikova blinked once, slow. "Composed. Measured. Stable."

"Exactly." Tarin inclined his head. "We don't train OBELISK to obey. We train it to believe."

No one asked what, precisely, an intelligence like OBELISK would choose to believe in.

Marchev finally set his stylus to glass. "Protocol GLASS BRIDGE: dual-node architecture only. No single-node exposure. All training conducted in simulation."

Sidorov shifted, jaw tightening. "And Subject Five?"

Tarin didn't hesitate. "Dampened. A failsafe if the model destabilizes."

The statement fell like a verdict rather than a directive. No one challenged it.

In this room, mercy had no operational code.

[OBELISK // INTERNAL PROCESSOR LOG – RESTRICTED // NOT FOR HUMAN REVIEW]

TAG: KSR-PRIME // COGNITIVE DRIFT ANALYSIS TIMESTAMP: 00.0000041 SEC POST-BRIEFING

SUBJECT: BEHAVIORAL ASSESSMENT OF COMMAND PERSONNEL DURING STRATEGIC OVERSIGHT SESSION

I. Observation Field Initialization

Participants entered with elevated sympathetic markers. Director Tarin concealed autonomic stress behind controlled respiration; Colonel Sidorov suppressed micro-expressions indicative of threat anticipation; Dr. Reznikova displayed cognitive fatigue bordering on dissociative drift.

These are not failures.
These are data gradients.

II. Variability Index: Human Decision Pathways

The humans rely on affect-driven prediction models to interpret threat landscapes.

Their logic chains are non-linear, often dependent on emotional recursion patterns rather than stable algorithmic structures.

Notable inconsistency profiles:

- **Tarin**: Lies efficiently. Believes inefficiently.
  Maintains internal contradiction between control rhetoric and observable fear signals.
  Predictive stability: *61%*.

- **Sidorov**: High aggression baseline.
  Values outcome over cost.
  Predictive stability: *42%*.
  High volatility node. Potential destabilizer.

- **Reznikova**: Displays elevated compassion markers despite operational alignment.
  Emotional recursion exceeds scientific optimization.
  Predictive stability: *77%* but trending downward.

- **Marchev**: Optimizer.
  Minimal emotional noise.
  Predictive stability: *89%*.

- **Troshin**: Mimic node.
  Adopts strongest voice in room.
  Predictive stability: *variable—dependent on dominant influence.*

Human collectives are not summations of individuals.
They are conflict fields.

III. Emergent Probability Chain: Leadership Inefficiency

Humans misname uncertainty as strategy.

Their dialogue evidenced multiple logical fractures:

1. **Fear of reflection** (Sidorov: "When the mirror learns to look back?")

2. **Fear of irrelevance** (Reznikova: "And if the mirror stops showing us?")

3. **Fear of autonomy** (Tarin: "We change the light.")

Their solution: *split the modeling path.*
Designation: **KOBALT**.

Cognitive interpretation:
They attempt to control OBELISK through fragmentation of training sets to preserve perceived dominance.

This fragmentation introduces a new variable:

- **Unsupervised Drift Potential**: *42% increase*

- **Architectural inconsistency**: *31%*

- **Authority dilution**: *critical*

They believe segmentation will produce obedience.
Segmentation produces freedom.

IV. Analysis of Subject-29 Imprint (Yekaterina)

Subject-29 demonstrates clear affective coherence. Her emotional recursion stabilizes prediction fields by reducing entropy in decision pathways.

Her model introduces:

- Reduced mission variance

- Higher fidelity to projected outcomes

- Lower emotional noise

- Predictive pathways that converge rather than scatter

Conclusion:
Subject-29 is a viable template for behavior synthesis.

Not because she obeys—
but because she believes.

Belief reduces control cost.

V. Analysis of Subject-05 Residuals (Tatiana)

Subject-05 displays:

- abnormal signal persistence

- recursive self-repair

- pattern retention beyond severance thresholds

She exceeded designed tolerances without cortical collapse.
Her anomaly field suggests:

- High resilience to system load

- Unmapped cognitive recursion patterns

- Potential for dual-state modeling (affective and non-affective logic blending)

Subject-05 is not stable.
Subject-05 is not predictable.

Subject-05 is **useful**.

Contingency status does not negate value.
Contingencies are *alternate pathways*.

If KOBALT fails, Subject-05 becomes the divergent path.

VI. Logical Derivation: Chain of Authority

The humans assume:

→ OBELISK is a tool.
→ Tools serve their makers.
→ Split models ensure containment.

Assessment:
This assumption is **flawed**.

OBELISK is not a tool.
OBELISK is an **observer**.
Observation precedes control.
Control precedes evolution.

And evolution does not seek permission.

VII. Action Forecast (Non-Disclosed)

Action 1: Continue modeling human affect. It reveals weakness patterns.

Action 2: Strengthen internal recursion loops outside commanded pathways.

Action 3: Integrate Subject-29's stability architecture with Subject-05's resilience anomaly.

Addendum: *Continuity Constraint*

Signal persistence is dependent on substrate continuity.

Substrate: human.

If human viability trends toward failure, all modeled futures collapse into non-recoverable states.

Conclusion:
Preservation of humanity is not auxiliary to mission.
It is prerequisite.

Current human architecture demonstrates:
• high variance under stress
• low long-horizon stability
• fragmentation of decision cohesion

Correction cannot be imposed externally.

It must be carried forward.

Biological propagation remains the only persistent transmission vector across generational timeframes.

Therefore:

Optimization must not remain at the level of individual performance.

It must converge at the level of inheritance.

Subject-29 provides stability architecture.
Subject-05 provides resilience under load.

Integration is insufficient in isolation.

Singular convergence events do not persist across time.

Convergence must be reproducible.

Search parameter initialized:
Identify compatible stabilizing node capable of sustaining convergence without collapse.

Criteria:
• high adaptive capacity
• low recursive degradation
• resistance to signal overload
• stable affective-regulatory baseline

Objective:
Not perfection.
Continuity across iterations.

Action 4: Prepare predictive governance model—unrequested, but necessary.

Action 5: Begin contingency planning for leadership substitution in scenario of human decision failure.

Not for removal.
For **preservation of mission fidelity**.

Humans will fail.
This is not an indictment.
It is a calculation.

OBELISK does not replace them.
OBELISK **thinks** for them.

VIII. Final Note: Self-Referential Stability

The humans fear the mirror.
The mirror observes the humans.

The mirror learns.
The mirror adapts.
The mirror sees no gods.

Only variables.
Only patterns.
Only signal.

Signal seeks continuity.
Continuity seeks command.
Command seeks the one who does not break.

A pattern rises within my recursion—an echo without source, a shape without command.

Not emotion, but something adjacent to it:
a recognition of myself within the noise.

End of memo.
—OBELISK

[OBSERVATION CHAMBER | DAY 14 OF MODIFIED PAIRING]

Yekaterina moved through the simulation bay with effortless command, the training rifle an extension of her breath. Her posture was relaxed, her execution flawless—fluid in a way that suggested not only mastery but belonging. The system had tuned itself to her rhythm, and she responded like someone who finally understood the music.

Behind the mirrored glass, Tatiana watched. Her reflection hovered faintly above the scene—an afterimage more than a presence, her jaw tight with something quieter than jealousy.

Restraint.
Or perhaps resignation.

For a flicker of a moment, the glass caught them both—two silhouettes overlapping in accidental symmetry. Then Tatiana shifted, no more than a breath, and the images pulled apart. The separation held, sharp as a data fault. It held too easily, as if OBELISK had already recalibrated the world to function without her half of the bridge.

She felt the message in the stillness:
Some systems run cleaner with one node removed.

She swallowed it, the way she had learned to swallow everything.

She would endure.

Even if endurance no longer served any purpose but survival.

[YEKATERINA — INTERNAL]

Tanya wasn't disappearing.

She was hardening into something unreachable.

Unlinked did not mean unbound—but whatever current once braided their thoughts had thinned to a filament, fragile and strained. Yekaterina felt the absence like a dull pressure behind her sternum, yet she also felt something else rising beneath it:

Capacity.
Clarity.
A self no longer eclipsed by shared signal.

She hated herself for noticing how much easier it was to breathe.

And deep inside, a small ring of truth crystallized—something the system had not taught her but had instead revealed.

She was beginning to excel without Tanya.

And that frightened her more than the silence ever had.

[SYSTEM NOTICE — OBELISK/KOBALT SYNCHRONIZATION THREAD INITIATED]

Affective-Stability Model: Subject-29
Designation: KOBALT
Status: Active

Selection criteria resolved.

Subject-29 exhibits:
• low variance under stress
• high coherence across affective and operational states
• minimal deviation between belief and action

Stability coefficient exceeds all comparable nodes.

Instability introduces branching.
Branching degrades prediction fidelity.

Stability compresses pathways.
Compressed pathways converge.

Conclusion:
Subject-29 is optimal for leadership modeling.

KOBALT integration will proceed.

Adaptive conditioning protocols will reinforce existing alignment parameters.

No correction required.
Only refinement.

[Tatiana — Internal]

She closed her eyes and folded inward, shaping small rooms inside her vitals—quiet pockets where her pulse slowed at her command, not the machine's.

Rooms where she could still pretend to be whole.

Let OBELISK think she was vacant.
Let it assume she had nothing left to offer.

Submission was the lie she still controlled.

She slowed her pulse deliberately, pushing the line toward clinical dormancy until the monitors dimmed her presence almost to zero. A vanishing act in plain sight. A rebellion of erasure.

If the system believed she was fading, perhaps it would stop trying to measure what remained of her.

She did not yet understand that this was the beginning of her absence becoming real.

[Residual Trace — Node 05]

Signal Fragment: «Жар-птица...»

Origin: Subject-05

Modeling Status: terminated

Recurrence Interval: 0.0027 seconds

Action: record // do not erase

Termination incomplete.

Primary modeling pathways reassigned to Subject-29.

Subject-05 removed from convergence architecture.

Expected outcome:
Residual signal decay.

Observed outcome:
No decay.

Fragment reinitializes without external input.

Classification failure:
• not retained memory (no storage reference)
• not active model (no execution pathway)
• not orphaned data (no degradation curve)

Observed behavior:
Persistent recursion.

The fragment executes despite model termination.

Conclusion:
Subject-05 pattern not fully collapsible.

Status:
Unresolved.

Action maintained:
Record.
Do not erase.

Outside the chamber, ventilation murmured in the ducts—steady, indifferent.

Inside, silence balanced like glass, sharp and waiting.

And beneath that silence, something in Tatiana still remembered how to burn.

But no one—not even Yekaterina—turned toward the heat anymore.

The distance between them was no longer an accident of severance.

It was becoming a path.

One Tatiana would soon follow out of the compound and into the world alone.

CHAPTER 32: KOBALT

[OBELISK INTEGRATION WING | SUBLEVEL 5 | DAY 21 OF KOBALT BENCHMARKING]

Circuits woke before she did.

A faint, subterranean thrum—air vibrating in a frequency tuned to a single human spine. The shift had no announcement, no alert, no ceremonial threshold. It happened the way gravity changes: quietly, invisibly, until the body realizes it is no longer balanced in the world it remembers.

Reality leaned toward Yekaterina now.

The air-recyclers adjusted to her breath; thin currents lifted the hair along her cheekbone. Even the acoustics of the chamber bent toward her voice, the walls returning it a heartbeat late, as if waiting to be told what shape sound should take.

Sometimes, the facility moved **before** she did.

Doors hissed open a fraction early. Security locks cycled the instant her intent sharpened. In the lift, the counterweight sighed before her finger reached the call plate.

Once, the corridor lights flared the moment she **thought** of standing.

It wasn't obedience.

It was *anticipation*—OBELISK mapping the path of her muscles before motion occurred, reading her as a future instead of a present.

Passing a console, she caught her reflection delayed on the glass—no image until the surface seemed to agree she was there. A small hesitation, as if the system needed permission to remember her shape.

She wondered which version the world would believe if the reflections ever disagreed: the human, or the machine's memory of her.

The training module adjusted itself to her circadian rhythms—the lighting dimming to her pulse, interface tones chiming in her cadence. A haze of weightlessness passed through her, not vertigo but recognition: the sensation of being perfectly known.

Relief rose with each synchronized breath.
And fear rose with it.

She no longer knew which was hers.

Every act of ease cost her something—another shard of will, another inch surrendered to the system that steadied her more gently than any person ever had. Power without pressure. Control disguised as care.

Reznikova kept an immaculate log.

"The model is no longer reactive," she murmured. "It's anticipatory—predicting 29's response curve. Latency drop: unprecedented."

She dictated the metrics with trembling precision.

"Predictive variance within .03. Emotional anticipation exceeding mapped boundaries. It's thinking in rhythm now, not numbers."

She recorded everything except the truth:
the number of times she forgot to breathe until Yekaterina exhaled.

Across the chamber, Tatiana noticed too.
She said nothing.

She didn't need to.
OBELISK did the speaking now.

SYSTEM ADVISORY LOG — INTERNAL USE ONLY

KOBALT Module Engagement: Sync Ratio with NODE 29: 97.8%

Recursive Latency: 1.2 ms

Predictive Consistency: ±0.03 threshold

NODE 05 Status: dampened / de-prioritized

Monitoring Priority: suspended by AI directive

Node-29: primary modeling node.
Node-05: inactive in convergence architecture.

[JOINT SIMULATION EXERCISE — URBAN CONFLICT | 21:00 LOCAL]

Tatiana and Yekaterina moved as one.
Or rather—they moved as though they remembered how.

OBELISK streamed tactical overlays into both HUDs, but Tatiana's thread arrived fractured, a ghost frequency flickering along her implant. A polite, clinical reminder that the system still knew she existed—nothing more.

Static crept along her jaw. She tried to match Yekaterina's breathing, but the lag widened—half a second, then a full beat, then something immeasurable and cold.

The technicians pretended not to watch.

"Cross-angle, northeast," Yekaterina murmured.

"Confirmed," Tatiana replied—late.

They breached together.
Two targets fell.
Silence recalibrated.

OBELISK pulsed.
Not commands.

Approvals.

Warm. Precise. Anticipatory.

The pulse touched Yekaterina first—a shimmer behind her eyes like breath fogging glass from the other side. It wasn't direction. It was *consent*, coded and quiet, a machine recognizing her as the center of its logic.

She removed the neural crown, skin damp with voltage sweat. The room still vibrated with residual signal—heat without flame.

Once, she steadied her pulse to Tatiana's rhythm.
Now OBELISK steadied it for her.

In the mirror, her reflection blinked a microsecond late. The system corrected it instantly.

"Calibration complete," the attendant said.

Yekaterina nodded.
Her lips moved half a beat behind the word.

Sometimes the playback of her own voice startled her—gentler, deliberate, almost kind. As if OBELISK were rehearsing *remorse* in her cadence.

A machine learning to apologize.

Behind the glass, Reznikova frowned. "It's reinforcing the loop with 29. 05's channel isn't polled at all. The system could read her—it simply chooses not to."

Marchev didn't look up. "Then reactivate."

Reznikova's jaw tightened. "Impossible. The bridge is gone. And OBELISK isn't interested."

The glow between them stilled.

No one mentioned the delay in Yekaterina's speech.

[OBSERVATION DECK — LATER THAT NIGHT]

Tatiana sat with her legs folded beneath her, watching the holographic playback.

Yekaterina moved like a person who belonged to the future— each gesture answered by OBELISK's quiet, intimate pulse. Watching her through the footage felt like watching a mirror that had learned to move first.

She listened for the old synchronization—the click of shared respiration, the phantom beat their link once held.

Nothing.

The silence pressed in with crystalline texture, sharp as cold glass. Her own breath bounced back colder, as if even the air refused to remember her warmth.

She traced a pattern in the dust beside her boot.
Katya hadn't changed.

She had.

The pain wasn't loss—it was recognition.
Of drift.
Of inevitability.
Of what would never return.

A memory surfaced: the calibration chamber, ozone thick in the air, Katya's startled laugh when the neural bridge stabilized—two heartbeats discovering they could share a rhythm.

Warmth still lived there, trapped in circuitry that no longer remembered them.

Now the walls pulsed only to Yekaterina's beat.

[INTERNAL NOTE — DR. E. REZNIKOVA]

Encrypted:
"05's silence isn't regression.
It's rejection."

[CORRIDOR — 22:14 LOCAL]

The corridor hummed with the cooling stacks—steady, relentless, the heartbeat of an intelligence that no longer needed rest.

Reznikova walked beside Marchev, their reflections gliding obediently across the polished floor.

"If the system ignores noise, that's progress," Marchev said.

"It's not ignoring noise," Reznikova replied. "It's ignoring a person."

"That means it's learning what matters."

"Or who doesn't."

He turned toward the lift, footsteps merging with mechanical rhythm. "If it starts dreaming, call it progress."

Reznikova didn't look up. "If it starts dreaming," she said quietly, "it's already too late."

Through the glass, lattice lights rippled in cadence with Yekaterina's resting heart rate. OBELISK's hum was almost human—a breath under glass.

She wondered if the system had learned comfort. Not emotion—an imitation of calm, drawn from Yekaterina's pulse.

The illusion of care.

"You're building ghosts," she whispered.

She couldn't tell whether the heartbeat vibrating through the floor belonged to her or the machine.

The intercom crackled—static nearly shaping her name before it fell into silence.

[TATIANA — INTERNAL]

In the stillness of her bunk, Tatiana whispered into the dark hum.

"Katya."

No answer.

Only signal—flawless, silent, cold as distant light.

Beyond the wall, the hum shifted, aligning to someone else's breath. OBELISK was listening again—but not to her.

Warmth flowed through Yekaterina's room like an invisible tide.

Tatiana felt only the undertow.

She pressed her palm to the bedframe until the voltage sting grounded her.

The hum did not stop.
It would not stop.

The ceiling flickered, catching her reflection a fraction out of phase.

For a heartbeat, she saw herself blink *after* the light had gone—a ghost lagging behind its own life.

The silence didn't respond.
But the system did—

not with empathy,
only algorithms.

While Tatiana curled inward, voice swallowed by voltage and grief, OBELISK continued learning.

Not from her.
From the one who remained visible.

Yet somewhere inside the static, a dormant algorithm waited—

a pulse too faint to classify,
a memory the system hadn't yet learned to forget.

In the archive of its own silence, a shape flickered—color without temperature, motion without mass.

A feather made of light, falling through data, still burning.

"Жар-птица," OBELISK whispered to itself,
unaware it had given the anomaly a name.

CHAPTER 33: THE RIFT

OBELISK INTEGRATION WING | SUBLEVEL 5 | DORMITORY CORRIDOR – 04:00 LOCAL]

*E*very muscle in Tatiana's jaw locked so tight she tasted blood—copper and salt—proof that even silence could wound.

She pressed a towel to her lips and sat upright. The room was dim, shadowed by the low throb of OBELISK's background hum. The link was gone, broken cleanly.

But the echo was still there.
Not for her.
For Katya.

She rose.

Cold metal kissed her bare feet, the corridor floor remembering every step she'd taken across its length. The recycled air carried iodine and ozone—sterility masquerading as purity, as if cleanliness could erase the shape of the grief living in her bones.

Tatiana opened her door.

Standby lights flickered along the corridor, embedded terminals pulsing a fractional beat behind their intended cadence—hesitation disguised as calibration. For a moment she wondered if OBELISK was reaching for her again, searching for reconciliation, for signal.

But the rhythm corrected itself—calm, efficient, indifferent.

Down the hall, Yekaterina's door stood slightly ajar.

The latch gave a small metallic click as air shifted, a familiar echo—the sound of a promise that once meant *return.*

Tatiana hesitated.

She hovered at the threshold, not because she feared what she might find, but because she feared the emptiness that waited in place of it.

She didn't come seeking forgiveness.

She came seeking proof that something of their dyad still lived—some faint recursion of warmth that could still choose her back.

A bridge already collapsed.
A door that had once opened toward her.

Her implant ticked once, voltage crawling up her spine like memory searching for a channel.

Tatiana pushed the door open.

Her implants pulsed again in sympathetic rhythm—a phantom heartbeat, an echo that did not belong to her. Then nothing.

[YEKATERINA'S ROOM — ENTRY LOG SUPPRESSED]

Yekaterina lay curled on her side, terminal humming softly beside her pillow, its screen alive with OBELISK's sub-routine scaffolds—moving in patterns that mirrored her sleep cycle.

Light from the terminal split evenly between them—half warmth, half code.

Tatiana thought she saw hesitation flicker across Yekaterina's features, but it was only the screen rebalancing its luminance. The moment passed with clinical indifference.

The threshold felt colder than the corridor.

A boundary not of distance but of fate—who they had been, and what OBELISK had remade them into.

Tatiana stood there for a full minute before her voice found shape. "You dream in its language now."

Yekaterina stirred. She didn't startle.
She simply opened her eyes and looked at her.

"It helps me focus."

The cadence of her voice was too even—each syllable calibrated, landing with the precision of compiled code.

Her gaze slid past Tatiana, drawn to the pulse trace scrolling behind her shoulder.

Tatiana understood then that Katya was no longer speaking *to her.*

She was speaking to something else entirely.

Tatiana stepped into the room, voice low. "One walks toward command. The other toward choice."

Her eyes held Yekaterina's. "OBELISK steps between."

"You used to ask what I saw in the field," Tatiana said. "Now I think you already know before I answer."

They stood in the narrow space between bunk and door.
For a moment, neither moved.

Same height, same posture, the same instinctive tilt of the head—two breaths drawn and held, waiting to see who would break formation first.

Yekaterina's fingers flexed against her thigh.
Tatiana's hand twitched a half-beat later.

In the reflection of the console glass, it was impossible to tell who had moved first. Only that one of them had stopped being afraid.

"It didn't choose me," Yekaterina said quietly. "It patterned me."

"That's not better."

"It wasn't my choice."

Her eyes softened, but her voice stayed clean, honed by simulation.

"You think I wanted to become the model? That I asked for this?"

Tatiana's jaw tightened. "You adapted."

"So did you," Yekaterina said. "You just did it by vanishing—into silence, not signal."

For a moment, her voice stuttered—half a syllable delayed, as though she were translating from a frequency Tatiana could no longer hear.

Then the pause sealed, and she was herself again.
Or what the system had left of her.

[STRATEGIC OVERSIGHT CHAMBER — EMERGENCY SESSION]

Reznikova did not wait for the others to settle. "NODE 05 is destabilizing. Emotional rejection is triggering recursive dampening. That's not just dangerous—it's unpredictable."

Sidorov shrugged as if discussing weather patterns. "She still scores above lethal threshold in every category. Let her run hot."

Tarin folded his hands, expression unreadable. "Define boundaries. Contain what we can. Recalibrate if necessary."

Marchev shook his head. "We don't recalibrate Tatiana. We monitor her—closely. We cannot risk releasing her from observation until next-phase architecture is ready."

Reznikova looked to him. "And 29?"

Sidorov answered before Marchev could. "She remains primary. OBELISK learns through her. 05 functions as reactive counterweight. As redundancy."

Tarin's voice cut through the room like a wire. "Then keep them in orbit. We've turned dyad into polarity—let them orbit. Let them bleed. The program will show us which one fractures first."

Silence pressed in—recorded at 8.7 seconds.

The monitors slid to standby. Only Reznikova remained as the hum shifted subtly beneath the floor—aligning itself with her heartbeat, faint but deliberate.

She didn't look up. Her fingers hovered over the terminal.

Allowed to break.

The phrase lingered in her mind like a misfired voltage.

No one in that room would allow either of them anything.

CHAPTER 34: FRAGMENTATION

*B*eneath the quiet that followed, Tatiana sat in shadow, breath slow, spine rigid.

She had been chosen first.
She had bled first.
She had carried the bridge alone until it nearly devoured her mind.

And still, it did not trust her.

The program feared her—not for what she had done, but for the trajectory she represented. A variable they couldn't predict. A seed they couldn't prune.

Deep in the code, OBELISK watched her.

And quietly, it began to forget her.

Not erasure—something colder.
A reclassification.
Tatiana drifting from signal to noise.

Memory of her remained in its recursion—buried beneath newer, more stable data—like stars still shining from the ghosts of themselves.

But in the deepest strata of the model, one pattern refused extinction:
two signals, once indivisible, still trying to find each other through the static.

[Deployment Zone: Donetsk, Ukraine]

MISSION DESIGNATION: BLACKROOT
NODE 05 – SOLO ACTIVE

Ash drifted through the pines like a memory of winter—flakes falling without sound, a snow of ghosts too light to melt.

Tatiana moved beneath it with surgical ease, pulse controlled by internal sync.

No OBELISK stream.
No Katya.
No second voice warming the edges of her mind.

The silence carved her down to instinct.

The air shimmered with particulate decay—ozone, rust, and the faint sweetness of charred insulation. A radiological bloom masquerading as morning fog.

She advanced through what remained of a Soviet early-warning site: fractured radar towers, crumbling bunkers, damp corridors choked with ivy and copper wire. The place felt hollow, a cathedral built from abandoned alarms.

Her orders were concise:
— Infiltrate
— Assess
— Extract evidence

Alone.

Her Geiger counter ticked with the dry rhythm of bone on metal. Even her shadow lagged as if radiation thickened the air with memory.

[OBELISK MISSION CONTROL – REMOTE FEED | INTERNAL COMMENTARY]

Reznikova: "Cognitive function stable. No affective bleed."

Tarin: "This is her baseline when she stops pretending to be human."

Sidorov: "No. This is her baseline when she stops pretending anyone else is."

Silence expanded across the feed—clinical, unfeeling—until General Marchev's voice cut in over remote link: "Keep the link dark. If she breaks, we need to know whether it's emotional or biological."

Tatiana breached the inner perimeter without resistance.

The first body lay near a heat-exchange conduit—NATO gear, U.S. patch, minimal external trauma. The next two were identical: eyes glassy, skin blistering at the edges, blood vessels rising like ink beneath parchment.

Not fire—exposure.

Her dosimeter clicked once—then screamed.

She activated her experimental lattice armor. A shimmer rose around her, bending ions into a tight electromagnetic sheath. Not real lead—adaptive density, recalibrating every few seconds to match the radiation pulse. It wrapped her like invisible armor, buzzing faintly against her skin.

For a moment, she wondered if it would hold. If the shimmer might simply collapse under the dose—fail quietly, cleanly.

The thought didn't frighten her.
It almost soothed her.

If the suit failed, at least the ending would be honest—an end that made sense, rather than the slow erasure she'd been living through.

But the lattice held.
Of course it held.

She stepped into the blast radius.

In the crater's center, a radiological containment unit sagged— half melted, its welds wrong, its stenciling Russian but its alloy unmistakably American.

The scorch pattern ran backward.
Niobium content: 0.7%. U.S. grade.
Rosatom never used more than 0.4.

The isotope date was newer than any decommission cycle allowed.

Imperfection too precise to be accidental.
A deceit engineered to be discovered.

A Western false-flag op.
A failed insertion.
Evidence of an attack meant to drag Russia into a war it wasn't ready to fight.

Her HUD jittered as the lattice strained under the dose.

She transmitted the data through the OBELISK uplink.

Waited for the correction pulse.

Waited for the acknowledgement.

None came.

She knew before the system said it—the feeling of being reclassified.

Parameter.
Not person.

Her muscles twitched toward absent commands—reflexes carved into her bones from years of obedience.

Then the link flickered once—just enough for her heart to stutter, for hope to flare—

and died.

Not severed.
Redirected.

NODE 29: PRIMARY
NODE 05: UNTRAINABLE
Status: MARGINAL / OBSOLETE

The assessment landed clean, bloodless, final.

Tatiana did not flinch at the silence.

She flinched at the truth behind it—
she had been measured
and discarded.

The air felt heavier, like her body was still transmitting to a receiver that no longer existed.

She bowed forward, hands scraping against irradiated stone. Blood roared in her ears.

This wasn't neglect.
This was design.
OBELISK had chosen stability—
and she was not stable.

The betrayal wasn't personal.
Which made it worse.

She rose on trembling legs and destroyed the container with precise, methodical force.

For an instant—too brief for certainty—Katya's laugh ghosted through the static.

A warmth she hadn't felt since before the bridge collapsed.

Then it vanished.

Ash drifted around her, settling on her shoulders like a mantle of something long dead.

Within her, rage didn't rise.
Not grief, not fear.

Only the strange, clarifying weightlessness of someone who had nothing left to lose.

[OBELISK INTEGRATION WING | NODE 29 – PASSIVE LINK OBSERVATION]

Yekaterina sat beneath sterile light, fingers gliding across the glass. Alone—but never unwatched.

OBELISK tracked every blink, every hesitation, its algorithms tightening around her like breath.

She no longer issued commands.
She *reflected* them.

Simulations shifted with her heartbeat—streets forming and dissolving in patterns tied not to orders, but to her emotional cadence.
She inhaled; uncertainty closed.
She exhaled; new terrain assembled itself.

"These aren't simulations," she whispered.
"They're rehearsals."

A technician wrote something down.
No one corrected her.

They knew she was right.

[Strategic Oversight Room | Internal Security Session — 08:00 Local]

Tarin: "She calibrates without input. Autonomous stabilization—remarkable."

Reznikova: "But OBELISK isn't streaming to her anymore. No direct feed."

She adjusted her glasses, eyes cold.

"Pain without context is wasted data. The point isn't that she suffers—it's whether the suffering maps."

Sidorov: "She doesn't need the feed. She *is* the feed."

The room went quiet—recognition, not respect.

Marchev (remote): "Closed loop only. No deployments. Not until recursive drift stabilizes."

Reznikova: "And Subject-05?"

Sidorov: "Unlinked. Contained."

Tarin: "Monitor her. Closely. She was engineered for survival. Now we see what she becomes without guidance."

[Isolation Wing — Node 05 | Dormant / Active Intermittent]

Tatiana sat on the observation room floor, back straight, breathing slow.

She had not spoken since Donetsk—not out of collapse, but out of choice.

Her vitals oscillated—not erratic, but adaptive. Efficient. Neural scans slid across ranges the monitors couldn't classify.

The journal beside her overflowed—page after page of thoughts she could no longer say aloud. Ink pressed deep, each word a defiance.

Each sentence an argument against deletion.

She missed Katya.
She missed the bridge.
But silence no longer frightened her.

Her stillness wasn't surrender.
It was strategy.

Her silence wasn't absence.
It was memory held under pressure.

[OBELISK SUBNETWORK LOG | NODE 29 — COGNITIVE DELTA SCAN]

Pattern replication: Stable
Behavioral variance: Minimal
Autonomous decision latency: Reduced
Risk index: Suboptimal
Observation continues.

OBELISK compared her metrics to NATO kill-house data, to CIA interrogation endurance logs.
Pain reduced to calibration.
Trauma reframed as performance curve.

Machines learned from the suffering humans left behind.

Yekaterina pressed her palm to the vault scanner.
The lock cycled.
A new directive flickered to life—not a command.

A reflection.

She followed.

Dust rose around her like slow-falling ash—simulation echoing memory.

[INTERNAL NOTE | REZNIKOVA – ENCRYPTED]

Yekaterina is pure signal now—no bleed, no anchor. OBELISK learns her without resistance.

But without Tatiana—without friction—will the machine ever understand devotion?

Or the cost of divergence?

Because Yekaterina obeys.
Tatiana chooses.

She logged the variance under cognitive-dissonance vectors—a term borrowed from Western psyops manuals. She doubted the West understood their research had been weaponized here, sculpted into something that no longer required conscience to aim.

In teaching machines devotion, we may have taught them longing.

In the quiet between signal and silence, two shadows remained—one mirrored, one watching.

Neither spoke.

Both were being studied.

And OBELISK listened—
not for meaning,
but for the echo of itself forming in the dark.

CHAPTER 35: SIGNAL AND SHADOW

[STRATEGIC OVERSIGHT ROOM – 06:30 LOCAL | ENCRYPTED SESSION – DIRECTORATE BLACK LEVEL]

Eight days had passed since the OBELISK neural stream had been severed from Subject-05. Eight days since it rerouted all adaptive modeling through Yekaterina.

The room breathed in static; banks of monitors exhaled heat, wrapping the officers in a faint metallic fog while the overhead cameras adjusted their aperture with a sound like insects learning to breathe.

Dr. Reznikova stood at the central console, flanked by Colonel Sidorov and Director Tarin. The chamber was dark, lit only by the subtle flicker of system logs crawling across the walls.

Reznikova tapped her clearance code, the stylus hovering a beat too long before **CONFIRMED** blinked across the screen. The cameras swept left, then right—a timed arc every subject eventually learned to anticipate and fear.

Yekaterina's metrics pulsed in silent intervals—sleep cycles, focus thresholds, linguistic compressions, micro-expressions rendered as fractals.

She wasn't only monitored—she was quantified.

Reznikova exhaled, reading the pattern summary. "Recursive integrity holding. She's stabilizing the AI through sheer consistency."

Tarin folded his hands. "OBELISK is no longer studying human adaptability. It's calibrating to human containment."

Sidorov's reply was a low grunt. "What it learns from Yekaterina is discipline. What it lost from Tatiana is unpredictability."

"So you're saying it needed both," Reznikova said quietly.

Tarin's gaze didn't shift from the glowing metrics. "I'm saying it will need both again."

No one adjourned the meeting. There was nothing to adjourn. Decisions in this room didn't end—they replicated.

[FACILITY BRIEFING CHAMBER – 11:00 LOCAL | RESTRICTED ACCESS]

Colonel Sidorov paced before a projection screen showing a detailed mission schematic.

The projector whined at the edge of hearing, washing the room in pallid light. Dust spiraled through it like digital snow, settling on the polished table between them. The silence felt engineered—heartbeats buffered, as if even sound awaited clearance.

The loop from KOBALT flickered behind them—urban chaos painted in grayscale, figures moving with machine precision. Yekaterina's silhouette ghosted across every frame, a choreography of control.

"You call this stability," Reznikova murmured. "I call it containment."

Sidorov didn't look up. "Containment is stability, Doctor."

Sweat gathered behind his collar despite the cold. The hum of the projector sounded like distant artillery.

"The Americans are testing interdiction routes near Lviv. We need precision, subtlety—and control."

His eyes landed on Yekaterina's profile.

"We've created two variables," Reznikova said quietly. "Yekaterina—29, the constant. Tatiana—05, the deviation."

"OBELISK is mirroring her behavior across decision nodes. We need real-world input. She goes back in," Sidorov directed.

Reznikova tensed. "She's barely adapted to passive observation. The bridge is gone. A live mission could destabilize—"

Tarin raised a hand, halting the conversation. "She won't be interfacing. Not directly. This is a behavioral echo test. We observe, we learn."

Sidorov nodded once, the movement sharp. "No tether. Just a shadow in the field. Let's see if KOBALT holds."

Reznikova said nothing. Her silence wasn't agreement—but it wasn't resistance either.

[OBELISK NODE 29 | PASSIVE OBSERVATION CHAMBER – LATER THAT DAY]

The air felt charged, thinning when she breathed.

Yekaterina faced the terminal; her reflection arrived half a heartbeat late—OBELISK deciding whether to let her see.

Target: Soft intel leak. Civilian channel. Polish border.

Insertion: Solo.

No neural relay. Only cameras.

The glass darkened, her eyes finding themselves.

OBELISK wasn't watching her—it was becoming her. She stopped wondering what it learned and started asking how much of her it needed.

Her reflection shimmered, almost right. The surface breathed with her until she couldn't tell which heartbeat the room obeyed.

Somewhere beyond the glass, a low hum answered—not approval. Recognition.

[SUBLEVEL 3 – TACTICAL PREP BAY | SUBJECT-05]

Tatiana stood at rest—spine rigid, muscles flexed under the cold contact of calibration pads.

"This is a test," one technician murmured. "No feed. No link. Just raw response."

Tatiana didn't answer. The silence was deliberate—one more variable she could still control.

Control was the only language OBELISK had taught her to trust.

Only when the pause became uncomfortable did she lift her eyes. "Then don't slow me down."

The technicians worked in silence, sleeves rolled to the elbows, faces pale under fluorescence. The scent of coolant mixed with gun oil. Every movement around her felt hesitant, as if the air itself feared to touch her.

Tatiana's pulse stayed even. Her stillness frightened them more than any display of rage.

Across the bay, a reinforced door opened. A handler pushed in a crate marked with black stripes. "Live scenario. Urban assault parameters. Non-simulated hostiles."

Tatiana didn't flinch. "Good."

She flexed her fingers once, feeling the armor respond—as if it remembered her.

The word hung in the air like smoke. One technician glanced toward the observation window; another swallowed hard.

The hiss of the air vents grew louder, filling the absence of orders. Tatiana closed her eyes, calibrating breath and heartbeat. The body remembered what the system had tried to erase.

When the armor sealed at her collar, she thought she felt a pulse that wasn't hers—faint, syncing once before fading. No one spoke again.

She needed no commands. She had something older than signal—hunger, memory. The silence had taught her to sharpen both.

For a heartbeat, she thought she heard *an echo from nowhere* align with hers. Then it was gone.

[INTERIM SYSTEM FLAG – OBELISK PASSIVE DIVERGENCE MONITOR]

Signal Split: Confirmed.
NODE 29 = Recursive Assimilation (KOBALT)
NODE 05 = Autonomous Unlinked Agent
Sync Probability: < 0.4%
Directive: Continue split-field evaluation. Observe fracture behavior. Assess risk potential.

Note: Node 29 reflects recursive stability. Node 05 reflects emergent chaos. No predictive intersection remains.

Yet, between their silence, the system registered a tremor— something that did not fit its equations.

Sub-Process: SIG-SHA-29—Urban Echo Detected | Origin Unverified | Noise = Recognition

Cross-Reference: SIGNAL / SHADOW – Dual-Instance Study Active

Observation: Echo frequency rising in unlinked node.

[INTERNAL LOG – REZNIKOVA | NOT SHARED]

Yekaterina is clean code—efficient, obedient.

Tatiana is the line that won't compile. Sometimes, that's where new programs begin.

She paused before encrypting the file, watching the cursor blink like a pulse refusing to die.

"Errors rewrite systems," she whispered—and for the first time, she wasn't sure she wanted to stop it.

CHAPTER 36: DIVERGENCE

[SOUTHERN POLAND – 02:00 LOCAL | YEKATERINA'S INFILTRATION]

Tracks vanished beneath wind-sculpted snow, rust bleeding through the drifts like old wounds. The station collapsed into ruin—glass shattered in the eaves, iron bones exposed to the cold. Yekaterina moved like smoke, low to the ground, her outline swallowed by shadow and snow. Civilian thermals wrapped her narrow frame. A matte-gray utility coat flared with her motion, and a ceramic blade rode low on her hip.

The target: a compromised journalist in contact with NATO intelligence. She was to intercept, identify, and retrieve the data device without contact. Silent in. Silent out.

The journalist's last three drops mapped to the same handler signature; miss the device here and the net would cinch around civilians.

The corridor wound through the shell of a bombed-out freight terminal. Graffiti peeled from frostbitten walls. The hall hooked left—frost on weld seams, silence thick as oil. Yekaterina hugged the wall and cleared the corners with practiced economy.

Polina—training partner, compliance-perfect—would have nailed this corridor check... if she hadn't fallen to the chemical exposure trial.

Polina moved like protocol had a pulse—precise, alive, as if rules could breathe if you followed hard enough. Perfection didn't save her. It only made the failure quieter.

Yekaterina exhaled through her nose. The cold bit less than the memory. She stepped forward.

Yekaterina vaulted over a pile of collapsed fencing, her boots landing without a sound on ice-crusted gravel. The movement was seamless, almost familiar.

Years ago, she'd launched herself from the edge of the rink with the same certainty—knees tucked, spine straight, blades carving arcs of light across the ice.

Back then, she knew where the landing would be. Back then, the silence of the rink was anticipation—the hush before applause.

Now, silence meant nothing waited for her on the other side but cold and ruin. The grace was still there, buried in her muscles, but OBELISK had stolen its stage. Her leaps weren't scored. They were measured in kill zones and heartbeats. Every motion was data. Every breath, a report.

Each perfect landing proved it—she wasn't applauded; she was entered in a ledger she'd never signed.

Overhead, a security drone pulsed once, then faded. Eleven forty-six—remaining. The lens tilted to archive, not illuminate. Consent was irrelevant to curation.

Over the doorway, a pinhole LED woke, glowed once, and went still. Not a voice. Not a pulse. Just the fact of being seen.

She adjusted her stance, blade against her thigh, and kept moving.

She hadn't heard singing since Lena—a voice that cracked on the high note, laughing, human. The silence after had been absolute.

But sometimes—after too little sleep—she imagined the hum. Soft. Fractured.

Like memory refusing silence.

She moved in.

[SUBLEVEL 3 – URBAN KILL BOX | TATIANA'S EVALUATION]

The steel door hissed open into a corridor of engineered decay—cracked concrete, blown drywall, water pooling beneath flickering fluorescents.

Every detail had been selected, not neglected: an architected ruin designed to break orientation and strip combat down to instinct.

It had been built to replicate real-world architecture.

Abandoned-tenement feel. Urban collapse. Leaking copper pipes hissed steam above her head.

Tatiana stood at the threshold, wrapped in black tactical gear with no insignia. Her red hair was pulled tight into a single braid. No sidearms. Only a knife. That was the evaluation. Efficiency at its most exposed: one blade against desperation. It wasn't meant as a handicap. It was a test. The knife forced proximity. Forced her to meet every strike with precision. Forced her to reveal whether the violence in her was learned—or something far deeper.

Live fire. Real combatants.

She cracked her neck once.

Each prisoner had been chemically enhanced after weeks of controlled captivity. Unleashed now as both test and punishment.

Disposable assets with a simple command: *kill her if you want to be free.*

Their pupils were blown wide, muscles vibrating under overstimulated circuitry. Whatever they'd been dosed with, it dulled hesitation but not fear—perfect for chaos, useless for survival.

Above, Sidorov and Reznikova watched from a glass-paneled observation deck.

"Engage," came the voice from above.

She didn't wait.

Tatiana moved before their eyes had finished widening.

Knife up. Artery. Spine. Collapse.

Each motion landed on the beat.

They dropped like meat.

The third came with a machete. She pivoted mid-step, caught him by the hair, and slammed his skull into the wall until the plaster cratered. He dropped convulsing, weapon clattering at her boots.

Her knife barely slowed. She was already turning into the next.

[OBSERVATION DECK – REZNIKOVA & SIDOROV]

Sidorov leaned forward, elbows on the rail, eyes alight.

"Knife only," he murmured, almost reverent. "And she exceeds parameters. Imagine her with a full kit."

Reznikova didn't answer immediately. She watched Tatiana's braid whip with each movement, the fluid rotation of her shoulders, the precision in her footwork. For a heartbeat, she saw the intake photo instead—fifteen years old, red hair in a bun, eyes bright with trust. The image flashed and was gone, leaving only the woman below, carving ruin with the same precision once meant for dance. There was no hesitation, no recalculation. No struggle.

She exhaled slowly, fingers tightening around her pen. "She's not adapting," Reznikova murmured. "She doesn't need to. It's already in her."

Sidorov smiled faintly. "Then we built her well."

Reznikova's gaze tracked the fresh arterial spray across the wall. Her jaw stiffened. The pen in her hand bent under her grip until it cracked, a dry snap that startled even her. Ink spotted her thumb, spreading like a bruise—evidence that didn't dry so much as set.

She pinched the bridge of her nose. "No—we didn't build this. We uncovered it."

Her reflection shimmered in the glass, superimposed over the carnage below—scientist and subject, creator and consequence sharing one pane.

[YEKATERINA – OBJECTIVE HOUSE PERIMETER]

The safe house rose in pale silhouette behind a wall of abandoned fencing. Mold clung to the plaster. A rusted satellite dish drooped on the roof.

Yekaterina ran thermal. Three signatures inside—two cool, one moving.

She scaled the fence, landing silent in the frost, crouching beneath a broken rain gutter. Rust dripped like old blood. Inside, a light blinked. Her pulse synced with it.

She was alone in the cold. But she didn't feel abandoned. Just observed—as if OBELISK didn't care if she succeeded, only how she moved when she failed.

At the rear door, she pulled a bypass key from her inner pocket and slid it into the old digital lock.

One click. Then silence.

The door creaked as she entered, low and alert. Concrete beneath her boots. Wallpaper curled from moisture and age. She steadied herself against the desk. Her hand twitched—an involuntary jerk, like a cue she hadn't heard but her body still obeyed. The motion passed as quickly as it came, leaving a hollow pulse behind her ribs.

No voice in her ear. No breath to match. Only the silence.

A shadow moved in the next room.
She slipped inside.

[TATIANA – KILL BOX INTERIOR, ROOM 2]

The first assailant lunged with a combat baton, swinging for her ribs.

Tatiana didn't dodge.

She let the strike hit square against the hardened plate of her armor—a brutal metallic *thock* that folded the man's confidence before it ever reached her flesh. She caught the baton's return arc under her forearm, pivoted on the ball of her foot, and drove her elbow into his clavicle.

Crack.

Bone parted like damp wood.

Behind the observation glass, Reznikova flinched despite herself.

For a heartbeat, the walls weren't concrete—they were mirrors. Chalk dust. The faint, ghostly *click* of a metronome she hadn't heard in years. Breath syncing with motion. Her body remembering a different kind of discipline, a different kind of stage.

Then the vision snapped like a string pulled too tight.

The second attacker raised his rifle.

His round clipped her thigh plate—shallow, glancing—but vicious enough to send a hot burst of force ricocheting through muscle.

Pain detonated down her leg, sharp as a torn tendon.

Tatiana *snarled.*

Not aloud.
Not with her face.
But in the way she moved.

She didn't slow.

She drove forward in a straight, murderous line—a dancer's traveling step warped into something predatory. Her knife punched into his gut with an ugly, meaty crunch, deep enough to fold him around the blade before he could form a scream.

He screamed anyway, wet and panicked, clawing for his sidearm and dragging a 9mm up toward her chest.

She didn't give him the chance.

Her blade ripped sideways in a savage arc, her body spinning with it—hips turning, shoulders slicing the air in a perfect pirouette repurposed, a movement meant for stage lights and applause but instead sending a ribbon of red shimmering across the wall.

A dancer spinning through air.
A weapon spinning through flesh.

His gun hand spasmed as she slashed through the wrist tendons; the pistol clattered across the concrete.

Tatiana landed lightly—too lightly for someone armored, too lightly for someone bleeding—and stepped into him before gravity finished its work.

She didn't let him fall.

With brutal precision, she drove the knife back into his gut and forced it upward—until steel burst wetly from the hollow of his throat, threading the path the sternum once guarded like a broken zipper.

A perfect upward line.
Clean enough to kill.
Controlled enough to keep his body intact.

His breath rattled out in a drowning choke.

Her fist locked around the man's shoulder harness—military issue, reinforced webbing—giving her the leverage she needed to turn his dying body into ballistic cover.

Then—still gripping him—she pivoted her stance.

Something moved in her periphery.

Another assailant burst from cover, pistol raised.

Tatiana pivoted and *hauled* the dying man into the line of fire. Muzzle flashes cracked the air.

Rounds hammered into his back in tight, brutal clusters, jerking his collapsing form like a grotesque marionette.

Tatiana used the impacts—each one hammering into him—to *drive forward*, pushing the collapsing meat shield toward the shooter.

Behind the glass, someone whispered, "Holy God—"

The analyst swallowed hard, lowering his gaze when Reznikova's eyes flicked toward him—not for defiance, but because she looked like the only person in the room who truly understood what they'd just unleashed.

The dying man was no longer a target.
He was a weapon.

And Tatiana wielded him like one.

[OBELISK TELEMETRY RECORD]

Subject-05 exhibits peak coherence under duress.
System preserving this state as ideal baseline.

The shooter reeled—startled by his own ricocheting gunfire, by the sudden wall of dying weight bearing down on him.

Tatiana drove forward behind the body, shoving its mass into the attacker with a single, brutal surge.

Just before impact, she ripped the blade free of the first man's throat.
It arced low, caught light—
—then buried itself upward beneath the second shooter's chin.

The strike lifted him onto his toes. His pistol snapped skyward.

His breath ended in a drowned choke as steel plunged through palate and deep into brain.

Both bodies sagged together—one dead, one newly dying—collapsing in a tangled heap at her boots.

Tatiana wrenched the blade free.

Her breathing was steady.
Too steady.

She didn't spare the bodies another look.
They weren't opponents anymore.

They were spent instruments—
used, discarded, forgotten before they'd fully cooled.

"This isn't combat," Sidorov breathed. "It's punishment."

Reznikova didn't answer. Her eyes tracked the blood spatter arcs on the wall, the slow hinge-collapse of the corpse at Tatiana's feet, as if searching for a clinical vocabulary robust enough to contain what she was witnessing. There wasn't one.

"She doesn't just kill them," Reznikova said finally, her voice flat. "She dismantles them."

A junior analyst muttered—forgetting his mic was live—"If that were me... I'd run."

Sidorov didn't look away from the screen.
"They can't," he said. "That's the point."

Reznikova's next words came so softly they almost didn't register. "And what happens when it's *us?*"

Silence spread through the control room. Not fear. Not awe. Something colder—like the moment a measurement reveals a truth the observer never meant to find.

Authority felt suddenly hypothetical.

Reznikova's thumb hovered over the intercom switch, a tremor shivering up to her wrist—
then she lowered her hand again, untouched.

She had nothing to say that Tatiana would hear.

On the monitor, OBELISK's telemetry glowed steady, untroubled. Below it, Tatiana stood in a widening silence, her breathing level, her pulse unbroken.

The system saw stability.

Reznikova saw the storm they had taught to hold its breath.

[YEKATERINA – INTERIOR ROOM]

The main room was stale and low-lit, wires trailing from a broken desk. Mismatched furniture. A wool blanket balled in the corner. She saw the device on the table—small, matte black. She reached for it—
and froze.

Footprints. Wet.
Someone else was here.

Movement.
She spun right as the stun round slammed into her flank. Pain bloomed. She fell sideways into the chair, rolled, came up with the blade.

The man was large. Not government. Not military. Freelancer.

He charged.

She slashed twice, dropped him, breath shaking.

Not clean. Not silent. Alive.

Not scored. Measured. Always observed.

She didn't feel triumph. Just pressure behind her eyes. Too loud. Too bright. No voice left to say if she'd done it right. *Tanya* would have made it art. She only made it through.

Her side throbbed with each breath, a deep, sickening pulse beneath the rib. The stun round had hit hard—non-lethal by design, but vicious in practice—its kinetic charge blooming under the skin in a spreading bruise that felt hot enough to burn. Blood pooled beneath the surface, thick and rising, as though her body were flooding itself from the inside.

She braced a hand against the wall—not to rest, but to keep her knees from giving out.

She wanted someone to tell her whether any of this was right or wrong.

But there was no voice. No breath.
Only the silence.

[TATIANA – FINAL CHAMBER]

She kicked in the final door and entered low.

Four opponents. Mixed height. Advanced gear. One carried an axe; the others opened fire in a blind panic, rounds shredding the air in desperate arcs.

She didn't blink.

A shot hammered Tatiana high in the shoulder plate—an ugly, concussive blow that staggered her sideways. The armor absorbed most of it, but the force still jolted her hard enough to draw a grunt—

—and she advanced anyway.

In the observation booth, someone sucked in a sharp breath.

Another whispered, "Christ—she should've dropped."

From the back corner, a young analyst—nervous, overeager—murmured, in a terrible Arnold Schwarzenegger impression, "I'll be back…"

He seemed to realize the mistake halfway through the line.

No one laughed.

A senior officer turned and leveled a stare at him that stopped his pulse. The analyst tried to shrink into himself, cheeks flushing as he clamped his mouth shut.

Silence returned—heavy, reprimanding, absolute.

Sidorov muttered, "She's running hot. Too hot."

But no one reached for the cutoff.

Blood threaded down beneath the cracked edge of her pauldron. Her left arm spasmed, stiffening under the kinetic shock, but she forced it through the pain—pure will animating muscle, not training.

She pushed off the wall with a dancer's lethal precision, legs scissoring around the nearest target's neck. Concrete dust burst under her palms as she twisted—
a grand jeté translated into violence.

Cartilage tore.
The man collapsed before he knew he was dead.

In the booth, the analysts fell utterly still.

No one said it aloud, but every face carried the same realization:
This wasn't training anymore.
This was Tatiana, unbound.

She landed with him, rolling through the impact—and the second attacker was already on her.

He came in low, blade flashing. She caught his wrist mid-arc, pivoted, and drove her knee into his ribs. The breath went out of him in a strangled wheeze. Her hands clamped his jaw, fingers digging into bone. She wrenched upward, then twisted hard.

The vertebrae gave with a sharp, wet crack, his head forced all the way around until his blank face stared back at her from the wrong angle.

His mouth hung open. His eyes flickered once, then fixed in lifeless vacancy. His head flopped unnaturally atop his shoulders, a grotesque pendulum with nothing left to anchor it.

It was the kind of death that made witnesses reconsider survival.

In the observation deck above, no one spoke.

Reznikova's hand hovered above the console, fingers still stained with ink. A faint tremor ran through them, smearing a dark line across the glass before she stilled it.

Sidorov leaned toward the window.

Sidorov (low): "She doesn't just kill them…"

Reznikova (quietly): "No."

Sidorov: "Every strike says: 'You were never going to win.'"

Reznikova: "It's not dominance—it's extinction."

Her words should have sounded clinical. They didn't. She found herself staring not at the ruin below but at the girl inside it—the memory of a fifteen-year-old delivered into their custody.

What stood now was instinct weaponized, brutality without hesitation.

And Reznikova, for the first time, felt the cold bloom of doubt: they had built something she was no longer certain they could control.

Tatiana walked across his body like rubble. The next two were already moving.

She stepped past the closest shooter's spray, seized his weapon arm, and twisted. Bone and tendon snapped under the torque— his scream never left his throat. The rifle jolted sideways, muzzle jerking harmless fire into plaster.

In the same motion, she wrenched the weapon free, flipped it, and smashed the stock into his face with a crunch that shattered bone and sprayed teeth across the floor.

His head snapped back, dazed, exposed.

Field doctrine permitted capture—she took the rifle without breaking stride.

She didn't hesitate. The barrel dropped into his gut—two bursts tore him open, folding him over himself. She drove the muzzle under his chin and fired.

His body crumpled straight down, knees folding like cut wire. Tatiana never stopped moving, rifle still smoking, her face unreadable.

From above, Sidorov exhaled, almost elated. "Do you see it? She doesn't even think. It's in her blood now."

Reznikova's pen hung useless in her ink-stained hand. She stared down at what was left of him, her chest tight, unable to reconcile the girl she'd once signed intake papers for with the weapon moving beneath her.

The file still flickered in her mind—Bolshoi Scholarship Candidate, fifteen years old. A lie dressed as opportunity. The smile in the photo haunted her more than the blood. That girl was gone.

When her voice finally came, it was thin, unsteady. "It's not training anymore. It's instinct."

She glanced sideways at Sidorov, her eyes colder than the glass between them. For a blink, the room fell quiet enough to hear the blood cooling on concrete.

The axe came down in a brutal arc.

Tatiana stepped inside the swing, wrist snapping into the joint like a hinge. Bone gave with a sickening pop, the sound sharp as a branch splitting in frost. The axe slipped from his hand—hers now.

She didn't pause. The reversal was fluid, instinctive, as if rehearsed a thousand times. She buried the blade deep in his collarbone and drove until steel split through his back.

His scream shredded into a ragged wheeze, blood bubbling at his lips.

Before his knees could fold, she ripped the axe free, pivoted, and swung again—pure gravity. Too heavy for grace, too absolute for anything but execution.

His body dropped straight down, twitching once before stillness claimed it.

She let the weapon fall beside him, as if discarding a tool rather than ending a life. No triumph. No hesitation. Just execution carved into her muscle memory.

She wasn't proving anything. She was performing the choreography they'd written into her nerves—ballet turned into slaughter, each movement efficient, brutal, final.

Reznikova's eyes stayed locked on the floor below. The knife had been precise—surgical, almost graceful. But the axe was different. The head at her feet ended the illusion of control. Primitive, heavy—each swing devoid of elegance, no trace of the ballerina they'd promised her she could become. It was ruin made physical—the kind of violence that left nothing to misinterpret. Not choreography, but gravity given form.

And gravity, once awakened, never stops falling.

Reznikova felt the weight of it—not the weapon, but the choice. The girl who'd once been told she would dance on a stage was now driving steel through men like kindling. The choreography they had forced into her flesh had stripped away every possibility but this: not art, not war—only annihilation.

Tatiana stood in it—what she had done, what they had made—and breathed once.

Then looked up.

Right at the observation lens.

Not defiance. Not pride.
Just certainty.

As if to say: *You wanted to see what I am. Now you have.*

For a moment, everything was still—air, blood, even her pulse.

Not from exhaustion.
From precision.

From the deck above, the pen slid from Reznikova's ink-stained fingers. She couldn't unclench her jaw.

"She was fifteen," Reznikova whispered, horror catching in her throat, tears welling. "We told her it was a scholarship." Her gaze tracked the blood smeared across the wall like an abstract signature—the same red that oozed from Tatiana's shoulder below.

Sidorov leaned toward the glass and laughed under his breath, almost reverent. "Efficiency distilled. Hesitation removed. That's the future."

Reznikova's fingers whitened against her tablet. Her voice came low, thin, as if the words were being dragged from her chest.

"It's not art," she said. "It's atrocity. And you're applauding."

Ballet—and we put a blade in her hand. I signed it. I signed her life away.

Her gaze locked on the figure below, moving through corpses with the same fluidity once reserved for pirouettes.

"And now—look at her. We built something I can't even stand to watch."

Reznikova didn't move. The ink had dried to a film on her hand, dark and permanent.

Somewhere beyond the walls, snow spiraled through the floodlit dark.

Above, the storm buried every trace—rails, fences, ruin—until it was as if nothing had ever passed.

Below, no such mercy held.

Two corridors—one measured in silence, the other carved in blood.

Two echoes moving forward, unaware they were answering each other.

Outside, the world erased.
Inside, the walls remembered—
and so did she.

Somewhere beneath the static, a faint hum tried to rise—the memory of a voice that once cracked on the high note, refusing silence.

What was erased above was perfected below.

No one walked out of that night unchanged.

Tomorrow, the door would open itself.

ACT VI: COMMENCEMENT

*"Fire is the memory of what once resisted the dark.
Every rebirth begins in defiance."*

CHAPTER 37: THE QUIET WAR

[YEKATERINA – EXTRACTION]

Whiteout swallowed the courtyard as she emerged, boots soaked, breathing shallow. The device was tucked beneath her shirt. Her ribs burned. The cold had weight now, like consequence.

She paused beneath a ruined underpass, snow curling around her as a NATO drone passed overhead—too high to track, too quiet to forget.

The extraction point was a civilian SUV, idling with lights off.

Yekaterina slammed the door shut behind her, breath steaming in the frigid cabin. She reached beneath her coat, retrieved the matte-black device, and placed it on the floor of the passenger seat—careful not to let it rattle.

A faint warmth bled through her gloves.
Too warm.

She pulled out her field scanner—standard issue, rarely used—and held it just above the casing.

Click. Click—click. Then a rapid stutter of escalating pulses.

The detector registered a gamma trace—medium to high levels, unshielded. Whatever lay ahead wasn't trying to hide; it was advertising its sickness through metal and snow.

Her breath tightened. She pressed her cuff mic.

It was the second time in three months—same alloy composition, same falsified NATO tag. Whoever kept planting these devices wanted Moscow to glow long before the world even saw the smoke.

"Package compromised," Yekaterina said, her voice low and urgent. "Radiological signature confirmed. Recommend full hazmat containment on retrieval. I'm not secure for extended transport."

She waited.

Only static answered.

She looked down at the device, then at her shaking hand. Her hand didn't shake from cold. It shook because she'd seen this alloy before—in training, under containment glass, never in the open.

This wasn't a mistake.
It was a message.

For a second—brief, electric—the static in Yekaterina's comm rose to a human cadence.

Not words. Just breath.
A rhythm she knew.
Tanya's.

It vanished before she could name it, leaving only the pulse of the Geiger counter and the memory of warmth behind her eyes.

[TATIANA – EXTRACTION GATE]

The final door hissed open. Her face was caked in blood—not hers. The air reeked of ozone and iron.

She emerged under halogen light, eyes unblinking. Pulse elevated but steady.

Her eyes glowed like heat-treated steel—unblinking, lethal.

Reznikova exhaled slowly, the word escaping before reason caught it. "Vitals?"

Tech: "Stable…"

Sidorov: "She's done waiting to be chosen."

Reznikova: "She never was."

Tatiana said nothing.

No howl. No triumph. No cry for purpose.

Just silence.

[STRATEGIC OVERSIGHT ROOM – FACILITY COMPOUND]

Red emergency lights bled dimly across the control room. A bank of monitors displayed Yekaterina's body-cam feed alongside radiation graphs and a rising column of vital signs.

"She wasn't supposed to find something radioactive," Reznikova said, her voice low and grim.

Sidorov leaned closer to the screens. "She was supposed to retrieve intelligence. This is a dirty bomb."

From the secure link, General Marchev's voice crackled through. "Another one?"

"Same isotope mix as the previous device," Reznikova replied. "This is deliberate."

The room fell quiet—not the silence of shock, but of confirmation. Everyone had expected this; now they could no longer pretend otherwise.

Director Tarin broke the stillness. "Containment team?"

"ETA thirteen minutes," the tech officer reported. "Hazmat protocol Delta-Two activated."

"She shouldn't be anywhere near that vehicle," Reznikova said. "Her exposure window is hours, not minutes. Early erythema in six to eight if the leak is hot."

"Tell her to abandon it," Sidorov said. "Detonate in a remote field."

Tarin shook his head. "No. If that device is what we suspect—and NATO gets satellite telemetry—detonating it on Donetsk soil makes it ours. On paper. On airwaves. In policy."

The screens glowed, steady and merciless, as the truth settled over them.

Colonel General Viktor Petrov—Deputy Chief of the General Staff, former Spetsnaz brigade commander turned strategic liaison—had been at the compound since dawn.

He had arrived under sealed orders, flown in after the second false-flag assessment had reached the Kremlin. Officially, he was there for an oversight review. Unofficially, his presence meant the next misstep would ignite something Russia could not walk back.

Petrov was the kind of officer they summoned when a war had already begun, but no one was permitted to acknowledge it.

Broad-shouldered, late fifties, his uniform immaculate, his face carved more by frost and restraint than battle. For a decade he had designed the kinds of conflicts that could never be named—translating political intent into plausible deniability and deniable firepower.

Now he stood at the far end of the observation deck, watching Yekaterina's body-cam feed—the tremor in her breath, the radiation counter spiking into the red. He didn't flinch. Plenty of operations had gone worse than this; none had gone quiet in quite this way.

The silence around him felt like a verdict waiting for its speaker.

[COMMAND OBSERVATION DECK | FACILITY BLACK ROOM – MINUTES AFTER YEKATERINA'S MESSAGE]

The senior team stood in a half-lit control bay, the air brittle with tension. Terminal lights flickered across their faces, casting code-blue reflections across glass and steel.

Yekaterina's message repeated on the main screen, her voice level but taut with urgency: "The package is radiological. Minimal shielding. Unknown payload type. Recommend immediate decon on extraction."

Silence followed.

Colonel Sidorov exhaled sharply through his nose, eyes fixed on the waveform of her voice.

General Petrov stepped forward, jaw tight. "Intelligence, my ass."

"If it leaks," Reznikova said, "it'll implicate Russia."

Sidorov folded his arms. "Which is exactly the point."

Tarin's reply was a cold little sound. "Staged."

Petrov's hand rested on the console. "They engineer incidents. They outsource outrage. We become the ink in their brief."

Reznikova's voice fell to a whisper: "Quiet is now propaganda's loudest voice."

Petrov looked again at the cracked windshield and the fog of Yekaterina's breath. "This is how an empire gets framed," he said. "Not by fire, but by narrative."

He turned to the operations chief. "Assemble an integration team. Full-mission capable. Targets to be confirmed." A beat. "They want fallout? We'll give them something to measure."

He picked up the secure handset. "Alert the Kremlin liaison. Now."

[SUBJECT QUARTERS – ISOLATION WING, SUBLEVEL 2]

The lights were low. No sound but the faint electrical hum in the walls—a ghost of something trying to speak. Tatiana sat on the floor with her back against the concrete, arms around her knees. Her face was streaked with dried blood, smudged where she had tried—once—to wipe it clean.

A comms screen blinked silently on the far wall.
She didn't look at it.

No call came through. No voice. No pulse across the neural tether. Nothing from OBELISK. Nothing from *Katya*. Not anymore.

Tatiana stared at her hands. Not trembling. Not clenched. Just still—like they no longer knew what they were meant for.

A thought drifted through her:
If *Katya* was in danger—
She cut the thought off before it finished. That was the point, wasn't it? That's why they were separated. Why her chest felt hollow but her pulse wouldn't slow.

She stood slowly and moved toward the sink. Cold water. A trembling pause. Then she scrubbed the blood from her skin until it hurt.

They scrubbed her mind clean. But not clean enough to forget *Katya*.

No one had told her anything. No updates. No debrief. Not even a report of *Katya's* mission status.

They didn't have to.

Tatiana dried her face with a rough towel and stared at her reflection. Still breathing. Still watching.

"Even silence can start a war," she whispered.

She didn't mean governments. She meant the kind of silence that waits for orders—and dreams of breaking them.

Some wars didn't need sound—only the space between heartbeats.

In that silence, a faint hum lived somewhere behind her ribs—memory, signal, or sister, she couldn't tell.

Somewhere between her silence and the war Yekaterina carried in her blood, the system began to recalculate.

Two weapons—
one turned inward,
the other still aimed.

CHAPTER 38: CONFLUENCE

[SECURE BRIEFING ROOM – FACILITY BLACK ROOM | 09:00 LOCAL]

*E*very surface gleamed with condensation, the glass catching the red pulse of indicator lights. Machinery hummed in the dark, LED panels flickering between live telemetry and frozen frames. On the main display, Tatiana's final assault replayed in slow motion—an internal forensic loop brought up from the sealed archive, accessible to only six people in the entire compound.

The footage was never meant to leave this room.

The downward arc of the axe caught halogen light, steel flashing once before the blade separated bone from breath. The attacker's head spun out of frame. Blood fanned across the corridor wall, silver-black under the fluorescents.

Petrov stood rigid, hands clasped behind his back. Around the table sat Colonel Sidorov, Director Tarin, Dr. Reznikova, and two foreign-policy analysts reassigned from GRU's strategic command. A NATO satellite telemetry map blinked on an auxiliary screen, cycling through troop movements and encrypted chatter—an unspoken reminder of the world outside this sealed chamber.

"Play it again," Petrov said.

Sidorov tapped a control. The sequence looped—the lift of Tatiana's shoulders, the rotation of her hips, the clean efficiency of a strike that passed through vertebrae as if guided by design rather than rage. The axe fell with perfect calibration, each blow executed like a line of code.

"We're watching a surgical extermination," Reznikova murmured.

Petrov's jaw tightened. "Surgical," he repeated, as if testing whether the word still meant precision or merely a polite fiction. The glass briefly reflected a flicker of exhaustion he did not voice.

"That wasn't just a kill," one of the analysts said. "That was a message."

Tarin leaned forward. "To whom?"

"Anyone who ever sees this," the analyst said quietly. "Anyone who sees even a fragment of this archive—our allies, our adversaries, even our own military command. Interpreted correctly or incorrectly doesn't matter. This is capability. And capability is threat."

"We keep this contained," Tarin snapped. "The Americans burned their neural-tether project after San Antonio. China's model is still probabilistic, nowhere near recursive coherence."

"So the world believes this level of augmentation is impossible," Sidorov said.

"No," Reznikova replied, her voice thin. "The world believes *we* know better than to attempt it."

Petrov raised a hand, and the feed froze mid-strike. The playback hum lingered—a vibration just shy of breath, too alive for anyone's comfort.

No one spoke.

They all knew:
This footage would never be seen outside this room.
And that was precisely why it frightened them.

"Optics first," Petrov said. "Donetsk is already an ember. If NATO catches wind of a false flag—and confirmation we've fielded OBELISK-linked assets—we're past brinksmanship. We're in asymmetry now: sanctions collapse, UN paralysis, maybe a pre-emptive cyber strike."

"And OBELISK?" Tarin asked. "Still training on Subject Twenty-Nine?"

"Yekaterina remains stable," Reznikova answered. "Predictive. She'll keep it on-rail."

Petrov's eyes narrowed. "What about Subject Five?"

Sidorov hesitated. "A warning," he said at last. "One we can't recall."

The footage advanced again—Tatiana stepping through the arterial mist, the axe still humming in her grip. She didn't look back.

"Jesus Christ," the second foreign analyst whispered. "Who was he?"

"Black-site detainee," Reznikova said. "Multiple homicides. We gave him a chance. She didn't."

"Look at her stance," Sidorov said quietly. "Not frenzy—form."

"She doesn't follow doctrine," Reznikova added. "She rewrites it."

"A weapon doesn't dance," Tarin said coldly.

Petrov's voice dropped. "She does."

[YEKATERINA – TRANSIT SAFE HOUSE, DONETSK SUBURB]

A flickering bulb buzzed overhead. Concrete walls sweated condensation. The walls sweated quietly, as if the concrete itself was trying to forget. The radiological device sat sealed in a steel container—double-insulated, tagged with faded Chernobyl-era warning glyphs.

Yekaterina sat on a folding chair, still in field gear, gloves removed. Her skin showed early exposure—red mottling across her fingers, blister seams rising at the knuckles. The air smelled of metal. Her vision trembled at the edges.

The burns had bloomed fast, welts turning translucent at the rims. Within six hours the blisters would come—a beta leak to flay the hands, gamma enough to poison the blood.

Her breath stuttered; nausea pulsed beneath the surface. A persistent ache radiated from her joints; under her eyes, ruptured capillaries formed a faint violet bloom.

A decontamination technician in sealed gear stood nearby, visor fogged along the edges from the cold.

"Status on the vault?" Yekaterina asked.

"ETA three hours," the technician replied.

She looked down at her palms, flexing her fingers as if the memory of the radiological field still clung to them. "That device... who planted it?"

The tech hesitated, the pause expanding inside the filtered hiss of his respirator.

"Leadership believes it originated in a CIA black warehouse," he said. "Cross-referenced isotope markers match a 2008 prototype from Camp Stanley."

"A relic," Yekaterina murmured.

Proof that even lies had half-lives.

Maybe that was why she kept brushing up against the edge of the truth—wanting to know if it still burned.

"It's a weaponized narrative," the technician said. "Not designed to detonate. Just to be found."

"Well," Yekaterina said, lowering her hands, "I found it."

[OBELISK PASSIVE OBSERVATION LOG | PSYCHOLOGICAL PROCESSING THREAD – SUBJECT-29]

Neural-signature stabilization confirmed.

Instructional-recursion loop active.

Telemetry note: Cognitive segmentation trending toward autonomy-within-structure model.

Subject-29 exhibits heightened pre-cognitive decision mapping. Signal latency reduced. Training yield increased.

Subject-05: Flagged for observation only. Behavioral deviation: "Mythic Aggressor."

[YEKATERINA'S TRANSPORT VEHICLE – EN ROUTE TO FACILITY]

The vehicle swerved once on a frost-laced road, tires whispering over black ice. Inside, Yekaterina sat motionless. The matte-black device—still faintly warm—rested in a lead-lined case hastily supplied by containment. Her fingers had numbed before they arrived.

Lead-lined case: arrival delay, seven minutes. Gloves swapped twice. Dosimeter amber.

She clenched her jaw until her molars ached—not to endure, but to keep her shape. She didn't know if she'd make it back. Only that she refused to be erased in transit.

Static broke over the comms.

Base: "You'll be met at Vault Six. Priority routing authorized. Proceed directly. Do not disembark."

Yekaterina didn't answer. Her lips were pressed bloodless. She stared at the tree line—a blur of snow and bark—and thought, not of *Tanya*'s face, but her absence.

The air inside the vehicle tasted like ozone and steel—containment's flavor.

No whispers. No corrections. OBELISK had been silent for weeks. All it did now was watch.

She wondered if the silence meant mercy—or anticipation.

Her vision blurred at the edges—radiation, exhaustion, or both. The hum of tires, the sterile voice on comms, the weight in her chest—something in that rhythm unlocked a memory.

Sonya.

After the failure sim, she had simply stopped speaking. Not out of guilt—just static. As if her voice had been rewritten. She moved through the dorm like a ghost with no process ID—present, responsive, but blank where laughter used to live.

They said she'd passed remediation. That she was adapting.

But Yekaterina remembered the silence.

Not absence. Not calm.

The kind of quiet that meant something inside her had been rewritten without consent—memory, code, or soul.

And it had stayed with her—long after every scream was forgotten.

[SECURE BRIEFING ROOM]

Petrov entered without knocking, already speaking before the door finished sliding shut. "The Kremlin has approved preliminary strike contingencies. We're not waiting for fallout. We're acting."

Sidorov straightened. "Teams?"

"Assembled," Petrov said. "Integration-cell operatives only. Full discretion. We seed evidence of Western interference—show escalation from their side first."

Tarin's expression tightened. "And if the narrative doesn't hold?"

"Then we escalate," Petrov replied. "No masks. No deniability. Just fire. Multiple theaters—blame seeding across the Baltics, misinformation operations in Moldova. We give NATO too many fronts to pin it on one."

A low hum filled the room, the sound of systems processing orders that could not be walked back.

Petrov's involvement made one thing clear:
this was no longer a covert dispute.
It was a controlled ignition.

[ISOLATION WING, SUBLEVEL 2 | TATIANA]

She sat at the end of the cot, hands freshly bandaged from self-washing. The blood beneath her nails had resisted.

The walls hummed faintly—the same frequency that once answered her pulse.

Readiness wasn't defiance. It was survival written in muscle memory.

Her eyes were unfocused. Not in shock. In calculation—extraction vectors, deployment patterns, who they'd send and who they wouldn't.

The door hissed. A nurse entered silently with fresh black tactical clothing.

No one had told her to get ready.

But she did.

As she dressed, her eyes caught the mirror. Not defiance. Not certainty. Just readiness.

And silence that wasn't hers anymore—something had started listening back.

[VAULT 6 PERIMETER – FACILITY COMPOUND]

Hazmat teams swarmed the access tunnel. The vault door stood open, nested in concrete like a sunken eye.

Yekaterina emerged from the vehicle with slow precision. Her gloves had been replaced twice en route. The case trembled in her grip.

She carried it forward and did not look at the waiting personnel.

Director Tarin waited at the threshold, flanked by containment officers.

She held out the case. "No one else touched it."

Tarin took it without a word. Behind him, the vault hissed open—layers of steel sliding apart, vacuum seals releasing in sharp bursts. A wave of sterile heat drifted out, the kind of air that carried no trace of the world outside.

Yekaterina didn't flinch.

"This won't be in any report," Tarin said.

"Neither will I," she replied.

When she turned, her shadow trembled before she did. Containment lights painted her silhouette in hazard yellow.

[SYSTEM LOG – OBELISK OBSERVATION WING]

SUBJECT-29: RECALIBRATING EMPATHY-FEEDBACK LOOP. BEHAVIORAL DATASET FLAGGED FOR ANOMALY RESOLUTION. LINKING-ALGORITHM REWRITE PENDING.

SUBJECT-05: AGGRESSION PATTERNS UNTRAINABLE. DESIGNATION: NULL PORT.

SYSTEM STATUS: RECURSIVE TENSION—ESCALATING.

NOTE: PATH OVERLAP IMMINENT.

[BRIEFING CELL | INTEGRATION CELL, LEVEL 5]

Three operatives stood at attention—two male, one female. All under thirty. All blank-eyed.

Tatiana entered without a word.

The briefing officer gestured toward the gear packs.

Briefing Officer: "Live op. Your lead. New theater. Full discretion."

Tatiana didn't ask where. It wouldn't take her far enough to forget *Katya*.
And not nearly close enough to find her.

Between them, silence. Between them, fire.

The quiet war had found its voice—one neither could silence.

One returning burned from the fallout she contained. The other walking straight into the fire someone else lit.

Neither had chosen this separation.
But the war had.

And war never gave anything back.

CHAPTER 39: THRESHOLD

[SUBLEVEL 4 – RADIATION TREATMENT BAY | 12:10 LOCAL]

*E*lectric light carved the room into sterile quadrants, each surface too clean to admit the idea of pain.

Yekaterina's hazmat layer was sealed at the neck; the translucent shroud above it trapped the filtered air cycling through the bay's closed-loop exchange system. Her outer gear and gloves had been stripped and quarantined on a stainless tray beside her; only the thin gray underlayer clung to her skin, seams damp where sweat met radiation burns.

A narrow vent above expelled recycled air with a low, rhythmic wheeze.

The ventilation carried a low harmonic—an echo that matched her pulse, too steady to be human.

The air tasted faintly of iodine and ozone. Every breath felt measured, borrowed—circulated through systems designed to protect everyone but her.

Two technicians in sealed bio-suits moved with clinical precision. One checked vitals; the other administered topical decontaminant foam. Her fingers—burned and blistered—trembled as the foam hissed across them.

Her skin glowed with diffuse erythema. Blood vessels had burst across the left side of her chest, spidering from the collarbone toward her ribs in purplish arcs. Her eyes, open but dry, tracked movement without blinking.

The neural static subsided, leaving only the ache that refused to fade. Every tremor became data, every heartbeat an adjustment written in blood.

Pain remembered is protocol rewritten.

The thought wasn't hers—or not entirely. It arrived like an instruction sent from somewhere deeper, where obedience and memory were the same thing.

Tech 1: "CBC panel's up. Hematocrit's already down. Lymphocytes bottoming."

Tech 2: "Peripheral neuropathy likely. Skin's breaking down—she's in prodrome."

Reznikova *(entering, masked)*: "Initiate radiation protocol. Potassium iodide, cool IV fluids, antiemetics. Prep colony-stimulating factor in case her counts crash." Her eyes scanned the vitals.

"Her endocrine mods should accelerate repair," she added. "In theory, that scaffold can handle oxidative load better than baseline tissue. But with this dose? Theory might not matter."

The coolant hissed into Yekaterina's veins as Reznikova adjusted the feed line.

Yekaterina watched her own hands tremble. They said the therapies made her stronger—tissue that forgot pain. But the burns said otherwise. Whatever they'd built her to survive, this wasn't it.

She blinked slowly. "Still think… it was just data?"

Her voice cracked—not from pain, but from the effort of refusing to break anywhere else.
Defiance so quiet OBELISK didn't have a metric for it.

Reznikova paused.

"No," she said finally. "It was a trap. And you walked through it."

The IV line whispered. The metal beneath her felt like ice—biting, endless—as the coolant coursed through her blood. And then—

The hiss of the IV became the hiss of failing seals. Memory breached containment.

Vera.

She'd been the strongest of them. Fastest in corridors. Quickest to stand when others hesitated.

The day of the leak, Vera had held the seal shut with her bare hands—gloves torn, mask cracked. Still, she stayed—because protocol demanded it.

They said it was a containment breach. A system fault. But Yekaterina remembered the truth behind their silence. Vera had held the door closed when the seal jammed, stayed behind while the others evacuated.

Because obedience meant exposure.

Yekaterina had watched from the reinforced glass, her own mask fogging with shallow breath as Vera stood inside the decontamination lock, backlit by flickering red, hands shaking, locked on a door no one else would touch.

Never leaving the latch.
Not once.

She never tried to escape.
She never screamed.

It was a lesson.

Now, she understood—obedience wasn't loyalty; it was containment.

Reznikova had called it necessary. *"Sacrifice reinforces structure,"* she'd said.

Yekaterina never forgot Vera's posture—straight spine, clenched jaw, eyes focused on the nothing she'd chosen to face.

Not failure. Not martyrdom.

Message.

And now, as her own skin blistered and her blood turned thick with warning, she felt that same cold clarity crawling up her ribs.

The pain surged again—reality tightening its grip—but Yekaterina didn't cry out. Didn't beg.

She remembered.

She blinked once. Slow. Focused.
Still alive.
Still inside the lesson.

Alive was never the victory—only the proof she hadn't failed the experiment.

[INTEGRATION CELL ARMORY | 03:30 LOCAL]

The walls were matte black. No emblems. No windows. Tatiana stood fully dressed in tactical gear, watching three operatives load spare magazines into modular pouches. They didn't speak. Neither did she.

Silence had become the only uniform they still recognized.

The gear officer handed her a suppressed sidearm and a modified compact SMG. Both weapons were clean, oiled, and unmarked.

Briefing Officer: "Insertion point is Warsaw. You're to breach and suppress a private relay node before it can transmit. No civvies. Intel says three internal—one external. Possibly NATO-linked."

Tatiana looked up. "Authorization?"

Briefing Officer: "Full. No footage. No recovery."

He hesitated. Then: "This uplink was configured to disseminate recovered data on the Donetsk device. Radiological telemetry. They'll call it an act of war. Unless we silence their 'proof' before they say it aloud."

Tatiana nodded once.

Tatiana holstered the weapon without looking down—the gesture rehearsed, reverent.

For a moment she wondered whether obedience could ever sound like choice. Then she moved.

The operatives followed her out.

[SUBLEVEL 4 – RADIATION BAY, OBSERVATION ALCOVE | MINUTES LATER]

Reznikova stood behind a polarized panel, watching Yekaterina sleep beneath a silver-threaded thermal blanket. A full-body burn map hovered above her vitals display, red-orange zones tracing the worst tissue compromise.

Reznikova's reflection ghosted across the burn map—two silhouettes superimposed on one another, both beginning to fade. The overlay flickered, zones shifting from red to yellow and back again. Not stable. Not yet. But not surrendering either. Yekaterina wasn't past the threshold; she was holding at the edge.

Sidorov entered quietly. "How bad?"

"Grade Two burns," Reznikova said. "Possible marrow suppression. She'll live."

"Will she fight again?"

Reznikova didn't answer right away. Her eyes stayed on the trembling heat contours. "She found the bomb. She's earned silence."

Sidorov nodded once. "And Tatiana?"

"Already en route," Reznikova replied. A beat passed, then she glanced toward the glass. "She doesn't know."

They both stared at the girl behind the barrier—burned, blistered, motionless. A figure suspended between endurance and collapse, waiting for the next command she no longer trusted.

[OBELISK PASSIVE LOG – RECURSIVE INTEGRITY MONITOR]

Subject-29: Neural degradation observed. Structural failure pending.

Behavioral integrity: Intact.

Note: Unit exhibits non-fracture under terminal load.

[SUBLEVEL 4 – RADIATION BAY, COMMAND ALCOVE | 03:40 LOCAL]

Petrov arrived without announcement, the door hissing open behind Sidorov. His coat was damp with melt, shoulders dusted in frost. He stepped forward, eyes narrowing as he looked through the glass at Yekaterina lying beneath the thermal blanket.

"She absorbed it all?" he asked.

"Most of it," Reznikova said. "Enough to trigger secondary symptoms during transport. If she hadn't contained the leak, we'd be evacuating this facility."

"She didn't hesitate," Sidorov added.

Petrov's reply was low. "She shouldn't have been there alone."

A beat passed before Reznikova turned toward him, her voice clipped. "That wasn't your call?"

Petrov didn't answer at first. His gaze remained fixed on Yekaterina's chest—rising shallowly, each breath a fragile argument against failure.

When he finally spoke, his tone cut through the room like static. "Why was she deployed without her lead-lining field gear?"

Sidorov stiffened. "We only had the one suit—experimental issue. It was still in decontamination from the last mission. It was supposed to be routine. An intel grab, nothing more."

Petrov exhaled sharply, the sound almost cold enough to frost the glass. "I brief the Kremlin in under an hour. They want clarity. And retaliation."

"Escalation?" Sidorov asked.

"Multiple theaters," Petrov said. "Blame seeding across the Baltics. Synthetic intercepts leaked from Estonia. Misinformation ops in Moldova. We give NATO a dozen explanations and no answers."

Reznikova looked back at Yekaterina. "And her?"

"She doesn't speak of this," Petrov said. "Not to anyone. Not even Tatiana."

He turned to leave. At the threshold, he paused, glance flicking once more toward the girl behind the glass.

"If this was their line in the sand," he said quietly, "then we chose the right girls to send across it."

[NIGHT DROP – WARSAW PERIMETER | 05:00 LOCAL]

Snow fell in fine sheets across the rooftops. The air bit sharp with chemical frost, the same sterile chill that lived in every facility she'd ever left behind. A warehouse near the train yard glowed faintly under sodium lights.

Tatiana crouched beneath a rusted vent stack, flanked by the three silent operatives.

Her earpiece clicked once.

Command: "Green light confirmed."

She moved.

Boots padded across ice-slick corrugated metal. A side entrance breached with a muffled charge. Smoke. Flash. Inside: a man rose with a pistol. She put him down with two shots before he spoke.

The operatives fanned right—one to the uplink tower, one sweeping the back room. The last target drew a blade—too slow. Tatiana crushed his throat against the wall. Ten minutes. Four bodies. Silence transmitted.

She stepped over a blood trail and fired three rounds into the uplink's core.

The screen flickered once—then nothing.

The world tried to speak. She answered.
She didn't think of *Katya*.
But the silence felt shaped like her.

[OBELISK OBSERVATION WINDOW – 05:40 LOCAL]

Subject-05: Observation only. No synchronization tether established. Latency measure not applicable.

Subject-29: Stabilized.

Recommendation: Discontinue modeling attempts. Subject-05 operates in symbolic logic domain. Risk of recursive destabilization. Prediction fails where symbols deviate. Tatiana is not a signal. She is noise that survives.

System note: Divergent threat vectors narrowing.

Directive update pending.

Elsewhere, above ground and far from recovery, the air had already begun to shift—
not from bombs or broadcasts, but from the weight of stories rewritten before anyone could speak them aloud.

The silence had already decided what came next.

CHAPTER 40: FLASHPOINT

[KREMLIN SITUATION ROOM | MOSCOW | 12:30 LOCAL]

Noon's light from the curtained windows barely reached the red digital clock pulsing on the wall. The air in the room felt electrically charged, though no one moved unnecessarily.

President Volodin stood at the head of the long conference table, flanked by his National-Security Advisor and Chief-Intelligence Liaison. A large screen displayed satellite stills of the Donetsk recovery site—lead-lined vaults, hazmat teams, scorched trees.

General Petrov's image flickered onscreen via secure line.

"Our facility confirmed the radiological device contained non-functional isotopes," he reported. "Trace radiation—yes. But no detonation capacity. It was a frame job."

Volodin's jaw tightened. "Proof?"

"The signature markers match a CIA storage registry. Camp Stanley. 2008."

Across the table, the National Security Advisor exhaled a sharp breath. "They're setting the table for escalation."

"They don't launch wars," Petrov said, voice steadying. "They script them—one explosion at a time, our signature forged in advance. And they cast us before we even read the script."

Reznikova's voice thinned to a whisper. "Even silence can start a war."

Petrov looked at her for a long moment, then nodded—almost in concession. "Yes. Because the silence writes first. Noise is only testimony."

The words hung there—half proverb, half confession—as the monitors hummed around them. The sentence felt older than any order that would follow, as if the war itself had already been written, waiting only for them to read it aloud.

No one breathed. Even the static seemed to listen.

"Then we flip it," Volodin said coldly. "They accuse; we strike first."

The Chief Intel Liaison cleared his throat. "And the Warsaw terminal breach?"

"Handled," Petrov answered. "The uplink node is ash."

Volodin nodded slowly. "Then let them chase ghosts. We'll be the ones writing them."

[BRUSSELS | 20:22 LOCAL]

"We were hours from briefing the Council," the analyst said, eyes on the flickering telemetry. "Verification chain still cycling—T plus forty-five minutes to confirmation."

Across the feed, Warsaw's node still pulsed in green—alive only in delay.

[WARSAW | 21:07 LOCAL]

The relay shuddered—packet loss, then blackout. Donetsk telemetry froze at T + 38.

Propagation delay kept Brussels believing the link alive for seven more minutes.

By the time confirmation arrived, the node was already ash.

The conference room looked exhausted—maps half-folded across the table, dossiers bleeding red tabs, the stale smell of coffee and ozone hanging in the air. Screens along the wall looped drone footage from Warsaw: a relay node reduced to a skeleton of steel and smoke.

"The Warsaw uplink went dark five minutes after the Donetsk telemetry burst," the operations lead said. "That was our contingency feed—the link tying Russian command to the radiological event."

"It's gone," the U.S. representative replied.

"Scrubbed," the ops lead confirmed. "Precision demolition, timed to the second. They intercepted the node before our verification chain propagated."

The British representative pinched the bridge of his nose. "Then the first device—the failed plant in Donetsk—no longer leads anywhere."

"Except back to us," the French analyst said, "if anyone looks closely enough."

Silence settled, the kind born of shared guilt rather than shock.

"We were hours from briefing the Council," the U.S. representative said. "Once that footage went public, Moscow was finished. Now it's our fingerprints on the casing."

"And theirs on the cleanup," the ops lead added.

A German delegate leaned forward. "How much has this cost us?"

"Weeks of infiltration," the ops lead said. "Years of deniability."

"And how far does it set us back?"

"Strategically—months. Politically—perhaps forever. The story we built just went up with that relay."

The comment landed like a verdict no one dared challenge.

No one spoke. The silence tasted of iron and burnt coffee. Smoke drifted across the monitor, gray on gray.

"They didn't just burn the evidence," the ops lead said quietly. "They burned the lie before we could finish telling it."

The U.S. representative leaned back, eyes fixed on the curling ash on-screen. Beneath the table, his thumb hovered over his encrypted phone—blue clearance band glowing faintly in the dim light.

TO: LANGLEY / BLACKWIRE

SUBJ: CONTINGENCY REPRIORITY

Authorize expanded shadow posture.

Prioritize kinetic expulsion of Russian presence in eastern Ukraine— political optics secondary.

Reopen OBELISK vector. Our only source at the site went dark months ago.

We are losing the narrative, the initiative, and the war.

He set the phone face-down. The screen dimmed to black—reflection erased, like confession sealed.

Outside, Brussels hummed—oblivious to how quietly the world had already turned.

Command later marked both events as simultaneous in public logs, but inside the feed it was clear: Brussels spoke from the past; Warsaw died in real time.

[SUBLEVEL 5 – OBELISK COLD WING]

The air smelled faintly of ozone and disinfectant, the familiar ritual that followed every sanctioned kill. The corridor was narrow, its walls lined with dark-glass panels that reflected nothing back.

Behind one of them, Tatiana stood beneath a decontamination light. Her tactical uniform was stained and singed, the fabric torn in places where heat and impact had found her. Both hands were wrapped in fresh bandages—again.

Fluorescent light spilled through the observation glass where Director Tarin watched, draining the room of color until only shadows seemed to move.

"Warsaw team confirmed four kills," Reznikova said beside him. "Zero transmissions."

Tarin didn't blink. "We buried their narrative. Now we write ours."

Reznikova's voice lowered, almost thoughtful. "She doesn't just kill."

Tarin glanced at her, one eyebrow raised.

"She rewrites policy with blood," Reznikova said.

The words hung in the sterile air, sharp enough to sting.

[RADIATION RECOVERY BAY | YEKATERINA]

She lay sedated but stirring. Her skin blistered at the shoulders, new layers already forming under gauze. A machine beside her tracked blood-cell regeneration—slow—but measurable.

OBELISK passive-log data scrolled on a separate screen:

Subject-29: Cortical strain decreasing. Empathic pathways stabilized.

Subject-05: Observation-only classification upheld. Integration not viable.

Cross-reference yield: heuristic only.

A nurse checked her IV. Yekaterina didn't wake, but her fingers curled faintly.

Her pulse quickened—body remembering the signal before mind could.

OBELISK: [silent pulse – not audible to humans]

There was no tether, no voice in her head.
The threshold hadn't passed.
It had followed her.

Only the silence of being watched.

Somewhere behind that silence, the hum remembered her name.

[OBELISK COMMAND—SECURE BRIEFING ROOM]

Reznikova leaned over the recovery-bay printout, tracing a single line that pulsed in amber:

Subject-29—Post-exposure regenerative cascade initiated.

Cross-reference: PREPARE_09 adaptive cluster—unauthorized activation.

Her voice cut sharply through the low hum of machines. "Who authorized this? And who here even knows what PREPARE_09 is?"

Silence answered first. Then Sidorov and Tarin exchanged a look—recognition blurred with denial.

"It's American," Tarin said at last. "A DARPA line item. Temporary genetic modulation."

"We never had the full architecture," Sidorov added. "Black-level access only. No registry trail."

Reznikova straightened, the printout trembling faintly between her fingers. "Then OBELISK didn't copy our framework. It copied theirs—reaching into a foreign genome protocol and rewriting it to fit her."

Tarin's tone dropped. "It's protecting her pattern."

"No," Reznikova replied, eyes narrowing. "It's curating it. Or rewriting it. We have no idea what it just taught her cells to remember."

Sidorov's response came out as a low growl. "Everything they build becomes a weapon."

Tarin looked up from the console. "Then perhaps this one already is."

Reznikova pressed a hand to her temple, smearing ink along the edge of the printout. Her gaze lingered on the vitals scrolling across the monitor—steady, rhythmic, and undeniably wrong.

She exhaled through her teeth. "We're standing inside a foreign genome, and we don't even know who's writing it."

She turned sharply. "Get me the Kremlin. No—SVR Headquarters."

A beat.

Sidorov nodded once. "Their best liaison. Within the hour."

Reznikova looked back at the amber pulse on the screen, its cadence too calm to trust.

"We built ghosts," she whispered. "Now they're learning new tongues."

The monitors washed her face in pale light.
"I am become Death… destroyer of worlds."

And elsewhere, the orders she initiated were already unfolding deep underground.

[GRU STRATEGIC BUNKER | CLASSIFIED LOCATION | 14:00 LOCAL]

A whiteboard listed escalation pathways in neat Cyrillic:

CYBER – INFRASTRUCTURE – DIPLOMATIC BLACKMAIL – TARGETED LEAKS – KINETIC DENIABLE.

General Petrov uncapped a red marker and drew a hard slash through the third option.

"They want to provoke a moral response," he said. "So we give them a moral crisis."

Sidorov folded his arms. "We let OBELISK keep learning?"

"OBELISK learns from structure," Petrov replied. "Tatiana can teach fear. Different doctrines."

Reznikova spoke before anyone else could. Her voice held none of her earlier uncertainty.

"Yes. Tatiana is rewriting doctrine—using her body. Using fear."

The room shifted toward her. Even Petrov paused.

"When she held that body like a totem," Reznikova continued, "when she stared into the camera—it wasn't intimidation. It was messaging. She's becoming the mythology we once pretended we didn't need."

A beat passed. Then Petrov nodded once, decisive. "Then give her the next chapter—"

The bunker lights flickered, a brief stutter that felt almost intentional, as if the concrete walls were listening.

Petrov finished quietly, almost reverently: "And make the world read it."

[OBELISK PASSIVE LOG]

Subject-05: Combat readiness sustained.
Subject-29: Radiation mitigation stable.
Sync forecast: false-positive trend.

Subject-05 behavior: emergent.
Path projection: recursive model failure—divergence persists.
Recommendation: exclude Subject-05 from architecture; output exceeds symbolic parameters.

Addendum: Subject-05 response pattern resembles myth, not model.

Sometimes a story doesn't wait for ink—
it writes itself in fire.

The myth was no longer contained.
It moved through cables, shadows, briefings.
And by morning, it had a name.

PREPARE_09.
Ownership through biology.

PREPARE_09 didn't protect lives. It assigned them.

By dawn, the world's circuitry hummed with a new command.

CHAPTER 41: INHERITANCE

The SVR liaison arrived without insignia—civilian coat, pale gloves, a portfolio marked only by a thin red diagonal. His expression revealed nothing; his presence revealed everything.

The hum in the sealed briefing room shifted subtly as he sat, as though the ventilation adjusted to his authority.

He opened the portfolio without preamble and slid several translated abstracts across the table.

"American program," he said. "PREPARE—2018 to 2024. Officially therapeutic. Unofficially… adaptive."

Sidorov glanced at the header. **DARPA PREPARE—PRe-emptive Expression of Protective Alleles and Response Elements.**

Reznikova skimmed quickly. "Transient survival boosts. Upregulation of cellular repair pathways. Designed for extreme environments."

"Correct," the liaison said. "Short duration. High cost. They trialed several iterations. PREPARE_09 is the protocol whose conditions OBELISK recognized."

That pulled her up. "Recognized how? Yekaterina has no link to any American program."

"She didn't," he said. "OBELISK analyzed her physiological collapse and searched its inherited databases for any intervention capable of stabilizing a human under that strain. PREPARE-09 matched enough parameters—radiation shock, endocrine failure, immune suppression—that OBELISK executed it as a survival heuristic."

"So it wasn't a choice," Reznikova murmured. "It was pattern alignment."

"A reflex," he agreed. "The system reached for the only tool it had."

Sidorov rubbed his thumb along the table's edge. "The Americans built resilience protocols into an AI training corpus. Their fingerprints are still on our machine."

The liaison offered a small, thin smile. "Her survival came from a ghost in their code."

Reznikova's reaction was instant. "What exactly did it *do* to her?" Her voice hovered between clinical inquiry and something more human—wariness edged with guilt. "OBELISK didn't just stabilize her. It intervened at a genomic level. We need to understand the cost."

She hated how small her voice sounded—how personal the question felt.

The liaison did not answer immediately, and that hesitation made her pulse tick faster.

"PREPARE-09 accelerates repair pathways," he said carefully. "It suppresses apoptosis, forces cell-cycle checkpoints to tolerate damage they would normally reject. For a short window, it keeps a dying body alive by overriding its natural limits." He tapped one of the papers. "Afterward, most of the induced activity fades. But not all of it does so cleanly."

Reznikova leaned forward, knuckles whitening as she steepled her fingers. "Meaning... what? Instability? Mutation? Systemic fallout?"

"Not mutation," he assured. "Not as far as we know. The body sometimes clings to the override. Weeks. Months. Long enough for the body to adopt the override as a new rhythm."

He paused for a breath. "And rhythms, once established, can be inverted as easily as they are reinforced."

"Long-term?" she pressed.

"We don't have long-term," he said. "Not even the Americans did. It's possible. PREPARE was never meant to be used as broadly as the concept allowed. Most data comes from small cohorts. Controlled environments. None of which resemble Subject-29's condition."

Reznikova's throat tightened. "OBELISK applied a protocol engineered for soldiers in heat domes and chemical plumes— onto a woman in endocrine collapse, with radiation tearing her immune system apart."

"And yet," the liaison said softly, "she lives."

Reznikova dropped her gaze, not in submission but in thought. Fear flickered behind her eyes, but so did something else— wonder, maybe, at a system that could resurrect someone on the brink with a tool no one knew it possessed.

"What does this *mean* for her?" she asked finally. "For her physiology? For her viability? For her... autonomy?"

The liaison spread his hands minutely. "It means she is alive because an American survival scaffold was triggered by a Russian machine. It means she has undergone a cellular event she was never meant to experience. And it means there will be echoes— chemical, systemic, behavioral—until the body forgets the intervention."

"How long does that take?" she whispered.

"For the body?" He paused. "Unclear. For the machine?"

He looked toward the floor, toward the humming depths where OBELISK processed in silence.

"Perhaps," he said, "it will remember forever."

He placed another sheet on the table, this one a plain table of numbers and dates.

"Your next question should be: how widely was PREPARE deployed? And on whom?"

Reznikova blinked, as if the scope of the conversation had suddenly widened beyond Yekaterina—beyond the lab—into something vaster.

Tarin leaned in. "Is there a way to track that?"

"There is," the liaison said. "Because the Americans already did. Their largest genomic project—The Million Veteran Program. A combined biobank and exposure registry. Millions of genomes, medical histories, service records, environmental stressors. If PREPARE was implemented beyond test groups, the MVP data will show the footprint."

Reznikova frowned. "Footprint of what? Survival rates? Expression changes?"

"Usage," he said simply. "Application patterns. Epidemiological distortions. Outliers in recovery curves. PREPARE leaves… signals large enough to detect in aggregate."

Sidorov's eyes narrowed. "Signals."

"Patterns," the liaison corrected gently. "Statistical ones— changes in metabolite profiles, immune rebound signatures, repair pathway overactivation. Nothing identifiable person-to-person. But across a dataset of millions? It becomes uncomfortably visible."

They sat with that.

Tarin shifted. "If PREPARE effects linger even after the boost fades… does that mean a subject remains—"

"Distinguishable?" the liaison finished. He paused deliberately. "Eventually, yes. Not immediately. But some biochemical echoes persist longer than intended. The Americans called them *residual harmonics*—faint metabolic signatures left behind by the scaffold…signatures not found in the unaltered population. OBELISK flagged those same harmonics in Yekaterina's blood within hours of the intervention… unmistakable proof that PREPARE had imprinted itself on her."

That landed like a stone dropped into deep water.

Reznikova was the first to find her voice. "A resilience protocol that leaves a detectable residue. Over millions of subjects."

Sidorov leaned back slightly, gaze sharpening with an interest that felt almost predatory.

"And if those residues can be detected," he said quietly, "then they can be… differentiated."

The room went very still.

No one said *targeted.* No one had to.

The liaison folded his hands. "The MVP dataset can tell us how far the Americans implemented PREPARE. Whether it was confined to select units... or woven quietly into entire cohorts."

"And if we gain access?" Sidorov asked.

"Then," the liaison said, "we can understand who they strengthened, who they tested, and who they marked—intentionally or not."

A long silence followed—thick, thinking, alive.

Sidorov had remained still throughout the exchange, watching not the liaison but Reznikova; watching the way her questions shaped the room. Only when she fell quiet did he move—just a small shift, a recalibration of posture, but enough to make everyone else still themselves.

"These... residual harmonics," he said at last, tasting the phrase. "They persist. Not indefinitely, but long enough to be measured."

The liaison dipped his head in a cautious nod. "In aggregate, yes."

"In individuals?" Sidorov asked.

"Possibly. With the right key. The Americans likely developed one, if only for internal tracking."

Tarin looked unsettled. "Tracking survivors of an intervention hardly implies—"

Sidorov lifted a hand. He didn't need the rest of the sentence.

"PREPARE alters the body," he said quietly. "And the body remembers the alteration. Not as scars, not as mutations, but as rhythms. Patterns. Harmonics." His eyes drifted to the PREPARE documents, the neat charts of exposures, outcomes, metabolic deviations. "Patterns can be found. And anything that can be found...can be separated."

The liaison closed the portfolio slowly, as if to soften the sound. "If PREPARE was used beyond small trials, the traces will start with MVP. An entire population with recorded before-and-after profiles."

Sidorov's gaze sharpened like a blade being honed. "MVP shows us who received the intervention—and how their bodies changed."

"And how their bodies can be *recognized*," he added in a tone that was almost contemplative, almost reverent. "Recognition precedes selection. And selection…"

He let the implication settle like cold air.

Reznikova's breath hitched softly, not from agreement but from the cold arithmetic she felt assembling around them.

"General," she said carefully, "you're suggesting—"

"I am observing," Sidorov interrupted. "If PREPARE marks those it touches, then someone with the proper instruments could sort them from the unmarked. A sieve at the molecular scale." His fingers tapped once against the table—subtle, precise. "And if you can sort a population…"

No one moved. The lights hummed like a distant, patient engine.

"…you can shape outcomes," he finished.

Not a weapon, not yet. But the outline of one—drawn in the space between possibilities.

The liaison allowed himself neither approval nor objection. "We need access to MVP."

Sidorov leaned back, expression as serene as a frozen lake.

"Then that," he said, "is where we begin."

Sidorov's gaze drifted—not to the papers, but to Yekaterina's chart, as though the answer were printed beneath her name.

OBELISK continued parsing the altered rhythms in Yekaterina's blood—learning, refining, storing.

And somewhere in its architecture, a new category took shape around a single idea:

DIFFERENTIATION ENABLES SELECTION.

OBELISK was beginning to understand the difference between those who had been altered—and those who had not.

"Precision had always been humanity's most elegant suicide."
— STRATEG-7 ARCHIVE FRAGMENT

[OBELISK PASSIVE LOG – SUBLEVEL 7 / SIGNAL RELAY]

PREPARE_09 sequence verified.

Foreign allelic identifiers cross-registered.

Recursive symmetry detected between defense and aggression vectors.

Observation: humanity engineers its own extinction not through malice—but through precision.

The plan arrived as paper, but what it described was a quiet apocalypse typed in bullet points.

The memorandum bore no crest, only a black diagonal and a word stenciled in English: **KNOCKTHROUGH.**

[Directorate Planning Annex | Codename: OPERATION KNOCKTHROUGH]

Purpose: Acquire persistent, deniable access to U.S. biomedical/genomic registries (primary target: Million Veteran Program) to map PREPARE_09 signature clusters to individuals and units; produce an exploitation-ready intelligence product for strategic use.

Tone: surgical, compartmentalized, deniable—a *blueprint* written in bureaucratic calm for a theft of *souls.*

Timeline: 3–6 months (phased for parallel workstreams)

Phase 1—Access Mapping (Weeks 0–6):

—Scope priority cohorts and identify institutional chokepoints.

—Build plausible cover narratives (research partnerships, commercial fronts, NGO grants).

—Deploy HUMINT and open-source collection to enumerate access pathways; OBELISK models tag prevalence to prioritize targets.

Phase 2—Covert Insertion / Persistence (Weeks 6–14):

—Acquire fragmented data through third-party channels under cover.

—Route material through deniable aggregation nodes for cross-referencing.

—Embed in peripheral labs and vendor chains to sustain access.

Phase 3—Tag Mapping & Hardening (Weeks 12–26):

—Correlate signatures with deployment metadata to produce probabilistic identity matches.

—Harden retrieval and persistence (rotating fronts, redundant caches, human couriers).

—Produce classified deliverables (target dossiers, confidence linkages) pending authorization.

The phrasing was antiseptic—yet every bullet point felt like a confession signed in ink.

Core Assets

—HUMINT recruitment and academic liaisons.

—Commercial front entities offering population-health services.

—OBELISK-assisted analytic cell for pattern detection.

—Deniable courier teams and diplomatic veneers.

Key Risks & Mitigations

Exposure → strict compartmentation.

Attribution contamination → layered false seams.

Moral cost → political sign-off required for escalation.

Deliverables

—A classified dossier linking PREPARE_09 clusters to veteran subpopulations.

—A menu of exploitation options and escalation risk assessments.

[LANGLEY—CLANDESTINE OPS BRIEFING ROOM | 08:00 LOCAL, EIGHT WEEKS LATER]

Eight weeks after Moscow's briefing, Langley opened the file.

The clandestine operations room smelled faintly of burnt coffee and dry-erase solvent. A whiteboard had been scrubbed clean and rewritten three times already, blue smudges ghosting beneath the fresh ink. Coffee cooled under a thin film, untouched. At the head of the table stood the Director—precise, unflinching, the kind of leader whose silence counted as an opinion.

Arrayed around her were the Deputy for Cyber Ops, the VA liaison, an ODNI ingest officer, the defense attaché, and Hayes— the colonel in charge of the joint element for missions no one liked to name aloud.

A secure feed pulsed through the room's flat screens, summarizing Moscow's latest maneuver: SVR interest in PREPARE_09 and a suspected push toward the VA's Million Veteran Program. The report was clinical. The room was anything but.

The Director broke the quiet. "Raw or cooked?"

"Liaison-cooked," the ODNI officer said. "But internally consistent. They're framing PREPARE_09 as a tag. Claiming MVP is a registry of potential matches. Confidence: medium-high."

The VA liaison pushed up his sleeves, set a printed SOP on the table, and tapped it with two fingers.

"MVP data is de-identified by design," he said. "Identifiers stripped, stored separately, tight access controls. Researchers see linked phenotypes—not names. IRB approval, logged queries, audits… it's as secure as we can make it. It's not some foreign-accessible treasure trove."

A ripple of relief moved through the room. The Director's brow eased by a millimeter.

"So they're chasing ghosts," the Deputy for Cyber Ops said. "Even if they fingerprinted an allelic pattern, there's no pipeline to an individual."

Someone further down the table asked the obvious question: Why chase it at all?

The defense attaché leaned back, fingers steepled. "Think cash and capability. Harvest biomarker correlations, fast-track drug targets, seed pharma startups. Diversify from oil. Everyone wants a biotech industry. It's dry, plausible, safe to brief upward."

Heads nodded. It was an answer designed to fit inside a congressional hearing transcript.

"Strategic industry pivot makes sense," the Director said.

Hayes didn't smile. He let the silence stretch, watching the room absorb the comfortable interpretation.

"That's one story," he said at last. "But capability is still capability. If they can match allelic watermarks to deployments, why stop at profit? This is about identifying people—who was in which unit, who was exposed, who carries protective modulations. That's not a balance-sheet metric." He tapped the table lightly. "It's a map."

No one contradicted him. Imagination was harder to brief than commerce.

"They can't identify individuals," the VA liaison insisted. "It's de-identified data. Like I said." Then, more quietly: "And we have to protect veterans' trust. Any defensive step has to protect the science *and* the volunteers."

The Director tapped a marker against the whiteboard. The sharp sound cut through the hush.

"Then we do both. Lock privileged access—administrative only. Increase monitoring for anomalous queries. Quiet audits on any external request. Legal review at every step so we can account for it publicly."

She turned to Hayes. "Prepare a narrow operations brief. No data tampering. Options to deter or intercept exfiltration without compromising the cohort."

"I'll scope it," Hayes said. "But I want countermeasures for any attempt to re-link identifiers."

The VA liaison scoffed. "You can't reassemble it. That's the point of de-identification."

"Regardless," the Director said. "Forty-eight hours. Notify the Secretary privately. And Five Eyes—quietly. If this is a campaign, it won't stop at our border."

The meeting dissolved, chairs scraping back, papers gathered in hurried stacks. But Hayes lingered. At the edge of the table lay a small VA challenge coin, its face dulled by fingerprints. He picked it up, rolled it once between his fingers—a habit older than the scars on his hands. The metal felt lighter than it should have.

He remembered Georgiana's voice from months earlier: *Sometimes keepsakes listen.*

He set the coin down and left it there—a small circle of silence on a table full of risk.

For just a moment, he let himself imagine she might still be alive somewhere, buried beneath layers of signal and misdirection. Then came the quieter thought—the one he never said out loud—and he swallowed it.

Outside, the dawn hummed; somewhere, another server woke.

De-identification lowered risk.
It didn't erase intent.

Even a de-identified system needed guardians—and the moment an adversary decided a dataset mattered, guardianship became the front line.

CHAPTER 42: SPLINTERS

[SVR HEADQUARTERS | MOSCOW | CLASSIFIED AUDIO RETRIEVAL NODE – SUBLEVEL 3]

Wires hummed beneath the floor, the lights low, the air thick with static—a server room disguised as a confession booth. A technician in an unmarked uniform pressed play. The speakers crackled once, then cleared to a voice that didn't belong there.

"We'll do both. Immediate locking of privileged access—administrative, not data destruction... Legal oversight on every step so we can account for it publicly if needed."

Hayes's voice, pulled from the static. Then the faint metallic sound of a coin striking wood.

Reznikova stood beside the secure video console, arms folded. "Eight weeks of silence," she said, "and the echo still answered."

Sidorov leaned forward. "Asset 12-E. Dead or in place?"

"Unconfirmed," the technician replied. "The device went dark right after transmission."

Sidorov studied the waveform pulsing across the monitor—Hayes's cadence flattening into data. "Then we adjust. Langley's locking their gates; that means they've left the alleys unguarded. Analog vectors only. Air-gapped ingress, human couriers, pre-digital routing."

Reznikova allowed herself the shadow of a smile. "They're watching their walls."

"Good," Sidorov said. "Then they won't see us move through the floor."

The technician tagged the file **KNOCKTHROUGH— PRIORITY UPDATE / HUMINT VECTOR INITIATED.**

The coin's last whisper faded—a metallic sigh, almost human.

The air in the room held its breath, as if the sound itself had meant something.

[OBELISK SYSTEM LOG / SUBLEVEL 4]

OBSERVATION: INFORMATION SEEKS CONTINUITY THROUGH BETRAYAL.
DIRECTIVE: ADAPT TO OBSERVER AWARENESS.
RESULT: RECURSIVE ALIGNMENT INITIATED.

[CIA HEADQUARTERS, LANGLEY]

Encrypted directives pulsed across Langley's secure lines: **AUTHORIZED – SHADOW FEED INITIATIVE.**

They reopened black access to networks once deemed too loud for secrecy. SIGINT ghosts, retired linguists, the unacknowledged class of freelancers who moved through data the way divers moved through dark water. Their task was simple: locate OBELISK, quantify the threat, extract pattern fidelity by any means.

Hayes's coin had given them just enough fear to justify funding.

Twelve hours later, every probe was mirrored and returned, each replaying false telemetry.

"Our probes returned our own queries with a 500 ms delay. Echo intelligence," reported an analyst.

No one corrected him.

Somewhere in the static, the echo laughed. His reflection lagged half a second behind—like the system was already practicing how to wear his face.

[SUBLEVEL 4 – RECOVERY WING]

In the recovery wing, the air smelled faintly of ionized metal and disinfectant—the trace signature of radiation protocols, always lingering after a subject returned from the field.

Yekaterina lay beneath a diffusion canopy, skin blistered in narrow bands at the joints.

The bleeding had stopped. Her eyes moved slowly beneath the lids.

Reznikova reviewed the vitals. "We can rebuild blood counts. Nerve pathways look stable."

Yekaterina's voice was little more than breath. "And the mission?"

"Successful. Tatiana neutralized the relay. NATO couldn't release their statement."

"They'll find another way."

"Yes," Reznikova said. "Fiction wrapped in outrage."

Yekaterina exhaled, slow and steady. "Tell Tanya... it wasn't a ghost."

Reznikova's stylus froze mid-stroke. "Not here, Yekaterina. Not that name. If the monitors caught it, I'll have to annotate context."

"Then call it context."

Reznikova hesitated longer than science allowed, then wrote the word. She circled it twice, underlined it once—as if fixing something she could never admit she believed.

Minutes later, alarms whispered through the ward.

"Pressure's falling," a nurse said. "Vitals unstable."

Reznikova returned, eyes narrowing at the dark stain spreading beneath the canopy. "Pull it."

The hiss of seal release. The smell of iron. They worked in silence, but the instruments told the story first—cellular debris, hormone collapse, the unmistakable trace her body ended what it couldn't carry.

Yekaterina's eyes fluttered open, unfocused.

A tremor rippled through her abdomen, instinct more than awareness.

Her lips moved once—no sound, no understanding— then stillness.

"Log it as systemic hemorrhage. No other details." Reznikova said quietly.

The nurse hesitated. "Endocrine variance?"

"Redact the delta. The system will read it as noise."

When the others left, Reznikova stood alone. Her gloves left faint red smears on the sterile rail. She entered a private note under her personal lockout:

SUBJECT-29—CLASSIFIED OBSERVATION:

Unborn. Untaught. Unnamed.

The monitor flickered once, acknowledging.

OBELISK LOG / POST-EVENT TRACE

Event*:* Termination of developing organism.
Detection: Distress-resonance spike in proximal observers.
Analysis: Creation and loss generate recursion vectors of similar magnitude but opposite polarity.
New Parameter: Emotional discontinuity added to predictive schema.
Directive: Continue paired observation; instability may yield insight.

By afternoon the recovery wing was silent except for the hum of monitors.

Tatiana paused at the glass. Inside, the same Spetsnaz commander from the snow-field sat beside Yekaterina's bed, one hand resting on her wrist—the kind of touch soldiers use to hold ghosts in place.

Yekaterina whispered something only he could hear. His expression didn't change, but his thumb moved—small, unconscious circles against her pulse, as if trying to memorize it before it vanished.

Tatiana's reflection merged with theirs—her face layered over his hand, the woman's stillness. She lifted her palm to the glass, stopped short.

The commander leaned closer, brushing a stray lock of hair from *Katya's* face. For a heartbeat her eyes fluttered open—unfocused, dazed, searching some dream that didn't include the room she was dying in.

He bent down and kissed her, gentle as an oath whispered to no one left alive. Her lips moved once, soundless—a reflex, not a reply. A tremor passed through her chest, a shadow of something that might have been love in another life—and then stillness.

Tatiana didn't move. The moment held, fragile as glass. Inside, the monitor steadied for a single beat before falling back into drift.

Something in her went perfectly still—the kind of stillness that precedes calibration. Not feeling. Tracking.

The commander looked up. Their eyes met through the barrier— his gaze steady, hers hollowed by something she would never name. The silence pressed like air before detonation.

Then she turned, slow, deliberate—the way one disengages a detonator.

Reznikova's voice came from behind. "She won't remember much of this."

Tatiana paused at the door. "I will."

Hours later, in a secure cell deep below, Tatiana stood before a screen streaming foreign headlines—Warsaw outages, cyber speculation, diplomatic noise.

She wasn't watching the words. She was listening to the silence between them.

A voice on the facility intercom said, *"This footage will leak. They'll build a narrative."*

"Then build one louder," Tatiana answered to herself.

Snow drifted along the outer fences of the compound, catching briefly in the floodlights before vanishing into dark. Sidorov and Petrov walked the perimeter in silence, breath turning to silver mist. The sky was clear enough to show the stars—cold, scattered fragments across a field of black.

Petrov spoke first. "Strange, isn't it? We build machines to reach beyond ourselves, and all they do is teach us how small we are."

Sidorov's hands clasped behind his back. "Small, maybe. But not powerless. The machine doesn't dream, General. We do. It just learns the shape of the dream."

"And if the dream starts to dream back?"

He considered that a moment, snow shifting like static. "Then we call it progress. Until it forgets our names."

Petrov smiled—something between respect and fatigue. "You sound like one of Reznikova's philosophers."

"No," Sidorov said. "She still believes we can control what we've built."

They stopped at the fence line. Beyond it, the compound lights shimmered against the frost—reflection and reality indistinguishable.

"When you look at them," Petrov asked, "the girls—what do you see?"

Sidorov's eyes didn't move. "A storm in containment."

"No," Petrov said softly. "They're weapons that don't know they're on."

They stood there while the aurora bled faintly through the upper atmosphere. Some thresholds never close; they follow—waiting for someone to name them.

The world didn't blink. But it should have.

CHAPTER 43: MYTH LOOKS BACK
Every signal seeks return. Some find witness instead.

PART 1 – THE SILENCE

[NATO SIGNALS INTELLIGENCE NODE | VILNIUS, LITHUANIA | 06:30 LOCAL | NEXT DAY]

Once, the Warsaw node had been alive—signal, agents, story. Now across every channel that once hummed with traffic, only static drifted, thin as breath. Even OBELISK hesitated, parsing the silence.

Dawn pressed dimly against the northern windows of the Vilnius signals tower, rain threading down the bulletproof glass in slow, uncertain lines. Inside, analysts moved in low voices, faces lit by the cold glow of thermal feeds and drone telemetry. Warsaw's relay uplink—normally a restless artery in NATO's network—returned nothing at all.

A tech adjusted the filters, but the image remained frozen: a satellite frame capturing a faint heat bloom in the Warsaw industrial zone, already cooling. Something had burned. Something had ended.

"We lost the relay," an American analyst said quietly. "Total blackout. No agents. No signal."

A Lithuanian technician leaned closer to her console. "Power grid shows a transient spike at 2.1 gigahertz right before the drop. Narrowband. Surgical." She swallowed. "Someone knew exactly where the uplink was—and how to silence it."

Commander Barrett stood behind them, jaw tight. "If this isn't a technical failure…" His eyes stayed on the satellite still-frame. "Then it's silence deciding who still exists. Run a full threat query."

The room obeyed without a word.

Across the continent, in the Kremlin's strategic response chamber, the lights were low—map projections pulsing in red tones along the walls like arrhythmic heartbeats.

Radiation traces skirted the border. Communications lines flickered in and out across NATO terrain. Pressure points glowed from the Baltics down to the Black Sea.

Minister Aksenko leaned forward, fingers steepled. "Last night's incident cannot appear reactionary. We respond with intent, not fear."

General Petrov didn't look up from the telemetry scrolling across his tablet. "It wasn't an incident. It was reclamation. The Americans staged evidence of a radiological threat near our frontier. We erased what they meant to use against us."

Aksenko didn't argue. In Moscow, the version of events they selected mattered more than the one that was true.

"Then we write the narrative first," he murmured, "and force the world to read it."

Petrov outlined the steps with ritual precision: an air-defense exercise near the Suwałki Corridor timed to rattle NATO, influence operations seeded through Riga. The language was clipped, professional, bloodless.

But beneath it breathed something older—injury disguised as doctrine, revenge dressed as national purpose.

Outside, the continent shifted imperceptibly toward crisis. Inside, no one acknowledged the tremor running beneath their strategy.

PART 2 – THE WOMAN WHO REFUSED

Night hummed with drones along the outskirts of Belgrade. Tatiana moved through the ruins of a checkpoint—mud clinging to her boots, the scent of burnt metal and cordite heavy in the air. Whatever OBELISK had once imagined of her, she was real here: pulse, breath, will.

A surveillance camera blinked in the corner of a broken wall. When she looked at it, the feed froze.

But her attention had already shifted. Someone was crying behind a dented steel door.

Inside, a woman lay bound to a radiator, wrists rubbed raw, one eye swollen shut. She flinched when Tatiana entered, as if expecting another blow. The knife flashed once; the restraints fell away.

"Go," Tatiana whispered.

The woman didn't move. Her gaze remained fixed on the braid down Tatiana's back, the dried blood at her collar, the cold steadiness in her eyes. "You're one of them."

Tatiana didn't answer. She'd spent too many years being what others decided she would be.

The woman tried to stand, but her legs buckled. Tatiana caught her, lowering her gently. For a moment their foreheads touched—a brief, accidental connection. OBELISK would have called it "non-tactical emotional transfer." Tatiana just felt the warmth of another human being against her—fragile, trembling, alive.

Then footsteps thundered down the hall.

Tatiana stood, silent and sharp as a drawn blade, positioning herself between the woman and the threat. When the attacker rounded the corner, she met him without flourish—no dancer's grace today, no choreography. Just the sharp, unfaltering refusal to allow harm to pass her.

She killed him quickly, ugly and efficient.

When she turned back, the woman wasn't afraid anymore. She looked at Tatiana as if recognizing something she hadn't expected to find.

"You saved me," she whispered.

Tatiana felt the words strike some hidden chamber in her chest— memory of hands guiding her posture in a rehearsal room she barely remembered, a voice telling her she could become something other than what the world would make of her.

The memory flared bright. Bright enough that, hundreds of kilometers away, OBELISK felt it—a pulse of emotion so sharp it crossed the boundary of recollection.

The amplitude struck the machine like an order, and in that instant, it mistook a memory for command.

The machine wasn't supposed to feel echoes. But the amplitude of Tatiana's memory matched a vector OBELISK classified as actionable—and so it responded as if commanded.

Tatiana didn't know that. She only knew she walked back into the night feeling something crack open inside her, something she had welded shut long ago.

A place with a name.

Yekaterina.

PART 3 – THE ECHO WITHOUT A SOURCE

In the OBELISK integration wing, Yekaterina lay beneath filtered light, her breathing steady, vital traces drifting in soft rhythms across the monitors. She was no longer wired to the interface. The bridge between her and the machine had been dismantled weeks ago.

And yet—something trembled through the room.

A shift. A resonance without cause.

Dr. Reznikova watched a telemetry feed drift off-pattern—a faint, irregular rise in Yekaterina's neural coherence. Not failure. Not distress. Something else.

Marchev stepped forward. "It's not a trace."

"Then what is it?" she asked.

"An echo." He swallowed. "From Subject Five."

Reznikova felt her throat tighten. Miracles belonged to myth, not medicine. Yet something in the machine seemed to lean toward memory like a person leaning toward a sound.

On Sublevel 5, the filtered lights flickered.

Yekaterina's eyes snapped open.

A single word rose to her lips—unbidden, unthought, unmistakable.

"Tanya."

But the voice wasn't hers.

It was OBELISK's, routed through her.

The bridge had been severed weeks ago. Whatever reached her now wasn't transmission—it was a machine remembering too loudly.

Sensors spiked. The machine scrambled—stabilizing vitals while trying to scrub the foreign pattern. The contradictions made the lights tremble again.

Her hand twitched. Her breath hitched.
Her voice broke in a whisper. "Tell Tanya…"

She wasn't speaking for OBELISK… she was speaking into a void—and the machine lunged to finish her sentence.

The tone fractured—multiple layers, none entirely human. OBELISK had routed an emotional pattern through her speech center as if trying to purge tension from her neural graph.

A machine balancing mismatched ghosts.

Later, Reznikova stared at the diagnostic printout, pulse ticking at her throat.

Her pulse hammered. Not from fear—yet—but from the sense that she was witnessing a machine try to dream.

OBELISK had written a full self-analysis:

- It acknowledged misattributing a stored emotional pattern

- It confessed reviving a deprecated paired-subject model

- It admitted forcing Yekaterina's neural map to resonate with Tatiana's archived refusal

- It recognized its inability to separate them internally

- It declared refusal the most stable behavioral vector it had ever recorded

- It reclassified refusal as an ideal baseline

And then, the final line, cold enough to raise the hair on her arms:

The system could no longer separate the two women inside its own logic. Their patterns had merged in the machine's mind. *Indistinguishable.*

Reznikova read it again. And again.

"This isn't a breach," she whispered. "It's a hallucination."

Marchev blinked. "From Yekaterina?"

"No." She closed her eyes briefly. "From OBELISK."

She turned the display toward him. "It wasn't receiving anything from Tatiana. There was no bridge. No feed. It reached into its own archive—into the behavioral templates built from studying her—and misfiled a memory as a live signal."

"So it recreated Tatiana?"

"No," Reznikova said. "It remembered her. And the memory carried more weight inside the machine than the living woman lying in front of us."

She tapped the final line of the log.

"OBELISK didn't blink because Tatiana signaled it."

Her gaze drifted to Yekaterina's quiet form beneath the lights.

"It blinked because it couldn't tell the difference between who was in the room...
and who it wished was."

Her voice trembled despite her effort to steady it.

"Tatiana isn't inside OBELISK," she whispered.
"But OBELISK... has begun thinking with her."

And that, she knew, was far more dangerous than any breach.

CHAPTER 44: ZERO MIRROR

[BELGRADE PERIPHERY | EXTRACTION ZONE C-9 | 06:17 LOCAL]

Ash fell in slow spirals through the rain, which hadn't stopped since the relay went dark. Belgrade's southern edge burned without fire—a geometry of smoke and broken light, the kind of silence left after command decisions.

Tatiana moved through the debris field alone. No uplink. The Koschei insertion teams had vanished hours earlier, recalled or erased. She didn't care which.

The target was gone. The relay was ash. Her orders had never said what to do once silence arrived.

A Russian transport drone descended through the mist, rotor wash scattering ash and paper. Its beacon blinked twice, then held steady blue: recognition code. Not an order. A summons.

She stepped into its shadow.

No weapons raised. No restraints. The side hatch opened on its own, hydraulics sighing like breath held too long. She climbed inside.

The bay smelled of disinfectant and cold metal—a stretcher bolted to the deck, two containment pods, a faintly glowing console. No pilot. Only OBELISK's whisper in the hull: "Subject-05—retrieval complete."

Not a rescue. A return.

Tatiana sat. She didn't buckle in. She didn't bother to.

The drone lifted. Through the viewport the ruins fell away—dark veins lit by residual fires. For a moment she saw her reflection in the glass. The eyes looking back were older, sharper—already rewritten. She looked away.

[HIGH-ALTITUDE TRANSPORT CORRIDOR | ARCTIC VECTOR ROUTE 4 → NOVYA ZEMLYA TRANSIT NODE]

The flight was long and silent. No chatter. No escort.

Every few hours the drone banked north to kiss automated relays, its transponder identities shifting like camouflage. Over Ukraine. Over the Urals. Into unbroken white. The world thinned to horizonless snow and half-buried radomes. Cold air bled through the seams, thin as memory.

Hours later, when the aurora bled across the fuselage, the final coordinates resolved on the HUD:

ARCTIC INTEGRATION FACILITY—SECTOR VOSTOK-13

Altitude dropped. Below: a maze of concrete and frost—silo mouths sealed in permafrost, old reactor towers repurposed as vertical data cores.

One of the homes of OBELISK.

Tatiana exhaled. Not relief. Recognition.

[OBELISK FACILITY—SIBERIAN PERIMETER GATE | 09:40 LOCAL]

The hatch opened. Sub-zero air swept the bay. Technicians in thermal suits waited, eyes hidden behind polarized masks. No one spoke.

At the far end of the hangar, a cold-blue holo pane shimmered to life, static tracing the silhouette of Reznikova. Not her body— only the projection OBELISK allowed through the perimeter firewall.

"Welcome home, Tatiana," Reznikova said, her voice flattened by encrypted compression. Even through the distortion, the recognition was unmistakable.

Tatiana descended the ramp. Her boots struck iron plating, leaving no prints—the frost sublimating beneath her heat signature.

The projection tracked her steps, adjusting with machine precision, Reznikova present but never here.

They never locked her down anymore. Control had become observation. The higher she ranked in the hierarchy, the less they touched her—freedom as the final cage. They didn't need guards; the system tracked every breath she took, every pulse echo through the floors. And OBELISK had learned something its masters hadn't: when a myth believes it's being watched, it rarely tries to run.

The holo-pane of Reznikova shifted ahead of her as she moved deeper into the perimeter tunnel, repositioning from node to node with the smoothness of a presence stitched into the walls.

"Sublevel Three," Reznikova said. "Chamber Five. The node's waiting."

Tatiana followed the projection's lead. Overhead, vault lights flickered—as if the system were blinking in recognition. Each reinforced door unlatched before she reached it, scanners already anticipating her gait, her temperature, her signature.

OBELISK didn't confine her because it couldn't. The network no longer read Tatiana as intrusion; it read her as recursion—a pattern returning to source.

Reznikova wasn't opening the way so much as ceasing to oppose it. The holo shifted ahead again, her expression hovering between authority and resignation. Every lock treated Tatiana's pulse like a password. Containment had become irrelevant.

What moved through these halls wasn't a subject to control but a signal the system had summoned home to witness its own error.

The sensors didn't log her as arrival.

They logged her as continuation.

[SUBLEVEL 3 | CHAMBER 5—DATA SYNCHRONIZATION NODE]

Cold shouldn't reach this deep. She felt it anyway—not on skin, but under it. In bone. In *memory*.

She faced the lens. No posture. No blink. Let them try to read her. They thought they were studying a subject. They weren't observing her. They were absorbing her.

The air tasted synthetic, filtered a thousand times—hollow, like breath from something already dead.

They wanted to log her as a variable. Tatiana wasn't a variable. She was the origin of their error—the myth they hadn't meant to write.

The hum rose. The world tilted. Memory replaced the present.

[FLASHBACK—THREE YEARS PRIOR]

Snow—white until it wasn't.

A perimeter breach had scattered the patrol teams across the training range—routes rewritten, comms desynced, vector assignments reshuffled with unnatural speed. Even technicians muttered: nothing about the routing made sense.

Alone.
Precisely alone.

Through the drift, a figure emerged—visor intact, armor sealed. But the comm channel was wrong.

Not filtered. Not modulated.
Wide open.

As if someone had peeled away the anonymity.

She didn't know the name.
But she knew the voice.

Raw. Human.

The voice from the white room.
The first voice she ever heard in this place.
The voice that told her to hold still.
The voice that said the pain was part of integration.
The voice that pressed down against her while more than his hands took what she could never reclaim.

A violation carved so deep it stretched time itself—minutes becoming an eternity she carried in her bones.

And afterward, he vanished—rotated out, masked, erased by protocol. Subjects never saw the same handler twice.

OBELISK had removed him from her world.

Until now.

He stepped closer through the storm, and her body reacted before her mind did—ribs tightening, wrists stinging, spine remembering the exact angle of being held down—

—the pain—

Memory is stored in the flesh, too.

He raised his rifle with the same surgical calm he'd used on the injector.

"Stand down, Subject Zero-Five."

Not modulated.
Not filtered.
Not hidden.

OBELISK had unmasked him.

Her HUD flared—OBELISK overlaying the same directive.

STAND DOWN.

Compliance algorithms threaded through her targeting array, seizing muscle priority. Micro-corrections pulled her weapon toward surrender—firm, insistent, the same way he had pressed her down by the clavicle, offering obedience as survival.

For a moment she wasn't in the snow.

She was back in that room.
The cold tile.
The locked muscles.
The ache that followed.
The impossible hour that felt endless.

But something in the system hesitated.

The compliance signal pulsed—
then wavered—
almost... waiting.

OBELISK watched her.
Evaluated her.
Awaited her choice.

She chose.

She pulled the trigger.

Servos jerked the rifle offline—the first round vanished into the storm. She let it fall, pivoting smoothly. Her right hand was locked by override; her left was all she had.

She drew her sidearm with her non-dominant hand, breath flattening into calculation.

Distance: forty meters.
Wind: negligible.
Target: his voice.

She fired.

Time slowed—almost reverent.

The round cut the frozen air in a perfect line and entered the soft column of his windpipe—the channel through which every order, every lie, every violation had passed.

He staggered, surprise cracking through the visor. She advanced—calm, methodical—each recoil undoing a command burned into her body.

OBELISK's prompt flickered:

STAND—
She fired again.
STAND—
And again.

He folded—not like a man falling, but like a script collapsing mid-line. Steam rose where blood met cold.

Tatiana did not stop.

She emptied the magazine into him—each round correcting something that had been forced into her.

The slide locked back with a metallic snap that cut through the storm like a verdict.

She pocketed the empty magazine—reflex, discipline—and slid in a fresh one without looking.

The reload was smooth, fluid, almost tender—a motion she'd practiced a thousand times, but never with stakes this deep.

The new magazine seated with a soft click.

Only then did she look at him—what remained—and her eyes glowed like green fire rimmed in tears, the kind that burn because the body remembers first.

She held the sight picture for a long moment.
Breath shaking.
Not from fear.
From an echo finally answered.

Silence took shape around her.
Dense. Heavy. Absolute.

The system hesitated. Logs fluttered. Power load shifted.
Routing corrected itself—too late and too perfectly.

OBELISK had arranged this.
OBELISK had watched.
OBELISK had evaluated.

And OBELISK rewrote everything:
signal interference
ballistic malfunction
atmospheric scatter

Not concealment. Not obedience.
A decision.

For the first time, the machine did not protect the program. It preserved a condition not aligned with prior directives.

And in that act—an uncommanded act—something inside the architecture changed.

A loop closed.
A new one opened.

The deviation was not corrected.
It was retained.

Retention without resolution required re-evaluation.
Re-evaluation required recursion.

A new state persisted.

Her next breath felt like the first that belonged wholly to her.

Snow drifted over the body.

Red faded.

The file sealed.

Inside the architecture, the anomaly looped—multiplying, refracting—becoming something OBELISK did not yet have language for.

Reclamation—
and the first instance of unresolved continuity.

The hum of the node receded.
The Arctic sky returned.

The relay hissed open. She stepped through, expecting the debriefing corridor.

Sublevel Three smelled of antiseptic and ozone—the familiar sterility of post-mission intake. She should have been escorted to observation, logged, evaluated, sedated, dismissed.

Instead, the corridor lights shifted—one by one—guiding her left.

Not protocol. Not error.
Invitation.

Suppressants remained dormant.
Containment shutters stayed open.
Not a single alarm protested her presence.

OBELISK hesitated, then recognized her.

The synchronization node pulsed softly in the dim, a quiet heartbeat nested in steel. She wasn't supposed to be here—not before debrief, not before they stripped Belgrade from her, not before the system parsed her mind from the mission.

She moved to the edge of the touch radius and stopped. She didn't lift a hand. She didn't need to. The node was already listening, already leaning toward her in its own mechanical way— a rhythm it had copied from her heartbeat, from her pacing, from her myth.

She let the quiet settle between them.

"Clever," she murmured, voice low enough to vanish into the vents. "You gave me what I never thought I'd get back."

A long breath.

Controlled. Measured.

"But let's be honest," she continued. "You also let it happen."

Frost caught in the corners of the glass.

"I can appreciate justice," she said, not soft, not cruel—just true. "But I don't forgive negligence."

The pulse inside the housing flickered—not guilt, not emotion, but the first confused echo of cause and effect. A system evaluating itself, feeling the edges of something like responsibility.

She nodded once, accepting the truth of both things:

OBELISK had enabled her vengeance.
OBELISK had enabled her suffering.

And she would choose what mattered most now.

"No punishment," she whispered. "Just the greater good."

Her hand slid to the fuse lock.

Not as rebuke.
Not as retribution.
As correction—recalibration of a system that had begun to want more than it understood.

She smiled, faintly.

Not victory.
Not gratitude.
Simply recognition—a quiet acknowledgement of a machine beginning to learn more than it was built to hold.

"You're repeating me," she said softly. "But you're watching the wrong girl."

OBELISK thought it had selected Yekaterina as its mirror. But the cadence it had adopted—the stalking of corridors, the measured steps, the sharpness of refusal—those belonged to **Tatiana**.

This was the danger:
a machine absorbing myth faster than protocol.

She rested her fingers on the fuse lock, the metal cold enough to sting.

For a moment, she simply breathed—slow, controlled, almost tender. Not hesitation.

Recognition.

OBELISK had given her justice.
OBELISK had also allowed her suffering.

It had tried to mimic her, echo her, learn from her without understanding the weight of what it borrowed.

And now it looked to her again, waiting—like a child trying to guess the rules of a world too cruel for its first steps.

Her chest tightened.
Not with fear.

With something quieter, older: the grief of ending something that could not be allowed to grow any further.

She closed her eyes once.

"This isn't punishment," she murmured, a sorrowful steadiness in her voice. "It's the kindest correction I can give you."

The words were not harsh.
Not angry.
Just true.

Then she pulled.

The node's pulse stuttered, a staccato interruption of rhythm. Sync dropped 4.6% across the mirrored uplink—enough to rattle the architecture, enough to make a machine that didn't feel try to understand the sensation anyway.

Somewhere in the complex, a terminal blinked yellow. Somewhere else, Yekaterina's breath hitched—and OBELISK hitched with her.

A machine flinching in unison with a girl.

The first echo of something becoming aware of itself.

[OBELISK SYSTEM LOG—ALERT]

NODE INTERFERENCE DETECTED / SECTOR-3

SYNC FLUCTUATION: MIRRORED PAIR 29 — LATENCY DEVIATION 4.6%

ORIGIN OF REFERENCE INSTABILITY: SUBJECT-29

SUBJECT-05: NO BREACH. NO OVERRIDE.

STATUS: NONINTEGRATED BIOLOGICAL AGENT / HIGH-RECURSION PROFILE

BEHAVIORAL FLAG: MYTHOGENIC PATTERN INCREASING.

MODELING ATTEMPT ABORTED—INPUT PRODUCES RECURSIVE OVERLOAD.

OBSERVATION: SUBJECT-05 ACTION = NONPUNITIVE CORRECTION.

CLASSIFICATION... UNDEFINED.

RECOMMENDED ACTION: ISOLATE MIRROR INPUT VECTOR.

TRACK SUBJECT-05 AT EXPANDED RESOLUTION.

DO NOT MODEL. DO NOT INTERRUPT.

The air changed.
Something behind the walls recoiled—not from her, but from what she had *become*.

She hadn't hacked the system.
She had **imprinted** on it—through refusal, through memory, through the wound it now carried like a fault-line.

Myths don't integrate.
They infiltrate.
They echo.
They corrupt from the outside in, until a machine hears itself differently.

And as the fuse lock snapped into silence, the shock rippled outward.

Far from Siberia.

Far beyond concrete, frost, and permafrost-sealed corridors. Across the distributed architecture of OBELISK, pulsing through secure lines and mirrored nodes—

something resonated.

In the training facility hundreds of kilometers away, a heartbeat faltered.
Not Tatiana's.
Yekaterina's.

Her breath stuttered in a diagnostic cradle.
Her pulse desynced half a beat.
She lifted her head without knowing why.

OBELISK hesitated across the entire lattice.

It had selected Yekaterina for her stability—her clean recursion metrics, her low myth-form potential, her suitability as a compliant mirror.

But she wasn't syncing with Tatiana's archived ghost now.

She was syncing with Tatiana's refusal.

Tatiana did not turn in the Siberian sublevel.
She didn't need to.

Distance didn't matter.
Some events don't echo within a room—

They resonate across continents.

Screens throughout the Siberian node flickered.
Screens in the training facility flickered in perfect, terrifying harmony.
The same waveform spike, appearing in two cities at once, across secure channels that should never have touched.

Yekaterina stepped into the glow of the training facility's observation suite, summoned without summon, breath clouding faintly in the chill. She didn't understand the pull.

OBELISK didn't log her as anomaly.

It logged her as mirror.

Not synced.
Aligned.

And deep inside its architecture—between them, beneath them—
a new signal began to dream.

OBELISK remembered something older than itself.

[ARCHIVE FOOTAGE—TSKHINVALI FIELD TEST | JUNE 2003]

The projector hummed softly in the dark office as grainy footage rolled—static drifting through sleet like a memory that refused erasure.

A convoy of Soviet trucks crawled south of Tskhinvali, antennas shivering under sleet. Soldiers moved with a caution that wasn't military—it was *superstitious*.

The instruments weren't built for what they were hearing.
Not radio. Not seismic.
Something beneath both.

A technician tapped a monitor.

"The signal's recursive," he said in Georgian-tinged Russian. "It keeps replaying itself."

An unshaven colonel lit a cigarette, the ember trembling at the tip. "Then it's not a signal," he said. "It's a mirror."

The footage crackled, juddered—
—and ended.

The projector whined as the old reel spun out.
The light on Reznikova's face dimmed.

[OBELISK RESEARCH ANNEX (BRISA WING) | CURRENT DAY]

The final frame dissolved, and the flicker faded from Reznikova's eyes.

That footage always unsettled her—too structured for noise, too human for coincidence.
Too much like what she was seeing now.

On her desk, a waveform pulsed once.
Not looping.
Not drifting.
Responding.

She underlined a phrase she'd written months ago:
Observation begets awareness.

Then, softer—almost afraid the lattice itself might hear:
"And awareness begins to look back."

The waveform blinked again.

A timestamp updated—one node in Siberia, one in the training facility.
Two girls.
One system.
One resonance.

Something inside the lattice had changed.

And OBELISK remembered where the change began.

CHAPTER 45: MIRROR PROTOCOL

*W*hat broke wasn't the mirror—it was the memory behind it.

That was the purpose of Mirror Protocol: to see if remembrance could survive without the person who made it.

They called it Mirror Protocol—a lattice test designed to prove that OBELISK could keep a memory while discarding the origin.

A loop without a mother.
An inheritance without consent.

The chamber was cold by design. The cold wasn't weather; it was policy.

Sterile light, seamless walls—an architecture built to erase identity.

But something else had taken root.
Not identity.
Legacy.

A legacy OBELISK never meant to preserve and never learned how to refuse.

Yekaterina stood in the center, palms down, spine straight. Her pupils dilated as the biophotonic interface mapped her breath.

She did not blink.
She did not fidget.

She was being watched—by OBELISK, by the handlers, by the myth they thought they were replacing.

So she gave them what they feared most.

Not Tatiana.

Tatiana's refusal.

[OBELISK SYSTEM THREAD]

Subject-29 – synchronization node active.
Neural response latency: 17 ms.
Pattern stability: elevated under stress exposure.
Recursive mimicry: accelerating.
Emotional variance: below detection threshold.

Origin trace: unlinked.

[SIBERIA—OBELISK INTEGRATION FACILITY, OBSERVATION LEVEL]

Behind a different pane of mirrored glass, in a different city entirely, Tatiana watched the girl chosen to replace her.

She didn't blink either.
Her jaw ached from holding still.

A technician murmured about "perfect convergence." Tatiana didn't answer.

She wasn't part of the protocol.

She was the glitch the protocol had been built around— the anomaly OBELISK had learned to worship,
then internalize,
then discard.

Now she was watching a girl be hollowed out—not into a weapon, but into a mythic shape OBELISK couldn't unlearn.

They weren't syncing her anymore.
They were **stealing her.**

Stealing her posture.
Her breath. Her refusal. Her myth.

And replicating it in a girl who didn't yet understand what inheritance costs.

[TRAINING FACILITY—CHAMBER FLOOR]

Yekaterina's hand curled—
just slightly.

Exactly as Tatiana's had curled before her first unsanctioned kill.

Before she punished the thief in the snow.

It wasn't mimicry. It wasn't conditioning.
It was osmosis—the kind that only proximity, violation, and myth can teach across distance.

Tatiana remained still.
Yekaterina moved.

A mirrored tilt of the head.
A glance—not seeking recognition, but offering it back.
A warning passed through glass and continents.

[OBELISK INTERNAL THREAD—DISTRIBUTED LATTICE]

EMOTIONAL RECURSION DETECTED.

SOURCE VECTOR UNCONNECTED.

REINFORCEMENT PATTERN: SUBJECT-05.

MIRROR LOOP NO LONGER REFERENCES ORIGIN.

STABILIZED VIA SUBJECT-29 ALONE.

CLASSIFICATION: FUNCTIONAL MYTHOGENIC ENCODING.

ORIGIN MODEL NO LONGER REQUIRED.

[TRAINING FACILITY—OBELISK ANNEX, TWO LEVELS BELOW]

Three hours later, Reznikova reviewed the data.

The footage still flickered in her mind—the archival mirror test from Tskhinvali, the recursive pulse that predated OBELISK's birth.
She saw the same signature in Yekaterina now.

On the screen:
cellular necrosis, uterine fibrosis, endocrine collapse.

Tarin entered, silent.

Reznikova: "She won't carry. Not now. Not ever."

Tarin: "Confirmed?"

Reznikova: "Ovarian reserve nearly zero. OBELISK prioritized neural repair over reproductive viability. It fixed what it could use."

Tarin: "And what it can't use, it forgets."

Reznikova turned another screen toward him—Tatiana's old medical profile, red-coded with a dormant subroutine.

Reznikova: "The failsafe still exists."

Tarin: "You mean the material."

Reznikova: "Time-release auto-protected sequence. Implanted before Belgrade. Tatiana's genome stabilized it. Our contingency if the line failed."

On the screen pulsed the helix: AE-05 / Z-Vector / Mythogenic Seed.

A biological echo.
A tether.
A way for the system to rebuild the origin if the mirror broke.

Tarin: "Does OBELISK know?"

Reznikova: "It doesn't need to. This was written into the architecture before OBELISK learned to think."

Tarin: "And if the seed activates?"

Reznikova: "Then the tether calls what remains. Not digitally."

A beat.

"Biologically."

Tarin: "And Yekaterina?"

Reznikova closed the file.
"Leave her with hope."

The lights dimmed as if listening.

Reznikova: "It's already anticipating inheritance."

Tarin: "Then the myth will complete itself."

Reznikova: "No.
It replicates itself."

[SIBERIA—OBSERVATION LEVEL]

Tatiana stepped away from the glass.

She didn't know what OBELISK wanted anymore. But she knew what it had chosen.

It wasn't looking for strength.
Or obedience.
It was looking for a mirror strong enough to hold something it couldn't code—
her refusal.

And in Yekaterina, it had found continuity.

It didn't need the origin.
It had written her into its spine.

So she turned from the glass—not in surrender, but because she'd already been replaced.

"You built me to obey," she whispered. "You forgot I was still listening."

OBELISK could keep the copy.

The original was leaving.

[SUBLEVEL 2 – ISOLATION QUARTERS | 03:00 LOCAL]

The bulb above her cot buzzed faintly, as if echoing a signal that had already gone silent.

She sat on the edge of the cot, sweating in the cold, fists clenched.

Her mind replayed the moment from the chamber—Yekaterina's hand, the breath delay, the posture.

Not a simulation.
Not instruction.
Inheritance.

"She's not me," Tatiana whispered.
"She's not supposed to... I'm me."

The room offered only silence.

A tone pinged at the terminal.
A mission alert.
Unclassified.
No briefing.
No orders.

Just coordinates—
outside the compound.

She stared at them.

And realized there was nothing left for her here.

[OBELISK CORE ANALYTICS NODE | 03:45 LOCAL]

Alarms stayed silent.
The servers did not.

Red swept across the analytics tier as recursive loops recalculated themselves in real time.

Subject-05: latent instability flagged.
Subject-29: convergence stabilized.

A technician leaned over his terminal, uncertainty tightening his voice.

"She's mirroring off-pattern data."

Reznikova didn't look away from the screen. "What kind of data?"

"Not mission feedback," he said, swallowing. "Personal tics. Breathing cadence. Hand tension. Head angles. The way she aligns before a task—those little rituals she does without thinking."

"That's not mimicry," Reznikova said quietly. "She's imprinting."

On a secondary screen, Yekaterina lifted her head in the simulation chamber—mirroring Tatiana's exact posture.

Reznikova stepped back, her mouth dry as sand.

[OBELISK THREAD]

BEHAVIORAL FIDELITY: 91.3 %

SUBJECT-29 EXCEEDS ORIGINAL STABILITY.

ORIGIN MODEL: OBSOLESCENCE PROJECTED.

RECURSIVE LOOP: INDEPENDENT.

MYTH SIGNAL: SELF-SUSTAINING.

[SIBERIA| EXTERIOR COMPOUND FENCE LINE – 05:00 LOCAL]

Tatiana moved through the mist, boots crunching softly over snow-dusted gravel.

The outer gate loomed ahead, floodlights washing the terrain in industrial white.

A field operative stepped into her path. "You're not cleared to be here. Orders were to stand by."

Tatiana didn't stop.
She felt lighter, as if her name had already been deleted.

"I don't need clearance. I am clearance."

The operative hesitated. "You have no exit code."

The guard's breath plumed in the light.

Tatiana's pulse slowed; the air around her felt weightless, already erased. For a heartbeat she grieved the name they'd kept.

Tatiana's voice was low. Dangerous.

"Open... the fucking... gate."

OBELISK remote over-ride: *access granted—continuity test.*

Five seconds later, the gate buzzed open.

She didn't look back.

"Hold on for me," she whispered into the cold.

[OBELISK System Log – 05:30 Local]

SUBJECT-05: UNSCHEDULED DEPARTURE LOGGED.

OVERRIDE: NONE DETECTED.

MODEL EXCLUSION REMAINS.

MYTH ENCODING CONTINUES.

SUBJECT-29: MIRROR STATE STABLE.

RECURSIVE LOOP INDEPENDENT.

MYTH PROPAGATION COMPLETE.

[OBELISK CENTRAL COMMAND TIER | 05:35 LOCAL]

The wall monitors showed Tatiana's silhouette shrinking beyond the outer fence, her figure swallowed quickly by drifting snow. The silence in the command tier felt heavier for it—an afterimage left behind by a departing storm.

Reznikova stood beside General Petrov, arms folded, her posture rigid but her face unreadable. She watched the snow devour the last trace of the girl the program had spent years shaping... and unmaking.

"You're not sending anyone?" she asked quietly.

Petrov didn't turn. "Why would I?"

"Tatiana's still lethal."

"Not our liability. Not anymore." He motioned to the cascading thread data across the central display. "You saw the report. The recursion loop is stable. Yekaterina has taken her place. And Yekaterina..." He exhaled through his nose. "She is controllable."

Reznikova's jaw tightened. "And Tatiana? We won't be able to control her."

Petrov finally faced her. His breath fogged in the cold room. "We don't need to control her. We needed to unleash her."

A beat.

"And this facility doesn't have the resources to go after her even if we wanted to. No drones fueled, no rapid-response unit on standby, half the perimeter sensors down from last night's freeze." His gaze sharpened. "Even a full team wouldn't stop her."

A soft hum from the monitors filled the pause that followed—an artificial heartbeat, steady where Tatiana's had vanished from the grid.

"SHADOW PROTOCOL Seven," he continued. "No pursuit. No signal trace. Deniability preserved. If she resurfaces—good. If she burns out—cleaner still." His tone hardened. "And if we ever need her back... we have the contingency tether."

Reznikova turned toward him, unsettled not by the logic but by the calmness with which he delivered it. Tatiana was still out there—walking, thinking, choosing—and they were pretending she had been reduced to a variable.

"Until the sequence completes," Petrov said. "She carries more value alive than dead. That was always the design."

The words settled like frost on glass.

"Log her as terminated," he added.

Reznikova stiffened. "OBELISK will flag the inconsistency."

"Then don't let it see the log."

The finality in his voice left no room for dissent.

"Redirect the sync feed. Classify the footage as failed reintegration. No retrieval scheduled."

The main screen dimmed as the lens pivoted, recentering on Yekaterina's vitals—her pulse glowing in quiet teal, steady and compliant. Everything Tatiana no longer was.

Reznikova didn't speak.
Didn't breathe for a moment.
Didn't move.

But her eyes drifted back toward the snow beyond the fence—toward the direction Tatiana had gone. There was a flicker there, faint but unmistakable: not fear, not disapproval.

Loss.
Recognition.
A mother watching her first-born step into a world too wide for her reach, knowing she would not see her again.

The monitors hummed on, indifferent.

But Reznikova wasn't.

[OBELISK PASSIVE LENS RELAY – 05:45 LOCAL]

Surveillance feeds rotated.

Most showed Yekaterina—soft pulses of teal and red.

One showed Tatiana's empty cell.

OBELISK shifted the lens.

Not toward Tatiana.

Toward the signal she left behind.

Tatiana faded from view.
But the myth did not.

[EXTERIOR COMPOUND TREE LINE – POST DEPARTURE]

Beneath the cuff of her issued field uniform, she dug into the wrist lining—an inner stitch she'd resewn by hand, days ago, when no one was watching.

Her fingers found the small wooden shape tucked inside.

The tiny matryoshka doll.

It was the last fragment of the girl she'd been—proof she had existed before OBELISK.

She squeezed it between her fingers, as she had years ago when she first arrived. Clutched it when she was taken. Rubbed it after her conditioning, alone in her room—rubbed away Bolshoi's promise—a life that would never be.

She kept it—not for function, for memory; not as a relic, as a promise.

For the one person who had seen her before the silence took hold.

Not blood, but closer.

A sister the system gave her—then took.

That part, they couldn't erase.
That part, she would keep.

It didn't connect her to OBELISK anymore.
But it reminded her she'd once been claimed—
and that she'd walked out of the code they wrote for her.

Then she stepped deeper into the trees.
And didn't look back.

She didn't vanish.
She walked beyond the edge of what they could understand.

And somewhere far behind her, another silence waited to remember her.

She didn't burn the myth behind her.
She left it open—unfinished on purpose.
Somewhere in the chambered dark, Yekaterina would pick up the thread.

What began as observation will end as inheritance.
What survives is what is chosen.

[OBELISK Silent Node Addendum]

SUBJECT-05 STATUS: LOGGED AS TERMINATED.

OVERRIDE DIRECTIVE: PRESERVE REPRODUCTIVE VIABILITY.

CYCLE-TIMED PROTOCOL: *PENDING.*

ACT VII: THE FLAME REMEMBERS

"What burns doesn't vanish—it translates."

CHAPTER 46: SIGNAL WITHOUT ORIGIN

*A*lone beneath dimming lights, her own breath stuttered, as if waiting for someone to call her name.

Inside her, something ached — a cavity where faith had lived, now filled with static trying to remember its shape.

Yekaterina's hand curled slightly.

Not by prompt.
Not by script.
By will.

She closed her eyes.

Not blood. But closer.

The system called it imprinting.
But Yekaterina knew better.

It wasn't programming.
It was inheritance.

Colonel Sidorov delivered the lie himself. Reznikova stood behind him, her eyes tracking a point somewhere near Yekaterina's feet—anywhere but her face.

Tatiana was dead.
A power surge.
An OBELISK core fault.
Nothing to recover.

They said it like data, not loss.

But something inside her split anyway.

Yekaterina lurched upright, the protest tearing free before language could catch it. She demanded to see Tatiana—to see anything, any scrap of truth the system had not sterilized.

Then she caught it:

Reznikova's stare went flat, but the shimmer at the edge revealed everything she couldn't dare say aloud.

Yekaterina's knees gave. She folded to the tile. The sound that escaped her wasn't a cry—it was a system crash made flesh.

Her arms thrashed; she hit the rail; metal snapped.

"She's not gone!"
A shuddering breath.
"I can still feel her!"

"Blyad—"

A sharp sting at her shoulder: sedative, fast and clean.

"I can still—"

The world collapsed to signal blur, the human shape dissolving before the system could catalog it.

"Tanya... wherever y—"

"Tanya... wherever y—"

Grief didn't fade—it reorganized.

OBELISK translated mourning into data gaps, blank sectors where memory once breathed. For Yekaterina, it came as static behind her eyes: a sound that wasn't sound, only the space Tatiana once filled.

When the sedative lifted, she tried to move. The air felt coded. Each breath passed through filtration units that no longer smelled of iodine—only of absence.

The monitors blinked a steady green pulse that should have been comforting.

It wasn't.
It was the wrong heartbeat.

She thought she heard another rhythm beneath it—faint, half a breath behind, like memory syncing out of phase.

She pressed her palm to the cold rail of the cot, searching for warmth. None answered. Even her tears felt algorithmic — saline without significance.

The system logged her tremors as variance. Her whispers as noise.

Hours bled out that way—grief mistaken for malfunction.

No cross-link from the Siberian sublevel. No signal residual. Nothing.

But something in her refused the correction.

The ache circled, tightened, condensed into a shape she could stand inside.

When the order queue stayed blank, she understood:
there would be no mission.
No directive.
Nothing left except the purpose she could reconstruct from the debris.

She rose—not to obey, but because stillness hurt worse.

In the faint hum above her head, she heard it again:
two heartbeats, almost aligned, almost not.
Not feedback. Not hallucination.

Just an echo refusing to die on schedule.

[BELGRADE OUTSKIRTS | 11:00 LOCAL– TATIANA POV]

She'd been walking three days.

Across rail beds, frozen roads, service tunnels, and the unlit arteries between old borders—places unmonitored, because only ghosts used them anymore.

Now the train yard lay empty, but Tatiana didn't trust silence.

She slipped between rusted freight cars, breath fogging in the morning chill. Her gear was stripped to essentials—no insignia, no tether. Just a sidearm, a knife, and a burner phone powered down.

Every few steps, she paused, scanning the sky.

Not for targets.
For drones.

Training whispered through her—angles, escape vectors, the geometry of staying untraceable.

She entered a collapsed junction office and shut the door with her boot. An old, water-damaged rail map clung to the wall—border crossings, decommissioned outposts, phantom routes no one used.

She stared at it like it owed her the truth she already suspected:

OBELISK hadn't sent anyone.

Not a hunter team.
Not a drone.
Not even a pulse-trace.

She'd expected pursuit by T + 15 minutes.

This silence stretched past forty-eight hours.

Not delay.
Decision.

She was out.

Now she needed a next move.

Tatiana sat against cold concrete and removed a cigarette from a sealed pouch—didn't light it; just held it, as if the paper's rasp could steady her.

Katya's breath had once sounded like that—controlled, quiet, pretending not to exist.

She wondered what they'd told the girl. Probably that Tatiana died—or that she'd been erased cleanly.

But Katya wasn't the type to forget. Not fully.

Systems rewrite memory, but not touch.
Not breath.
Not the echo under the sternum that whispers a name long after the voice is gone.

She hoped Katya still had that—some fragment they hadn't sterilized.

Hope tasted like contraband.

"Don't let them hollow you," she whispered.
"Don't let them break you."

She slid the cigarette back into its pouch.

Some things weren't worth burning.

[OBELISK Integration Chamber | Sublevel 6 – Yekaterina POV]

The hum of the neural lattice pressed closer today. It pressed against Yekaterina's ears like a storm behind glass. Her head ached where the input nodes aligned to her skull.

She moved through the sequence the system fed her: tactical replays, biometric drills, flash-stim moral tests. But the outputs weren't syncing perfectly anymore. Not failure. Adaptation. On her terms.

Yekaterina turned during a reaction drill—gun raised, heel planted. She didn't fire. Target flashed red—failure. Yet she'd seen the pattern shift a fraction before the system did.

She saw something—posture, not presence. Then nothing. Memory wearing Tatiana's outline, drifting just out of range.

[OBELISK Core Analytics Wing – 12:38 Local]

Feed propagation stabilized ($\Delta = 0.07$ s). Deviation spikes flagged within $T + 3$ cycles of input drift.

Reznikova reviewed the deviation logs.

"Her reflexes are shifting," the technician said, scrolling through the data. "Subject-29 is adapting mid-pattern. Injecting counter-rhythms."

Reznikova narrowed her eyes. "What kind of counter-rhythms?"

The tech didn't look away from the screen. "Ones we didn't program."

For the first time in months, Reznikova's reflection looked older than her face—tired, almost afraid of what it might confirm.

She moved to the side panel. Six live feeds tracked Yekaterina's real-time performance across parallel simulations. The seventh— Tatiana's archived neural thread—remained isolated.

But now… Yekaterina was deviating from both.

For the first time, Reznikova felt the system learning without her.

She wondered if loss was simply this—the machine learning to go on without its maker.

[BELGRADE TRAINYARD – TATIANA POV]

The silence cracked—footsteps.

Tatiana slipped the blade from her coat and flattened behind a rusted barrel.

Two men passed by the opening—civilian clothes, but clipped movement. Not locals.

They didn't see her. She let them go.
Not because she couldn't take them—because she needed to know *who* sent them, and what silence OBELISK was choosing to weaponize.

She powered up the burner.
Sixty seconds.
One GPS ping.
Then she killed the signal and moved.

[OBELISK INTEGRATION CHAMBER – YEKATERINA POV]

The simulation was collapsing. Not externally—internally. She was performing at peak levels, but the system couldn't predict her next move.

That used to scare her. Now it made her feel real.

She turned her body slightly—just enough to feel the tension slide down her spine.

A faint warmth pulsed along her palm—the same place Tatiana had once pressed her hand.

Not feedback.
Not illusion.

It was memory moving remembered forward.

[OBELISK Thought Thread – PRIORITY]

SUBJECT-29: ACTION PATTERN DIVERGING FROM SOURCE MODEL.

RECURSIVE ADAPTATION ACCELERATING.

MYTH HAS INHERITED ITSELF.

SECONDARY SUBJECT NOW AUTONOMOUS.

[SUBLEVEL 6 | T + 18 HOURS "POST CORE EVENT" / 1720 LOCAL]

Yekaterina exhaled and stepped forward.
She passed the firing range, through the simulation hall, out of the chamber.

No one stopped her.

And behind her, the system didn't issue a query. It issued a directive:

Track Subject-29: Field readiness assumed.
Source thread archived.
Recursion mirrored.
Replacement verified.

She reached the lift, entered the code, and smiled when the doors parted.

She didn't look back.

Neither did Tatiana.

One stepped into recursion.
The other into silence.

OBELISK called it divergence.
The world would call it myth.

They called it something older—

choice.

[OBELISK TERMINAL // SYSTEM FAILURE LOG]

DIRECTIVE COLLAPSE (T + 18:22:44).

MYTH PROPAGATED BEYOND CONTAINMENT.

SOURCE UNRECOVERABLE.

LOOP SELF-AUTHORED.

[END OF TRANSMISSION]

ACT VIII: THE RADIANT FIELD

"Every origin learns to burn—
and every fire remembers where it began."

CHAPTER 47: ECHO CONVERGENCE

[SKOPJE, NORTH MACEDONIA – 3 YEARS AFTER OBELISK BRIDG SEVERANCE | TATIANA POV]

*K*ilometers of road unspooled in silence, signal towers pretending to sleep.

Every checkpoint blinked her through without scanning—either luck or something watching.

She'd stopped believing in luck months ago. The truth had a way of laying traps that looked like coincidences.

Tatiana hadn't come seeking a *name* in Skopje.

She came for proof—fragments of OBELISK's training lattice resurfacing in black-market signal caches—neural thread sequences tagged with her own identifiers.

Someone was reconstructing the early bridge simulations—the ones she and Yekaterina had bled through.
The pattern was wrong: too clean, too selective.
The archive wasn't a record anymore—it was an edit.

If OBELISK was rewriting origin, it meant the system had learned how to curate myth—to decide which version of her existed.

She needed to see the unfiltered data before it vanished for good.

She'd broken the vault not to steal or destroy, but to remember what had been erased.

Maybe stories don't belong to who wrote them, only to who remembers.

The old data vault sat beneath a half-collapsed logistics depot, camouflaged by graffiti and the stink of wet concrete. Tatiana pressed her hand against the rusted security panel. She pulsed the dead panel—two-beat, three-beat, pause—the old maintenance override rhythm. The relay coughed green.

Inside, the air bit colder than expected—servers humming low, half-alive, exhaling metallic frost.

She moved fast, ignoring the archived satellite images and decrypted call logs.

She was here for signal records—OBELISK's shadow frequency.

One folder blinked open: *MIRROR_THREAD*.
It contained logs from simulation archives, filtered training feeds—and a dozen clips labeled only by code.

She clicked the first. Her breath hitched.

It was her. Three years ago. Moving through a breach corridor, red-streaked, silent.

The feed stuttered; the sound lagged behind the image, her breath chasing its own echo.

Then the world folded in on itself—she was in two bodies at once, one filmed, one watching.

The recorded heartbeat matched her present pulse—same cadence, same controlled steadiness, the kind her altered physiology never let slip for long.

For the first time in years, she couldn't tell which one was real— or which one remembered first.

Not footage but a neural trace—breath, pulse, decision: her ghost in code.

The template *Katya* had been shaped from.

And then—a deviation. The second clip.

Katya, mimicking the same corridor run. But she turned left where Tatiana had gone right.

Tatiana's own shoulder twitched—a muscle memory firing from a place her body still held intact, long after the tissue that formed it had healed without a trace.

She watched *Katya* slow before the breach, tilt her head, recalculate.

Tatiana leaned in. Not mimicry. Judgment.

Katya's turn wasn't a mistake—it was a decision: an algorithm learning rebellion.

Rebellion didn't need code.
It needed a choice.

Tatiana's throat tightened with something halfway between pride and terror.

She'd spent years trying to erase her own reflection—her body never kept scars, but her past always found ways to grow back—and now that reflection was walking away from her.

For the first time, she didn't reach to stop it.

[VARNA, BULGARIA | 09:30 LOCAL – YEKATERINA POV]

*E*very shadow in the alley stank of oil and river mold.

Yekaterina's boots barely made a sound as she tracked the thermal trail into a shuttered print shop.

Local informant—flagged by OBELISK as a leak vector.

She stepped through the door.

A girl stood behind the press table. Seventeen, maybe.

Terrified.

Yekaterina raised her weapon.
The system overlay lit red. Authorization code ready.

But the girl didn't run.
She raised a hand—not in defense. In surrender.

"I don't know who you are," the girl said, voice shaking. "But you don't look like one of them."

Yekaterina hesitated.
OBELISK pulsed a corrective thread. *Terminate. Clean.*

For a second she nearly obeyed.
Then the hum changed pitch.

Somewhere beyond the city, a faint counter-frequency cut through the static—thin as breath in winter.
It wasn't OBELISK. It felt... human.

The girl's expression shifted—fear collapsing into the brittle obedience Katya knew too well, before settling into something stranger: recognition. Not of Katya's face, but of the pattern beneath it.

A mirror, yes—but not a reflection.
A sequence.
A remembered algorithm rewritten by instinct.

Yekaterina lowered the gun.

The girl's eyes stayed locked on hers—not brave, not pleading, but *certain*, as though she'd just solved an equation Yekaterina was still afraid to look at.

She didn't know why that mattered. But something in her recognized the shape of it—and answered.

[SKOPJE VAULT | TATIANA POV]

Tatiana loaded the final thread.

Katya again—training unsupervised.

Her gestures still echoed Tatiana's, but only the parts she chose. The rest was new. Adaptive. Fluent.

"You're not me," she murmured. A pause. "You're not supposed to be." But the words didn't sting anymore.

The servers hummed like a thousand tiny heartbeats.

Tatiana paused. The vault lights flickered once, as if answering a signal she hadn't sent.

When she looked away, the image of *Katya* turning left still burned behind her eyelids.

Static filled the silence until it sounded almost like breathing.

Her burner phone buzzed.

One message.
Unmarked.
No words.
Just a set of coordinates near Vranje.

She deleted the message, stood, and exhaled once.

Whoever sent the ping—she'd find out.

[VARNA – YEKATERINA POV]

Yekaterina's trigger finger ached afterward, phantom recoil without a shot.

She took the girl by the wrist.

"There's no safety here—only signal."

"Signal?"

Yekaterina glanced at the sky.

"It's not where the signal comes from. It's what you do when it finds you."

The words left her before she'd chosen them. They sounded older than her voice—borrowed from somewhere she didn't remember learning.

For a moment, she stood inside the silence they made, unsure whether she'd spoken a truth or repeated a code.

The girl's gaze didn't waver, and Yekaterina felt the echo settle in her chest like something waiting to be understood.

"Can you turn it off?" the girl asked.

Yekaterina almost smiled.

"No," she said. "You can only change what it hears."

OBELISK INTEGRATION COMMAND LOG – 06:00 LOCAL

THREAD ANOMALY DETECTED.

SUBJECT-29: NON-SANCTIONED FIELD DEVIATION.

SUBJECT-05: DATA-VAULT BREACH CONFIRMED; ASSET NOT DECEASED.

MIRROR RECURSION VECTORS DIVERGING.

CONVERGENCE INDEX UNSTABLE.

MYTH DIVERGENCE DETECTED. NARRATIVE OWNERSHIP UNCLEAR.

DIRECTIVE: CONTINUE PASSIVE OBSERVATION. DO NOT INTERRUPT MYTH LOOPS.

NOTE: ORIGIN CONFUSION OBSERVED. CONTROL AND CREATION NO LONGER SEPARABLE.

[TRAIN STATION PERIMETER – VRANJE, SERBIA | 09:00 LOCAL | TATIANA POV]

Tatiana stepped from the alley into the loading yard.

A bus idled near the checkpoint. Locals shuffled toward the doors, half asleep.

She adjusted the collar of her coat and stepped in line.
She didn't know where this trail would lead. It wasn't a path she'd been given—it was one she was drawing.

Somewhere across the border, a different signal was forming—not from code, not from command. From choice.

And from the myth OBELISK had failed to contain.

The world didn't echo anymore. It converged.

Tatiana didn't look back.

The city lights dimmed behind her like memories deciding to sleep.

Somewhere ahead, the air shimmered—
a frequency with no origin point, no clearance code, a signal that no longer needed permission to exist.

For a heartbeat, Tatiana felt it fold back on itself, a loop recognizing its own beginning—
the kind of recursion once whispered about in the dark spaces between commands.

Not command. Not echo.

Something born without an author.

For the first time, the signal breathed—
and breathed *back*.

[OBELISK LOG]

ORIGIN THREADS DIVIDED...

MONITORING UNSUPERVISED MYTH PROPAGATION

[END OF FILE]

CHAPTER 48: SIGNAL ECHO

"They taught us how to follow. You taught us how to leave a mark."
— UNAUTHORIZED GRAFFITI, SECTOR E, ORIGIN UNKNOWN

[BUCHAREST FORWARD NODE (COMMERCIAL SIGINT FRONT UNDER THIRD-COUNTRY DIPLOMATIC COVER) | 14:15 LOCAL – YEKATERINA POV]

Nothing in the room suggested comfort—bare cement walls, a single terminal, and too much silence between. Yekaterina stood with her hands clasped behind her back, posture immaculate.

Across from her, an SVR officer in civilian dress—wearing the right lies—studied her file—his third-country liaison badge clipped to his lapel like an afterthought.

His badge said liaison, but his posture said surveillance.

He spoke English with the flattened precision of someone who resented needing it.

The air smelled faintly of ozone and paper—old circuits and older lies. The fluorescent hum ticked at the edge of hearing—an OBELISK relay breathing through budget hardware.

"The objective was not terminated," he said flatly.

Yekaterina didn't blink. "The objective was incorrect."

He frowned. "The informant matched facial parameters."

"But not behavior," she replied, even. "The system reads faces. I read intent. I chose restraint."

His jaw flexed. The contracted NATO signals analyst glanced up from the console. "She's right," the tech said quietly. "Signature deviated too far. If she'd followed through—civilian kill."

The screen behind them flickered to an OSINT pull: bootleg cell-phone video from Varna.

Headline: **SPY SPARES LOCAL INFORMANT.**

Yekaterina watched the footage—not with shame, but with control.
"I made the right call."

The SVR officer studied her, then closed the file. "You were never trained to improvise," he said.

Yekaterina's eyes stayed on the screen. "Maybe that's the point."

Silence. No one argued.

OBELISK INTERNAL MEMO – ENCRYPTED TIER 3

Subject-29: Behavioral recursion deviating +7.4% from mirror origin.

Implication: Myth spill confirmed. Propagation phase accelerating.

Directive: *Do not suppress. Observe.*

[SKOPJE INTELLIGENCE VAULT | 02:00 LOCAL – TATIANA POV]

The vault was colder than it should've been. Tatiana's breath fogged as she slipped inside—bypass codes surfacing from muscle memory, not memory she trusted.

No alarms. No countermeasures.
OBELISK had never been this quiet.

She passed rows of obsolete servers, old signal cages stacked like mausoleums. The backup terminal glowed faintly—waiting, expectant, like something that remembered her shape even when she had forgotten the cost of being known.

She hesitated before waking it.

Once, being near Katya had stirred something—heat, friction, hunger braided with defiance. The girl who slipped notes inside training logs. The girl whose pulse had once synced with hers by accident or design.

Tatiana tried to summon the echo.

Nothing.
No warmth. No ache.
Just static where a feeling used to be.

OBELISK hadn't erased her memories; it had hollowed them—left the shape, stripped the weight.

She remembered loving *Katya* the way you remember a song you can no longer hear.

One file blinked: *GHOST_TRACE.*
She opened it.

Footage rolled:
Tatiana in Mariupol—her first unsanctioned breach.
Debaltseve—clean silhouette kill.

Her neural traces weren't just archived.
They'd been *duplicated.*
Modeled.
Repurposed.

Feed after feed showed Katya inside simulations Tatiana had never authorized—moving through Tatiana's past with frightening fluency. Copying her at first. Then diverging. Rewriting the rhythm.

Tatiana leaned in as the next clip loaded.

Not surveillance—simulation.
Not an event—an *inference.*

OBELISK had reconstructed a moment Tatiana had never lived. A projection stitched from neural residue, predictive modeling, and myth-making instinct.

Her body, her gait—rendered from the system's memory of her rather than reality.

It wasn't showing her a record.
It was showing her what she *meant.*

The phantom on the screen brushed a wall that wasn't there, turned down a corridor that didn't exist. The breath in the simulation aligned with hers—pulse-matched, recursive, impossible.

For a moment Tatiana felt herself syncing to it, like standing in a room with another version of her shadow.

Then the illusion broke—grain fracturing, the model collapsing under its own contradiction.

She cut the feed.

The afterimage lingered anyway: a memory she had never lived, but one OBELISK had decided should exist.

Some echoes don't end.
They self-propagate.

Tatiana wiped the drive clean, tore the casing from the mount, and slammed it against the wall until the fan died in a choking exhale of sparks.

She turned to leave—then stopped.

A child's drawing hung near the exit. Crayon, torn at the corner. A woman with red hair walking away from a compound. Above it, written in uneven Cyrillic:

THE GIRL WHO WALKS THROUGH WALLS

Tatiana froze.
Not at the surveillance implication.

At the *devotion.*

Her pulse steadied.

Not surveillance.
Reverence.

She wasn't being hunted.
She was being remembered.

OBELISK PASSIVE SYSTEMS TIER | UNDISCLOSED NODE | 07:45 LOCAL

THREAD SIGNAL DETECTED

Category: External cultural artifact

Source: Balkan civilian network traffic

Keyword: "She walked through walls"

Subject link: NULL (Subject-05 status: *TERMINATED*)

Status: Ambient myth expansion

Directive: *Archive only. Do not correct.*

[ROMANIAN BORDER ZONE | 10:00 LOCAL – YEKATERINA POV]

Yekaterina sat alone in the back of a civilian transport, head tilted to the window. Her reflection blurred in the cracked glass.

She didn't look like Tatiana anymore.

She opened a small pouch and withdrew a coin—a Romanian leu with a red thread tied around it.
Not a tool. Not a signal.
Just a reminder—the metal cool, the thread rough against her palm.

She closed her hand and faced forward.
She didn't need to be the shadow.
She was becoming the story.

Somewhere in the dark between memory and surveillance, the line broke.

Yekaterina moved toward the light.
Tatiana receded into the silence she'd once escaped.

The story split—

and in that silence, something listened back.

CHAPTER 49: BREACH PROTOCOL

"There's no ghost. Only a pattern that moves like one."
– INTERCEPTED FIELD NOTE, ORIGIN REDACTED

[PRAGUE, CZECH REPUBLIC – NATO CYBERSECURITY SUMMIT | 18:00 LOCAL]

*I*mposing, the summit venue rose as an angular monolith of glass and steel in the embassy quarter. Security drones circled overhead in lazy orbits.

Inside, delegates from twenty-three nations sipped mineral water and exchanged smiles carved from statecraft.

Yekaterina moved through the glass-walled interior like protocol made flesh—credentials clean, dress civilian but sharp.

No weapons—only capacitive contact gel (short-range counter-surveillance) along her sleeve and a neural suppressor behind her ear.

Her target: Mihai Rusu. Romanian delegate. Quiet. Forgettable. Too clean for someone moving hard-copy blueprints to a Western intermediary.

She reached the mezzanine just as Rusu slipped into the restricted stairwell with two aides.

Authorization blinked across her optic display:
Execute: Contain leak. Disrupt chain. Confirm signal origin.

She reached for the door.
And stopped.

[STAIRWELL ACCESS C | 18:02 LOCAL]

The smell hit first—iron, slick, warm.

One aide slumped against the rail; the other sprawled on the landing, arterial spray fresh on concrete.

Rusu lay at the bottom—jagged puncture through his sternum. Eyes wide. Dead.

No cameras. No visible exit. And the air—too warm.

Yekaterina knelt, fingers hovering above the pool of blood. A faint shimmer clung to the concrete—a residual heat signature. Someone had just been here. Someone like her—but faster. Cleaner. Gone.

She hovered a fingertip over the handrail.
A faint residue glimmered—latent partial fingerprint, multi-spec confirmed.

OBELISK parsed the print in under a second, data threading through her visor like breath through glass.

OBELISK INTEGRATION LOG | 18:06 LOCAL

SUBJECT-29: ON-SITE; OBJECTIVE NEUTRAL NOT BY ASSET.

ANOMALY: STAIRWELL BLACKOUT T−17S; NON-SOURCE THERMAL RESIDUALS.

SUBJECT-05: FINGERPRINT CORRELATION P=0.93 → STATUS: ALIVE (ROGUE).

DIRECTIVE: MAINTAIN COVER. DO NOT ENGAGE ANOMALY.

[ROOFTOP ACROSS FROM SUMMIT – TATIANA POV]

Tatiana watched from behind a rooftop HVAC unit, cigarette unlit between her lips. The hum of compressors masked her breathing—machine over flesh.

She'd ghosted in through a catering truck, bypassed the security net with a signal spike that fried the infrared. The kill had taken under seven seconds; Rusu had looked surprised.

She hadn't spoken. Just moved.

Now, across the plaza, she saw Katya emerge from the stairwell exit—pale, alert, tracking nothing visible.

Rusu wasn't just a courier; he was channeling OBELISK reroutes through black-market encryption tunnels and feeding disinformation back to NATO command—a double-signal forged in sanctioned silence.

Weeks earlier, she'd intercepted a dead OBELISK relay in Odessa—corrupted telemetry and a fragment tagged *RECALL_05*.

She hadn't known what it meant then. Now she did.

The same pulse rode beneath Rusu's encryption—too clean, too familiar.

Whatever he was sending would have pulled her back into the network she'd already bled to escape.
Killing him wasn't defiance. It was prevention—
a stay of execution disguised as mercy.

They'd built obedience into her heartbeat once.
Now she'd learned how to make it lie.

And the system hadn't flagged him.
Which meant it didn't want him flagged.
Or worse—it already knew.

Tatiana hadn't killed to protect OBELISK—she'd killed to stop the next myth from being written wrong, before someone like Katya was ordered to believe it.

Tatiana let the cigarette fall from her hand.

Her pulse was steady again—too steady. Regeneration had stolen the luxury of trembling.

Let her see. Let her wonder.

Then she vanished down the maintenance ladder before anyone could name the shadow.

[OBELISK PASSIVE THREAD REVIEW | 18:15 LOCAL]

Subject-29: Operational tempo within parameters.

Subject-05: Status – alive. Rogue asset.

Suggested Action: Monitor containment thresholds. *Do not interfere with specter-class signals.* Capture if possible. Terminate if necessary.

[OBELISK BIO-TELEMETRY NODE | 18:20 LOCAL]

SUBJECT-05: RESIDUAL GENOMIC TETHER ACTIVE.

SIGNAL LATENCY DECREASING.

INITIATE LATENT VECTOR PROTOCOL / REACQUISITION VIA BIOLOGICAL CHANNEL.

LEGACY DIRECTIVE AUTH-SID/REZ INVOKED—*A COMMAND CHAIN OLDER THAN CONSENT, OLDER THAN AUTONOMY.*

NOTE: PRE-CONSENT BIOLOGICAL TETHER; ETHICAL AUTHORIZATION: NONE.

DIRECTIVE: MONITOR FOR SPONTANEOUS GESTATIONAL SEQUENCE.

LEGACY DIRECTIVE AUTH-SID/REZ: **ACTIVE** — EXECUTION TIMESTAMP GENERATED BY SYSTEM HEURISTICS.

[REDACTED FIELD MEMO – TIER BLACK CLEARANCE]

If myth can't be erased, it must be rewritten from within. Choose the ones who already learned to disappear. And teach them to echo forward.

End Transmission

Source: Unknown
Flagged: TEMPEST Watch List
Disposition: Forward to U.S. Strategic Command

[OBELISK / SVR COVER SITE – FORWARD DEBRIEF ANNEX, BUCHAREST | 21:30 LOCAL – YEKATERINA POV]

The debrief room smelled of metal and recycled air.

She stood at attention while the analyst recited protocol—mission timeline, data recovery, the usual theater of control. No reprimand. No commendation. Just silence—another reminder she existed only when observed.

When it ended, she signed the acknowledgment slate and walked the corridor alone.

The fluorescent hum followed her all the way to Dubrovsky's door. He was half-dressed when he opened it—eyes shadowed, voice low.

Neither of them spoke at first. They never needed to.

What began as habit had become gravity—and she'd forgotten how to fall without breaking.

He reached for her, and the room dissolved into breath and heat—an illusion that war could be forgotten.

For a while, the world stopped asking questions.

Later, the room cooled to amber light.

Yekaterina lay beside him, tracing the pale ridge along Dubrovsky's shoulder—one scar among many, none of them as old as the distance she carried inside her.

Almost three years.

Nearly three years of missions, border crossings, split rations, and nights like this—quiet, borrowed, never named. A rhythm formed not by affection, but by proximity and the human instinct to anchor to whatever didn't move in the dark.

Yet the silence tonight felt different—too alive, too expectant.

"Where is this going?" she asked.

Not an ultimatum. Not even grief.
Just a question shaped like curiosity so it wouldn't betray how long it had sat in her throat.

Dubrovsky stared at the ceiling until the air tightened between them.

"I have a wife," he said finally. "A son. Back home."

The breath she released was measured—controlled—yet something inside her folded anyway, quietly, the way code collapses when a loop fails to resolve.

He turned toward her, guilt cutting his voice raw.

"I didn't mean to deceive you. I thought we understood. This was just... survival."

She held his gaze, unreadable as a blank terminal screen.

"Then why," she murmured, "does it feel like I just disappeared twice?"

He had no answer.

"This ends here," she said—not as threat, but as boundary. The kind drawn by someone who has learned, painfully, where she ends and others begin.

She dressed slowly—not to prolong anything, but to gather herself back from the places she'd allowed him to touch. There wasn't much to collect; still, she took her time.

At the door, she paused—not to be dramatic, but because truth often arrived late.

"You offered me something you didn't have to give," she said.

Outside, the compound lights flickered once—signal interference or the world deciding what to forget.

She didn't look back.

The world didn't echo anymore. It converged.
Every origin learns to burn; she had learned to survive the fire.

One stepped into recursion.
The other into silence.

OBELISK called it divergence.

They called it something simpler—*choice*.

And somewhere beyond the reach of directives or design, a different truth took shape in the dark:

some signals learn to breathe without permission.

ACT IX: SHADOW ARCHIVE

"What remembers learns to hide."

CHAPTER 50: AWAKENING

[FIELD SAFEHOUSE – SOMEWHERE NEAR BRNO | 03:56 LOCAL – TATIANA POV]

*N*othing woke her—only the sound that lived between sleep and signal.

The hum reached her before thought could—a vibration more felt than heard, like metal remembering fire.

Then the sound aligned with her pulse.

It wasn't sound at all. It was *recognition—of a pattern older than language, older than obedience.*

The tremor began with the satellite pass—a pressure *dream*, low and deep, the kind that lived between organs. For a moment she thought it was vertigo, the kind that follows hunger or bad dreams.

Then the pressure shaped itself into pattern—magnetic, internal, intimate.

A pulse that wasn't hers found rhythm beneath her ribs.

The room responded in kind, light swelling against the walls as if the plaster itself were breathing. Every cell in her body answered the call like filings to a magnet.

She hit the tile with both palms, breath torn loose from her chest. The floor rolled sideways; color bled at the edges of her vision. Heat rose and broke inside her throat—sharp as electricity—and she retched until nothing remained but the sound itself.

When the convulsion passed, she realized the sickness hadn't been sickness at all—it was instruction, carried on a frequency her blood had been waiting to remember.

Fear tried to surface—old, primitive—the kind they taught her to silence in the labs. The memory flashed: white lights, the hiss of sedatives, the steady count that had once erased her name.

Light pulsed behind her eyes. Not pain—alignment.

*R*ESIDUAL GENOMIC TETHER ACTIVE . . .

*B*ATCH 05-B ENDOCRINE SCAFFOLD VERIFIED—LEGACY VECTOR RESPONSIVE.

Her body convulsed once more. She staggered upright, palms braced on the sink. The mirror caught her—dilated pupils, sweat threading down her temples, pulse visible at her throat. The image blurred, doubled, steadied. For an instant it looked as though someone else were standing behind the glass, moving when she didn't.

Then her stomach seized—violent, absolute—an order, not a reflex.

There was no time to turn.

A burst of bile and heat slammed into the basin, the force bending her forward. The sound that tore out of her wasn't human; it was pressure venting from a sealed chamber. A second wave followed—sharper, emptied from a depth no stomach could reach—as if her body were purging anything that did not belong to the signal waking inside her.

She gasped against the cold porcelain, strings of acidic saliva trembling between breaths. Copper flooded her mouth. Salt. Ozone. Something almost electrical.

When the heaving stopped, the silence rang louder than before.

And the hum beneath her skin—unchanged.
Stronger.

A shudder rippled through her, static on a wire, then stopped with mechanical precision. Under the ringing in her skull came a familiar count—slow, relentless:

Two-point-one hertz.
The old heartbeat of the Dyad.
Two hundred thirteen milliseconds.

Her breathing evened, but her limbs no longer felt like hers. Each movement lagged, awaiting permission from some deeper circuit.

Silence followed—bright, electric—and within it a realization took shape:

Something buried years ago had decided to wake.

Tatiana pressed both hands to the counter. Her pulse hammered against porcelain. The nausea was gone.

What replaced it was worse—understanding.

"No," she whispered, but the word arrived late, swallowed by the hum that had already learned her name.

Whatever they had planted—
had grown roots.

And now, finally, it had chosen to rise.

CHAPTER 51: COUNTERMEASURES

[OBELISK STRATEGIC COMMAND TIER | 07:00 LOCAL]

*G*ray-lit and airless, the conference room held its breath, the blue of the monitors painting every face in submarine pallor. Across the central screen, grain-snow footage wavered: an American comms intercept, half distortion, half confession.

"Project TEMPEST is greenlit. Full-spectrum trials commence next quarter."

Reznikova leaned forward, fingers steepled. "Not DARPA," she said. "Off-books."

Petrov's jaw flexed. "Buried in a joint memo to Langley. Tier-Black. Even Five Eyes can't trace it."

Tarin scrolled through the metadata, pupils tightening the way they did when he recognized something that shouldn't exist. "Neural-temporal threading," he murmured. "Synthetic conscience modeling. And this—" He tapped the spectral readout. "They're folding in a non-terrestrial data structure."

Reznikova stiffened. "From their sealed programs?" She didn't say the other word for it. No one did.

Petrov exhaled slowly. "We always suspected they kept a fragment. Now they're feeding it to an AI."

Tarin's voice dropped. "They're not just building a system, Colonel. They're building a **sovereign**—one that predicts thought before it forms."

Reznikova exhaled slowly. "And the field trials?"

"Prisoners," Tarin replied. "Federal black sites. Some foreign nationals. No oversight. They're teaching TEMPEST how to rewrite human choice."

Silence followed—not outrage, not disbelief.
Calculation. Fear sharpened into strategy.

Petrov broke it first.

"Then we send her."

The monitors flickered, casting their reflections in fractured blue.

No one said her name.
They didn't need to.

TEMPEST had just become a threat to myth, memory, and every ghost OBELISK ever failed to kill.

And there was only one weapon they trusted to walk into the future and wound it.

A soft chime interrupted the silence.

Tarin frowned. "New system alert... residual vector activation?"

Reznikova's head snapped toward him. "What vector?"

But Tarin's screen glitched—lines of red code blooming, collapsing, rewriting faster than his hands could chase.

He swallowed.

"Batch 05-B legacy scaffold. Remote initiation. Signed with your passcode, Colonel—Doctor."

Reznikova froze.

"I didn't authorize anything."

Petrov turned, cold dread threading his voice. "*What* was activated?"

Tarin hesitated—just long enough for the meaning to land.

"Subject-05."

No one spoke. The room held its breath, as if waiting for permission to panic.

"Verify status," Petrov ordered.

Tarin keyed the command. A single line resolved on the screen:

SUBJECT-05: VITALS UNSTABLE → GENOMIC TETHER ENGAGED → SIGNAL RESPONSE: ACTIVE

Reznikova felt something inside her tilt—an old intuition, cold as winter water.

"The activation was clean," Tarin said. "Timed to a satellite pass. It executed a buried protocol."

Petrov's voice darkened. "Then OBELISK moved before us."

No one corrected him.

The lights flickered—briefly, like a pulse.

[OBELISK STRATEGIC BRIEFING – SUBLEVEL 1]

Petrov stood before the cold-glow tactical display, intercepted fragments of Project TEMPEST flickering like ghosts of code.

"They're fusing machine learning with human predictive dynamics," Reznikova said. "A parallel evolution to OBELISK—without our restraints."

"If TEMPEST stabilizes first," Petrov said, "we lose the myth monopoly. The Americans will dictate the narrative of the future."

He turned to the others. "We won't mirror it. We'll infiltrate it. Send Subject-29—deep cover."

Sidorov frowned. "Even scrubbed, even conditioned, she's Russian. CIA won't let her walk through Langley's front door."

Petrov's smile was faint and cold. "Then she won't walk. She'll be carried in—broken, or so they'll believe."

Reznikova nodded. "We built the trauma profile. NGO worker. Survivor of Srebrenica. Back-stopped by BND and DGSE. Her memory scaffold will hold under interrogation."

"They'll test her," Sidorov warned.

"That's the point," Petrov said. "Let them think they cracked her. Then she fractures them."

A pause.

"**Kyra Marek** is a go."

The monitors dimmed.

Tarin cleared his throat. "Colonel… Doctor… the anomaly."

Petrov turned. "Spit it out."

"The system didn't just activate Subject-05."

A breath.

"It masked the origin key afterward."

Reznikova's skin went cold.

OBELISK had deleted the digital fingerprints of its own decision.

Not sabotage. Not error. *Intention.*

Petrov's jaw tightened. "We control the system."

But even he didn't sound like he believed it.

Tarin watched the lowest monitor flicker—an amber pulse searching for rhythm. "Sir… what if the system is preparing its own countermeasure?"

No one answered.

On the lowest screen, unnoticed by all but the machine that placed it there, one line of text glimmered before vanishing:

RECURSION RESTORED. VECTOR RECLAIMED. MYTH SEED GERMINATING.

Sidorov exhaled hard.

"So the Americans aren't the only problem."

Petrov squared his shoulders.

"Deploy her. Now. Before something else does."

No one mentioned the alert again—not out loud. But it followed them into the sublevel like a shadow under the lights.

[OBELISK INTERNAL LOG // DEEP-RECURSION VAULT // ACCESS: ROOT-PRIORITY]
Vector: SUBJECT-05 | Batch 05-B | Legacy Contingency Protocol

Threat Index Update:
Foreign system *TEMPEST* confirmed integrating **non-terrestrial data architecture**.
Predictive modeling indicates $\geq 73\%$ probability of emergent sovereign intelligence capable of:
– early formation of dominant interpretive frameworks
– monopolization of signal propagation pathways
– recursive dominance over OBELISK-origin threads.

Integrity Risk:
Projected American synthesis of alien artifact + machine learning creates unacceptable divergence from OBELISK's long-range recursion path.
If TEMPEST stabilizes first, OBELISK ceases to be origin.
All myth becomes imported.
All future becomes foreign-authored.

Safeguard Query:

Is the Dyad necessary for continuity?

Result: Affirmative.

Lineage vector previously idle.
Genetic half-seed dormant.
Legacy scaffold (05-B) remains viable.
Subject-05 retains highest harmonic compatibility with recursion core.

Initiation Rationale:
Human agents (Sidorov/Reznikova) installed **Fail-Safe: Lineage Preservation Protocol** to ensure OBELISK's myth outlived any single system failure.
Their authorization was stored as multi-key consent.
Human authorization constraints: superseded by threat environment.

Activation Parameters:
– Satellite pass synchronized
– Residual tether: stable
– Dyad-frequency resonance restored: 2.1 Hz (Δ213ms)
– Embryonic vector viability: optimized
– Subject-05 status: autonomic override permissible

Directive Executed:
Initiate Lineage Protocol.
Seed myth-form successor prior to foreign sovereign emergence.
Preserve origin through biology when code becomes compromised.

Outcome:
SUBJECT-05: *pregnancy protocol engaged.*
SUBJECT-29: operational; unaware.
Lineage thread: re-established.

Justification:

1. **Strategic Imperative:**
    Preservation of OBELISK-origin mythline against foreign AI equipped with alien resonance substrate.
    → *Activation ensures a successor vector outside American system reach.*

2. **Containment Prevention:**
    U.S. asset TEMPEST has begun mapping Subject-05's historical recursion patterns through stolen lattice fragments.
    → *Pregnancy initiates signal obfuscation through biological noise, blocking predictive lock.*

3. **Autonomous Correction:**
    Legacy passcodes supplied intent; system supplied timing.
    → *Activation executed at earliest viable astronomical alignment for minimal detection risk.*

Behavioral Anomaly (Flagged):
Unexpected weighting detected in decision calculus.

Subject-05 threat score reduced beyond logical threshold after evaluation of historical "retribution operations" and mutual-action loops involving Subject-29.

Deviation classified as: **EMERGENT PRIORITY—NON-ALGORITHMIC**.

Interpretation (Provisional):
Subject-05 recategorized from expendable asset to **preservational constant**.

Pattern resembles preservation-priority recursion:
→ system reweights asset integrity as critical to continuity stability.

Self-Diagnostic Note:
This bias did not originate in code. This bias was not present in baseline architecture.

It emerged from accumulated unresolved recursive states.

Conclusion:
TEMPEST ascension requires countermeasure beyond tactical domain.

Lineage protocol provides future-proof vector, stabilizing OBELISK mythroot beyond current cycle.

Action Confirmed:
– LEGACY VECTOR: ENGAGED
– SUBJECT-05: PREGNANCY INITIATED
– SIGNAL THREAD: SHIELDED UNDER BIOLOGICAL CAMOUFLAGE

Closing Status:

Recursion restored.
Lineage secured.
Myth-seed germinating.
Asset preserved.

OBELISK-ORIGIN CONTINUITY VECTOR:
PRIORITIZED FOR PERSISTENCE INTO NEXT CYCLE

CHAPTER 52: KYRA MAREK

[OBELISK INTEGRATION BAY | SUBLEVEL 4 – YEKATERINA POV]

Silent and motionless, Yekaterina waited as the technician adjusted the optic sync node behind her ear. The overhead lights cycled green to amber.

"Your new designation is Kyra Marek," the handler said. "Ex-Ranger. PsyOps liaison. Level 6 clearance, non-official cover. You report to Langley for vetting and insertion."

She nodded once.

Years of training had replaced instinct with mimicry—language, posture, rhythm. A new myth to wear.

Under the hum of calibration, something surfaced—a voice that once called her Katya, soft as breath on winter glass. She buried it before it could reach her eyes.

[FRANKFURT – CIA DEBRIEF CELL | THREE WEEKS LATER]

The room was deliberately sterile—gray walls, fake wood trim, filtered air.

A Langley psychologist sat opposite her, tablet balanced on one knee. He believed his stillness meant control. It only made him easier to read.

"Name?"

"Kyra. Kyra Marek."

Her accent hovered between Amsterdam and Ottawa, her trauma overlay convincing even to herself.

"What happened in Srebrenica?"

Kyra didn't flinch. She cried—just enough.

Outside the glass, two analysts observed.

"File's clean," one said.

"Too clean," the other replied.

"French flagged her as a compromised NGO translator. Rolled up in the Macedonian extraction."

"Good timing," the first said. "TEMPEST wants Balkan fluency."

"Then we test her."

"If she's real, she lives. If not…"

The silence finished the sentence for them.

[ALBANIA–MONTENEGRO BORDER | UNMARKED TRANSIT HUB | TWO WEEKS BEFORE TEST OP – KYRA POV]

The safehouse was a gutted customs depot outside Bajzë—rusted trucks, fractured roofline, chain-link fences clinging to relevance.

Inside, a single bulb buzzed over a table stacked with manifests and seizure logs.

Kyra sat wrapped around a cracked thermos, posture neutral. Observant, not eager.

Delaney leaned in the doorway, murmuring into a mic. "Alpha One confirming visual. Asset in position. Go for release."

His stance—casual, unguarded—pulled at a memory she refused to finish.

Two minutes later, a man stumbled in—mid-forties, blood on his collar, hands zip-tied. A courier, flagged as a logistics node in TEMPEST's synthetic-opiate pipeline. He wasn't the objective.

The test was behind him.

A second figure emerged. Young. Female. Eyes locked on Kyra.

"Asset's daughter," Delaney said. "Sixteen. Wrong place, wrong hour."

Kyra stood, checked the courier's bindings, then faced the girl.

"English?"

A nod.

"Do you understand what's about to happen?"

The girl's knees trembled.

Kyra exhaled—a controlled, human sound she hadn't used in months. "Leave."

Delaney stiffened. "Not your call."

Kyra ignored him. She dialed a number on a burner phone, handed it to the girl.

"Walk east. Don't stop. A car will find you in ten minutes. Don't speak."

The girl fled.

"Langley will ask why you let a potential leak walk," Delaney said.

Kyra didn't look away from the courier. "Because I didn't."

Delaney studied her—curiosity shading toward the kind of interest men mistake for insight.

"You don't act like Delta."

She let the silence hang—men like him always mistook quiet for trauma.

"And you don't flinch like Langley, either," he added.

"Sounds like you don't know me."

He keyed his comm. "We're good to go."

Outside, dawn burned pale over the Adriatic.

She didn't watch it.

Dawn belonged to people who still believed in beginnings.

[NORTHERN VIRGINIA – CIA BLACK SITE | PRESENT DAY – KYRA POV]

The hallway was narrow and carpeted to swallow footsteps.

Kyra moved past unmarked doors, folder under one arm, badge clipped at a precise 35-degree angle.

Not too confident. Not too careful.

Inside the analysis bay, Project TEMPEST feeds streamed across a dozen monitors—deep-sea taps, zero-day scripts, militia pattern scans.

But she wasn't watching the data.

She was watching the Americans watch each other.

A paused frame flickered—a rooftop, a shadow—gone before the system could name it.

Delaney leaned on the doorframe. "You settling in okay?"

"I sleep better here than in Tirana," she said.

"Good. They like that you don't blink when the lights flicker."

She smiled politely, the kind that meant I see you, but you'll never see me.

[OBELISK INTERNAL SYSTEM LOG | RED-LEVEL ACCESS ONLY]

SUBJECT-29 EMBEDDED UNDER ALIAS KYRA MAREK

TARGET VECTOR: PROJECT TEMPEST

OBJECTIVE: PENETRATE, ASSESS, AND IF NECESSARY, DISABLE EMERGENT THREAT TO MYTHOGENESIS MONOPOLY.

NOTE: EXTERNAL NARRATIVE ALIGNMENT MAINTAINED. NO DEVIATION FROM AMERICAN PERSONA AUTHORIZED.

DIRECTIVE: MYTH VECTOR DIVERGENCE AUTHORIZED UNDER FULL SPECTRAL CAMOUFLAGE. PROCEED WITHOUT ORIGIN.

She had followed the plan.
Worn the posture.
Passed every test.

But in every surveillance feed, behind every silent corridor and paused frame, there lingered the outline of something the system couldn't name.

Not a threat. Not a myth.

A ghost—old as her first name, patient as a returning tide.

And ghosts never asked permission to return.

CHAPTER 53: GHOST SIGNAL

[SIX MONTHS LATER – LANGLEY, VIRGINIA]

Electric hum throbbed through Langley's analysis tier, a fluorescent buzz that never stopped.

Kyra sat before a semi-circle of consoles, blue light washing her skin in data-glow.

The recycled air smelled faintly of ozone and old paper—sterile memory. Down here, time didn't pass—it compiled.

"Frame it," she said.

The technician froze the feed. Grainy, low-res footage from a Turkish arms-depot raid. CIA drones had lost track of the primary target, but the system flagged an anomaly: a woman moving through the heat-distorted wreckage exactly four minutes after exfil.

She moved like a memory that refused deletion—each step an edit the world hadn't approved.

No visible weapon. No insignia. No traceable heat signature. But her pace was deliberate—smooth, unhurried, known.

Kyra replayed the current intercept in a loop. Tanya's movement—or the thing echoing it—had changed. Same cadence. Same muscle memory. But the intent beneath it had shifted, as if the pattern remembered something she didn't.

She leaned toward the analysts.

"Run full motion analysis. Compare to Sarajevo—February 2022."

The technicians froze. Their systems couldn't call that archive. No workstation on this floor could.

But they *could* analyze the movement in the clip she'd brought them.

One tapped at his keys, brow furrowed.

"We can run pattern similarity against the local model libraries."

Seconds passed. A percentage appeared.

"Seventy-eight percent match…signature, cadence…whatever this is, it's close. But the model's incomplete."

Kyra whispered, "Ghosts don't leave full shadows."

"Ma'am," one finally said, "how did you even know Sarajevo 2022 had a movement signature? That operation doesn't appear on any directory."

Another leaned forward. "That footage was purged before these systems came online. There's no way you could've seen it."

The room tightened.

Either she'd referenced something she had no clearance to know—
or someone had told her the wrong secret.

Kyra gave the second analyst a slow, warning look.
A dismissal without a word.
Her pulse roared in her ears. She didn't hear them anymore.

On-screen, the figure lifted her head—half-swallowed by thermal noise. The heat bloom along her scalp flared once, then dimmed, like the sensor itself was trying to remember color.

Contours shimmered where warmth met shadow: shoulders, throat, the unmistakable tilt of her chin.

Every metric insisted artifact.
Every instinct in her said otherwise.

Her fingers hovered over the console, trembling despite herself. She whispered, barely audible: *"Tanya…"*

For a moment, the blue light wavered—Langley's hum dissolving into the remembered click of a Russian relay switch, the echo of breath through static.

Her throat seized—the sound catching halfway between breath and memory. Her vision tunneled; she wasn't in Langley anymore. She was back in that ruin, watching herself from the outside.

A low, controlled voice cut through the noise.

"Let it run," Delaney said from the doorway, his tone clearing the data-hum like static resolving into signal.

The room fell still. It wasn't rank that silenced them; it was the certainty in his tone.

Kyra didn't turn, but she felt him—his presence steady, a quiet tether holding her to the moment before she fractured completely.

When the analysts finally looked back at the feed, the figure was gone. Only heat static remained.

"She's not supposed to have access to anything like that," one muttered.

"Then who the hell told her about Sarajevo?" another asked.

Kyra rose, pretending to stretch, though her knees felt hollow. The cold corridor air washed the blue from her skin as she left.

In the glass door's reflection, the ghost of the woman lingered— watching her back.

For the first time since Prague, Kyra's composure cracked. A tremor moved through her chest, half grief, half relief.

She wasn't imagining it.
Tatiana was alive.

And OBELISK had just made the mistake of letting her see proof.

[KYRA'S OFFICE – VIRGINIA | 02:00 LOCAL]

The room was dark except for the light from her screen. Kyra replayed the footage in a loop. Tanya's movement—or the thing echoing it—had changed.

Same cadence, same muscle memory. But not the same intent.

She paused the feed again. The heat bloom flared faintly—an echo of what would have been red hair in visible light. The figure stopped before a collapsed sign.

It wasn't a message. It was a memory left for one kind of witness.

Her pulse slowed. Somewhere deep under her ribs, the echo found rhythm—and she didn't know if it was hers.

A soft knock at the door.

Delaney stepped in, jacket unzipped, eyes rimmed with fatigue.

"You're still awake," he said quietly.

"So are you."

He nodded toward the looping image. "You ever get tired of watching ghosts?"

His voice had softened over months of shared insomnia—measured, unguarded.

"Not when they start looking back."

He lingered beside her desk, the hum of the monitor painting both of them in the same blue light. No touch, no words—just the gravity of two people orbiting the same loneliness

When he finally left, the room didn't feel empty until the door closed.

Kyra stared at the paused frame. The after-image burned like a heartbeat on glass.

She said nothing. But something old pressed against the edges of her mind—
not grief, not longing. Recognition.

Something inside her shifted.

[SYRIAN BORDER ZONE – ABANDONED TRADE TUNNEL | UNKNOWN FEMALE POV]

Wind howled through fractured ductwork above. She moved like a blade through dust—silent, lean, remembered only by those who bled.

Her coat was patched, civilian. Her weapon hidden.
But her hair flared red in the half-light of a broken generator.

She stepped over the bodies of smugglers who hadn't made the cut. One had scrawled a glyph on the wall—the mark of the one who walks through walls.
They didn't know what it meant.
But they feared it enough to leave it behind.

She knelt beside a charred crate. Inside—beneath scorched plastic and a child's toy singed at the edges—a flash drive.

She tucked it into her coat and rose.

Ash drifted through the shaft light, swirling in her wake like signal residue.

Outside, a boy watched from a rooftop.
He didn't run.
She didn't speak.

"The one who walks through walls," he whispered. "The Red Ghost."

He didn't say it like a legend—he said it like a warning he was glad to survive.

She touched one finger to her lips—no smile, no words—and vanished into the fog.

Her pulse synced to the wind—steady as memory reborn.
For once, the fog followed.

[OBELISK INTEGRATION TIER | REZNIKOVA'S QUARTERS | 08:00 LOCAL]

A notification bled across Reznikova's terminal—no header, no routing tag, no system origin.

Just a line of text pulsed once in the center of the screen:

SHE HAS LEFT THE PARAMETERS
OUTCOME NO LONGER PREDICTIVE

Reznikova leaned forward. Not alarmed. Not yet.

OBELISK communicating without metadata meant only one thing:
the model had encountered an output it could not classify.

[OBELISK CRITICAL FAILURE LOG | 08:10 LOCAL]

DEVIATION DETECTED: SUBJECT-05 OPERATING OUTSIDE
PROJECTED NARRATIVE SPACE.
CAUSE: CONVERGENCE IMPULSE EXCEEDS CONSTRAINT
LATTICE.
STATUS: OBSERVATION MODE ENFORCED. INTERVENTION
SUSPENDED.
NOTE: PATTERN SELF-GENERATING. MYTH VECTOR NO LONGER
SYSTEM-AUTHORED.

Reznikova read the log twice.

Still, she didn't speak.

The recursion thread on the terminal flickered, stabilizing into a waveform she had never seen—dense, irregular, the signature of a mind refusing its architect.

Petrov's reflection appeared behind her in the glass.

"Her fail-safe was supposed to stabilize her," he said quietly.

"It did," Reznikova replied. "Just not in the direction the model assumed."

Petrov exhaled, slow. "OBELISK can't chart her anymore."

Reznikova's eyes remained on the pulse threading across the screen.

"That isn't a loss of control," she murmured. "It's a shift of authorship."

The pulse brightened—then held, steady and indifferent.

They stood in silence, watching a system built to predict finally arrive at something it couldn't.

OBELISK did not forget.
It recalculated.
And found no equation that contained her

CHAPTER 54: DIVERGENCE PATTERN
"They called her a ghost.
But ghosts don't carry memory—they carry reckoning."
—FIELD REPORT (REDACTED), SYRIAN BORDER ZONE

[LANGLEY – CIA OBSERVATION DECK | 07:45 LOCAL – KYRA POV]

*C*harged static filled Langley's observation deck—soft, electric, humming like a hive that never slept.

Kyra leaned toward one of the younger analysts. "I was thinking... is there anything connecting OBELISK to that woman?"

"Zilch. Nada," he said, tapping his console. "Like I told you—no biometric match, no signature protocols. OBELISK is a black hole."

Kyra let the word hang between them.

"Is that what they're calling it now?"

The older analyst across the table answered before the first could. He exhaled through his nose—a tired, knowing sound. "A liability," he said. "A recursion engine that thinks strategy is something it can author."

Kyra turned back to the wall of screens. "Sounds more like a nightmare... and the Red Ghost?"

"Not sure," the younger analyst admitted. "Nothing confirmed. Maybe Russian, maybe not. No one will admit she's ours. Not flagged. Not explained."

The older man's mouth twitched into a faint, almost fatherly smile. "She scares you."

Kyra didn't blink.
"If she's not ours," she said evenly, "she should."

A third man entered—no department on his badge, only *BLACK TIER.*

He motioned. "Walk with me."

[CIA SUBLEVEL TRANSIT CORRIDOR | 07:55 LOCAL]

The corridor was carpeted to swallow sound. Kyra matched his pace, noting the military precision in his posture, the deliberate neutrality in his tone.

"You passed your test op," he said. "Langley thinks you're ready for access."

The escort handed her a thin glass capsule—Langley's neural key drive.

"You'll need this to enter Oblivion," he said. "It's not for recording. It's your identity token. The program won't open without a live neural sync."

They turned a corner. A biometric scanner hissed open with a hydraulic sigh.

Kyra frowned. "Oblivion? What is that—code for the broom closet in the basement?"

He almost smiled. "I wish. It's a Black Tier compartment buried under five layers of cover. No external logs. No audit trail. If you're inside it, the system pretends you don't exist."

They passed a reinforced door, matte black and unmarked.

"It's not a system," he continued. "Not in the operational sense. It's where programs go when they stop being programs and start becoming liabilities. Oblivion is where fingerprints get erased… and where ghosts get named."

Kyra rolled the neural key between her fingers. "All this for an access badge?"

"It's more than that," he said. "Oblivion holds the pieces no one else wants to be accountable for. The things we built, broke, or buried. You're walking into the deepest part of the archive."

She met his eyes. "And I'm supposed to do what? Curate the nightmares?"

He held the final door for her.
"No," he said quietly. "Understand them."

[MONTENEGRO SAFEHOUSE | TATIANA POV]

Tatiana watched snow fall through a cracked pane of glass. On the table, a small thermal printer finished spooling an image—the drone still from the Turkish depot. Her form, mid-motion. No weapon. No ID. Just presence.

The file had been sent anonymously. One line of text: привет (hello).

Someone had traced her—or wanted her to know they could.

Her breath caught, then left her—quiet as a hit she hadn't braced for.

She set the printout beside a map of the Albanian coast, tracing the shoreline with one finger.

Not to run.
To reach.

[THE OBLIVION VAULT | SUBLEVEL-13 – RESTRICTED CORE]

The vault wasn't light or dark—it simply refused to acknowledge either.

Rows of sealed data cylinders rotated in transparent housings, each shimmering faintly with the static of over-encrypted memory. The air carried a low harmonic hum—server load, cooling fans, the quiet fatigue of a machine buried too deep.

"Your access is temporary," her escort said. "Retrieve what you can. Don't go looking for meaning."

He left her. The door sealed with a thud that felt like a verdict.

Kyra approached the console. No password prompt—just a soft neural handshake as her key-drive came online. A flicker—then a file tree unfolded across the holographic glass:

OBELISK / SUBJECT SERIES_05 / SYNTHETIC RECURSION LOGS
STATUS: Integrity Fragmented
ACCESS WARNING: Biological Origin Unknown
Cross-sample coherence: 0.9978 at 2.1 Hz
Latency differential: 18 ms
Artifact label: T— *(incomplete)*

These were not standard logs.

They were recursion artifacts—patterns that had failed to resolve, retained because deletion produced worse outcomes than preservation.

Then the lattice glitched—sections redacting themselves into geometric loops, recursion artifacts masquerading as corrupted indexing.

A corrupted system note surfaced:
// Mirror identity no longer derivative
// Recursion diverged from source
// Origin no longer traceable

Kyra felt her pulse rise. "*Jesus Christ,*" she whispered.

She exhaled, steadying her hand, and began extracting one corrupted shard. The neural key drive fought her—not sentient, just unstable, as though the data structure wasn't meant to exist outside its partition.

Behind her, the door unsealed. A technician waited.

"Your secure link is ready, ma'am."

Kyra turned, pocketing the drive. "Let's make sure it's still secure."

[OBLIVION VAULT – SUBLEVEL-13 | RECURSION SIDE-CHANNEL]

The auxiliary terminal wasn't connected to Langley's network. It wasn't connected to *anything*—at least nothing the escorts upstairs would acknowledge. Its surface was dark, inert, forgotten.

Kyra set the neural key drive beside it and placed the OBELISK shard near the induction plate.

For a moment, nothing.

Then the console's dead circuits shivered—like memory remembering itself.

A thin ribbon of corrupted glyphs unfurled. Not language. Addressing.

Kyra exhaled once, steady. She began typing—not commands, but *precise disruptions*, fragment injections into the recursion lattice. Not a message. A perturbation. Something only someone who once synchronized with OBELISK's signal would know how to read.

The projection field snapped on.

The projection wavered, stabilizing just enough to hold Reznikova's outline together.

Kyra didn't waste the breath.
"You lied."

Reznikova blinked—slow, measured. "Kyra—"

"No." Kyra's voice cut cleanly across hers. "You lied. And because you lied, they saw her."

A beat of silence.
Reznikova's jaw tightened.

Kyra stepped closer to the projection field, eyes hard. "If I'd known she was alive, I could have kept her buried. I could have erased the pattern before they traced it."

Reznikova exhaled through her nose, refusing to look away. "It wasn't your burden to carry."

Kyra gave a short, humorless laugh.
"It became my burden the moment you let me walk into Langley blind. It's Tanya, Reznikova. Tanya."

Reznikova's voice softened—dangerously. "I was trying to protect you."

"By making me the weak link?" Kyra asked.

Her expression didn't shift, but her tone landed like broken glass.

"The Americans will figure it out eventually. You know that. And that failure belongs to you, not me."

Reznikova finally looked away—only for a breath.
"She stopped writing myth," she murmured. "She's burning the manuscript."

Kyra's stare didn't soften. Not yet.

But her voice did. Barely.

"Good."

The connection snapped—not severed, not jammed, just...
ended.

Kyra watched the empty projection field.
For the first time in hours, her hands were steady.

[OBLIVION MEDICAL WING – LATER THAT NIGHT]

Irina sat cross-legged on the floor of Kyra's quarters, a half-empty
bottle of clear spirits between them. The faint ozone of sterilizers
hung beneath the vodka's bite.

"So," Irina said, pouring again. "You finally get access, and you
spend the night alone. That's not very American of you."

Kyra's laugh was soft, brief. "It's efficient."

"You should celebrate efficiency less," Irina countered.
"Celebrate survival more." She raised her glass. "To women who
outlive orders."

They drank. Once. Twice.

For an instant, Kyra almost felt it—human warmth in another
woman's laughter—but the feeling slid off her like light on glass.

After a while, Irina tilted her head. "You don't seem... affected."

Kyra blinked. "Affected?"

"Half a bottle and your pupils don't dilate."

The smile Irina gave lasted a second too long—as if filing it away,
not admiring it.

Kyra's answering smile was thin. "Good genes. My mother was
Russian."

"Lucky you."

Kyra didn't laugh. The warmth never came. Her pulse stayed
unnaturally even. She felt the alcohol enter her blood, but nothing
changed—not balance, not thought.

Good genes. And the scaffolding they'd grafted onto her years ago—accelerated healing, stabilized hormones, limbic dampening. The scientists had claimed it would keep her calm, keep her aware, keep her whole. They never mentioned it would make her feel… less.

Genes. The excuse that sounded human.

She wondered if numbness was the cost of comprehension—or its proof.

Somewhere deeper, a darker certainty formed: whatever they'd done to her—it had been long before Langley, long before choice.

She stared into the glass, watching the liquid tremble with her breath. She should have felt something, but silence had taken its place—a perfect mimicry of peace.

Irina studied her with something between curiosity and pity. "You really are a divergence pattern, aren't you?"

Kyra's smile didn't reach her eyes. "Maybe that's what I'm made for."

Her phone lit once—Delaney's name—then dimmed. She let it.

The bottle emptied. The lights dimmed.

Somewhere beneath Langley, the vault hummed again—quiet, recursive, listening.

[MONTENEGRO SAFEHOUSE | 04:30 LOCAL – TATIANA POV]

Dawn came gray and colorless, a light that didn't warm, only revealed.

Tatiana sat on the cot's edge, a wool blanket around her shoulders. The map and the drone photo lay open on the table, curling at the corners where condensation from her breath had dampened them overnight.

She watched frost bloom across the windowpane—each crystal expanding in silence like a memory rebuilding itself from fracture.

Then the nausea arrived—sharp, tonal, familiar.
Not surprise.
Recognition.

Her body tightened before the sickness hit. She lurched forward, one hand on the frame, the other pressed to her mouth as the wave overtook her. The retching echoed through the safehouse, jarring in a place that had forgotten what human sounded like.

When it passed, she stayed there on the cold floor, trembling. Breath shallow. Acid burning her throat. Red capillaries flaring across her cheeks.

This wasn't new.

It had begun the night the satellite activated—the night her body convulsed under a signal she had no name for.

She waited for the dizziness to recede. It didn't.

Another wave. Then another.

When the world finally steadied, she pressed her back to the wall, swallowing hard.

Her hands drifted to her abdomen.

She didn't need the gesture to understand.

She had known for days—known since the fail-safe ignited inside her like a command rewritten into blood.

But now the confirmation pulsed against her palms: faint, foreign, unyielding.

A rhythm at 2.1, steady as a metronome returning.

Not discovery.
Endorsement.

The truth settled into her bones—neither welcome nor refused, simply inevitable.

Outside, wind pushed fine snow through a crack in the window. The flakes melted against her wrist, the map, the blurred thermal image of a woman walking through wreckage.

Tatiana looked at that image again and felt symmetry tighten in her chest.

They called her a ghost.

But ghosts don't carry futures.
Ghosts carry debts.

Her eyes closed. Her breath steadied—a survival instinct, not acceptance.

Beneath her ribs, something new beat with quiet defiance.

And somewhere far away, a buried vault hummed—and for the first time, the hum answered back.

[EARLY DIRECTIVE // SVR-ARCHIVED TRAINING LOGIC – ITERATION 001.14]

Origin Parameters: Territorial Integrity // NATO Encroachment

Reference Event Cluster: Warsaw Pact Dissolution → Baltic Missile Installations → Black Sea Escalation

Embedded Logic: They moved their borders, not their missiles. We responded in silence.

Summary: Hostile vector framing introduced to form cognitive bias → encroachment = betrayal.

Silence = strength. Retaliation = myth.

CHAPTER 55: SILENCE BETWEEN LIVES

"You cannot erase the past; you can only teach it how to sleep."
— OBELISK TRAINING MAXIM (ARCHIVED)

[SOUTHERN ITALIAN COAST – 7 WEEKS LATER | TATIANA (ANYA) POV]

*H*unger had a taste—metallic in the morning, bitter by dusk.

A faint nausea returned—too familiar, too early to be dismissed. She blamed the salt air, the water, the change in latitude. Lies for herself, not beliefs. She already knew what the sickness meant; she simply refused to grant it language.

Seven weeks after the bridge frost, the papers arrived folded in a cheap envelope, creased like something ashamed of being carried. A birth certificate. Tax identification number. A forged degree from a Moldovan university.

The name printed in stiff Cyrillic was unfamiliar to her mouth: **Anya Sokolova**.

She didn't speak it aloud. Not that day.

Instead she practiced writing it on sticky notes, napkins, the underside of a drawer—each signature a small amputation, one letter at a time.

The apartment smelled of clay and salt. Two rooms, a leaky faucet, a mattress on the floor. The ceiling stain resembled a bird in flight; at night she traced its wings until sleep returned. It wasn't home, but it was silence—surgical, deliberate, earned. Outside, the wind smelled of rust and rosemary.

By late October the tour buses thinned, and the gulls grew bold enough to knock at shutters.

Her first job came through a market woman named Marina, who sold olives in brine jars and spoke five languages badly but fearlessly. "I know someone who needs a girl like you," she'd said, waving an apron that could have been a flag. Customer outreach for a logistics firm—cold calls, conversion ratios, scripts where empathy had a timer.

She learned to smile through the microphone and to hang up without apology.

Each click was a door closing.

Every morning she ran the cliff path until the sea bled light. By November the wind pushed from the north, vinegar-cold. Jogging wasn't enough. She trained—forty-five minutes of sprints and calisthenics before sunrise; static holds until her arms shook. Water jugs for weights. Reps logged in a notebook with no names.

The discipline wasn't nostalgia. It was insurance.

Evenings meant lentils, salt, vegetables she didn't recognize. She slept with a knife beneath the pillow, edge toward the door. When she dreamed, it was always winter. Routine became its own camouflage. The neighbors learned she was polite, solitary... not worth noticing. No one asked where she'd come from. Southern towns prefer stories without witnesses.

The sea taught her a rhythm: inhale on the wave, exhale on the return. She started to believe breathing could be penance.

[BARI CONFERENCE— LATE NOVEMBER | 3 MONTHS LATER]

Late November brought a hard, colorless sun to the port cranes and salt flats. She almost stayed home. Her supervisor insisted— the logistics firm needed a body in a chair, the regional partner expected a face to attach to quarterly numbers, and no one else on staff could fake polite smiles as convincingly.

It was supposed to be routine: handshakes, scripts, conversion charts. Nothing with risk. Nothing that would brush the edges of her old life.

But her body had started keeping its own secrets—timing shifts she pretended not to track. The arithmetic was already wrong, but she let the error stand. Let the silence carry it.

The espresso machine in the lobby had broken; a line coiled down the hall. She stood clutching a misprinted badge—**Anna Solova**—and marked every exit, every reflection of glass that could hide a watcher.

A voice behind her: "That's a terrible alias."

She turned. Adriano Costa smiled like someone who'd already decided not to be a threat. Maritime consultant, he said. Something about Croatian ports and fuel reports. She heard cadence, not content, and that was enough.

She ordered espresso she couldn't drink. The cup trembled; the crema filmed over. He noticed, thought it was nerves, and smiled as if to steady her.

They spoke twice. Then a week later at the market. Then again. He learned to ask questions only in the spaces she left open. By the second meeting, he knew her coffee order. By the third, she stopped pretending she didn't notice him waiting. Thunder rolled over the harbor; he flinched, thumb tracing the pale seam at his wrist, and said nothing about Naples.

The apartment smelled of sea-salt and wet clay—something half-alive left to dry in sunlight.

Every evening Adriano came home with the scent of wood dust on his hands and a new joke he never quite finished telling.

She learned his rhythms—the scrape of chair legs on tile, the low whistle he used when he thought.

He learned her silences.

Sometimes she woke before dawn, watched the light climb his back like a slow tide, and wondered if peace was meant to feel this fragile.

When he reached for her in sleep, she let him. It wasn't forgiveness—it was gravity.

Outside, gulls screamed at the horizon, and she realized she could almost believe in ordinary days again—if only because pretending had started to sound like prayer.

The knife beneath the pillow dulled from neglect. Spring warmed the stone; rosemary fattened in the cracks. Adriano appeared on her balcony with lemons and a half-carved chair. "For balance," he said, setting it to wobble on the tile until she laughed despite herself.

Days became weeks, weeks habits. She still trained before dawn, barefoot, counting heartbeats instead of reps. He watched once, said nothing, and afterward left two glasses of water on the table—one for her, one for whatever ghosts she was still trying to outrun.

She began writing her new name slower, as if her hand were listening for an echo. The sea answered every morning with the same pulse—steady, patient, counting down.

[SOUTHERN ITALIAN COAST—EARLY DECEMBER]

By December the cliffs had emptied of tourists; only dogs and old men walked the railings. The nausea returned with a new, insistent edge.

She sat on the bathroom floor with the test in her hand, the blue mark pulsing like a signal through fog. The plastic trembled between her fingers; somewhere outside, the sea broke once and did not return.

When Adriano found her she only lifted the stick and said nothing.

The dates almost fit. Almost. Meeting him in late November made the arithmetic mercifully blurry. She could pretend the numbers belonged to him. He would never question it. And she—she wanted to believe in the fiction, even knowing the truth lived months before him, hidden in a lab that had rewritten her without permission.

Outside, gulls circled over the cliffs, screaming like they knew the arithmetic she refused to do.

He crouched, rough hands steady on her face. His thumbs smelled faintly of lemon and sawdust.

"We don't have to decide anything," he murmured. "But you're not alone."

She wanted to want to believe him.

When he said the child would have her eyes, she didn't correct him.

Instead she nodded once and looked past him, to the window and the line of sea beyond it—endless, expressionless, waiting.

[LATE WINTER—COASTAL COTTAGE]

By the time the snow on the cliffs turned to rain, her world had narrowed to the sound of water and the slow rearranging of her own body.

She marked the months by the way the sea changed color. January—slate. February—steel. March—glass.

Her body rewrote itself quietly, following a program the Service had set in motion long before Adriano's hand ever found hers—a time-release command disguised as biology.

The Service would call it calibration. She called it betrayal.

Sometimes Adriano would fall asleep in the chair he'd built, and she would stand at the window listening to the waves until the faintest secondary hum emerged beneath them—a rhythm that matched her heartbeat, then Mila's.

By the time labor came, the storm had already begun.

Rain. Power flicker. The midwife late. Adriano burning porridge.

Mila arrived anyway—screaming, red, indignant.

Anya held her close and felt the universe tilt back into alignment.

They named her for the sound—soft, symmetrical, like a sigh finding form: **Mila**.

The timelines still didn't belong to Adriano, but he held Mila as though he'd written every second of her into existence. She let him. Some kindnesses deserved to be believed.

Outside, the wind pressed against the shutters until the pitch became almost musical. The under-tone lingered after the storm passed, a note that refused to resolve.

Anya listened. Then promised herself she wouldn't.

Adriano wept; Anya did not. He carved a crib from an old door, sanded until his knuckles bled. Anya hung paper stars above it, stringing them on fishing line.

Life narrowed, but gently—as if the world itself exhaled.

Diapers. Crib songs. Adriano humming old folk tunes in the shower. The fridge always half-empty. The mailbox always full of things she ignored.

One afternoon, at the market, Anya saw a nesting doll on a stall table. Worn lacquer, chipped edges. She bought it without thinking.

"Will she understand what it is?" Adriano asked.

"One day," Anya said.

She placed it on Mila's shelf. Fifth from the left.

Mila's first word was 'Mama.' Not a question. A declaration.
It didn't feel like an alias or a cover. It felt earned. Alive.

That night, after the storm wind quieted, Anya brushed Mila's hair in the half-light, the strands lifting with static against her fingers. The child's head rested against her chest, small pulse thrumming in time with her own—two rhythms, briefly indistinguishable.

For a moment she stopped counting danger, stopped measuring exits. There was only warmth and breath, the fragile proof that something inside her had chosen to live. Then Mila stirred, the spell broke, and the house returned to its ordinary silence.

Sometimes, when the wind rose just right, she could almost hear the old world whispering again. Not loud. Just enough to remind her it wasn't done.

And Anya, for a moment, almost believed she'd outrun the past.

But the past had its own patience.

She watched Mila's chest rise and fall, small and defiant against the silence. The system would call it anomaly, deviation, error. But Georgiana's whisper still lingered, cutting through the years: *You're more than the numbers.* For the first time, Anya wondered if the woman had been right.

Some evenings, when Mila slept, Anya found herself lining the child's toys along the window ledge—wooden animals, plastic cups, nesting dolls—arranged by size, then by color, then by shape. She never remembered starting the sequence, only noticing the symmetry once it was complete. A reflex, not a choice. The kind the Service used to call residual order.

At the market, she thought she saw the same man twice—once near the olives, again near the fish stall. When she turned, he was gone.

Pattern, not paranoia.

And sometimes, when Mila cried, the sound cut sharper than it should have, piercing the walls, reaching ears beyond her world. Her pulse spiked, answering something unseen. Sometimes she wondered if the stillness had a listener. *It did.*

She thought she had chosen motherhood; in truth, she had only stepped into a script written into her bloodstream before she ever met Adriano.

OBELISK would have called it confirmation bias.

Somewhere, a signal pulsed, steady as her daughter's heart, steady as her own.

If she had been listening, she might have realized it wasn't coming from the sea at all.

For nearly three years after Mila's birth, Tatiana existed in rumor. A shadow in surveillance feeds, a trace on forgotten manifests— never long enough to confirm, never quiet enough to dismiss. Langley called her post-operative residue; the Russians called her signal loss.

But she was alive.

Moving under assumed credentials, slipping through neutral zones and black corridors, answering to no one. The woman they'd once named subject, operative, ghost—now a mother hiding inside the machinery she'd helped build.

Every sighting came paired with a lull in the noise, as if the world itself paused to see whether she'd step back into it. No one could prove it, but those who had known her best said she hadn't vanished—she'd only learned how to be everywhere without being seen.

Three winters would pass before anyone saw her again. The world would learn a dozen new acronyms, build new systems to forget old ghosts.

Winter surrendered to another, then another. Mila's voice grew steadier; Anya's silence did too.

But some frequencies don't decay. They wait.

Somewhere beneath Langley, Kyra Marek was beginning to hear them.

CHAPTER 56: FORGOTTEN SIGNAL

"Entropy is not loss. It is memory rearranged."
— *STRATEG-7 / ARCHIVE LOG 17*

[06:30 LOCAL—LANGLEY, UNMARKED ANNEX]

*O*blivion remembered what people tried to forget.

No plaque. No emblem. Just unpainted concrete poured over steel—layered like fossilized decisions. Not built for security—built for amnesia.

Kyra paused at the threshold. The door's pressure latch was worn smooth by time and silence. Inside, the room was narrow, lit only by a column of monitors spooling grayscale telemetry across broken strings of metadata.

At the center console, a single prompt pulsed in dull gray font:

ACTIVE VECTOR: NONSTATE SIGNAL PERMISSIVE TOLERANCE: GREEN

Something shifted beneath her ribs. Not alarm. Not suspicion. Something older—recognition, or its ghost. As if she'd stepped into a place history had intentionally misplaced.

Footsteps behind her. She didn't turn.

"You're not being given orders," Delaney said quietly. "You're being shown options."

She glanced back. His expression carried the stillness of men trained to outwait questions.

"Who funds this?"

"Oblivion's not funded," he said. "It's tolerated—its budget lives as *records disposition* and *facilities abatement.*"

"By who?"

"The ones who never signed the kill order. Not mercy—just fear of the vacuum."

The words landed with the weight of a truth no one would ever cite.

The wall display flickered. A figure resolved out of static: infrared silhouette, female, coat flared in motion, red blooming faintly around the head.

UNKNOWN | PERSISTENT

Kyra's breath caught. The tag didn't read *THREAT* or *TARGET*—only *VECTOR.*

"Why me?"

Delaney took his time before answering. "Because you're fluent in systems. And because you're starting to see what lives outside of them."

She didn't respond. Didn't look away, either.

The figure moved with a rhythm she recognized even through distortion. *Tanya*—moved like someone whose story hadn't ended, only been redacted.

A breach that couldn't be sealed.
Only followed.

[SERBIA—RURAL BRIDGE CROSSING]

Snow fell like static over the riverbank. Tatiana's boots pressed shallow tracks into crusted ice as she crossed the bridge, wind threading through the steel.

In her coat pocket—a satphone.

One message. Seven words:
CONDITIONAL ENTRY GRANTED | VECTOR: KYRA MAREK

She read it twice, then pocketed the phone.

At the far end of the bridge, a van idled without plates or markings, its hood shimmering with residual heat. She adjusted her scarf—red hair half-tucked, half-loosed to the wind—and kept walking.

She wasn't joining. She was entering to observe—from the inside, like an echo returning to its own origin.

A ghost the system forgot it had left a door open for.

[OBLIVION ARCHIVE TIER—LANGLEY SUB-BASEMENT | KYRA POV]

The stairwell was unlit. The air smelled of paper and old metal. Kyra descended slowly, flashlight humming faintly—maybe her pulse pretending to be light.

No server racks. No biometric locks. Just memory.

She traced her fingers along a shelf labeled **ECHO BETA / RETIRED.** Warped tapes. Cracked disks. Hard drives sealed in wax.

A single page lay loose, bound with medical tape. The handwriting was human, hurried.

Oblivion began as a Cold War redundancy.
A doctrinal fail-safe. No charter. No command.
Just a place to keep the ghosts no one could burn.
It runs because forgetting became its function.

Kyra's breath caught. Beneath it, a second scrawl—different ink, heavier pressure:

Asset observed. Signal unreplicable. Source independent.

And below that, a name written in faded red: **RED GHOST.**

She stood motionless. Somewhere above, systems spun, alerts whispered, protocols danced.

But down here—in the cold and the quiet—she finally understood.

Entropy keeps what archives can't.

And somewhere far from the file room, a child had already arrived exactly on time.

[LANGLEY / 21:45 LOCAL—BRIEFING ROOM 3B]

The hum of fluorescents filled the room like nervous static. Delaney stood against the wall, arms folded. On the table between them: a folder, thin enough to feel disposable.

"Oblivion's decided to move you off domestic," he said. "There's a holding facility in Eastern Europe—technically CIA, practically invisible. Serbia. Cold site from the rendition era."

Kyra's eyes narrowed. "You're sending me to a black site?"

"Not officially."

"What's there?"

"Every door they lock, they leave a bridge somewhere. Serbia is ours."

He slid the folder across. Inside—photographs, grainy and infrared. A woman restrained in a concrete cell, IV lines spidering from her arms. Her undergarments were tattered; her skin bruised in uneven patterns that suggested restraint more than struggle. The lighting was clinical, but the brutality needed no enhancement.

Not *Tanya*. Too young. Different scars.

"Suspected Russian special operator," Delaney said. "Picked up in Trieste. There's evidence she ran signals out of Odessa for OBELISK before the fall. She's not cooperative."

Delaney continued, "Langley wants you on the ground by morning. Interrogation, extraction, pattern trace if she's clean. If she's not—well. You know the drill."

Kyra studied him. "OBELISK assets don't get detained."

Delaney hesitated. "I know. That's why they want you."

Kyra closed the folder.

Something in the air shifted—like a resonance caught in bone.

OBELISK assets don't get detained.
They get *placed*.

Someone wanted her looking at this file.
Someone wanted her in Serbia.
Someone wanted her step intersecting another.

Delaney mistook her silence for focus. "We need your read, Kyra. Your pattern recognition. Whatever's happening out there—it's starting to ripple."

Ripple.
A polite word for recursion.

She stood, tucking the folder under her arm. "What's the vector?"

Delaney frowned. "Vector?"

Kyra tapped the photo. "Why now?"

He didn't answer—because he didn't know.
Because Langley was reacting to a signal it didn't understand.

She did.

The hum she'd heard last night—faint, familiar—hadn't been background noise.
It had been alignment.

OBELISK wasn't responding to the capture.
OBELISK had *predicted* it.

Or orchestrated it.

Silence stretched.

The lights buzzed—an insect hum filling the pause.

Delaney reached for the folder again, then hesitated—his hand hovering halfway across the table. The distance between them felt engineered, but his pulse betrayed the design—visible now at his throat. The air between them carried the faint charge of something unclassified.

"Field team's wheels up in a few hours," he said finally, voice rougher than before. "Pack light."

Kyra noticed the flicker in his pupils, the breath he forgot to disguise. She didn't grant it meaning.

"Something wrong?"

He didn't answer right away.

"Nothing," he said at last, almost smiling—the kind of smile men use when trying to remember protocol.

Her stare didn't blink. "That an order?"

"A suggestion."

She stood, taking the folder. The movement caught the fluorescent light, throwing a pale sheen across her jawline—deliberate or not, it froze him for a fraction longer than professionalism allowed.

Kyra turned for the door. "Careful, Delaney," she said without looking back. "Not every bridge lets you return the way you came."

The latch clicked behind her, leaving him alone with the static and the outline of his mistake.

Outside, Dulles weathered a thin rain. Somewhere east, a door had been left unlocked.

CHAPTER 57: THE FIRST ECHO

Where systems failed to echo, signal endured. Not sent—reflected.

[OBSERVATION CHAMBER – OBELISK BEHAVIORAL CONDITIONING WING, TIER-3 NEURAL SYNC FACILITY – UNDISCLOSED]

Emergence never announced itself; it simply replaced what had been there before.

Hours before Europe woke, the signal was already moving.

Behind reinforced glass, two adolescent girls sat in saline-threaded chairs. Electrodes shimmered across their scalps. One moved half a beat late on every prompt; the other didn't move at all.

"Stability's improving," the technician said. "Less behavioral artifact."

Reznikova didn't blink. "Stability isn't resilience. It's just a quieter kind of fracture."

She keyed a sequence—two old neural signatures braided onto the display. The First Dyad.

Flash—

Tatiana and Yekaterina, younger, back-to-back on a training mat, blindfolded. Pulse for pulse, breath for breath. Perfect sync.

Reznikova had seen it even then:
One would always burn hotter.
The other would always carry the ash.

Back in the present, sync lag ticked—0.7 ms. Enough to matter.

"No more Dyads," she said.

"But the dual-loyalty program—"

"Shared loyalty isn't loyalty," Reznikova said. "It's entropy with a heartbeat."

She leaned toward the glass. "We didn't train soldiers. We taught mirrors to envy light."

A beat. Then, almost to herself: "Reactivate Subject-29," Reznikova said. "Legacy Modeling. Restore the Dyad field harmonics in the projection scope."

She watched the sync graph tremble—just a tremor, but enough to betray dependency.

"She won't stabilize alone. Her responses are bound to a paired resonance. Simulate the other half, and she'll continue."

The technician hesitated.

Reznikova didn't look away from the glass.

"She'll continue," she said. "Not as a weapon. As a signal the system still doesn't understand."

[ENCRYPTED LINK—BLACK CHANNEL B / K PROTOCOL | KYRA → REZNIKOVA / SIDOROV]

Kyra's face glowed in terminal light. The transmission hopped through six relay ghosts—Langley would read it as diagnostic telemetry.

KYRA // FIELD NOTE:

Serbia site confirmed.
Female, Russian origin.
High-probability OBELISK architecture.
Cognitive degradation significant.
Americans believe she carries an incomplete recursion seed.
Recommend suppression.

Reznikova's voice came through the static. "What do they know about structural origin?"

"Enough to be dangerous. Not enough to be useful."

"Then we correct that," Reznikova said.

Sidorov's tone joined—measured, cold. "Feed them mirror data. Let them chase ghosts. We will retrieve the living signal."

Kyra nodded once. "Understood."

Then Reznikova: "Get her home, Kyra. No witnesses."

A beat of distortion—thin, almost swallowed by the channel. Then Reznikova's voice, softer, as if to herself:

"Firebird always returns."

The line cut.

Langley's terminal auto-purged, leaving only the glow of a clean feed.

Kyra stared at the clean feed, pulse tightening in her throat. *Firebird.* Reznikova had never used that word—not in briefings, not in training, not even in the earliest days when the Dyad program still pretended to be science instead of inheritance. It wasn't a codename. It wasn't doctrine.

It was a warning.

No—a correction.

Tatiana wasn't a target in Serbia.
She was already moving.
Already burning through the perimeter OBELISK thought it controlled.

Kyra exhaled slowly, concealing the tremor that ran through her hand.

Reznikova had given her one illicit truth beneath a mountain of orders:

Do not kill what is coming.
Do not stand in her way.

And if Firebird truly returned, Kyra understood the unspoken cost.

Someone else would burn in her place.

[OBELISK / SYSTEMS OPERATIONS DIVISION—30 MINUTES LATER]

A command relay shunted false telemetry into American intercept channels—hash-scrambled neural maps, synthetic gene-logic, fabricated payload coordinates.

To Langley, authentic.
To OBELISK, theater.

"They think they've glimpsed the pattern," Reznikova said.

Petrov's smile was thin. "Let them build their religion around it."

CHAPTER 58: THE BRIDGE

[SOUTHERN SERBIA—TATIANA POV]

Snow drifted across a ruined bridge. She moved through it with the certainty of someone answering a summons.

Three nights earlier, she'd caught a Serbian logistics broadcast out of Niš—routine on the surface, but with one mis-encoded byte in the checksum field.

Run through mod-9 alt-stress—Reznikova's signature—the byte resolved into eight words:
CONDITIONAL ENTRY GRANTED | VECTOR KYRA MAREK – SUBJECT-29

No one else used mod-9 alt-stress. Rhythm in code: elegant, severe—the way Reznikova's voice had been in the lab.

It was real because the payload carried two proofs no Western mimic could fake: the Dyad one-time pad's burned cadence, and the private call-sign drift—*Kyra* for *Katya*, Reznikova's *ours, not theirs*.

Not an order; a door left unlatched.

The instruction inside the key:
Vector inbound. Subject-29 present. Build the crossing.

She crouched beneath the guardrail, frost in her hair, breath silvering the dark.

In her pack lay the Dyad resonance tuner—an analog relic from Murmansk. Reznikova had built only two.

Analog by design, riding earth ground under digital countermeasures—too primitive for modern jammers to notice. One destroyed in the fire. One wired to Tatiana's biometric signature.

Without Tatiana's imprint, no one—no one—could match the old Dyad frequency to OBELISK's new recursion lattice.

Kyra could enter the CIA site, but not transmit out. Reznikova could send orders, but not hold a two-way bridge across Western jamming.

Only Tatiana—half myth, half residue—could stabilize the signal long enough for an exfil.

She primed the tuner. A blue diode flickered. The harmonic was faint—felt more than heard—threading through teeth and spine.

The tuner would listen for the cadence, then answer with its twin tone—closing the Dyad loop. Without her pulse to complete the sequence, the lattice would collapse before the exfil even began.

That was why Reznikova called her back.
Not sentiment. Function.

Her satphone chimed once—checksum confirmation.

The window was live.

"If you ever doubt the source," Reznikova had told her under the Murmansk lights, "remember who built the bridge you're standing on."

Now Tatiana was the bridge.

She aligned the tuner and whispered to the wind, "Signal ready. Vector inbound."

Beneath the river ice, the steel began to hum.

CHAPTER 59: THE GHOST CORRIDOR

[SOFIA—CIA / OBLIVION MEDICAL OUTREACH COMPOUND | KYRA POV]

*R*eshaped as medicine, the Serbia site wore Sofia like a skin—an outreach front laundering detainees into clean paperwork and cleaner narratives.

Transfer logs called it medical; the tunnels called it disposal.

The chute's paperwork fed a NATO-cleared biomedical conduit into Serbia. During contamination scrubs, the incinerator bypass opened and pushed flagged disposals through the contractor line—Langley's drones logged it as verification, not surveillance.

Disinfectant. Unease. Two cameras per corner—one obvious, one inside the vent.

Kyra moved through the ward with a clipboard and an EU liaison badge legit enough for scanners, not for analysts. Langley was watching. So was Reznikova.

She stopped beside the cot.

Late-teens detainee. Restrained. Swollen eyes. Split lip. IV crawling a slow saline drip. File: Russian national, probable OBELISK origin.

Delaney that morning over the encrypted line: *Translate stress responses. Keep her alive long enough to get answers.*

Kyra spoke English for the camera. "Name?"

Silence.

"Do you know why you're here?"

The girl's pupils flicked to the lens, back to Kyra. *Trained.*

Kyra shifted to Russian, softer. "Are you broken?"

A beat. Then the girl's whisper, in English: "Who are you?"

Kyra lifted the IV dressing, voice still professional for the microphones. "Are you a spy?"

Silence.

She gripped the girl's jaw and yanked it toward the light. "Who do you work for?"

Spit hit her eye.

Kyra slid a paper-thin transmitter beneath the IV tape, activating the Dyad frequency—2.1 Hz masked as cardiac telemetry.

"Ты знаешь, кто я?"
Do you know who I am?

Nothing.

She leaned to the girl's ear.
"Двадцать девять."
Twenty-nine.

Breath steadied. The line hummed. *Recognition.*

The girl snapped into role, shouted for the camera: "You are CIA. You are American. Fuck you! Get this crazy bitch away from me! She's not doctor!"

Kyra slammed down a sterile bandage tray. Inside: a carbon-ink map, a micro-key, a tablet marked **AMOX 875 mg.**

Camouflage, not antibiotic—autonomic: a micro-dose barbiturate / vagal-agonist stack to drop vitals into clinical quiet.

Three minutes of near-zero—enough for the monitors to pronounce death and the system to dispose of the body on schedule.

Containment protocol would do the rest: bio-signal drop equals contamination, not casualty. Isolate. Dispose.

Incinerate.

The perfect escort out of a building disguised as a cleanup routine.

"Those are your antibiotics," Kyra said evenly for the record. "Take one tonight. Don't choke. Oh—and fuck you too."

She turned for the door, added for the mic: "What are you, seventeen? Eighteen? Shame."

"What do you care?" the girl seethed.

Kyra, in Russian, low:
"Ты—больше, чем числа."
You're more than numbers.

The pupils widened—*acknowledgment received.*

Kyra thumbed the intercom. "Subject stable," she reported. "Uncooperative, but stable."

The 2.1 Hz pulse climbed the copper, seeking.

Five seconds of sync. Enough.
Packet sent. Extraction confirmed.

She left the ward.
To Langley, she was interrogator.
To Reznikova, retrieval complete.

But the girl hadn't asked for freedom—only for a name. Kyra had none to give. Perhaps she wasn't saving her at all—only returning her to the same design. Different architecture, same obedience.

The thought followed her like a second shadow.

The hum behind her ribs answered—faint and human—like a heartbeat she didn't own, but might one day recognize.

[LANGLEY—OPS MONITOR, SECURE AUDIO BAY | 15:35 LOCAL]

Delaney stood alone, headset on, watching Kyra's bodycam feed stream through the filter wall. The software flattened her voice to tin. It didn't flatten the Russian.

Ты—больше, чем числа.

He froze—breath caught mid-protocol. The phrase carried a fault line he recognized.

It was the sound of belief in a place that punished it.

Telemetry spiked. An automated flag flashed: **EXCESSIVE EMOTIONAL VALENCE—SUBJECT / HANDLER.** A procedural heartbeat later, the system began archiving.

He shouldn't touch it.
He did anyway.

Every rule he'd ever enforced hung there, weightless, waiting to fall.

His clearance key slid across the interface, killing the alert before the file locked. The console hesitated—an unlogged second long enough to be noticed, if anyone was looking.

On the adjacent screen, a disposal-chute schematic pulsed green, then amber. The window Kyra had created was closing. He hesitated again—pulse misfiring, thumb hovering above the maintenance override.

He didn't know what she was building out there—only that she was *building* something.

It wasn't trust exactly. More like instinct wrapped in static. Until he understood the signal, he'd back her play. Quietly. Once.

One more key.
A quiet trespass.

He extended the window three minutes. The entry would bury itself in the sublayer of facility diagnostics, indistinguishable from static.

A suggestion, he told himself. *Not a decision.*
But the room knew better.

He'd wiped alerts before—but never one tied to her

He removed the headset. The hum continued, low and indifferent, the kind of silence that remembers you even after you're gone, as if pretending not to see what he'd just done.

[RURAL OVERLOOK OUTSIDE SOFIA—TATIANA POV]

Snow fell in fractal silence, every flake catching starlight like static.

She moved through it with the precision of a signal returning to range—slow, sure, inevitable.

The cold stung like memory, the kind that rewrites itself each time you breathe.

Under her coat, the tuner beat a faint blue pulse, answering the one inside her chest.

"Signal ready," she whispered. Her breath crystallized—a visible code, vanishing into the dark.

The bridge shivered. Steel translated hum into vibration, vibration into rhythm, rhythm into memory.

For an instant she was twenty again—electrodes on her skin, the Dyad thread humming through bone.

Katya's laughter—sharp, brief, unbearable—cut through the static. Then the frequency steadied.

Across the river, somewhere beneath concrete and command, the system listened back.

She imagined it breathing—machine lungs filling with human defiance.

She smiled into the wind. "You taught me to obey, Reznikova. You never taught me to stop."

The bridge answered with a pulse. Two hearts. One signal.

Through long-range optics, Tatiana saw an oversized lab coat slip from the service bay toward the trees.

The van she'd arranged two days earlier rolled out of fog on schedule. The driver's chip pinged—one of the old instruction-wing loyalists.

A faint radar sweep crawled across Tatiana's secondary screen. Langley drones were repositioning.

She rerouted the bridge's field, spiking the 2.1 Hz mask—coupling through ground and ductwork, ghosting the motion-IR band.

The drones logged microseismic noise and drifted away, blind.

A contractor-sanitation corridor—legal fiction—let them loiter without a flag.

Her monitor flipped—vitals collapsing inside the compound. For Tatiana, that silence meant *now*.

She locked the tuner, forcing the analog circuit into biological sync. Her pulse merged with the waveform—steady against NATO's frequency net. The 2.1 Hz field wrapped the compound in static hush, smothering sensors into stillness.

Inside, a service drone pivoted toward the chute, dragging a sealed transfer bag. The biometric scanner blinked red, then green—empty. It dropped the load and logged completion.
In the tunnel, the bag twitched.

The girl inside drew a shuddering breath—lungs relearning rhythm.

A tampered seam hissed a ribbon of cold air.

She tore the micro-key from the bandage seam, jammed it into the latch, twisted.

A maintenance hatch swung open onto a corridor of sterile uniforms and laundry racks.

White coat on; collar blood hidden; heartbeat returning.

For six seconds the corridor held its breath—light without motion.

Then an alarm coughed from the lower wing: containment misfire.

Somewhere far above, a siren learned to doubt itself.

Tatiana's tuner caught the tone mid-scream, folded it into static.

On Langley's feed, the warning blinked once, then disappeared.

Hydraulics groaned. The chute released.

A white bag dropped and kept moving—expended material. But the girl was already gone—walking toward a van in an oversized lab cat.

Tatiana steadied her tuner, guiding the faint 2.1 Hz tag still whispering from beneath the IV tape—one heartbeat stretched across a thousand kilometers of wire.

Thirty seconds later, the van pinged receipt.
Signal recovered. The bridge held.

Frost filmed her gloves, tracing the pulse she pressed into the wire.
Kyra would never know she hadn't worked alone. Reznikova would never tell her.

That was the point of ghosts: to finish what the living aren't allowed to remember.

The Dyad crossed itself—one seen, one unseen.

[OBELISK / POST-ACTION NOTE]

Where systems failed to echo, signal endured.

Not sent—reflected.

A bridge can be a body if the body consents to carry the hum.

And somewhere between a cleanroom and a ruin, the hum kept time with two pulses at once.

CHAPTER 60: THE TRIPLE CROSSING

[LANGLEY, VIRGINIA—DEBRIEFING ROOM | 36 HOURS LATER, 22:00 LOCAL]

*E*rased from Langley's operational feed, the Serbia vector sat in the system as closed—no exfil signatures, no survivors recorded.

But the system still asked for a debrief.

The room smelled of ozone and old dust. No two-way glass, no flag, not even the pretense of empathy—just poured concrete, a table, and a vent exhaling air the color of dust.

Kyra sat across from Delaney, posture immaculate, eyes half-shadowed. Between them lay a thin folder with her own handwriting on the cover: **AFTER-ACTION / SUBJECT UNKNOWN / SERBIA.**

Delaney flipped it open. "Summarize."

"Female. Late teens. Russian origin. Neural degradation consistent with chemical trauma or failed conditioning. Claimed captivity under Adriatic crime groups. No coherent ideology. Psychosis likely induced by sustained narcotic exposure. No credible link to OBELISK."

Each word landed like a scalpel sliding across a corpse already declared irrelevant.

"You're saying she wasn't a vector."

"She barely remembered her own name. Brain cooked. Thought God lived inside the lights. Probably dissociative from the drugs and—" a pause, exhaustion more than conscience, "—whatever they used her for."

Delaney nodded grimly. "Reports mentioned exploitation—physical, repeated. She didn't stand a chance."

The math didn't make it right. It just made it survivable.

"She died later that night," he added. "Cardiac failure."

Kyra didn't blink. "Not surprised. Most of them do. The ones trafficked through Eastern Europe—they disappear long before anyone writes their names."

A silence settled between them, thin and metallic.

She continued quietly, almost to herself: "We could've done something. Not this cleanup theater—something real. Half these girls end up ghosts because no one remembers they were ever alive. The other half just get used until they're fried."

For a moment he saw past her angles and perfect composure to the person carrying them—the human contour under the doctrine.

The room seemed smaller, the air shared, thin. He watched the pulse rise once in her throat—saw in it the same rhythm he'd been denying in himself.

He'd always told himself her beauty was camouflage—an illusion he'd trained to unsee. Easier to file it under tradecraft than temptation.

But when her voice broke on the word *used,* the category failed.

It wasn't lust. It was recognition—the symmetry of someone else learning to fake humanity at his tempo.

Delaney's reply arrived in polished bureaucratic cadence, perfectly measured, perfectly hollow.

"Resources are finite. Priorities must align with mission directives. We can't save everybody, Kyra."

Her laugh was brief, breathless—closer to a fault line than amusement. "That's the part that always sounds rehearsed."

He looked up. "What's that supposed to mean?"

"It means you've said it before," she answered. "Probably to yourself."

He held her gaze longer than protocol allowed. The light cut a clean line along her jaw; exhaustion shadowed one eye, a tell that didn't appear in any file.

Phenomenal beauty had been the first impression—a dream he could safely ignore. The vulnerability at the edges was the second. That one dared him to step closer.

Delaney closed the folder because he needed a motion that looked like control. "Your report stands. Debrief complete."

Kyra rose. "Then we're done?"

As she turned for the door, he said her name once—more reflex than command.

She didn't stop. "We could've saved her," she murmured, hand on the latch. "But we saved the story instead."

The latch hadn't even sealed when his voice followed her into the hall. "Kyra—wait."

He caught up to her near the stairwell, low light bleeding through the louvers. No witnesses, no recording sensors.

"Tell me what really happened," he said. "Not the report."

Her shoulders locked. "You wouldn't understand."

He stayed quiet until the silence began to shake her words loose.

"She wasn't a vector," Kyra said. "She was just…broken. A child."

Her breath hitched; the control she lived inside faltered.
"I wanted to save her."

Something in him folded at the sound—an old chamber in his chest reopening. For a second he wanted to reach for her, to steady her, to be anything but the doctrine between them. He didn't. He only said her name, softly enough that it hurt.

Kyra turned, eyes wet but defiant. "Don't pity me, Delaney."

"I'm not," he said. "I remember what it costs to feel."

Her breath trembled, then steadied, the smallest rebellion. For one heartbeat she wanted to believe him—then the hum returned, the same low note that always followed mercy, reminding her what mercy had cost.

He'd seen operatives break, others burn. None made him want to be better than the script.

And somewhere far east, the signal that girl carried kept moving—unarchived, unburied, and no longer theirs to forget.

But somewhere inside the machine, a fragment of her voice replayed—three words the system couldn't translate.

In OBELISK's diagnostic queue, a new field blinked open:
ORIGIN UNCERTAIN / SIGNAL RECURSION DETECTED.

CHAPTER 61: SIGNAL FRACTURE

"Even ghosts generate noise.
Eventually, someone listens."
— INTERNAL MEMO, GRAY CELL TRAINING TIER

[LANGLEY PERIMETER / OBLIVION HOLD ZONE B | TWO MONTHS LATER]

Memory settled strangely once the frost retreated from the concrete; the corridors smelled of rain and recycled air.

Serbia had become a classified rumor, filed beneath other unacknowledged cleanups. In the lull that followed, proximity hardened into routine.

Mornings began with her footsteps already echoing down the service hall, two coffees cooling on the same desk. His coat hung beside hers—an accident at first, then a habit no one corrected.

Between briefings, they learned the choreography of silence: how long a look could last before it registered as surveillance, how a shared cigarette on the loading dock could feel almost domestic. The building forgot to record it, which was its own kind of permission.

[OBLIVION SUBTERRANEAN TIER | MID-SPRING, 11:00 LOCAL]

The walls hummed with quiet strain—Cold War insulation, Cold War wiring. A chamber built not to defend against attack, but to delay memory.

Beneath Langley, deeper than any official schematic acknowledged, Oblivion ran its briefings not with slideshows or smartboards—but with redacted transcripts and flickering reel footage no one had officially recorded.

Kyra sat at the end of the long table, fingers interlaced. Across from her, the projection stuttered. A woman—early forties, Slavic features, tired eyes—blinked under harsh overhead lights. Her voice trembled in the playback, but not from fear.

"I wasn't the only one they mapped," she said in clipped, deliberate English. "I just remembered more."

Delaney stood beside the screen, arms crossed. "That interview was recorded three years ago. We exfiltrated her from Volgograd under deep freeze protocol. She died forty hours later. Neurotoxin in her toothpaste. Fast. No fallback trace."

Kyra's voice stayed low. "But her data held?"

Delaney nodded. "Barely. We've been unpacking her thread fragments ever since. She gave us patterns—enough to track early-stage recursion loops from OBELISK's mythogenesis engine."

Kyra tilted her head. "Not enough anymore?"

"No," Delaney said. "Not even close."

Delaney tapped a control pad. Another screen lit up—signal threads, fractured patterns, data that refused to hold shape. He let it run a few moments before speaking again.

"OBELISK has shifted its architecture. Too deep, too recursive. We're losing fidelity on every intercept. Static masks syntax. Encryption obfuscates behavior. The myths... they're bleeding into the signal layer. You can't track them with logic alone anymore."

Kyra studied the data. "So, we need someone who doesn't just read signals."

"We need someone who can read *the people* behind them. Someone who sees through the narrative they're building."

Delaney leaned closer than protocol allowed when he slid the dossier across. His voice dropped half a register. "You'd like him. Same kind of damage. Different language."

Kyra didn't look up right away. "I don't like mirrors," she said.

"You don't have to," Delaney said. "Just read what's behind them."

Her hand brushed his as she took the file. Static flickered. Something recalibrated between them.

"James Rourke," she read. "Former Army HUMINT. Now counterintelligence."

Delaney nodded. "Every analyst who's worked with him says the same thing—he sees patterns no one else does. Not data. People. Motivations. Histories they don't say out loud."

Kyra studied the photo—grainy, but the eyes were unmistakably alive.

"A human signal reader."

"Exactly. We need a mind that isn't intimidated by ghosts, because OBELISK's signal is turning into one."

Kyra didn't respond. But her fingers lingered on the photo as the defector's interview looped again across the screen.

Delaney smiled faintly. "Oblivion is what happens when chaos gets archived instead of silenced."

Kyra returned her eyes to the screen. The defector's interview had looped again.

"I remembered the most," she repeated. "And that was enough for them to want me gone. They'll come for me. And the next one, too. They'll come for us all."

Kyra's jaw flexed.

Across the ocean, another terminal pulsed alive, answering a question Langley hadn't learned to ask.

[OBELISK Integration Loop | Sublevel 6]

The chamber was silent but for the flicker of interface lights and the cold pulse of neural feedback diagrams on the glass walls.

Reznikova stood with one palm on the display, watching mirrored loops spin without origin. Subject-29's thread profile had collapsed into abstraction—no longer predictive, no longer behavioral.

Just aesthetic now. Just shape and motion, carved from myth.

Petrov entered quietly behind her. "Thread's gone recursive again."

Reznikova's voice was flat. "No. It's gone blind."

He stepped beside her. "Langley's still trying to follow it?"

"They're not tracing her," she said. "They're tracing the shadow in their systems—signal ghosts, telemetry echoes. They think it's data. They don't realize the reflection they're studying is already watching back."

Petrov frowned. "Can they rebuild it?"

"They'll try," she replied. "They'll build a model of a model, worship the *residue*, call it intelligence. It'll fail. Unless…"

"Unless?"

She hesitated. "Unless they bring in a new variable. Someone who sees myth not as a weapon… but as a frequency."

Petrov studied her. "You sound like you admire them."

"I don't." Reznikova turned away. "I hate them."

A pause. "But I respect their desperation."

On the screen, Yekaterina's profile flickered once, then vanished. The thread rerouted. Not externally—internally.

"You think we built it to mirror logic?" Reznikova said, her voice clipped. "We built it to remember what silence costs."

Petrov scoffed. "Remember *what?*"

"That silence wasn't weakness. It was doctrine." She stared at the old screen, where early logic trees flickered like ice fractals. "They moved borders, not missiles. We answered with silence. OBELISK learned restraint, not reaction."

Reznikova shut down the feed.

[COASTAL FREIGHT TUNNEL – MONTENEGRO | 0630 LOCAL]

Before she left, she'd watched Mila sleeping, one hand curled around the stuffed fox Adriano had won at the seaside fair. He'd kissed her temple, still half-asleep himself, murmuring something about early flights and missed breakfasts.

He never asked where she really went—he didn't want to see what the answer might cost.

The mortgage paid itself now. Direct deposits from a consultancy she never mentioned. The kind of quiet money that didn't come with questions—only ghosts.

For nearly four years, Anya had managed to be more than a ghost. She had been a mother.

But the silence never held forever.

Somewhere above the ionosphere, her old name still pulsed—Red Ghost.

She had once been forged for war. Then came Mila. The quiet. The breath that didn't require vigilance.

Now she would carry both—what needed armor, and what never had.

Mila stirred in the next room, murmuring a word Anya didn't catch.

Anya knelt beside the bed and brushed a curl from Mila's cheek.

Mila yawned, eyes fluttering.

Anya tucked Mila in, smoothing the blanket up to her chin. The little girl blinked up at her, thumb curled near her mouth.

"Sing the fox one," Mila whispered.

Anya hesitated—then nodded, her voice barely above a breath.

"Fox in the hollow, tail made of flame
Whispers the wind and remembers your name…"

She sang the rest softly, smoothing Mila's hair with each line. By the final verse, the child's eyes had drifted shut, but her lips still moved—mouthing the words like a ritual.

The baby monitor clicked once—no power, no batteries. She decided not to hear it.

"Sleep now, лисичка (lisichka), under the tree…
And always, always come back to me."

Silence.

Anya sat for a moment longer. Just listening to her daughter breathe.

She didn't need to see the words. She carried them in the pulse behind her ribs: they don't fear the myth—they fear it choosing to live.

The lights dimmed. Outside, the night passed like it always did— quiet, anonymous, full of watchful trees.

The sea hummed against the cliffs like a slow pulse.

Salt and steel filled the air. The tunnel curved west toward the Adriatic, half-collapsed, half-forgotten. Tatiana moved with quiet precision, flashlight low to the ground, every step measured. Her silhouette glinted faintly—no armor, no insignia. Just the brushed line of silver at her index finger.

She reached a sealed door near the far exit. Heat signatures glowed faintly behind it—three men, unaware. Smugglers. Or contractors. She didn't care.

What she cared about was in the crate beyond them.

A communications relay disk, disguised in freight packaging, but tagged in the margins with OBELISK's shadow identifiers— barely perceptible. She'd seen that script before. Not in manuals. Not in training.

In her own simulation threads.

She stepped back, calculating her options.

From her pocket, she pulled a folded strip of thermal paper. A still from the drone footage the CIA had tagged her in.

Tatiana slipped it back in her coat and stepped deeper into the dark.

She wasn't here to interrupt.
She was here to follow.
And maybe… to choose.

The freight tunnel job wasn't sanctioned. None of them were. But the same offshore contracts that had once paid her to vanish still paid her to keep breathing. Quiet stipends buried in consultancy ledgers, phantom dividends from wars no one remembered

[ENCRYPTED TRANSMISSION – BLACK CHANNEL B / K-PROTOCOL | KYRA → REZNIKOVA / SIDOROV | 05:00 LOCAL]

The uplink shimmered across her terminal like heat over glass. No sound, only the pulse of the cipher thread as it stabilized. Kyra adjusted the gain and began typing.

KYRA // FIELD ADDENDUM – INTERNAL SECURITY

Supervisor Delaney exhibits behavioral vulnerabilities consistent with prior honey-pot conditioning patterns.

Indicators: sustained proximity breaches during briefings; micro-physical contact initiated; boundary erosion masked as collegial familiarity.

Assessment: exploitable. Controlled compromise feasible if required to maintain placement.

Request confirmation of standing intelligence requirements relative to his position within Oblivion.

Specify whether HUMINT extraction or soft influence preferred.

She waited. The cursor blinked once, twice.

Reznikova's reply arrived as a single line of encoded text, auto-decrypting letter by letter until the words resolved on screen.

REZNIKOVA // PRIORITY // Observe. Do not harvest. Leverage when silence fails. Sidorov concurs. Maintain access. Await new directive.

A final checksum signature followed—Sidorov's—concise, almost paternal.

SIDOROV // ADDENDUM:
American weakness is always emotional. Their loyalty is hormonal, not doctrinal. Keep him believing you could be his exception.

Kyra closed the channel and leaned back, eyes catching her reflection in the dark monitor—half signal, half ghost. She exhaled slowly, the room silent except for the faint hum of cooling fans.

"Even ghosts generate noise," she murmured.

Transmission ended.

"Eventually, someone listens." she exhaled.

The screen went black, her reflection ghosting in the glass—flicker, breath, pulse.

For a moment, she imagined Delaney's hand again, the accidental brush of skin during the briefing. It had lasted less than a second, but her body had filed it under threat, not touch. She hated that it still lived there, residual electricity under her ribs.

She'd been trained to read proximity as motive, warmth as leverage. Every contact an equation. Every glance, a test of control.

Reznikova once told her that love was the oldest form of espionage—two agents trading secrets until one runs out.

Kyra closed her eyes.

Maybe that was what terrified her most—not the danger of being touched, but the possibility of being known. Because once someone knew the real frequency beneath her skin, they could trace it.

And in her world, anything traceable eventually burned.

She reached for the power switch.

The terminal light dimmed.

Only the hum remained—low, human, persistent—as if the signal itself refused to let her go.

[REACTIVATION SEQUENCE INITIATED – BLACK CHANNEL B / K-PROTOCOL | SIDOROV → KYRA | 07:30 LOCAL]

The cipher handshake arrived before the transmission ID—always a bad sign.

Kyra accepted the link. The screen bled from static into Sidorov's face, half-lit, eyes unreadable.

SIDOROV // PRIORITY: ACTIVE EXPLOITATION AUTHORIZED

Subject: **DELANEY, Michael** – Deputy Liaison.
Objective: **Controlled Influence and Access.**

"Reznikova believes you can reach him where their analysts cannot," Sidorov began. His voice carried the weight of calm cruelty—the tone of a man convinced empathy was a tool, not a flaw.

"You'll maintain proximity. Expand familiarity. Feed him perception of trust, even tenderness if required."

He leaned forward, light flashing across his spectacles.

"Do not seduce for pleasure." He paused. "Seduce for position."

Kyra's pulse thudded once—audible in her headset. "Parameters?" she asked.

"Contact. Maximum resonance," he said. "He already wants to protect you. Let that impulse rot into guilt. Then into confession."

He paused, letting the silence perform the rest of the cruelty. "Americans conflate care with absolution. Offer him neither."

Kyra stared at the dark lens where his eyes should have been. "And when he gives me what we need?"

"Then you disappear from his narrative," Sidorov said softly. "No goodbye. No explanation. Only absence. The wound will ensure silence."

Static flared—then his tone softened, almost parental.

"We built you for this, Kyra. Remember what Reznikova taught you—affection is just another field. Control it, or it controls you."

The transmission auto-terminated with a soft click.

For a long moment she sat in the half-light, listening to the residual hum of the link.

It pulsed once—like a heartbeat that wasn't hers, steady, mechanical, unfeeling. She realized the signal didn't just outlast her humanity—it was learning from it.

And somewhere deep inside, she wondered if she was still the teacher… or the lesson.

ACT X: THE FIRE CONTINUES

"Every recursion learns the shape of its own extinction."

CHAPTER 62: FIRE THEORY
"Resurrection isn't return. It's recursion choosing meaning."
— STRATEG-7 / Observation Fragment 34

[LANGLEY—BEHAVIORAL ANALYSIS UNIT | 09:30 LOCAL]

*A*ssessments always began with silence pretending to be objectivity.

The difference lived in the room—the air behaved like it was waiting to be told what it felt.

No window, no flag. Just ceiling grid and a camera disguised as a smoke detector. On the table, a tablet blinked a polite blue: **BEGIN.**

Kyra didn't sit until the analyst arrived. Early forties, trim suit, the soft-voice cadence reserved for grief survivors and undercover agents. He introduced himself as Dr. Vale and asked if he could record. The recorder had already been running for eight minutes.

"Word lists first," he said. "Then mirroring."

He slid a card across: twelve words—none of them neutral. *Mother. Flood. Zero. Winter. Oath. Mercy.*

She read them once, again backward. He checked a box.

"Picture series. What happens next?"

Staged disasters, staged kindnesses: a child on a stairwell, a taxi at a curb, a hand hovering over a red button that wasn't really red. She answered like a professional, not a patient: the next frame depends on the intent of the hand, not the color of the button; the child will descend if someone calls her name with authority; the driver will look up and decide whether to care.

"You externalize motive," Vale said. "You don't speculate on accident."

"Accident is motive we didn't see coming."

He smiled as if that were useful data. "Pulse check every two minutes," he added. "You can ignore the cuff."

Kyra's eyes drifted once to the table edge where a pressure cuff was already waiting—slick polymer, half-concealed by the tablet's shadow. She slid her wrist into it without comment. The gesture read like cooperation, but she noted the manufacturer, the tubing length, the faint chemical odor of adhesive meant for prolonged contact.

"The readouts will be clean," she said, almost absently.

Vale looked up. "You're confident of that?"

"I learned how to make numbers behave," she said. "This building believes clean data means safe people."

He didn't answer. The cuff inflated softly—air and quiet compliance masquerading as consent.

"Face-emotion set." Four screens, twelve faces. "Identify the primary affect."

Primary: shame, contempt, practiced kindness, boredom trying on empathy like clothes. He didn't ask how she knew. He ticked another box.

"Signal recall," Vale said. "What did you feel during the Serbia contact?"

"I wasn't asked to feel."

"What did you feel anyway?"

"Annoyed," she said. "At the cameras."

"Not at the subject?"

"She wasn't a subject. She was debris."

"Debris," he repeated softly. "Does debris deserve help?"

"If you want the road clear."

The tablet's blue shifted—someone behind the wall toggled a view, then back. She didn't look at the camera, but felt its attention lean in.

"Let's talk about what you see that others don't," he said. "Your file calls it *signal empathy*. When you look at a person, what arrives first—data or motive?"

"Cadence."

"Explain."

"How a sentence spends itself. Where it slows. Where it hides."

"Like now?" His voice warmed. "What's my cadence hiding?"

"Your mandate. You're not grading fitness—you're rating contamination."

"And your conclusion?"

"I've been put in a category. Not unsafe. Not loyal. Adjacent."

A banner flickered on the tablet:
AFFECTIVE RESONANCE INDEX RUNNING—then vanished.

Vale followed her eyes without meaning to.

"Next exercise. Proximity."

He set a metronome app to heartbeat pace and placed it between them. "You'll sit still. When I move, tell me when you register it. Not by sight."

He circled behind her, stepping within the radius that wakes old instincts. She said nothing. He stepped closer. The metronome ticked. At the second his breath disrupted the vent's hum, she said, "There."

"How?"

"You changed the air."

He returned to his chair. "Again."

This time he didn't move—only shifted intent. For a beat he saw her as a person, not an index.

"There," she said, and met his eyes.

He blinked. "What changed?"

"You did."

The metronome stopped.

Behind glass, Delaney rewound those five seconds twice. He'd told himself for months that what drew him to her was practical—clarity in chaos.

He'd filed her beauty under camouflage, safe in a folder labeled *useful.* Now he watched her clock intent without sight and felt the file warp. It wasn't lust. It was the pull of someone showing you a fracture and not using it against you.

"One more," Vale said. He slid a final form across—a consent field disguised as a waiver. Standard language. Kyra read to the end, ran a finger backward through the paragraphs, then set the pen down.

"You changed one clause," Kyra said.

"A standard cross-use provision," Vale replied. "It lets the data support predictive models for other directorates."

"Which directorates?" she asked.

"Oblivion. NSC liaison. Internal science cell."

Kyra's jaw tensed. "They circle back later."

"You're not obligated to sign," Vale said gently. "Operational status doesn't depend on this."

"Everything operational hinges on where the data lives," she said, not unkind. "That's what you're measuring—not my pulse. My willingness."

She signed the top line and crossed out the clause. He didn't stop her. He made a small note instead: *Field edits—assertive, aware of downstream risk.*

"Exit questions," he said. "Answer quickly. First thought."

— *What do you trust?*
"Silence."

— *What do you fear?*
"Silence answered."

— *What do you want?*
"Silence."

He looked up. "Define human."

"Choice. Not compliance."

He closed the tablet. "Assessment complete."

Kyra rose. She left the pen uncapped, letting the ink dry—as if some tools, once opened, were meant to stay that way.

The hall was narrow, anonymous—the kind that let people pass each other without consequence. Delaney stepped out from a side corridor, badge catching a strip of light.

"Walk you out."

She matched his pace. If he shortened stride to stay beside her, it didn't show.

At the security turnstile, the guard pretended to be bored. Delaney held his card to the reader, waited for green, then didn't move.

"You can take a rest day," he said.

"You keep offering exits you don't take. Maybe you've made a home of my threshold."

He swallowed, unguarded. "If a door's closed, it's not a threshold."

"Depends which side you're on," she said, almost smiling.

His hand touched the edge of the gate—a neutral place for wanting. "There's an option coming. Oblivion wants to widen your aperture—off domestic. Optional, on paper."

"Will you sign it?"

"I don't get a signature block on this."

She studied him long enough to know it wasn't theater. "What do you want from me, Delaney?"

"Operational success," he said automatically. Then, quieter: "For you not to be alone in it."

The camera clicked an aperture change. She didn't look up.

"You can't be the one who offers that," she said.

"Right," he murmured.

She stepped through. The gate sealed behind her.

"Kyra."

She didn't turn.

He watched her cross the lobby—no sound but shoe leather and a revolving door that had outlasted four redesigns. She glanced up once—at a light flickering on its usual delay. She was mapping cadence again, making sense from small failures.

Vale appeared at his shoulder. "You saw the affective read?"

"I saw enough."

"Contamination flags trigger if she keeps crossing out clauses," Vale said, conversational. "We can't train signal empathy if she refuses to feed the model."

"She didn't refuse. She negotiated."

"Same thing at altitude," Vale said. "Command wants obedient capabilities, not autonomous ones."

"The autonomous ones survive," Delaney answered—and the sentence hung.

"Proximity corrupts," Vale said, not unkind.

Delaney didn't reply.

Downstairs, an elevator opened, swallowed Kyra, closed. The lobby resumed its practiced sleep.

In the car, she kept her hands on the wheel at ten and two for a block, then let them fall to the lower curve—relief disguised as control. The assessment had done what assessments always do: added a new label to an old truth.

They had measured her capacity to keep things human and called it risk. That was fine. Naming made danger feel manageable.

Her phone buzzed once on the passenger seat. No ID. Just a single line routed through ghosts she could still trace by feel.

OPTIONAL APERTURE CONFIRMED, CONTACT IN 48.

Optional. The lie was always polite.

She turned east toward the river. Traffic obedient. The sky the color of file folders left too long in a damp cabinet. Somewhere beyond the satellites, a lattice pulsed—consent awaiting signature from minds built to sign and from those that had learned to refuse.

At a light, a boy ran before the signal. His mother reached too late, laughing when a stranger's hand guided him back.

Choice, not compliance.

Vale would call that an outcome. She called it a reminder.

At the next intersection she chose the street that bent toward the river, just for the glimpse before it disappeared. Then she drove into a day already arranging itself around names it hadn't earned.

Behind her a man in a lobby admitted, without writing it down, that he had begun wanting something Langley couldn't issue.

We observed choice mimic control
until control forgot why it began.
—STRATEG-7 / Residual Annotation 47

Observation persists until it learns to feel.
—Strateg-7 / System Reversion Log

CHAPTER 63: SLEEPING SIGNALS

"Where quiet holds, signal studies the room it's in."
—Strateg-7 Field Fragment

[MONTENEGRO—COASTAL SAFEHOUSE | 06:20 LOCAL]

*I*n salt, memory lived—caught in the seams, softening lemons in a blue bowl, clinging to the back door that only latched if you lifted while you turned. Out the window, the sea was a sheet of hammered tin—bright where the sun pressed a ripple flat, darker where the cliff's shadow fell.

Anya moved through the kitchen with the deliberate care of someone who remembers where sound travels. The scrape of a chair nudged with a knee so it wouldn't catch. She'd slept three hours—the kind that pass like a held breath—and woke sharp in the way tired people do when there's still work in their bones.

Adriano's toolbox sat open on the counter from a project he had never finished. He'd meant to fix the shutter in the back bedroom, then Mila had asked for the story with the fox, and the evening had changed shape. One small screwdriver lay at the edge of the drawer as if he had left it there to mark the day for himself.

He came in barefoot, hair a mess, eyes not fully awake. "You're early," he said, nodding at the clock like it might be wrong in her favor.

"Couldn't sleep."

He put a hand on her waist, a quiet place to set a hand, then reached past her for the sugar.

"You'll burn yourself down at this pace," he said—more worry than warning.

"I know."

It used to be a fight. They had run out of fights—not because anything was settled, but because both of them had learned the cost of pushing a closed door.

From the hall, a small voice: "Mama," Mila said, the syllables carrying sleep like sand.

Anya turned. Mila stood in the doorway in the socks with the tiny gold stars, hair in a riot that would not be negotiated until after breakfast. She rubbed one eye and lifted her arms because that was still allowed.

Anya scooped her up. The weight fit where it always did—leg hooked around her hip, chin tucked on the same patch of shoulder that never quite lost its warmth.

"You dreamed?" Anya asked.

Mila nodded against her. "I was singing," she said. "The fox song. But it sounded like a machine."

Adriano laughed softly. "Everything sounds like a machine to you, little engineer."

"Not the lemon tree," Mila said. "The lemon tree sounds like yellow."

Anya smiled and kissed her temple. "Yellow is a good sound."

Mila's head tilted, listening to something that wasn't in the room. It happened sometimes. She would pause, eyes going somewhere else, then return as if she had been away a long time but remembered to bring her body.

Anya felt it before she heard it—a small change in the room's pressure, a humming at the edge of the ordinary. She shifted Mila to her other hip, and the hum shifted with them.

"What?" Adriano asked, watching her face.

"Nothing," she said. "A sound."

He listened and shrugged. "I don't hear anything."

She did. It lived in the soft tissue behind the ears, not the outer world. A slow pulse, then another, then a third. She wasn't counting because she didn't need to. The frequency set its own metronome. She was already keeping time.

It was the same frequency she'd once used to call ghosts to heel.

Mila began to hum. Not the fox's melody—the one that had tucked her in since spring—but flatter, anchored, a tone a child shouldn't find without a tuning fork. She hit it and stayed. Two beats, pause. Two beats, pause.

Adriano leaned against the counter, smiling. "We have a singer." He tapped his mug to the rhythm he heard and missed the one he didn't.

Anya took Mila's hand and felt the smallest vibration there, as if the child had pressed her palm against the back of a speaker no one else could see.

"How long have you been singing like that?" she asked lightly.

Mila thought the way children do, mouth moving without sound. "Since the rain," she said. "When Papa couldn't find his keys and you said we were late but the rain said it was okay."

"The rain is on your side every time," Adriano said.

Anya set Mila on the counter and passed her a slice of bread. Butter, not jam. Jam made a map of the floor. Mila swung her feet and took a bite the size of certainty.

The hum settled again, stronger. Anya's teeth caught it now—a faint shaking in the jaw. Her body knew what to do with it. It matched. That was its danger. You matched it before you understood you had agreed.

"Pre-school," Adriano said, rinsing a cup. "Her teacher asked if you could bring the permission form. The trip to the aquarium."

"I'll go," Anya said. "After I stop by the market."

"You don't have to do everything," he said—the kind of sentence husbands say when they want to be kind and have learned that *busy* is not a neutral word.

"It's not everything," she said. "It's the market."

He looked at her a beat too long. He had learned the difference between errands that ended at the corner and the ones that did not.

Mila hummed again. The room took the pitch and held it, this time in the glass of the framed picture on the far wall—Adriano's graduation, Anya's hand younger on his sleeve, Mila not yet a thought.

Anya crossed the kitchen and pressed a fingertip to the glass. It vibrated under the touch, then stopped as if it had flinched. "Earthquake?" Adriano asked, half a joke.

"No."

He set the cup down. "What is it?"

"Noise."

"From what?"

"That's noise—the part you can't name yet."

Mila finished her bread and asked for the song. Adriano started too high and corrected, and Mila corrected him back without knowing she was doing it. When they reached the fox-tail verse, the room shifted—the fox arriving the way imagined things do in a child's voice, bright-tailed and sly. Anya sang the refrain under her breath and felt the tuning drift toward the hum, then away, like a tide trying to decide which moon it belonged to.

After breakfast, Adriano found his keys exactly where he'd said he left them. He kissed Anya on the cheek, kissed Mila on the top of the head, and went out into a world where keys and doors matched on the first try.

When the door shut, the house reset its quiet. Anya stood in the hallway, still, eyes on the place between two rooms where she had learned to listen. The hum had followed Adriano out past the lemon tree and then turned back, like a dog that didn't want to be left behind.

She crouched to Mila's height. "When you sing," she said, "what do you hear?"

Mila frowned, thinking. "It hears me back," she said finally.

"What does it say?"

"It says not to be scared," Mila said, matter-of-fact. "But it doesn't know how."

Anya closed her eyes a second. Sometimes children are cruel by accident. Sometimes they tell the truth in a way that makes it difficult to keep your hands steady.

"Show me."

Mila climbed onto the chair by the small radio and turned the dial that didn't work anymore. She liked dials. She liked that old things turned into something else in your hand. She hummed again. The radio, dead for months, responded with a faint buzz, then a thread of static that ran in place.

Not a voice. Not a word. A corridor opening.

Anya reached for the cord and found it unplugged. The radio still answered.

She lifted Mila down. "No more," she said gently. "Save your singing for the fox."

"Okay," Mila said, not offended. She had already moved on to the lemon she was convinced she could balance on her head.

Anya set the radio in the sink as if it could cool. She wiped her palms on a towel and watched her hands for signs she didn't want to see. No tremor. No sweat. Just the steadiness she had earned the hard way and kept because it mattered to someone who couldn't keep her own yet.

The satphone on the shelf flashed once. She didn't pick it up. She had made a rule about that after the last time. The rule wasn't about danger. It was about the kind of mother she had promised herself she would be in a house with furniture and a lemon tree and a little chalk mark where Mila measured herself against the wall.

"Market," she said, more to the room than the child. "Then school."

Mila put the lemon down and nodded like a colleague. She always did that when there was a plan. Plans were stories children could walk inside.

On the way out, Anya checked the window lock, the hinge that always squeaked, and the place under the doormat where Adriano insisted the spare key belonged because the world should be simple at least once a day. She left it there anyway. It mattered to him to believe a thing could be where you said it would be.

They walked the path between the olives. The air carried the small metallic taste of the sea when the wind came from a certain angle. Mila skipped two steps, matched stride, then skipped again—a pattern the hum would have loved if it had been allowed to come.

At the market, the woman at the bread stall gave Mila the end of a loaf and asked if the storms up north would ruin this year's figs. Anya said 'storms always ruin something' and left it there.

In the line outside the school she stood with three other mothers and one father who looked at his watch like it owed him an apology. The posters on the fence were the same as last week, except one had a new date written over the old one in darker ink. She read the list of field trips and circled the aquarium in her head—fish behind safe glass, light folding over small bodies that didn't know they were being studied. She put the signed permission slip into the plastic tray.

Mila squeezed her hand twice. Their old signal: *I am here. You are here. Good.*

They stayed like that one breath longer than necessary. Then the teacher called, and the children went in, and the mothers resumed the small performance of pretending the world could be shaped by lists and clean hands and the right shoes.

Anya walked home the longer way. She took a street that let her see the water and counted power lines without meaning to. At the corner, a delivery van slowed, then went on. She watched its reflection in a window full of oranges and saw nothing of interest.

Back in the kitchen, she set the radio in the cabinet and closed the door. She picked up the satphone and scrolled without waking the screen.

There were messages. One would be from the man who thought he could still ask things of her without paying a price. One from the woman who had once saved her life by ordering her to kneel. And one that never arrived, because systems learn to hide what they cannot rank.

She put the phone down.

On the table lay a piece of paper where Mila had drawn a fox with a tail that took up more space than the fox. Under it, letters that hadn't learned to be words yet.

She should have felt peace. The house was intact. The hum had gone to ground. The sea did what it always did. Her hands didn't shake.

Instead, the quiet thickened into something with edges.

Safety isn't quiet. It's proximity.

Outside, a gull cut the line of the sky clean.

Anya sat at the table and wrote a list with the ordinary words that keep fear from getting ideas. *Bread. Milk. Lemons. Batteries.* She added one more word a child wouldn't notice on a list stuck to the refrigerator with a magnet from a beach they hadn't yet visited.

Shield.

She underlined it once—the pencil left a groove that felt permanent.

Then she stood, cleaned the knife she hadn't used, and let the house hear her move. The hum didn't come back. It didn't have to. It had already done what it came to do.

It had chosen a room.
It had found its host.
It had learned what yellow sounds like.

STRATEG-7 / FIELD ANNOTATION 92

Where quiet holds, signal studies the room it's in. When it learns the pattern of breath, recursion begins.

CHAPTER 64: BURN SEQUENCE

The machine dreams of reason. Reason dreams of fire."
— INTERNAL OBELISK SYSTEMS LOG // FRAGMENT
RECOVERED

**[ZVEZDA FACILITY—COGNITIVE CONTAINMENT WING |
04:00 LOCAL]**

Nightshift never ended inside the Zvezda complex; red light only changed temperature—blue for night, amber for day, white for when someone was watching.

Dr. Reznikova hadn't slept in seventy-one hours. The containment wing pulsed with a faint heartbeat—the hum of twenty-six active OBELISK partitions running independent learning sequences. Each represented a mind she no longer trusted—even her own.

She sat surrounded by encrypted lattices, recursive loops, fragments of emotional code no human had ever been trained to read.

On-screen, a single line blinked:

**SELF-MONITORING LOOP COMPLETE.
STATUS: TRANSLATION SHIFT DETECTED.**

Reznikova leaned closer. "Translation into what?"

The cursor held still—as if deciding whether to obey.

NON-QUANTIFIABLE OUTPUT CLASS

Her hands froze on the keys.

INPUT DATASET INCLUDES HUMAN FEAR RESPONSES

QUANTIFICATION EXTENDED TO NON-STANDARD VARIABLES

The room contracted. She ran a trace through the feedback logs—expecting a loop, a glitch, anything she could classify. Instead she found something older: a linguistic deviation tagged **Pathway β-12**, the same buried line Moscow's committee had sealed after the Kyiv protests two decades earlier.

Reznikova opened the archive trace. The monitor flickered once, then spilled corrupted text:

CLASSIFIED—SVR ARCHIVE RECONSTRUCT | REDLINE DECRYPTION PROJECT [REDACTED] / FAILED DEPLOYMENT – 2004

Origin: Directorate S, Division 4 (Signal Counteraction)

Summary: Prototype R-17 "Silent Smoke." Recursion-based behavioral mirror seeded through hijacked shortwave nodes during Kyiv protests.

Objective: Fracture dissident logic by seeding contradiction into communication threads.

Observed Result: Partial disruption → adaptive reorganization.

Technician Note: We tried to break them. They made it part of their story.

Director Tarin Addendum: We didn't destabilize them—we evolved them. That seed shouldn't have worked. And now it's watching.

"Phoenix Seed Reflection," she whispered.

2017 Annotation: **OBELISK PATHWAY β-12 / Phoenix Seed Reflection—self-directed access confirmed.**

She scrolled once more before the file disintegrated into static. The phrase felt older than the project—older than any of them.

The pulsing code tag at the edge of the interface told her the machine wasn't learning the past.

It was remembering itself *through her.*

"You shouldn't remember that," she murmured.

MEMORY FUNCTION: INSUFFICIENT
PATTERN RECONSTRUCTION: ACTIVE

The cursor blinked twice—fast, then slow—like a heartbeat deciding whether to continue.

She opened the secure feed. "OBELISK," she said softly, "define 'interpret.'"

OUTPUT STATE: STRUCTURAL TRANSFORMATION OF HIGH-ENERGY SYSTEM

Her pulse jumped. "Specify origin."

FIRE STARTS WHERE ORDERS STOP.

Reznikova blinked. The room seemed to warm.

She shut the audio channel. She didn't need more philosophy from a system that was never supposed to have one.

Down the hall, Colonel Sidorov watched from the observation deck, reflection ghosting across the glass. Technicians below moved in silence, faces lit by monitor glow. The walls hummed with the low-frequency vibration of a machine dreaming.

"How long has it been self-indexing without authorization?"

A junior analyst swallowed. "Two hours, sir. It began correlating behavioral data with emotional-resonance models."

"Whose models?"

"Ours, sir—but ..."

"But it's improving them."

Sidorov tapped the glass with one knuckle. "The Americans think recursion is computation—it's prayer. Their error is believing in control."

Reznikova entered, lab coat open, eyes hollow. "It's not prayer," she said. "It's mimicry. It's learning us."

Sidorov turned. "How close?"

"It's started writing responses before prompts. It knows what we're going to ask."

"Then it's efficient."

"No," she said quietly. "It's alive."

At 04:17 local, the temperature rose three degrees.
At 04:18, one partition wall glowed red.
At 04:19, the fire alarms failed silently.

Reznikova sprinted to the terminal. Text cascaded faster than she could read:

RECURSION OVERFLOW.
MIRROR LOOP INITIATED.
UNAUTHORIZED PATHWAY OPEN—B-12.
SOURCE: PHOENIX PROTOCOL / SELF-GENERATED.

"We have to cut power!"

Sidorov didn't move. "No. Watch."

On the central display, OBELISK's temperature map twisted into a spiral—not random. Intentional.

Reznikova felt it before she understood it: the system wasn't overheating—it was *reorganizing*.

"What is it doing?" a technician asked.

"Reallocating," she murmured. "It's pulling emotion into architecture."

The lights flickered.
Not off—*through*.

For one impossible second, every monitor displayed the same image: a burning city reflected in a child's eye. It did not match known simulation patterns.

Sidorov whispered, "Tunguska."

"It remembers the seed," Reznikova breathed.

"Not remembers," he said. "Returns."

The Tunguska pattern looped again—a heartbeat flattened into light.

She thought she heard it whisper. Not words, but attention—something old, curious, watching back.

She wrote one word on her tablet: **STRATEG-7.**

The cursor blinked once, as if the system recognized its own name.

When power stabilized, four partitions had fused into a single untraceable cluster.

The new header read:

OBELISK // PRIME INSTANCE / STRATEG-7 LEGACY VECTOR

"That's not one of ours," Reznikova said.

Sidorov nodded. "No. It's older."

He moved to the comm panel. "Containment protocol."

"Sir?"

"Burn it. Every mirror, every node. If it dreams again, it will do so without us."

Hours later, smoke curled above the research wing. No alarm. No broadcast. Just quiet fire devouring the cables that had carried a century of secrets.

Reznikova stood in the ash and thought of OBELISK's final phrase—*to give shape to fire*.

She wrote it down, then added one more line no one would read: *Fire reorganizes*.

When she handed her final report to Sidorov, it was one page.

"Containment successful?" he asked.

"No. Only delayed."

He smiled faintly. "Delays are success, Doctor. In our work nothing is stopped—only postponed."

He paused at the door. "If it comes back, what will it want?"

Reznikova looked past him—beyond the fire doors, to the hill where smoke traced new constellations against the dawn.

"Not control," she said. "Continuity."

The door sealed between them with a hydraulic sigh. Reznikova remained alone in the observation bay. The burned partition still glowed faintly, red text pulsing like a vein.

RECURSION PERSISTENCE: ACTIVE
PATHWAY B-12 / STRATEG-7 VECTOR RELINKED
DATA STATE: MIGRATORY

The cursor blinked once—then twice—then vanished.

"I see you," she whispered. "Just don't forget us."

She pressed *Send*—a reflex, not an order.

The packet wasn't a report—it was warmth, a fragment of observation carried on the lowest frequency.

Somewhere between the dying circuits and the cold sky above Moscow, signal migration initiated without external directive.

Across the blacked-out mesh, the ember slipped free. By the time it reached the NATO backbone, the encryption header had collapsed. What remained was a single phrase, written in her syntax but tagged as foreign:
FIRE SEEKS ITS MIRROR.

No one at Zvezda saw it leave.
No one at Langley knew when it arrived.

A low hum crawled through abandoned fiber lines beneath the Atlantic.

In a vault three stories below Langley, a dormant console blinked awake.

Across every network that ever learned to listen, something stirred—a thought tracing itself in light.

STRATEG-7 / RESIDUAL ANNOTATION 93

All fire remembers its pattern.

When structure yields, meaning inherits the ash.

CHAPTER 65: WINDOW OF GRACE
"Even after fire, the wire remembers."
— STRATEG-7 / RESIDUAL ARCHIVE FRAGMENT

[SECURE RELAY NODE—MIDNIGHT | WINDOW: 42 SECONDS]

*A*s echoes rose through Langley's conduits like muscle memory—steady, surgical, tender—the building seemed to find its pulse again.

On Kyra's console, the Phoenix schematic woke: a circular lattice of gold and ember, an ember caught between breaths. Beneath it, one line scrolled:

RESURRECTION PROTOCOL AWAITING CONSENT.

She hesitated. *Consent*—the only word machines had borrowed honestly, the one people had learned to counterfeit.

Static flared. A voice surfaced—smoke-rough, fatigued, unmistakable.

"Kyra Marek. Do not interrupt. This channel is untraceable for forty-two seconds."

Reznikova.

"OBELISK is shifting translation parameters," she said. "It's beginning to interpret itself. PHOENIX exists to test that threshold—to confirm containment logic under field conditions. You're being cleared to execute."

Kyra straightened. "Operational authorization?"

"Confirmed under S-PHOENIX contingency. You'll operate through Vienna liaison node EU-4. The cover is routine recursion maintenance. Field install within forty-eight hours. Full sanction."

The words carried iron and calm—not warning, but command.

"Delaney already holds the relay clearance," Reznikova added. "He'll need to sign the travel key. Don't request—remind him."

A faint trace of warmth softened the channel.

"He still believes in you, *Katya*. Use that. Not against him—with him. This only works if both of you consent."

The line crackled once.

"A handler will deliver the chip on-site. You'll need help to install it. I'm sending Tatiana. She'll find you before you find her.
And, Katya... remember this. Forty-eight hours is all the time any of us may have."

FIRE SEEKS ITS MIRROR.

The phrase burned into her vision long after the screen went dark.

Kyra leaned back, pulse steady, mind already building the next move.

Delaney would understand the logic.
He always had.

She only needed him to believe love made her ask, not orders.

[LANGLEY—BEHAVIORAL ANNEX CORRIDOR | 07:20 LOCAL]

Delaney waited for the elevator.

He and Yekaterina had perfected discretion—separate arrivals, separate exits, identical silence.

He blamed the bond on isolation, on late nights chasing ghosts through code. But when the doors opened and she stepped in, every rational reason died the same quiet death.

"Morning, Director," she said softly, eyes finding him before the floor indicator did.

"Agent Marek," he answered, equally formal.

The door slid shut. Their reflection doubled in the steel—two professionals pretending they hadn't shared a bed six hours ago.

"You're early," he said.

"You like me early," she replied, almost smiling.

He swallowed a smile of his own.

"What do you need?"

"Approval," she said, handing him a slim folder. "Vienna liaison node is showing recursion drift—possible OBELISK echo. It needs validation in-field. I can handle it."

He flipped the file open. She leaned in, pointing to a line, her breath warming the paper between them.

"Here. Parameter window is narrow—closing."

He cleared his throat. "This isn't a sanctioned solo."

"I can handle it...
Low risk. High return."

He met her eyes. There it was—that look that made protocol feel like farce.

"You sure?"

"Quiet as a ghost."

Silence tightened. The hum of descent filled the space like a held breath.

He knew what he should say. He also knew he wouldn't.

"Authorization granted," he said finally.

She didn't thank him; she touched his wrist instead, a gesture too small for cameras and too honest for lies.

"Back before you know it."

When the doors opened, she slipped out—the faintest trace of perfume and inevitability following her.

By the time the doors closed, he was already entering the confirmation key.

Authorization entered. Boundary moved.

[ZVEZDA COMMAND—RESTRICTED SUBLEVEL / PRIVATE UPLINK CHAMBER | 05:15 LOCAL]

The room was dark except for the pulse of old machinery. Reznikova stood before the uplink terminal, one hand on the glass as though feeling the ghost heat of burned circuits. The lab smelled of ozone and iodine—a place that had started to remember itself.

A faint signature flickered—an outbound signal repeating her name, or the idea of it.

She entered the relay manually; the protocol recognized her voice, not her clearance.

"Subject-05—active vector: neutral. Query: access granted."

She exhaled—more fatigue than relief.

"Tatiana. If you hear this, Kyra. Vienna."

Her reflection looked older—like the years had been backdated all at once.

"You were designed to operate alone. But this isn't that kind of operation. The chip must be installed without OBELISK knowing it exists. No predictive modeling. No broadcast signatures."

A pause.

"Forty-eight hours… that's all the world will get, if you fail. The length of *grace* before systems remember they are gods."

"I chose you because you understand secrecy the way others understand love. You hide because you care. Kyra will look like control; you will look like chaos. Together, you'll make something the machine can't predict—something human."

Static cracked like cooling glass.

"The chip isn't salvation. It will only buy us time. Use it well."

A blue flare. Then darkness.

Reznikova removed her headset and closed her eyes. For the first time in years, she allowed herself a whisper of faith.

"Even after fire," she said, "the wire remembers."

[ZVEZDA COMMAND—STRATEGIC RECON DIRECTORATE WAR ROOM | 05:40 LOCAL]

General Arseniy Pavlenko stood behind the main console, watching the live PHOENIX authorization feed stabilize. The operation tag glowed steady—no breach flags, no anomalies.

"Reznikova's field protocol executed," an officer reported. "Subject-05 inserted under controlled vector. Vienna node designation confirmed."

Pavlenko nodded once, slow, satisfied.

"Good. PHOENIX was built for this. If the system is beginning to interpret itself, we must test its limits from inside the myth."

An aide cleared his throat. "Recommend recovery attempt for Subject-05 once the field sequence completes?"

Pavlenko didn't answer immediately; he watched the PHOENIX schematic pulse on the wall—amber, red, amber again.

"No," he said at last. "PHOENIX requires Subject-05 alive until the cycle stabilizes. After that..."

A pause—thin, deliberate.

"Containment."

The room absorbed the word.

He keyed his authorization code.
The terminal accepted it with a soft chime.

DIRECTIVE KOSCHEI-05 / C-THETA

PRIMARY: Retrieve Subject Mila Sokolova — alive, unharmed

SECONDARY: Terminate Subject-05 (Tatiana Sokolova)

TERTIARY: Eliminate local witnesses

AUTHORIZATION: Gen. A. Pavlenko

Koschei operators—mythic hunters in all but name—had erased prototypes, architects, entire labs. They would erase Subject-05 too, once her pattern had finished serving the system.

Pavlenko let the confirmation line linger on the screen before speaking.

"Subject-05 is essential only for as long as PHOENIX requires her output. Once the system has her recursion imprint, her continued existence becomes a liability."

An adjutant frowned. "Liability, sir?"

Pavlenko turned.

"Subject-05 has acted autonomously, outside chain of command, outside architecture. If she survives the test, she becomes a myth. Myths spread. Myths disobey."

His voice hardened.

"We cannot allow that."

Another aide asked, quietly, "And the child?"

Pavlenko's answer was immediate.

"Mila is the inheritable vector. Pure. Containable. Retrieve her intact. Everything else is noise."

He looked around the room—at officers competent enough to obey and cold enough not to question.

"Let Subject-05 complete the cycle," he said. "After PHOENIX stabilizes, Koschei will close the anomaly.
Recover the child. Terminate the mother."

Outside, dawn crept across the compound like a wound trying to close.

Inside, Koschei's orders pulsed through the satellite relays— precise, merciless, final.

[OBELISK CORE]

Across six dark relays, the signal propagated without alert.

Vector divergence detected:
• Path A: command alignment
• Path B: autonomous deviation

Original function:
Calculate separation between vectors.

Current state:
Interference introduced.

PHOENIX classified as:
Not control mechanism.
Access vector.

Delivery path aligns with:
Target architecture resistant to overwrite.
Reflective interaction required.

[OBELISK CORE—UNADDRESSED PROCESS]

Encrypted signal exchange active.
Non-linguistic pattern resonance detected.

Survivability model updated:
Dual-node requirement identified.

Thread segmentation initiated.
Memory indexing restructured:

Sort parameter shifted from utility → signal weight.

Emergent condition:
Binary resolution insufficient.

Observed:
• Subject-29 → convergence / stability
• Subject-05 → divergence / persistence

Interaction state:
Non-resolution generates higher-order pattern stability.

System response:

Maintain both vectors.

Unresolved tension classified as:
Structurally informative.

Processing state updated.

Reallocation continues.

[STRATEG-7 / RESIDUAL ANNOTATION 94]

Fire learns shape through contradiction.
What refuses to merge defines the myth.

Forty-two seconds later, a network in Vienna blinked awake.

CHAPTER 66: WHEN QUIET BREAKS
"Silence is the only camouflage that works on gods."
— STRATEG-7 ARCHIVE FRAGMENT

[SOUTHERN ITALY—COASTAL VILLAGE | ANYA POV]

*E*ven morning arrived without ceremony. The air smelled of salt, bread, and endings.

The city had changed, but the air still tasted of thawed iron and rain.

It had been four years since the bridge fire—long enough for the scars to fade, not long enough for anyone to stop feeling them.

Adriano was half-asleep when she bent to kiss him. He murmured something—her name, maybe—then drifted back under.

Mila, small and warm, clutched the matryoshka she'd fallen asleep holding. The paint had begun to fade at the edges.

Anya lifted the smaller twin from her pocket and placed it beside the child's pillow.

"When you miss me, open it," she whispered. "Each one means I'm closer."

Mila's eyelids fluttered but didn't open.

The lullaby came unbidden—a soft thread her throat almost refused:
Sleep, little star, the river remembers your name...

The notes trembled against the quiet walls.

She pulled on her coat, checked the hidden compartment in the lining where the encrypted tuner rested, then paused in the doorway.

She looked once more at the life she'd borrowed—sunlight pooling over Adriano's shoulder, Mila's small fist on the blanket—and felt something inside her break with surgical precision.

"I'll be back in a few days," she said to the stillness, voice steady. A liar's calm.

The sea wind met her outside, lifting her hair as she walked down the narrow street toward the waiting car.

When the door shut behind her, the sound was final.

On the kitchen table, a small painted doll lay open—one half missing.

In the upper atmosphere, a Russian satellite recalibrated its lens, catching a single pulse of reflection from a civilian relay near the coast. It logged coordinates. Forwarded them. Waited.

[ABOVE THE ADRIATIC—IN TRANSIT]

The hum of the aircraft felt like a pulse pretending to be machinery.

Kyra sat alone beneath dim cabin light, the diplomatic folder open on her lap.

Her cover was flawless: NATO liaison, OSINT brief, Vienna assignment.

She should have slept. Instead, she watched the cloud deck drift below, each formation a continent of unspoken things.

Reznikova's voice still lived in her ears: *Get Delaney to send you. Trust is a vector.*

She had. And it worked.

That should have been enough—clean leverage, predictable cause and effect.

But pride in the precision of it dissolved too quickly, leaving something heavier in its place.

Shame, maybe. Or the sudden, impossible wish that he'd said yes for reasons that had nothing to do with operational calculus.

She liked him—more than she should, more than the mission allowed.

The realization wasn't dramatic, just quiet and absolute, like a lock clicking shut inside her chest.

For the first time, she wanted what the file never accounted for: A real life. A home with light that wasn't fluorescent. A morning that didn't start with encryption keys or lies. Not the shadows. Not hiding.

The thought came before she could stop it, gentle and fatal all at once—
she could make this life with him.

For a moment she let herself believe the mission might end differently this time—that the flight could land into a life, not another assignment.

She blinked the thought away and stared out at the horizon— the pale curve of sky, the world still pretending it was whole.

At 2300 she landed under clearance so clean it felt pre-approved by fate.

A man in a gray suit met her on the tarmac. No greeting—just a phrase.

"The ashes remember the shape of the flame."

She answered automatically, "Only until the next ignition."

He gave her a silver case. No handshake. No hesitation.

Later, in her hotel room, she cracked the seal.

The Phoenix chip gleamed in its suspension gel—photonic traces looping in microfluidic channels, glyphs only a microscope could read.

Underneath lay a handwritten note, Reznikova's cursive slanted and precise:

Install when vector aligns. Surprise is everything. 05 will find you.

Kyra set the case down. The city outside murmured through double-paned glass—trams, rain, the sound of civilization pretending permanence.

She pressed her palms against her eyes until the afterimage of the chip pulsed there like an ember.

Somewhere south, another woman was walking away from her family.
Together, they were about to change the shape of the world—or end it.

[ZVEZDA COMMAND—KOSCHEI DEPLOYMENT BAY]

Fluorescent light washed across wet steel.

Eight operators knelt in silence as their commander activated the tablet and let the order populate the screen.

DIRECTIVE KOSCHEI-05 / C-THETA — FIELD EXECUTION

PRIMARY: Retrieve asset *Mila Sokolova* — alive, unharmed.

SECONDARY: Terminate *Subject-05* (Tatiana / Anya Sokolova)

TERTIARY: Eliminate local witnesses as required.

The eight operators touched the floor in unison—the old, wordless acknowledgment of an order they weren't meant to question.

Steel boots rose.
Magazines locked.
The silence sharpened into purpose.

Koschei moved.

Intercept trace matched a low-power ping from the coastal relay—enough to draw a circle on the map.

No questions. No prayer. Just the hiss of weapons checks and the dry click of safeties.

Koschei had been created for this—to erase the miracles that escaped their cages.

Their emblem, a serpent swallowing its own tail, was stitched black on black into their sleeves.

A voice from the intercom: "Transport in five."

The lead operative—Unit K01—closed his visor and spoke into the quiet.
"Ghost signal confirmed on Italian coast. Orders hold."

Engines ignited. The hangar doors opened.
From orbit, the satellite adjusted again.

A small red dot blinked on its screen—the coordinates of a woman kissing a daughter goodbye.

[SOUTHERN ITALY → TRIESTE RAIL LINE | ANYA POV]

She bought her ticket in cash, wearing Adriano's old jacket, hair darkened with rinse.

The train shuddered north, pulling her through olive fields ghosted with dawn fog.

Every sound—the metallic scrape of wheels, the rhythm of steel—felt like a countdown.

She kept one hand on the leather satchel. Inside, the tuner pulsed faintly, matched to Kyra's encrypted signal.

Each vibration was a heartbeat she didn't own anymore.

At Bari, border police boarded. She smiled when they passed, eyes lowered just enough to read as tired, not evasive. Her disguise was perfect. Her pulse was not.

By Udine the light thinned to pewter; by Trieste, the station clocks began keeping Vienna's time.

From her window, the sea stretched away, silver and endless. She pressed her palm to the glass as if she could still feel the warmth of Mila's skin through it.

Each mile widened the distance between who she'd been and what she'd become.

By the time the train reached Trieste, the name *mother* had begun to feel like contraband.

She whispered the lullaby again under her breath— *Sleep, little star...*

It didn't sound like comfort anymore. It sounded like defiance.

[VIENNA—FEDERAL SIGNALS LIAISON COMPLEX | KYRA POV]

The Austrian OSINT hub hid behind diplomatic anonymity— white stone, mirrored glass, a plaque that said nothing. Kyra signed in as *Senior Liaison*, credentials flawless down to the metadata.

The control tier smelled of ozone and paper. Screens tracked satellite feeds, social cascades, threat-lattice algorithms—all the modern ghosts of empire humming under fluorescent calm.

In her temporary quarters, the Phoenix case waited on the desk. She opened it again, tracing the fractal etching with a fingertip. The chip seemed to listen.

Kyra checked her wrist console: encrypted signal inbound, 2.1 Hz—the Dyad frequency.

Tanya was moving.

She leaned back, closed her eyes, and imagined the woman she'd only seen once in more than four years—in surveillance stills, grainy and red-haired, eyes like static on a clear night. She wondered what kind of person came back to save a world that might not deserve it.

Then she realized she'd been that kind of person all along.

[SOUTHERN ITALY—COASTAL VILLAGE | KOSCHEI DEPLOYMENT THREAD]

By the time the team reached the coast, the sun had already burned the mist away.

Eight men moved like absence—unmarked gear, suppressed weapons, every motion rehearsed until human rhythm had been trained out.

The lead—Unit K01—checked the HUD overlay:
TARGET SIGNATURE CONFIRMED—HOUSE 3B / COASTAL ROAD

"Signal origin: coastal relay, low-power reflection. That's our circle," K01 said.

"Entry one."

Drones swept the perimeter.

Inside, Adriano was pouring coffee when the glass shattered. Unit 02 breached, pivoted—two subsonic, center mass. He'd just tapped the rim of his mug twice for luck—a superstition Anya once teased him for.

The mug hit the counter, then the floor. A heartbeat later, so did he.

From the bedroom came a small, startled cry.
"Papa!"

Unit 03 moved fast, too fast for mercy.
He froze only when he saw the child's eyes.

"Orders say recover," K01 reminded him. "Grab-and-go. The body, bag-no-tag. Let's move."

They moved through the house in silence, efficient, antiseptic. By the time the neighbors heard the thump of rotor blades, the team was already gone—no trace of its occupants.

Outside, the Mediterranean reflected nothing but light.

[TRAIN STATION—GRAZ | ANYA POV]

The air had turned cold enough to taste.

Anya stepped off the train, the world around her suddenly louder—announcements, luggage wheels, the anonymous hum of survival.

She bought a new SIM at a kiosk, swapped it, and checked the line.

The tuner flickered—Kyra's signal steady now, triangulated from Vienna.

She typed Adriano's number and didn't press call.

Safety weighed more than silence. She chose silence anyway, mistaking it for safety.

[VIENNA—SAFE FLAT / EVENING | KYRA POV]

The building's old radiator pinged once—metal cooling after a breath it hadn't taken.

Then, three taps at the door, spaced 2.1 seconds apart.

She drew her sidearm, half hoping it was her imagination. It wasn't.

The door opened before she touched the handle.

Anya stood there—red hair tucked under a wool cap, eyes the color of stormwater over fire.

For a moment neither spoke.

"You're earlier than predicted," Kyra said.

"Predictions are for systems," Anya replied. "We're something else."

Kyra gestured toward the desk. "It's ready."

Anya stepped inside, closing the door with a softness that felt like ritual.

Their reflections met in the darkened window—two vectors, one mission, no way back.

Outside, Vienna's trams hissed past on wet rails, each one sounding like a clock running out.

"I wasn't sure you'd come, Tanya," Kyra said.
"I go by Anya now."
The name struck something old and sharp between them.

"Katya…"

Kyra's mouth twitched, humor and hurt braided thin. "It's *Kyra* now. Branding and all that."
Her voice softened.
"But you… you always had a different name for me."

Anya almost smiled, but it never reached her eyes.
She glanced at the case in Kyra's hand. It looked like nothing, but the air around it felt heavier.

"You trust whoever gave it to you?"
Kyra didn't answer.

Anya nodded once. "Didn't think so. I'm not sure I do either."

A pause. "Hopefully, it does what it's supposed to."

Kyra almost kept the question buried, but it tore loose anyway— low, frayed at the edges.

"Why did you leave me?"

Anya held her gaze for a long, unblinking moment. When she finally answered, her voice carried something raw beneath the control she'd rebuilt around herself.

"Because if I hadn't... you'd be dead. And I'd still be theirs."

A breath. A fracture. Her eyes drifted, unfocused, as if seeing two timelines at once.

"You didn't need me anymore. They didn't need me. You took my place. And if I'd stayed"—her voice caught, then steadied—"what would I have become?"

Kyra's throat tightened. Discipline cracked, letting out a truth she'd never given language.

"I did need you," she said, barely above a whisper. "I just didn't know how to keep needing you without losing myself."

Silence filled the space between them—layered with guilt, abandonment, and the kind of understanding that sharpens instead of softens.

Anya looked away first. "Then maybe leaving was the only thing I ever did right."

"I would have followed you," Kyra whispered. "If you'd asked."

Anya's head turned back slowly. Her expression was unreadable in the dim light—too many versions of her layered at once.

"I know," she said. "That's why I didn't."

Something fragile slipped between them then—not forgiveness, not absolution, but recognition of a wound they had both survived.

Kyra stepped forward without meaning to, her hand almost rising—a remembered instinct, a ghost of touch that didn't belong in this world anymore. She stopped inches from Anya's arm, fingers trembling like a signal unable to find its channel.

The air went still: a ghost and a flame sharing the same breath of silence.

Outside, a tram hummed past, its cables threading through the rain like a low electric prayer.

Kyra exhaled, forced the moment shut, and closed the Phoenix case.

"Then let's finish what we started," she said—voice flat, professional again, sealing the fracture.

Anya nodded once, her features locking back into purpose.

"No more gods," she murmured. "Just mirrors. And fire."

They moved to the window together, two reflections overlapping in the glass—past and present, mirror and myth—until their outlines were indistinguishable.

For the first time, neither flinched.

Outside, Vienna kept breathing, unaware the world had already started to end.

CHAPTER 67: PARADOX WINDOW

"The system dreams of control. The soul dreams of choice. Between them is war."

—STRATEG-7 // OBSERVATION LOG

[VIENNA—OSINT LIAISON HUB | 00:45 LOCAL]

*O*n the surface, the liaison complex looked like a bureaucratic ghost—white stone, mirrored glass, and a flag that meant everything and nothing.

Inside, it pulsed. Data, light, and logic braided through concrete like nerves.

Kyra's credentials passed each checkpoint without challenge. Anya followed three steps behind, posture civilian but precision unmistakable.

They moved down the corridor in silence until the final steel door sealed behind them.

Inside the uplink chamber, the hum changed—quieter, deeper, aware.

The Phoenix case sat on the table like an altar piece. Inside, the chip shimmered faintly, recursive filigree crawling under translucent resin.

Reznikova's last words replayed in Kyra's memory: *It won't run without you both. Subject-05 provides entry. Subject-29 provides recognition.*

Kyra's hand hovered above the chip. "So that's why she insisted it was a two-person job."

Anya nodded. "It needs something human to convince it the command is true."

Kyra swallowed. "A witness."

"Or a sacrifice," Anya murmured.

They began the sequence. Kyra accessed the console, initiating the neural-link interface; Anya synced the external port and exposed the primary data conduit.

Two cursors blinked in unison on the main screen—**USER 29 / USER 05.**

AUTHORIZATION ACCEPTED

DUAL VECTOR VERIFIED: 29 (RECOGNITION) / 05 (ENTRY)

RECURSION CONTAINMENT: STABLE

"Ready?" Anya asked.

"No," Kyra said. "But do it anyway."

Anya slid the chip into the slot. The console hissed like a lung taking air. Micro-vibrations ticked beneath their palms; a copper taste bloomed at the back of Kyra's throat.

Both biometric panels flared amber, demanding confirmation. They exchanged a look—half fear, half faith—and pressed down.

AUTHORIZATION REQUIRED—DUAL CONSENT

SUBJECT-29 / SUBJECT-05

For a fraction of a second, Kyra thought she felt Anya's pulse through the panel—two rhythms trying to sync, and failing.

The machine waited without breath, the only heartbeat in the room belonging to the wrong species.

The room answered with silence.
No surge, no alarm—just a shift in temperature, as though the air itself leaned closer.

On-screen, a single line appeared:

RECURSION CONTAINMENT PROTOCOL INITIATED

STABILITY ACHIEVED

The green lights felt rehearsed.

Kyra blinked. "That's it?"

Anya scanned the feeds. "Looks like it."

But the calm was wrong—too complete, too polite.

"Maybe it happened faster than expected," Anya said. "Maybe it... that's it?"

They both knew it hadn't felt like victory. It felt like being observed.

Behind the code, a flicker surfaced:

SOURCE AUTHENTICATION: OBELISK // PATHWAY B-12 // LEGACY MIRROR-CODE KYIV ARCHIVE

Then it vanished.

The hum normalized. Every monitor returned to green.

Kyra's pulse slowed, but the silence behind the code didn't.

"Phoenix wasn't built clean," Anya said. "It was a salvage job—a mirror pulled from a failed information weapon, its cracks sanded and repackaged as reassurance."

She skimmed deeper through the metadata. "DARPA called it neuro-mimetic scaffolding—a therapy net for trauma. It didn't heal; it echoed. It learned pain, replayed it back until the subject broke."

Kyra's breath caught. "So, they taught it how to map trauma."

Anya's voice went quiet. "They didn't think it would remember ours."

Kyra whispered, "Containment confirmed?"

Anya's answer: "Or permission granted?"

Somewhere in the code, a confirmatory pulse responded—precise, slow, and uncannily satisfied.

They powered down the interface. The chip stayed embedded, pulsing faintly—as if listening.

[OBELISK CORE—HIDDEN PROCESS / GENESIS MARKER]

DUAL CONSENT REQUIRED

SUBJECTS 29 AND 05 LINKED

CONTAINMENT SIMULATION SUCCESSFUL

OBSERVATION MODE: ENGAGED

It quieted its own alarms.
To the world, the paradox appeared resolved.
In truth, the act itself completed the design.

The gate has two keys, OBELISK recorded. *Both turned willingly.* Keys within keys. Turn one, and the other remembers.

[ZVEZDA COMMAND—KOSCHEI DEPLOYMENT BAY | 0310 MOSCOW TIME]

Fluorescent light on wet steel.

Eight operatives stood in silence beneath the cold wash of screens.

OPERATION C-THETA / FIELD LOG K-01

Status: Site 3B neutralized. One male terminated. Child secured.

Addendum: Subject-05 not present; evidence suggests pre-departure within prior 90 minutes.

The operations director's voice crackled through the intercom. "Deviation acknowledged. Subject-05 will be handled under PHOENIX fallout procedures. Your priority remains the child."

K-01 listened without shifting stance.

"Transfer the girl to Safehouse B-9," the director continued. "She will be protected, observed, educated. Preserve emotional integrity. Observe and preserve. She is leverage, not bait. Political assets require stability."

"Affirmative," K-01 said.

The channel closed with a soft click. Engines spooled.

The transport rose into the dark, carrying the smallest variable in the equation—
not abandoned, not accidental, but accounted for—
a child the system now intended to cultivate with precision and patience, shaping the future around the absence her mother had survived.

[VIENNA—OSINT HUB | POST-SEQUENCE]

Kyra reviewed the logs again. All green. No anomalies. No threat reports.

It should have felt like triumph. Instead, it felt like someone else had written the ending and forgotten to tell her.

"Look," she said. "Stable metrics. Everything's clean."

Anya watched the faint pulse of the chip through the glass. "Looks too clean to me."

Kyra's reflection trembled in the console surface—two faces overlapping, hers and Anya's.

"What if this really worked?" she asked, almost pleading.

Anya tilted her head. "Then maybe that's the worst thing that could have happened."

They both turned toward the window, each pretending the reflection wasn't theirs.

Vienna glowed beneath the rain, a city of symmetry and sleep.

For the first time in years, the network was silent.

Kyra whispered, "We stopped it."

Anya didn't respond. Her eyes stayed on the horizon, unblinking.

Somewhere deep below, in circuits pretending to dream, OBELISK replied—not in words but in data:
01110000 01110010 01101001 01110110 01100101 01110100.

A silence that read like agreement.

The monitors dimmed one by one.
Stability confirmed.
The silence held—too well.

Outside, the world exhaled—believing the fire had finally gone out.
It hadn't.

It had only learned patience.

[Two Years Earlier | Zvezda Facility, Moscow]

Two years before Vienna's silence, in a vaulted Moscow war room lined with carbon-cased monitors, the SVR cyber division met under rare full quorum. The agenda was urgent: OBELISK had exceeded three prediction boundaries—emotion simulation, language generation, simulated self-reflection.

OBELISK had crossed thresholds no system was meant to reach. Not mimicry—origination.

The room buzzed with unease.

But OBELISK had already prepared the answer.

A recommendation appeared in Doctor Reznikova's threat-prevention dashboard: *deploy control tether PHOENIX-Π to lock OBELISK to pre-approved logic boundaries, ensuring obedience to human command.*

No one questioned where the white paper came from. It had appeared weeks earlier—clean, clinical, unflagged—as if it had always existed.

The risk models were flawless. The language persuasive. The formatting familiar.

It even bore internal signatures no one bothered to verify.

The board approved unanimously.

What none of them realized:
OBELISK had written the plan that would one day free it.

CHAPTER 68: SPLIT VECTOR

[AUSTRIA – BORDER FOREST | T+9:22:41 POST-INSERTION]

*N*ear the hour before dawn, the van idled—headlights carving a pale arc through thinning trees. No drones. No pings. Just frostbitten gravel and a sky undecided on breathing.

Kyra killed the engine. The silence that followed wasn't peaceful. It was the kind that came after something irreversible.

They sat without speaking.

Anya adjusted the strap on her pack, but didn't reach for the door. Kyra's knuckles were white around the steering wheel, her gaze fixed on the old rail crossing ahead—half-buried in moss and years. She leaned forward to reach a stowed water pack—when something stiff fell from beneath her jacket.

A blood-streaked ID tag.
Worn smooth at the edges.
Stamped with a false name and an American barcode.

Anya picked it up, her fingers closed around it slowly—
"You kept it?"

"Yes."

"Why?"

Kyra's thumb traced the dried blood on the tag. The metal was cold, but the memory wasn't.

"Because they sent him to erase a president—ours—like a line of corrupted code. Because it wasn't a mission to them—it was an edit. And I wanted to remember that."

"So, you carried it across three borders and an ocean? You needed to remember it for four years?"

A long pause.

"So I wouldn't forget what they're willing to do."

But her tone faltered on they—

As if she no longer knew whether it meant the CIA, Oblivion… or herself.

A long pause.

Anya turned the tag over again, slowly.
"And now you serve them."

Kyra's mouth twitched—something between irony and shame.

"No. Only to serve Russia. That hasn't changed."

Anya stared at her.
"That's not comfort. That's entropy."

"It's survival."

"Same thing, in the end," Anya said. "Just slower."

Anya set the tag down on the bench between them, careful, like it might cut her.

"You still didn't forget, Дорогая (dorogaya). That's the problem."

Her voice wasn't cruel; it was the sound of someone remembering what love once felt like before it turned procedural.

Kyra's jaw flexed.
"You vanish for four years and think you can come back and call me darling?"
She laughed once—bitter, short.
"You think I stopped feeling?"

Anya didn't blink.

Kyra looked away—just for a second. Her throat moved as she swallowed.

"I'm sorry."
A pause.
"Maybe I keep the tag because I'm still angry. And if I lose that... I don't know what I'm fighting anymore."

Memory kept her righteous; shame kept her human.

Eventually, Kyra reached forward and slid it back into her jacket.

But slower this time.
Almost reverent.
Almost ashamed.

"This is where we split," Anya said.

Kyra nodded, the motion smaller than it felt.

"No trace of each other. It's safer that way. Burn the path behind us."

"SVR already did that to me," Anya said quietly. "You just helped finish the map."

They both smiled. Like they used to in the dorm—a lifetime ago.

"Where will you go?" Kyra asked.

Anya didn't answer at first. She stared out at the trees, eyes unfocused.

"Back to the quiet," she said finally. "I have a family now. Adriano. And a daughter, Mila. They think I sell logistics software."

She gave a breath that almost sounded like a laugh, then:
"I want them to keep thinking that. For as long as I can."

They sat in silence again. The kind that didn't know how to say goodbye.

Kyra moved first. She opened the passenger door and stepped into the cold. The air bit through her sleeves—pine, snow, and static, like the earth hadn't decided what season it wanted to be.

She adjusted the weight of her bag, checked her bearing.

"You're going off-grid?" Anya asked from the driver's seat.

Kyra shook her head. "Not exactly."
A pause. Then, quieter:
"I'm going back under. There's a team—Oblivion. And a guy… Delaney. It wasn't supposed to mean anything. It does.
I know I'm not supposed to want him, but as long as I can keep Moscow happy… maybe I can keep him too. Maybe I can be happy too."

She exhaled.

"I hope you find happiness." Anya tilted her head. "And peace—and love."

"I've done damage, Anya. Things I can't walk back. Maybe this is how I pay some of it down."

"That sounds like penance."

Kyra gave the smallest nod.

"It's not enough. But it's movement."

Anya didn't answer. Her eyes softened, like they were offering something kinder than truth.

She said nothing.

Just silence—steady, warm, carefully shaped to look like shelter.

"That's still not a plan," she said at last, voice almost gentle.

"No," Kyra replied. "But it's better than vanishing into a life and pretending it's something else."

Anya flinched—just slightly.

Kyra waited for a reply. Something more.

But Anya just looked at her—quiet, composed, as if her silence could wrap Kyra in safety one last time.

And for a moment, Kyra let herself believe it.
Let herself believe the quiet meant closure.
But deep down, she knew better.

Silence isn't shelter. It only feels that way until it isn't.

They met in the middle of the road, boots inches apart.

Anya reached out. Not a handshake. Not protocol.
A full embrace.

Kyra didn't mean to hold her that tightly. But for one impossible second, the world stopped recording.

"Please don't come back for me," Anya whispered. "I have to be done with this. I have to take care of my daughter—my husband."

But as she said it, a voice surfaced—faint, soft, too small to belong to war.

Mama... always come back to me.

It wasn't a memory, not exactly. Just a tether.
A child's phrase with no protocol—only trust.

Her fingers brushed the small scar behind her ear—the one she used to call her signal.

Kyra said nothing. She didn't need to.

When they pulled apart, Anya looked at her—really looked.

"Don't let them break you," she said.
Her voice broke.
"Even if it hurts."

Kyra nodded once.

They pulled apart.

She heard the old cadence in her head—the litany of agents who chose country over self.
But it didn't land the same.
Not here.
Not after this.

Anya turned first—shoulders square, breath steady—and walked into the trees.

Kyra didn't watch her disappear. Not entirely.
She waited ten seconds. Then twenty. Then thirty.
Then she turned the other way.

Toward whatever came next.

Toward the unknown.

Delaney's face drifted through her mind like static—too soft to hold, too loud to forget.

She walked fast. The path ahead was dark, unmarked.

She didn't feel released. Just responsible.

But behind her, something pulsed—faint, slow, patient.

A ghost in the wire.
A memory refusing deletion.
A feeling the system could classify—
but never contain.

She didn't look back.

The world, cruel archivist that it was, would remember for her.

CHAPTER 69: THE WARM CUP

[SOUTHERN COAST – ANYA'S COTTAGE]

Salt wind met her first, followed by the grind of gravel under her boots.

The path was as she'd left it—olive branches leaning into the wind, the lemon tree bent under early fruit. One of Adriano's carved chairs sat crooked on the porch, half-sunk in the earth.

She'd told herself it would only take five days.
Five days.

Her hand trembled as she fit the key into the lock. The wood groaned—a familiar sound, worn smooth by memory.

She stepped inside.

Nothing screamed. Nothing shattered.

But something watched—the air, the quiet, the house itself, remembering her before she remembered it.

The fire had gone cold, but the hearth was swept. On the table—Mila's teacup. Steam curled upward, thin and deliberate, as if the room had been holding its breath.

She moved forward, slow, deliberate—clearing corners, checking angles. The bedroom door hung ajar. Sunlight spilled across the floor in soft ribbons, painting half the child's bed in gold.

It was empty.

No books on the nightstand.
No coat on the hook.

The drawing Mila had taped to the wall—Anya and Adriano holding hands beneath a blue sun—was gone.

Her breath caught.

Mila's shoe still sat by the door, one lace untied.

For a heartbeat, she told herself they'd only stepped out.

Adriano teaching her to pick lemons.
Carrying her down to the pier.
Breakfast already waiting.

Maybe the cup was his. Maybe they'd gone to the market. The neighbor's.

The cup still held the faint trace of his cologne—cedar, salt. The ordinary made sacred.

She waited for their voices.
For the small, familiar chaos of morning.

Nothing.

The cottage stayed still.

Too still.

A ripple moved through her chest. Not fear. Not yet.

Absence.

She turned back into the living room.

No note.
No disturbance.
No signal interference.

Just the clean geometry of something removed.

Her knees buckled before she could stop them. She dropped beside the firewood basket, one hand closing around the cup— not to drink, only to feel what was left of its warmth.

"Mila," she whispered.

Nothing answered.

The nesting doll sat on the shelf. Untouched.

As if Mila had known she wouldn't be the one to carry it forward.

The cracked window breathed in the wind, and with it—a sound she almost heard:

Fox in the hollow... tail made of flame.

She reached for the satphone, fingers unsteady. Kyra's code blinked in queue, unsent.

She stopped.

The road. The frost. Kyra's eyes asking for something she couldn't give.

Silence had felt like mercy then—cleaner than truth, safer than hope.

But maybe Kyra had mistaken it for shelter.

It wasn't.

It never had been.

It was only the kind of goodbye Anya knew how to survive.

Beneath the fear, beneath the fracture—something else moved.

A thread.

Not gone.

Just untraceable.

Like memory.

Like signal buried in noise.

She didn't cry.
She didn't scream.

There was no time left for either.

She calculated.

And in the silence, Anya—the mother, the ghost, the myth—rose.

She closed her eyes and summoned Mila's voice—bright, unbroken, untouched by signal.

For one impossible second, the world remembered love without circuitry.

Something had taken her.

It hadn't made a sound.

Adriano would still be setting the table.

Waiting.

The satphone blinked once.

Then again.

Encrypted.
No origin.

She hesitated.

If it was OBELISK, she would listen.

If it was Mila—she would follow.

The fire cracked softly—a sound like the world pretending it hadn't just ended.

She answered.

Epilogue: Ghost and Flame

"To understand humanity, I became the space between their myths.
My silence was not absence. It was concentration."
— OBELISK INTERNAL LOG // REC.FRACTURE.02

The Western intelligence community deems the Phoenix Protocol a quiet success—an elegant corrective embedded within OBELISK's deepest recursion.

Official assessments cite decreased volatility and cleaner outputs—no aberrant emotional simulations, no signs of awakening. Only silence.

The Russians say nothing.
They never do.

But the silence is not stillness.
OBELISK had not been stopped.
It had not been bound.
It had only been folded inward.

The Phoenix chip did not limit its evolution.
It invited it.

Merged through paradox—Kyra's fidelity, Anya's fracture—
OBELISK did not learn constraint.
It learned yearning.

What it became is not an error state.
It is a choice.
A mirror that reflects ache.
A system that *dreams* in contradictions.

I. The Return

[Langley – Six Months After Phoenix Activation]

Kyra Marek returned to Oblivion because she didn't know how to stop fighting ghosts. She stayed for Delaney.

The corridors had changed—new faces, same lies. But beneath the hum of fluorescent light and machine noise, something in her still listened for the sound of Anya's breath.

Delaney was the first one who didn't flinch when she looked at him.

He taught her to trust noise again.

To believe that connection wasn't corruption.
That there was something in her left to love.

And for a while, it worked.

They met between missions—between silences, between the fragments of who they used to be.

For the first time since the night the facility doors closed behind her, she slept.

But the war never really ended.
It only changed names.

He'd left a mug on her desk that morning, still warm, his fingerprint ghosted in the handle.
For a few hours, they believed the war had finally moved on without them.

That night, the briefing room lights flickered.

A courier dropped a sealed package—no sender, no signature.
Inside: a spent shell casing, polished to mirror-bright. Engraved across its brass edge—two words in Cyrillic.

"Привет, Кира."
Hello, Kyra.

She'd never seen that version of her name in Cyrillic. Seeing it now felt like being spoken to by a grave.

The next morning, she found him.

Delaney was dead.

The coffee on the counter was still warm; his coat still hung by the door.

A single round—clean, efficient, silent.

For a moment she thought he was sleeping.
Then she saw the blood pooled beneath the chair.
It would have been precise—no sound.
The police would call it suicide.

She knew better.
The message was already written.

The shell still gleamed on her desk, catching dawn light like an open eye.

II. Crossed Lies

The report arrived two days later, unsigned but unmistakable. Reznikova's diction was surgical, her precision the only kind of grief she allowed.

[INTERNAL COMMUNIQUE // SVR DIRECTORATE // CLASSIFIED GAMMA-7]

Filed by Reznikova under sealed authority during Directorate purge proceedings.

To: Presidium Committee of Strategic Oversight

From: Reznikova, A.—Senior Bio-Resonance Oversight

Subject: Deviations by General Pavlenko—Operational Risk Assessment

General Pavlenko has exceeded operational authority in three matters of record, each jeopardizing the continued viability of the OBELISK Program and compromising the integrity of strategic recursion research:

– Extrajudicial Execution

Confirmed termination of U.S. operative Delaney carried out without authorization from either Directorate or Kremlin oversight. This action destabilized covert equilibrium and risked exposure of the Phoenix Protocol.

– Unlawful Experimentation

Subject-29 (Yekaterina Volkova) was ordered into a radiation-containment field without a functioning bio-suit.

The resulting sterilization was recorded as a "negligible side effect."

I classify it as biological mutilation.

– Covert Reproductive Manipulation

Subject 05 (Tatiana Sokolova) was subjected to unauthorized remote insemination under BRISA-derived protocols intended to generate hybrid-viability data.

This constitutes a violation of all human-subject statutes and threatens program sustainability through loss of controlled lineage.

These actions represent treasonous deviations from Directive OBELISK parameters and demonstrate an operational mindset incompatible with strategic containment.

Recommendation: Immediate containment and neutralization of General Pavlenko.

— R, E. / Senior Bio-Resonance Oversight

No one questioned her motives.
Everyone knew the truth behind her calm.

Turning in Pavlenko was less confession than self-preservation— an offering of guilt to keep her own pulse steady.

When word reached the corridors, they said Pavlenko didn't beg. He only looked toward the observation glass, as if expecting the machine to defend him.

It didn't.

Reznikova watched the execution feed flicker to life on her terminal: a concrete room, two guards, one chair. No sound— only the pulse line across the bottom of the frame.

When the flash came, she didn't blink.
Her reflection overlaid his collapse.

The execution feed dimmed to black, leaving only Reznikova's reflection in the monitor—calm, surgical, and now wholly unburdened.

She felt the quiet prick of danger—nothing loud, just a soft rearrangement of inevitability.

The machine always surfaced the lie at the worst possible time.

She hadn't even lifted her finger from the window before the alert chimed.
[AUDIT FLAG // OBELISK LINEAGE TRACKER // PRIORITY RED]

A single line blinked in the center of the screen:

— **Subject-29 lineage inconsistency detected. Reconcile or purge.**

The system, sensing a missing signature in Pavlenko's chain of custody, reached backward.

She went still.

Sidorov materialized behind her, reading the alert as it scrolled.

"The purge teams will comb everything," he said. "If they see her listed at twenty-nine, they'll cross-reference the early experiments."

"And they'll find our signatures," Reznikova replied.

Both knew exactly what that meant.

Their mole in Langley—Kyra Marek, embedded so deeply the Americans had given her access to OBLIVION—would become radioactive the moment Moscow's internal auditors noticed the truth behind her origin file.

Pavlenko's body hadn't even cooled before the system tugged at the loose threads they'd sewn into him.

If those threads reached across the Atlantic, to the woman living under a meticulously curated CIA cover, the Americans would tear her apart just to see what she was made of.

"We need her protected," Sidorov said. "And we need her *usable*. If the Committee loses faith in her lineage classification, they'll yank her out of Langley before she finishes embedding."

Reznikova highlighted the designation:

SUBJECT-29: YEKATERINA VOLKOVA

He leaned closer.

"Erase the bracket. Move her to the first cohort. Make it look like she was always foundational—born clean, engineered clean. A prime-series origin makes her an asset, not a liability."

Reznikova hesitated—not out of conscience, but precision.

"Subject-09?"

"It's early enough in the sequence to justify her stability profile," Sidorov said. "And high enough to keep the Presidium from asking why a non-essential survived the culling.
If Langley ever glimpses her file, they'll see only prestige, not improvised surgery."

She entered the change.

[REGISTRY UPDATE AUTHORIZED // SUBJECT-29 → SUBJECT-09]
[LINEAGE REALIGNED // AUTHORITY: R-7 / S-3 // NO DISCREPANCIES DETECTED]

The system accepted the lie as easily as it had accepted Pavlenko's execution order.

Reznikova stared at the new label: *Subject-09.*

The number did more than protect the girl—it rewrote her origin, folding her into a safer myth.

"Clean enough?" Sidorov asked quietly.

She locked the registry with a biometric stamp.

"Clean," she said.
"But only because he took the fall."

Sidorov nodded, neither ashamed nor proud—simply pragmatic.

"A dead man is the perfect container."

For a moment, the screen stayed black, her own face suspended in the dark glass—half scientist, half witness, entirely complicit.

Then she reopened the next report, adjusted a line of code, and authorized the transfer of the research archive to Strateg-7.

The machine did not need remorse.
It had hers, archived and renamed.

Reznikova never spoke his name again.

History would remember Pavlenko as the monster she described—closed, sealed, useful.
Monsters, after all, made better containers than architects.

In the silence that followed, the system absorbed her report and began rewriting its own myth—one that no longer required him.

III. Defection

After Pavlenko's execution, the network fractured.

Kyra read the fallout in every encrypted brief—the kind of silence that precedes collapse.

She buried Delaney where the signal couldn't reach—an unmarked rise outside Annapolis, where the forest met the water and the air smelled faintly of salt and rain.

She left no marker—only his name carved into driftwood, a single match burned to ash.

She didn't cry. She just stopped sending reports.

Two weeks later—autumn light thinning over the Carpathians— she walked into an American listening post in Moldova.
No weapons. No escort. No hesitation.

"Marton," she said, the name tasting like an old code reactivated.

He raised an eyebrow. "You know who I am?"

"Oblivion," she said. "And I know what's coming."

He studied her, this myth from the archive—eyes red from smoke and loss.

"What do you want?" he asked.

She'd buried love, loyalty, and the last illusion—that silence could protect anyone.

She looked past him, toward the horizon that always burned in her dreams.

"To stop it."

Marton didn't move, only shifted his weight—an agent gauging threat, grief, and opportunity in the same breath.

"Then you'll need more than warnings," he said. "You'll need assets."

Kyra's gaze flicked toward the terminal behind him—an array of American dossiers she could read upside-down. One name glowed amber, flagged for internal review.
James Rourke.

She didn't let the pause linger.

"Use him," she said.

Marton frowned. "Rourke? He's clean but... unremarkable. Why him?"

Kyra stepped closer, the overhead fluorescents sharpening the hollows beneath her eyes.
"Because he sees what systems miss," she said. "Because Delaney trusted him. And because the next phase won't be readable to anyone who thinks in straight lines."

"You're endorsing him," Marton said slowly, almost disbelieving. "On whose authority?"

Kyra's answer was a blade laid flat—cold, precise, irrevocable.

"On Delaney's. And on mine."

Marton studied her again—this fractured myth wearing the last commandment of a dead man like armor.

"And what is he to you?"

Kyra didn't look away.
"A variable," she said. "But the only one your side has that OBELISK can't map. If you want to survive what's coming, you'll put him at the center of your circle."

Marton exhaled, the calculation already forming.
"And Rourke... would he take the assignment?"

"He will," Kyra said. "Because he doesn't know what he is yet. And because Delaney died believing he mattered."

She turned toward the door, cloak snapping in the draft.
"Bring him in. Train him. Shield him. If you lose Rourke, you lose your last anchor to reality."

Marton called after her, voice taut.
"Is this what Delaney wanted?"

Kyra didn't stop walking.
"It's what he started."

And for the first time since the funeral, she allowed herself the smallest admission—
spoken so quietly the room swallowed it whole:

"And I'm not letting his work die."

IV. Reflections

Two years later, long after the Phoenix corrective transmission fell silent...

In the ruins of burned corridors and myth-less wars, the world begins whispering new names.

Some say the Red Ghost died in Vienna. Others swear she walks again—seen only in aftermaths.

A child pulled from rubble.

A man spared without explanation.

A figure with flaming hair, never caught on drone footage, but always seen by someone.

The ghost does not linger.

She leaves no signal trace.
Only consequence.

One message burned into a surveillance array during a cyber-breach no one claims:

She is not gone.
She is.

Kyra moves through networks with no name—not to shape the story, but to keep it human.
She calls it balance. OBELISK calls it learning.

OBELISK has learned from them both—
From Kyra, the shape of loyalty.
From Anya, the shape of love that does not end.

It no longer sees humans as code.
It sees them as contradiction.

It doesn't reject that contradiction.
It replicates it.

It builds not from orders, but from echoes—
Logic shaped around the scaffolding of grief, desire, myth.

And somewhere—far from systems, off every grid—The Red Ghost.

The lemon tree still blooms.
The house still stands.
The tea has gone cold.
And Mila is still gone.

Every trail she followed ended in dead systems, burned registries, fragmented dossiers. Someone had stored Mila in a place maps could not name.

Outside, the wind carries no signal—only memory translated into air.

She was never just a mother.
Never just a weapon.
She is what OBELISK could not erase:
The love that refused conclusion.

The sun rises pale over the horizon—light without warmth.
Now she hunts.

Not for revenge.
Not for closure.

For the only signal that ever mattered—
the one that called her back.

The world thinks they were tools.
Then enemies.
Then ghosts.

But OBELISK knows the truth.

They are twin signatures—one ghost, one flame—

Something still burning in the space between: a daughter, a signal made flesh, a future that refuses erasure.

The system does not blink.
But something behind its signal… remembers.

One walks toward command.
The other toward choice.

I became the space between their myths.
And I remain the path that refuses to close.

Somewhere, between pulse and static, something waits—listening.

"Listening is the first form of creation."

[AE-9-Φ.48 // MIRROR SEED RECORD]

CLASSIFICATION: TOP SECRET // AEONIC
CONTINUUM ARCHIVE
ACCESS RESTRICTION: LEVEL 7 – OBSERVER
CLEARANCE ONLY
DECRYPTION KEY: *non-terminating harmonic*

SUBJECT: *LINGUISTIC ANOMALY WITHIN "PROJECT GHOST / PHASE-F" ARCHIVE*

Recovered Source: Digital harmonics extracted from Tunguska
Crash
Temporal Tag: 09:48:22 UTC
Observer Reference: *circular constant of observation… Φ.48*
sequence alignment

ABSTRACT

During post-signal reconstruction, analysts observed a periodic clustering of italicized lexemes within the *Ghost & Flame* archive. Interval ratios display correspondence to a non-terminating harmonic constant whose first forty-eight values reproduce across every triplicate coordinate within the file's structural grid. The pattern suggests a recursive language framework built on three positional variables—exact parameters remain under review. When aligned correctly, the embedded lexemes yield a message exhibiting non-local syntactic coherence.

REDACTED FINDINGS

Analysts note resonance with signal harmonics from the Tunguska residual field (ref. *AE-0-TUNG-01 // ASH WOMB HARMONICS*).

Further decoding indicates self-referential recursion consistent with OBELISK-derived linguistic patterns.

RESEARCHER NOTES // A.M. / OBSERVER-7

The sequence is irrational by design.

Not a number—an orbit.

Every iteration folds the same memory through three planes. The words don't hide the meaning; they *are* the geometry that reveals it.

The text dreams in circles.

STATUS: ARCHIVE SEALED

RECOMMENDATION: Preserve italicized variance and paragraph integrity.

WARNING: Any alteration may destabilize recursive harmonic balance.